Twenty-One Days

C. M. OKONKWO

Copyright © 2015 C. M. Okonkwo

All rights reserved. This book or any portion thereof may not be reproduced or used in any manner whatsoever without the express written permission of the copyright owner, except for the use of brief quotations in a book review or scholarly journal.

Laybels Publishing
laybels@gmail.com
2015

www.cmo29.com

ISBN-10: 1512038245

ISBN-13: 978-1512038248

DISCLAIMER

Although inspired by real locations, activities, programmes and schedules, all events and characters appearing in this work are fictitious. Any resemblance to real persons, living, dead, undead, in the before-life or in the after-life, will be deemed a compliment of the author's genius.

DEDICATION

This book is dedicated to all those who have served in the National Youth Service Corps —NYSC — scheme; those who served, but didn't really serve; those who are yet to serve; those who dropped out halfway through; and those who never plan to serve.

This book is also dedicated to the 2014 Batch B, Stream 1, Youth Corps members and camp officials. Thank you all for the twenty-one delightful days and the unforgettable experience; whether good or bad, it was worth it. There was no better place to get information, experience and an idea of camp, community or 'boarding-school' life than from the camp itself.

To Platoon Seven, team Unity, this one is for you... some of you. To my roommates in room 21, this one is for some of you too. To those in other platoons, whose short friendship meant a lot to me, this one is for you as well.

What happens in camp... stays in camp!

I do hope you enjoy it!

CONTENTS

	Acknowledgements	i
Prelude	Welcome home	1
Chapter One	Special treatment	7
Chapter Two	Remember me	21
Chapter Three	Call up	33
Chapter Four	Day one	43
Chapter Five	The rush	59
Chapter Six	Day two	77
Chapter Seven	Day three	95
Chapter Eight	Day four	113
Chapter Nine	Day five	133
Chapter Ten	Day six	153
Chapter Eleven	Day seven	175
Chapter Twelve	Day eight	195
Chapter Thirteen	Day nine	213
Chapter Fourteen	Day ten	229
Chapter Fifteen	Day eleven	247
Chapter Sixteen	Day twelve	269
Chapter Seventeen	Day thirteen	289

Chapter Eighteen	Day fourteen	307
Chapter Nineteen	Day fifteen	325
Chapter Twenty	Day sixteen	343
Chapter Twenty-one	Day seventeen	361
Chapter Twenty-two	Day eighteen	383
Chapter Twenty-three	Day nineteen	405
Chapter Twenty-four	Day twenty	427
Chapter Twenty-five	Day twenty-one	445
Chapter Twenty-six	Next step	463
	Glossary	481
	Other books by the author	485
	Author's note	487

ACKNOWLEDGEMENTS

I want to give a special 'thanks' to my wonderful family for their support during the period of time I was writing this book and not having enough time for them. Thanks always for your understanding and tolerance.

Thanks to the friends I called and sent messages to all the time, and even at odd hours, for details I had forgotten, especially my bunkmate in camp, Dunsin Adesipe... your prompt responses were very much appreciated.

A special thanks to my family and some friends, who went to other Orientation camps in and outside Lagos, but still thought to share their stories with me — Barrister Nneka Okonkwo, Ebere Okonkwo, Barrister Ifeyinwa Obienu, Rukky Dan-Egua, Ogochukwu Efobi, Chinwendu Ukoha and many others. The input added more fuel and juice to the storyline.

Many thanks to my many editors, especially Rukky and Priscie of Laybels Editing for the editing, and thanks to all the reviewers for their great input and feedback.

Thanks to the NYSC Lagos State SAED office and their amazing team, especially Mrs. R. O. Idaewor and Mr. Toni Oviosun for the time and support they gave to me during this project and for the creation of the Champions Club for writing.

An equally big thank you to the NYSC team in Agege Local Government, headed by Mrs. Adeola Abdul, and the NYSC contact person in the Admin and Personnel Unit of the Agege Local Government office, Mr. Ola Dokun for their time and support.

C. M. OKONKWO

Cover image credit goes to Miss Bilikisu Abubakar, and photo-editing credit goes to Mr. Oluwaseyi Nayin, and also to the best partner in the world, my one and only, Mr. Brandon Jossy José.

To the all-knowing God, who giveth everything... this would not have been accomplished without His grace.

PRELUDE: WELCOME HOME

Oluomachukwu had vowed to never serve Nigeria by registering for the National Youth Service Corps — NYSC — scheme, which many Nigerian youths had tagged as 'Now Your Suffering Commences' or 'Now Your Suffering Continues' depending on if the youth was already suffering or was yet to suffer before the scheme.

The few things she had heard about the NYSC scheme were negative. Not even one good comment, one positive feedback or one nice story; not one exciting experience.

However, many years later, as if she had forgotten her vow or she had suddenly gotten amnesia, Oluomachukwu woke up one Saturday morning, and as she lay on her bed, in her bedroom in central London, she decided she would do the NYSC programme, if not for anything, but for the experience... an experience of camping out in a community similar to a boarding school.

She went online immediately and researched on the programme, grateful that the NYSC had a website that was functional and was regularly updated. She saw that foreign-trained Nigerian students had to set up an account first to upload all their credentials and biometric data information before going to the NYSC Head Office at the Federal

Capital Territory in Abuja, Nigeria, for verification of the credentials. Oluomachukwu wondered why foreign-trained students had to travel to Abuja for such procedure, and not to their respective State of residence — Lagos State in her case. Only locally-trained Nigerian students had that privilege. Oluomachukwu wasn't really bothered about it. It was going to be an opportunity for her to visit and know Abuja.

When she talked to her mother about the decision in London, her mother was surprised, or rather shocked, and wondered why she wanted to quit her nice job in the UK for something as ordinary as the NYSC programme. Her mother might have even blamed the impulsive decision on her enemies back in the village or even on native charms, Oluomachukwu wasn't sure. Anyway, she regarded all the negative comments as a sign to follow her heart. Although people saw the NYSC programme as banal, she didn't. She wanted to decide for herself.

Oluomachukwu didn't have a lot of friends, but the few she had strongly discouraged her from signing up for the scheme. They shared their own experiences and also sent her links online where people complained about their terrible experiences in camp — how their personal effects and cash were stolen; soldier brutality; falling ill and every other terrible thing that could go wrong.

Oluomachukwu could have listened to them, cancelled her ticket and called her ex-boss to ask for her job back, but she didn't. She reasoned that if her friends had already done the programme and survived it, then she, too, was capable of doing the same.

As she packed her bags for Nigeria, she wondered what could be tough about spending twenty-one days in a camp with other graduates, young or old, male and female; what could be tough about waking up by 4:00am and going through vigorous physical activities and drills under the sun and in the rain, under the glaring eyes of army officers trained to instil discipline in a bunch of assumed youths.

Oluomachukwu smiled. Nothing could be tough about finally going to serve her country, even after staying away for basically all her life.

The experience was all that mattered.

***

Oluomachukwu landed safely in Murtala Muhammed International Airport, in Lagos, and felt the heat sting her as though she had just been dropped inside an empty pan that had been placed on an open fire. Given the duration of time she had spent out of Nigeria for her primary, high school and university studies, coming back home felt like she was visiting a foreign land.

The flight had gone smoothly, mostly because she had been asleep all through, only waking up once to eat, and then another time to use the lavatory before drinking a mini bottle of Irish cream she had gotten off an airhostess. She backed it up with two other small bottles of Martini Bianco, then nodded off after that until the plane landed.

At first when she woke up, she was both shocked and embarrassed at the same time. Someone had tapped her on the shoulder to let her know that the plane had touched down. Even the forceful landing of the aircraft hadn't moved her. The clapping and singing by other passengers to celebrate their safe landing hadn't come close to stirring her. The pilot's several announcements must have been like sweet music to her ears, because they didn't wake her up either.

Because of the way people rushed and didn't want anyone to join the line in front of them, Oluomachukwu had to wait on her seat for everyone to leave the plane before she pulled out her hand luggage from the overhead compartment. That way she didn't hit anyone with it.

However, sitting and waiting for others to leave hadn't been the best idea, because her head bounced from left to right as she fell asleep every little occasion she had. She was thankful that she didn't know anyone on the plane and it was the only reason why she wasn't really bothered.

But in order to curb her embarrassing sleep-nodding episode, she decided to stand up instead and wait for every passenger, before preparing to go out and breathe in the stale, hot air of Lagos State.

When Oluomachukwu got to the immigration point, she saw a queue of people in about six lines, which should have only been one line. There were two main immigration points — one for Nigerian passport-holders and the other for foreign passport-holders. The line for foreign passport-holders was empty, but the officer there didn't call for people from the overcrowded Nigerian passport-holders line. Maybe he felt that it wasn't his problem, he had been assigned to one desk, so he preferred to sit there idly. It was somewhat obvious that the officer was bored, because sometimes he glanced at his cell phone and other times he glared at the people as they were called to present their passports to the officers that checked Nigerian passports.

The idle officer would look at the confused faces of the people that were called, then at their backs, and finally, at their buttocks.

Oluomachukwu spent about two hours on the queue and when she finally got to the counter, the immigration officer made her wait until everyone had left, because she still used the old Nigerian passport and not the biometric passport. After threatening to send her back to the UK, the immigration officer finally let her go. He might have been expecting some sort of bribe, Oluomachukwu didn't know, but what she did know was that she wasn't going to give him anything.

When Oluomachukwu finally got to the arrival lobby, her family friend, Okechukwu, had been waiting for her for hours. He had gotten to the airport very early to avoid the long hours of Lagos traffic and had regretted doing that. His anger vanished when he saw her, having not seen her in years. He opened the trunk of his car and loaded her three suitcases — two massive bags that felt as though they weighed a hundred kilograms each and an equally very heavy hand luggage that could pass for a regular luggage.

Okechukwu wasn't surprised when Oluomachukwu mentioned that an airline staff almost collected the hand luggage from her while boarding the plane to check it in. It was too big and clearly too heavy for the overhead locker, and the flight was a full one. Everyone seemed to be going to Lagos, and flights to Lagos were always jam-packed, so it wasn't that surprising.

When they both entered the car Okechukwu closed the door and smiled at Oluomachukwu. He pulled her close and hugged her tightly. "Welcome home," he said.

Oluomachukwu smiled back at him, but she wished he hadn't gotten so close. The first and most important thing she remembered about him was the crush he had on her, from their high school days up until about two years ago. She had fancied him too, but not enough to want to date him; she had no idea why she didn't want to date him.

As soon as she fastened her seatbelt, Okechukwu drove off before the airport army security officer that had been intimidating people at the airport had the opportunity to flex his muscles with them.

They got to Okechukwu's house after a few hours, had dinner and had a few too many drinks before they called it a night.

C. M. OKONKWO

CHAPTER ONE: SPECIAL TREATMENT

The next day, Oluomachukwu got to the local wing of the airport at about 5:00am. She was sleepy and tired, and wondered why she had left home so early. She probably felt that she would be caught up in traffic and miss the first flight. The alcohol she had with Okechukwu the night before still lingered in her system and it made her weak, so weak that she wished she was still in bed. At the same time, she wanted to relive the fun moment in her head and smile, but she was too exhausted to even think. She hoped that she would get stronger before she got to Abuja and that everything would go well for her.

Everything seemed rushed, especially as she was going to register for the NYSC programme two days before the closing date, leaving little or no time for damage control, in the event that there were hiccups during the registration process. She had planned to go the NYSC office on the last day of registration, that was on Friday, but Okechukwu had spoken to his friend at the NYSC Head Office and advised against that, based on information privy to only insiders. Generally, it was published on the NYSC website that Friday was the last day of registration for foreign-trained Nigerian students, but in fact, Thursday was going to be the last day.

Anyone who came to the office on Friday was going to be asked to come back a few months later to register with the next batch, that is, Batch 'C,' and be sent back home, irrespective of where they were coming from.

Oluomachukwu had shaken her head sleepily when Okechukwu gave her the information, because he had also asked if she wanted to wait and join the next batch a few months later. She didn't know what 'a few months later' meant and she didn't trust the NYSC scheme enough to want to wait until then. She didn't want to just sit at home indolently while waiting extra months to register, simply because she came after the last day of registration.

The earliest flight to Abuja was to leave by 6:15am and Okechukwu reserved it. He also paid for it, even though Oluomachukwu protested. She had enough money in her foreign bank account and Okechukwu had told her that her ATM card would work in Nigeria, but at the same time, he didn't want her to pay for anything. He also didn't want to leave her stranded in Abuja, where she had never been to before. So he gave her some money for her return ticket as well, for her taxi in Abuja, for her feeding and for every other necessary thing he thought she might need.

Oluomachukwu needed a phone line. She had been in the country for only a night, so she hadn't gotten a phone line yet. She felt she could just get a SIM pack from the airport or from any hawker on the street, but Okechukwu told her it wasn't possible. A lot of things had changed in Nigeria since the last time she visited, so she had to buy a SIM card from a verified seller and register the line before using it. Alternatively, she could take an already registered line from a friend or family member. And just like many other Nigerians, Okechukwu had more than three lines. Since no one trusted phone line operators in Nigeria, most Nigerians had to have more than two lines in case of emergencies, so he gave Oluomachukwu one to use.

When everything was set, Okechukwu hugged her and

waited for her to pass through security check before he left the airport and went home to get ready for work.

***

Oluomachukwu arrived at Abuja airport an hour later. There had been only twelve people on the plane, including the pilot and co-pilot, and two airhostesses. One of the airhostesses had woken her up when the plane landed. She had slept all through the flight, so she didn't collect the breakfast pack that was served, which usually contained a sandwich with dried meat in it, a pack of fruit juice with a straw, a mini chocolate bar and a serviette. She was glad that no one woke her up for that.

She got to the arrival lounge and stopped to wonder if she knew anyone in Abuja that could take her around when she was done with her registration. She didn't know anyone. But when she stepped outside to get an airport taxi, she saw him, the most beautiful man ever. She had met him in London during one summer holiday and he had had the same effect on her as he did now in Abuja. They had ended up dating for a year and although she had wanted the relationship to last longer, it couldn't. The guy moved back to Nigeria without notice, and long distant relationships didn't sit too well with her.

He had come back to London for Christmas holiday, just to see her, then for Easter, and then the next summer. She hadn't heard from him since then, which was about three years back. She had cried a little bit and cursed him, but then she got a new job, which was the distraction she needed from the pain.

As Oluomachukwu approached the guy, she didn't know if she should talk to him or not. She hated him so much, even though he didn't know to what extent. After a brief moment of hesitation, she decided to be a stronger person and talk to him.

"Nnanna," she called, but the guy didn't turn around.

She moved quickly towards him and tapped him on the shoulder. "Nnanna."

The guy turned around and removed the earphones from his ears. "Yes?"

"Yes?" Oluomachukwu repeated, and the guy gazed at her. "You don't remember me?" She felt stupid for asking that and the hatred she felt towards him started to become stronger.

The guy squinted his eyes as if his memory box was in them, then he shook his head. "No, I'm so sorry. Do you know me?"

Oluomachukwu shook her head too. "No." She looked away and went to get the taxi.

It was indeed Nnanna, and after breaking her heart and causing her terrible pain, she wasn't going to allow him take her for a desperate girl.

Before she entered the taxi, she stopped and glanced towards the entrance of the airport with the corner of her eye and saw Nnanna holding a girl's hand with one hand and a hand luggage with the other. Even from a distance, Oluomachukwu saw the girl's face clearly; smile so bright that it looked like she had just been proposed to. Just then, she understood why he had acted so clueless about her. He had obviously come to pick up his girlfriend, or whatever she was to him, and didn't want to explain how he knew Oluomachukwu to her.

After almost one hour on the traffic-free road that led into the main city, Oluomachukwu got to the NYSC Head Office. The entire front side of the building had been barricaded with large cement blocks that were meant to prevent any stray vehicles from ramming down the gates and exploding. The terror sect, Boko Haram, was still on the loose and there was no telling where and when their agents would strike. It was better to be safe than sorry.

Whenever a vehicle got close to the cement blocks and stopped, security officers immediately stopped what they were doing to find out why. And when the driver zoomed off after dropping a passenger, the security officers would carry on with their business. Oluomachukwu and the taxi that dropped her off did not escape the scrutiny. She got out of the taxi quickly, and as she walked up to the gate, she met a lot of people waiting outside and hoped that they were not there for the same reason as she was.

One security officer on duty, who appeared to be rude, told her to join the crowd of people who were waiting to be attended to, as the registration office was not yet open to the public. She had arrived by 8:00am and the gates were going to be opened in two hours.

Oluomachukwu wasn't sure if she could wait, let alone scramble with the others to get into the building. If there was one thing she knew about her fellow Nigerians, it was that everyone was always in a hurry and they felt that the next person was constantly in a competition with them.

Oluomachukwu pulled out her cell phone to make a call after she had joined the crowd. The phone rang twice before it was answered.

"Hello?" the person on the other end of the call said.

"Oke," Oluomachukwu said. "It's Oluoma."

Okechukwu smiled and Oluomachukwu felt it even from over the phone. "Glad you got to Abuja in one piece. I was worried when you didn't call me."

"You should have called me as well." Oluomachukwu sulked.

"I should have, and I could have," Okechukwu replied. "But I didn't remember to collect your number. I got that line a while back and didn't memorise the number or save it on my other phones."

"Oh." Oluomachukwu felt very silly for a second, even though she shouldn't have. "That's fine."

"So, have you gotten to the NYSC Head Office or are you still at the airport?" he asked.

"I'm at the Head Office already."

"Really?" Okechukwu sounded surprised. "That was fast and early."

"Yeah, and the whole world is here. Plus I have to wait for another two hours to get in."

"Hmm," Okechukwu replied. "Do you have something to do while waiting?"

"I'm definitely not waiting out here. Can you please give me your friend's number? I want to see if he can let me in."

"I really don't think he can." Okechukwu sounded firm, the same way he had sounded when Oluomachukwu had said 'No' to him some years back, and that she wanted to date someone else, someone who she had met through him.

"At least let me try." Oluomachukwu wasn't prepared to give up. "This place is crowded. I can't stand for too long. Plus I'm hungry."

Okechukwu didn't budge. "Didn't you have anything to eat on the plane?"

"No, I slept all through and I'm tired. I feel like I might pass out."

"Okay, okay," Okechukwu responded. He didn't know what else she would say just to get his friend's number. "I'll text it to you right away."

"Okay, thanks." She hung up and waited for it. And when the text finally came in, she was already pissed off. 'Right away' had taken almost five minutes.

Oluomachukwu called Okechukwu's contact, a young man named Kayode. She assumed he was young because of the way he sounded, and also for the fact that he was Okechukwu's friend. When Kayode came out to meet her, he was indeed young, and it felt as though heaven was on a mission to bless her with the pleasures of the eyes. He was the definition of 'eye candy,' just like Nnanna was, but in another flavour.

Kayode led Oluomachukwu into the building, and as she entered, she could hear the crowd murmur things that sounded like "cheat; bribery and corruption; impatient Nigerians; thunder will strike you; we have connection in

Abuja too; prostitute..." Oluomachukwu ignored them all. She smiled as she walked into the building, clutching the file that held all her documents in one hand and her bag in the other.

***

The minute Oluomachukwu stepped out of the NYSC Head Office, she pulled out her phone and saw more than twenty missed calls. About two hours had passed and the registration process had gone smoothly for her. She never expected it to be that way, but she was glad that she wasn't stressed. The only reason it took that long was because she had to scan and upload a missing document to her NYSC online account and make a couple of photocopies, which someone in Kayode's office helped her to do. Apart from that, it was a peaceful process.

As she was looking at her phone and trying to figure out who had the number that had left her all the missed calls, the phone started ringing again. The same number was calling her back.

Oluomachukwu picked it up. "Hello?"

"Oluoma, I have been calling you all morning. You got me very worried, where are you?" The person sounded aggressive and Oluomachukwu didn't know who it was. It was a female quite all right, but that was all she knew. Plus she hadn't given her number to anyone. She wanted to ask who it was, but she didn't want to sound rude.

"Are you still there?" the person asked.

Oluomachukwu gnashed her teeth. At the same time, she was surveying the fleet of cars that moved slowly on the road in front of the NYSC building, hoping to see an empty taxi. But she didn't see any.

"Hello?" the person on the phone called out again.

"Yes, I'm here, sorry," Oluomachukwu finally said. "I just need to get a taxi, so I'm looking out for one."

"Are you coming over here?" the person asked.

Oluomachukwu had no other option than to ask who it was. "I'm sorry, please, who is this?"

"It's Akunna *nau*," the person replied.

"Oh, Akunna." Oluomachukwu was embarrassed that she hadn't recognised the voice. Akunna was Okechukwu's older sister.

"Oke didn't tell you that he would give me your phone number to call you?" Akunna asked.

"No, he didn't."

"Anyway, he said you were spending the night with me in Abuja."

"He did?" Oluomachukwu didn't recall telling anyone that she was spending the night in Abuja, except Kayode, and she didn't think he would tell Okechukwu or anyone.

"Yes, so I wanted to call and find out when you would be done with your registration. And since it seems like you are already done, when are you coming over? You can take a taxi to Prince and Princess Estate..."

Oluomachukwu wasn't listening to what Akunna was saying anymore, but she knew she didn't want to spend the night with anyone. "Umm, Akunna, let me ring you back," she interrupted her after a few seconds.

Akunna cleared her throat. "Why?"

"I still have some things to take care of."

"I thought you just said you were looking for a taxi?"

Oluomachukwu had said that, but she didn't remember in time. And it was difficult to keep track of what was said, especially if it was a lie.

"Yes, the cyber café around here is packed full, but I was told there is another one not too far from here. I want to get a taxi and go there, then be back before the NYSC office closes."

"Oh, okay." Akunna sighed. Whether she believed the story or not, Oluomachukwu didn't care, she was just glad that Akunna had accepted it. "Call me when you are done so that I'll know when you would be coming."

"No problem. I'll speak to you later." Oluomachukwu

hung up, then sighed.

***

Oluomachukwu settled in her hotel room and lay on the bed, wanting to take a quick nap before she did any other thing. She had found herself a taxi shortly after her phone chat with Akunna and it took her straight to the hotel. The hotel had been recommended by Kayode, since she didn't know anywhere in Abuja. She looked at her phone — thirty-five missed calls from Akunna. And as she was about to place the phone on the table, Akunna started calling again. Oluomachukwu did not pick up.

When her phone beeped once, she looked at it and saw a text message from Akunna asking if everything was okay, because she was worried. All Oluomachukwu wanted was some time to rest and didn't want anyone disturbing her, family friend or not. She looked at the time, it was 4:35pm, so she texted Akunna back, saying that she couldn't talk, because she was still at the NYSC Head Office.

Akunna simply replied "Okay." Oluomachukwu sighed, relieved. Before she finally placed her phone on the table, she heard a knock at the door.

She scooted off quickly, and after looking through the peephole, she yanked the door open.

"Hey," she said. She smiled at Kayode as she made way for him to enter.

Kayode returned the smile and entered. He was holding two big white bags. "I come bearing gifts," he said, then gave her the bags. One was heavier than the other.

Oluomachukwu was very excited. She brought out the takeaway from KFC from the lighter bag and six bottles of alcoholic drinks from the heavier one. She hadn't realised how hungry she was, so she quickly served the drinks, then they began eating, drinking and talking.

"Your registration was successful and as you requested, I worked your posting to Lagos State."

"Thanks," Oluomachukwu replied, not taking her eyes off the fries and chicken.

"Why do you even want to serve in Lagos?" Kayode asked.

Oluomachukwu shrugged her shoulders, then licked her fingers. "I don't know. Familiar territory, I guess."

"I doubt there's any familiar area in Lagos for you, or even in Nigeria." Kayode laughed. "I should have worked Abuja for you, so that you would stay with me."

Oluomachukwu looked up at him, with eyes that could shoot fireballs.

Kayode laughed again and raised both hands. "I was just joking, take it easy," he said, as he continued laughing.

"Okechukwu is the only one I have in Nigeria for now and he is in Lagos," she said.

There was a brief silence, which was interrupted by her phone vibrating on the table by the bed. It did the same thing about three times.

"Aren't you going to get that?" Kayode asked.

"No." Oluomachukwu was eating the last tiny bit of chicken on the bone she was holding.

Kayode went and took the phone, and Oluomachukwu didn't object. "There's just a number calling you, but no name. Who is it?" he asked.

"I don't know." She sounded quite annoyed. She had a feeling it was Akunna again. "Just put the phone down."

Kayode didn't put the phone down. He answered it, and the second he said "Hello," Oluomachukwu jumped up from the bed, hopped towards him and snatched the phone, angry. She had flung the chicken bone in the process, and with her greasy hand, she held the phone to her ear. Okechukwu was saying "Hello" multiple times. He had called with a different number that she didn't have.

She hung up, then looked at Kayode. "What was that for?"

Before he could reply, her phone started ringing again. Okechukwu was calling her back, but she didn't pick it up.

He called a few more times and she still didn't answer.

A few seconds later, Kayode's phone started ringing. He looked at Oluomachukwu. "It's your cousin calling me. He probably wants to know how everything went today."

Oluomachukwu didn't answer. For a second, she didn't understand what Kayode had said, because she didn't have any cousin who would call Kayode to ask about her or her registration. But then, she figured it was Okechukwu and was amused that he had told Kayode they were cousins. And she thought she knew why — Okechukwu obviously didn't want Kayode to make passes at her. But the only way Okechukwu would have guaranteed that was if he had told Kayode that she was his girlfriend, and even at that, it wasn't promised.

Oluomachukwu took her cell phone with her into the bathroom. Kayode had picked up his call, but she couldn't hear what he was saying. While in the bathroom, she called Akunna back to tell her that she was coming, even though she had no intention of going to Akunna's place. The call was brief and after Oluomachukwu hung up, Akunna sent her the address via text message and told her to get a taxi over there immediately. It sounded as though Akunna was afraid of Oluomachukwu being kidnapped, or even worse, being blown up in an untimely explosion.

Oluomachukwu replied "O.K. thanks" to her, then she remembered why she didn't like visiting or even staying with friends or relatives. Most of them were too bossy and nosy. They loved to order people around, especially if they were housing the people, or supposed to house the people, and they would make sure to constantly mention that they own the house and pay all the bills.

When Oluomachukwu went back to the room, Kayode had gotten off the phone.

"You didn't tell your cousin that you were spending the night at a hotel?"

Oluomachukwu's phone started vibrating in her hand before she replied. Okechukwu was calling back again. "I didn't," she replied. "And you shouldn't have."

"I didn't either," Kayode said defensively. "I told him I was still at work and that you have to come back to the office tomorrow to finalise your registration."

"Okay," she replied, then picked up. She placed her index finger over her lips, indicating to Kayode to keep quiet. She couldn't risk Kayode even breathing loudly and being heard. "Oke?"

"I've been calling you, where did you keep your phone? Akunna has been calling you too. Where are you?"

Oluomachukwu was offended by his questioning and tone. She suddenly didn't want Kayode to listen in on what she was going to say, so she went into the bathroom. At the same time, Okechukwu was asking if she was still on the line and if she was with someone.

"Oke, I've been busy with my registration," she started. "I had to leave the office twice to get some things done."

"I called before and a guy picked up." Okechukwu was evidently angry. "Who was it?"

"That's strange," Oluomachukwu responded, sounding clueless. "Because I'm not with any guy and no one picked up my phone."

"Okay, please, call Akunna. She's waiting for you and she's worried. She said she has been calling you and you're not picking up."

Oluomachukwu wanted to ask him why he had to tell Akunna that she was in town, but she decided not to. "I'll see Akunna much later."

"Okay, cool. Keep me posted," he said, then hung up.

When Oluomachukwu returned to the room, Kayode had already finished eating and was taking shots of brandy. Oluomachukwu went to join him without saying anything.

"Hmm," Kayode started, after he took another shot of brandy. "Your cousin sounds like he is your boyfriend."

Oluomachukwu couldn't help but laugh. " All the guys in my family are overprotective. So you can't blame them." She decided to play along with him.

Kayode grinned at Oluomachukwu mischievously and she also smiled at him. There was an awkward silence after that, so she looked down and closed her eyes only briefly. When she opened them, Kayode was staring at her, his eyes traveling all over her body. He licked his lips when his eyes met with hers. Her look was so intense that he almost dropped the glass he was holding. He then carefully put it on the table and turned his stare back to her.

Oluomachukwu also had some shots of brandy and it was burning inside of her — the type of burning only the touch of a man could temper. Kayode saw it in her eyes and approached her. He attempted to kiss her and she did not resist him. She wanted to blame it on the alcohol, but she had not drunk enough to make her that intoxicated.

They started to kiss slowly and gently, as they took off their clothes, and that was the last thing Oluomachukwu remembered of the moment.

C. M. OKONKWO

CHAPTER TWO: REMEMBER ME

Oluomachukwu and Kayode sat at the lounge in Rockview Hotel, having drinks. They had opted for soft drinks, because they felt they had drunk enough alcohol at her hotel room. Oluomachukwu's head was aching, between her legs was still sensitive and her phone hadn't stopped ringing all the while that she was with Kayode back in her hotel room. She wasn't sure how many times Akunna or even Okechukwu had called. She hadn't saved either of their phone numbers, so she couldn't tell which number belonged to whom at that instant. She then divided the over forty missed calls between both of them.

Oluomachukwu and Kayode sat down at a table close to the bar, from where they could see the clean swimming pool in Rockview Hotel, but the silence between them was awkward. She and Kayode weren't saying anything to each other. They had nothing to say, although they had talked a lot before he put out her fire. They now looked like total strangers who had been put on the same table and forced to be friends.

Before the moment could get any weirder than it was already, Oluomachukwu heard her name and immediately turned around. The frame of a tall, caramel-skinned hunk stood behind her, blocking the light so that she couldn't see his face, only his silhouette. She tilted her head slightly to the side and saw the person's face.

She gasped, then said, "Nnanna?"

The person nodded. "I wasn't sure it was you. I saw you heading towards the stairs when I was driving out. I contemplated coming to say hello at first, but I eventually decided to."

"Oh yeah?" Oluomachukwu tilted her head backwards. "Why?"

"I didn't think you would remember me," he replied.

Oluomachukwu rolled her eyes. "Okay, so why did you ignore me and act clueless at the airport today, then?" She wanted to ask if it was because of the girl he had met at the airport, but she knew not to.

"What airport?" Nnanna asked.

"Were you not at the Nnamdi Azikiwe Airport today?" Oluomachukwu immediately felt like the clueless one.

He shook his head. "No. I guess you saw my look alike. I didn't know there was anyone as handsome as I am in Abuja." He laughed. Oluomachukwu also laughed, but he didn't notice that it was a forced one.

There was something about Nnanna that made her legs weak. She had loved him and even after he broke her heart and put her through a painful path, she secretly wanted to see him again, ask him why he had left her and tell him everything that had happened since then, then give him a second chance, if he asked. She wanted to tell him that she was still mad with him and that nothing could change the past, but there was the present and the future.

Nnanna and Oluomachukwu kept quiet when they were done laughing and didn't say any other thing until Kayode cleared his throat.

"Oh, I'm sorry," Oluomachukwu said. "Nnanna, this is—"

"Kayode," Nnanna complemented, then extended his hand to shake Kayode, although it appeared to be forced.

"I hope you are good."

Kayode hesitated before stretching forth his hand, and immediately after he shook Nnanna, he withdrew his hand. "All is well. I didn't know you knew Oluoma."

"I didn't know you did, too," Nnanna said. "Oluoma and I dated a few years back."

There was another awkward silence — Oluomachukwu started to wonder why Nnanna had added the part where they dated, and if there was a sort of contest going on between them. She felt a rush of guilt for having made out with Kayode and wished she had just gone back to Lagos after her registration.

She looked at Nnanna and Kayode, they were staring at each other, so focused that they didn't even notice when she stood up and walked away. She went to the toilet and spent a few too many minutes in there. Her phone was still ringing nonstop. She picked it up and it was Okechukwu.

"Oluoma, my sister is worried sick. Where are you?" he asked. "Is that music I'm hearing in the background?"

"Please, tell her I'm not coming," Oluomachukwu said. "I'll just spend the night at a hotel."

"What?" Okechukwu exclaimed. "With who?"

"Alone." Oluomachukwu sounded firm. "Who else will I spend the night with? I'll take the first available flight to Lagos tomorrow after I finalise my registration."

"Oluoma, are you okay?" Okechukwu asked. "Because you sound strange."

"I'm okay. I just want to listen to music, think about this one-year I want to give to my country, then fall asleep. That's all."

"Okay, no problem. I'll call Akunna now and tell her not to expect you, then. Good night."

"Good night..." She wanted to add 'dear,' but he had already hung up. She didn't realise until that moment how much he cared about her.

Although she felt he and Akunna were pestering her, but in reality, they were just looking out for her. It was not going to make her reconsider him, though. She liked the attention and feared that it would no longer be there if she decided to date him.

When she stepped out of the toilet, she bumped into Nnanna. "Nnanna, you scared me," she said.

"I'm so sorry. I was just about to leave, so I wanted to collect your phone number and give you mine." He pulled out his phone and waited for her to give it to him.

Oluomachukwu didn't object. She should have, but she didn't. She also didn't know what Okechukwu would say if he found out that she had met Nnanna, had a conversation with him again and even exchanged numbers.

Nnanna thanked her and promised to call her later. But before he left, he told her something that would make her think for a while. "Be careful of Kayode. He is married."

***

Oluomachukwu got back to her hotel room, pissed off, angry and in a very foul mood, as she recalled how she had gone back to meet Kayode right after Nnanna left. She had asked him about his wife and he remained calm. He didn't accept the fact and he didn't deny it either. The only thing he did was to ask her how she got the information about his marital status. He wondered if it was from Nnanna, Okechukwu, or both. Oluomachukwu didn't even reply to his question, she simply turned around to leave without saying goodbye, shoving his hand away as he tried to stop her.

While in the taxi back to her hotel, Nnanna had called her to make her feel better and laugh a bit. He managed to get a few laughs out of her until he apologised for breaking her heart. He didn't give a serious reason why he did it. He said he was young and didn't know what he wanted, but it wasn't a satisfactory reason for Oluomachukwu. And as the conversation carried on, he managed to invite himself over to her hotel room and she didn't object to it.

While waiting for him to arrive, she arranged her things in her handbag for her trip back to Lagos. She then ate the rest of the chicken that Kayode had bought, drank a few glasses of wine and ignored more phone calls, which were probably from Akunna to ask why she didn't want to visit anymore or from Kayode to apologise.

When she was done, she slipped into her nightwear — a spaghetti-strap satin top and matching shorts, both black. The satin top was lined with pink lace that dropped down to reveal her full cleavage.

She slid into bed, as she took another glass of wine, and pulled out her phone to go through her emails, tweets and Facebook updates, but she saw even more missed calls and wondered if Okechukwu hadn't told Akunna that she was not spending the night at hers anymore. She then used the opportunity to save all the numbers on her phone so that she would know who was calling at all times.

She had saved only Akunna's number when her phone started ringing. She wasn't really sure if it was Okechukwu calling and wondered why he would be calling again.

She picked up the call and it was Kayode.

"Why are you calling me?" she asked.

"I'm calling to apologise. I didn't say anything to you at Rockview because I knew you were upset. I didn't want to say anything that would upset you the more."

"I don't understand," Oluomachukwu said. She hadn't even seen a ring on his finger all day. "Why did you make a move on me when you knew you were married?"

"I'm sorry."

"I don't know what that means." She was not satisfied with his reply. "And why did you also ask me to go out for drinks with you afterwards?"

"Your cousin wanted me to take care of you in Abuja."

"Did he also ask you to take care of my body and its needs?" She didn't expect an answer to that. "I am sure he only asked you to help me out with my registration, and he doesn't even know that we hung out all evening."

"Why don't you ask him?" Kayode asked. "He is your cousin after all."

"Okechukwu," Oluomachukwu spat out. "Okechukwu is his name."

"What?" Kayode asked.

"Stop referring to him as my cousin all the time. He has a name."

Kayode was surprised. "Are you okay?" he asked. "If I didn't know the two of you were blood relatives, I would have said that you were in love or something."

"That's disgusting," Oluomachukwu replied. "You just keep saying 'your cousin.' I have other cousins and you are overworking my brain. Besides, he is my family friend, and not my cousin."

"I'm sorry," Kayode said, then he took her by surprise when he added, "About not telling you I was married." He figured that was the reason she was annoyed. Whether he called Okechukwu's name or not wasn't the issue.

Oluomachukwu didn't want to hear any of it, and she didn't even know what she was thinking, having something to do with a man she barely even knew. She wished she could turn back the hands of time and not accept to spend the night in Abuja or even see him earlier that evening.

"So have you forgiven me?"

Oluomachukwu heard Kayode's voice, but she hadn't been listening to what he was saying to her, if at all he had been saying anything to her. In fact, his voice startled her, and the knock on her hotel room door at that instant also startled her.

"Are you expecting someone?" Kayode asked her. But before she could respond, he added, "Is it Nnanna?"

Oluomachukwu didn't reply right away. She stood up and went to check who it was through the peephole. It was Nnanna quite all right, looking as handsome as ever. She smiled, then remembered she wasn't supposed to be happy with him.

"It's Nnanna, right?" Kayode repeated. "Are you still

there?"

There was another knock at the door. Oluomachukwu hung up immediately after saying goodbye, not allowing Kayode to reply. She then opened the door and smiled as Nnanna approached and hugged her. He smelled nice and sweet, so sweet that she could eat him, but she controlled herself.

After Oluomachukwu let him in, he went straight for the drinks on the table. Her phone started to ring while she was getting settled down. It was Kayode calling her back. She declined the call, then declined a second and a third time before she switched the phone off completely.

"Hmm, so who is calling you?" Nnanna asked. "Don't break any hearts oh."

Nnanna laughed, but she didn't. Heartbreak wasn't a topic she wanted to joke about. Nnanna understood the message a few seconds later. And instead of apologising or changing topics, he pulled her closer and attempted to give her a proper hug. "I've missed you," he said.

She pulled away, and as she looked into his eyes, she saw fire burning in it — the same kind she had had earlier that evening — the one only the touch of a woman could quench. But she wasn't going to give him the pleasure and satisfaction that he was expecting to receive.

She slapped him twice on the same cheek. "I hate you," she said, sounding sincere.

Nnanna didn't feel the impact of the slap, but he held his cheek all the same. "What was that for?" he asked, as if he didn't know.

"You think you can just come back into my life after breaking my heart and even allowing me to..." She stopped when she realised she should have stopped at 'breaking my heart.'

"Allowing you to what?"

"Nothing..." She paused a bit. "Forget I said anything."

"Oluoma, you know I won't forget anything." Nnanna was starting to sound and look worried.

"Well, too bad, because I am not telling you anything." She got the glasses for more drinks. "And you and I know that you are not going to win this battle, so don't bother asking me again."

She brought out the remaining bottle of drink, as she planned to drink all that was left in the hotel room before going back to Lagos.

***

When Oluomachukwu landed in Lagos, she went to get an airport taxi that would take her to Okechukwu's place in Ikoyi. She could have called him to come and get her, but she didn't want to disturb him, especially as she knew that he might already be at work. She also knew that she didn't want to stay at his place anymore. After her night with Nnanna, she was reconsidering him. And if she was going to date him again, she would need her own place.

As she waited around for a taxi, she realised that her phone hadn't rang in a while. When she fished out the phone from her handbag that could pass for a travelling bag, she saw that it was switched off. She had forgotten to turn it on after blowing Kayode off the night before.

She managed to bargain a taxi, but she wasn't sure if they had cheated her. So before getting in, she turned her phone on to call Okechukwu, ignoring the multitude of text messages that came in.

The call didn't go through, because she didn't have sufficient airtime. So she walked towards a young girl that hawked recharge cards for various network operators, who stood not too far away from her, and bought one for her phone.

As she was waiting for the girl to scratch the card and reveal the secret pin, she decided to go through her text messages — they were mostly promotional text messages from the network operator, then some from Okechukwu and one from Kayode.

She didn't open any of the text messages yet. She took the recharge card from the girl and loaded her phone first, then called Okechukwu immediately, as the taxi driver was still waiting for her and getting impatient.

"Oluoma," Okechukwu said, as soon as he picked up. "Where have you been? Are you okay?"

"Yeah, I guess so," Oluomachukwu replied.

"You guess so?" Okechukwu thought her reply was strange. "Where are you?"

"At the airport."

"Which airport?"

"Lagos."

Okechukwu was surprised. He glanced at his phone screen and checked the time. "It's not even 9:00am yet and you are back already."

"Yeah." Oluomachukwu didn't know exactly where he was going with his comments.

"Didn't you say you had to finish up your registration today?"

Oluomachukwu could have answered, but didn't know what to say. So instead she looked at her phone, then hit the End Call button. She wasn't in the mood to explain, especially as it was going to be a lie. She knew Okechukwu was going to call her back, so she wanted to use the short time to think of something to say. In three seconds, as she expected, her phone rang. She hesitated a bit, then picked up.

"Hello?" she said.

"What happened?" Okechukwu asked. "Did you run out of airtime?"

"Yes," Oluomachukwu lied, then walked back to the taxi line and found the taxi man she had bargained her trip back to Ikoyi with. "By the way, how much does it cost to come to Ikoyi with a taxi?"

"I would say between 3,500 naira and 4,000 naira, but it depends. Why?"

"Depends on what?" Oluomachukwu asked. "Because

I'm about to get into a taxi now."

"On if you are a *Johny-just-come*." Okechukwu laughed. "They can spot a newbie and hike the price. How much is he asking you for?"

The driver opened the back seat door for her, already grumbling, and she entered. "Anyway, I bargained 4,500 naira, so I'm not that bad." They both laughed. "Okay, so I just got into the taxi now. Are you still at home?"

"No, but you can come to my office first, I'll give you the house keys."

"Okay, thanks." Oluomachukwu paused briefly when the cabbie fired the engine. It was too noisy, she could hardly hear herself. When the taxi driver started moving, she continued, "Please, can you text your office address to me?"

"I will," Okechukwu replied. "And please, can you call Akunna?"

"Why?"

"She might be angry with you because you stood her up yesterday."

"Stood her up?"

"She was worried."

"Okay, I'll call her now and apologise for not spending the night over at hers."

As if the second part of Oluomachukwu's sentence had just triggered something, Okechukwu remembered he had asked a question that she didn't reply to. "So why did you spend the night in Abuja, anyway?" he asked. "Because it was obviously not for your registration."

Oluomachukwu didn't reply.

"Or was it because of Nnanna?" he continued.

Oluomachukwu felt her heart stop for a second. "What do you mean 'because of Nnanna?'"

"Well, he said he saw you at the airport, so I assumed he was the reason," Okechukwu said.

"He said that?"

"Aha!" Okechukwu exclaimed. "I knew it was because

of him."

"I didn't even see him," Oluomachukwu replied, angry. Nnanna had lied to her, which meant that he was indeed at the airport and was with a girl.

Okechukwu laughed, but it sounded more like he had sighed. "So why did you stay back? Or didn't you complete your registration?"

"I did," Oluomachukwu said. "Kayode called me later and told me that the registration had been successful. They had a problem with my degree certificate, but it had been rectified, so he called to tell me. And the call came in too late to start coming back to Lagos."

"Hmm," Okechukwu replied.

"If you have something to say, please, say it."

"Kayode is married."

"How does that concern me?" Oluomachukwu replied, even though it concerned her. But it was already too late to feel sad about it. She was already feeling guilty.

"Nnanna is also getting married soon. Did you know that?"

Oluomachukwu froze on the seat. She didn't reply. She didn't have anything to say. She wished the call would end.

"The funny thing is that the girl he wants to marry used to date Kayode before. Nnanna met her for the first time at one event I organised, then he sort of snatched her from Kayode. In fact, I don't know who did the snatching." He laughed, then stopped immediately when he noticed that Oluomachukwu hadn't said anything. "Are you still there?"

Oluomachukwu wanted to cry, but she held back the tears. She sort of had an idea why Okechukwu was giving her that information. It was payback. Payback for blowing him off to date Nnanna some years back.

There was an awkward silence that was broken by the taxi driver when he turned around to ask Oluomachukwu for the specific address she was going to in Ikoyi.

Oluomachukwu saw it as the perfect opportunity to put an end to the call. "Please, can you text your office address to me so that I can give it to the taxi man?" she asked. "He has been waiting for it."

"I'll do that now," Okechukwu said, then hung up.

Oluomachukwu looked at her phone screen, the battery life was at three percent, but it was enough to do a couple more things on the phone. She received the text message from Okechukwu and gave the address to the taxi driver, then she opened and read Kayode's text message from the night before, over and over again, "Be careful of Nnanna, he is getting married soon." She let out the tears.

CHAPTER THREE: CALL UP

Two weeks went very fast for Oluomachukwu. She spent the time touring Lagos, trying her best to forget her moments of weakness in Abuja and ignoring all her phone calls. She hadn't spoken to her parents yet, she only sent messages, but she wasn't worried. She had told her parents not to worry about her. The only time they were going to receive a call was if something didn't go as planned, and she wasn't expecting anything to go wrong.

Oluomachukwu couldn't remember what day she did, but she finally called Akunna to apologise. The call didn't go too well and Oluomachukwu didn't want to even think about it. Akunna had refused to answer her calls the first five times, so Oluomachukwu didn't bother calling back a sixth time. And after about five minutes, Akunna called back, yelled her mind at Oluomachukwu, then hung up.

Oluomachukwu thought it was more of a monologue than a dialogue. The age difference between both of them was merely seven years, but Akunna always wanted to act like she was the surrogate mother of all her relatives and family friends, the most responsible one and the one that everyone had to fear and respect. Oluomachukwu didn't have time for that. With Akunna out of the way, she could now focus on other things.

On the NYSC website, Oluomachukwu checked what date she was supposed to pick up her Call-up letter. In the letter, she would know in what State she was going to serve. She already knew it was going to be Lagos State, because Kayode had worked it out for her that way.

She flagged down a taxi just a few meters away from Okechukwu's house and asked the taxi man to take her to the NYSC Lagos State Secretariat in Surulere. She didn't know the route to get there, even after she had toured Lagos. She had looked at most of the roads, but didn't really memorise anything. As she rode in the taxi, she didn't know if she was on track or off track, she was at the mercy of the taxi driver.

The traffic was so intense and the sun was very hot. It was already rainy season, but it had rained only a few days in the two weeks she was in Lagos, and when it rained, it poured. The heat was making her feel like she had been sitting in the car for more than two hours, but she didn't know exactly how long it had been.

There were hawkers selling all sorts of things on trays, hanging either on their shoulders or resting on their heads. Some had cartons with transparent nylon in front, where their items were displayed. But with the heat and the angry motorists that filled the streets, who refused to buy anything, the hawkers stopped moving about and dropped their goods, and some of them started to grumble. One of the hawkers even started eating the meat pie he was selling, looking angrily at anyone he thought was judging him.

After another hour, the taxi driver dropped her off, and she asked him to wait for her, so that he could take her back to Ikoyi after she picked up her letter. He agreed.

The wait inside the collection building wasn't too long. Oluomachukwu figured that it was for only foreign-trained Nigerian students, and that was why there weren't any long queues reaching the main gate. It didn't mean that the line moved fast, though. It was simply a short, but slow queue. The NYSC officials were calling prospective Youth Corps members to pick up their letters by the alphabetical order of their surname.

Oluomachukwu was on the queue for 'J,' and it was a rather empty queue compared to the ones for 'A' and 'O.' So some people that came in later than others got their letters and left before those who had been there earlier on the longer queues.

When Oluomachukwu got to the top of the queue, she was asked to present her international passport in order to collect her Call-up letter. Nothing of the sort had been written on the NYSC website, or even at the Abuja Head Office, but Oluomachukwu had been wise enough to take hers along with her. Some of the prospective Youth Corps members hadn't taken their international passports along and were asked to go home and get it. It was part of the NYSC office's way of knowing if prospective Youth Corps members were still in the country after registration.

Well, rumour had it that some of them register for the programme, then leave the country after paying someone to collect their Call-up letter, go to the Orientation camp for them and follow-up with the full service year for them.

Oluomachukwu presented her international passport and received her letter. She was posted to Lagos, and there was no surprise there. She folded the letter in two and put it inside her international passport, then in her handbag, not to be touched, until it was time to go to camp... in five days' time. Oluomachukwu felt the timing was too soon. And as the idea of her going to camp so soon hit her, she started to have cold feet. She wasn't sure she wanted to go to camp anymore.

As Oluomachukwu was leaving the building, her phone started ringing. She had forgotten to put the ring style to 'vibrate' as she normally did, so it wasn't surprising that everyone looked at her when the phone rang, especially as her ring tone was a song in a language, foreign to everyone around her.

It was Nnanna calling and she hesitated. That was the best move she had made, because when she looked up, she saw Kayode from a distance heading towards the building — she had no idea he was in Lagos. She froze for a few seconds, not sure what to do. She declined the call first of all and turned her ringer off, after which she stood behind the door and started looking into her handbag as if she was searching for something. She waited until Kayode entered the building and went to speak with one of the officials before she snuck out.

As she was leaving, she heard him asking if they had finished distributing all the Call-up letters for surnames starting with 'T.' She didn't know why he asked that, but at least she was glad he wasn't looking for her. When she was sure that he wasn't looking, she crept towards the taxi parked in plain sight and jumped in.

As she got into the taxi, her phone started to vibrate. Nnanna was calling her back. She picked up the phone. "Hello?"

"Babe, I've been trying to call you since yesterday," he said. "Are you okay?"

"Of course I'm okay." Even Oluomachukwu could feel the frostiness in her own tone. "How about you and your fiancée?"

There was a sudden scramble, as though someone was fumbling with the phone. Oluomachukwu looked at her phone, Nnanna had hung up. As usual, he still didn't have the courage to tell her the truth.

***

The weekend before going to camp, Oluomachukwu sat in Okechukwu's sitting room with him, having a few drinks. She realised she hadn't said much to him in days, and it seemed as if she was avoiding him. She didn't just want him to mention Nnanna's name again, or talk about Abuja or anything at that. She just wanted to go back to her room and sleep, or do anything that would keep her away from the sitting room, from Okechuwku and from the bottle of alcohol that refused to get empty. She stood up to leave.

"Oluoma, you've been avoiding me. Did I do anything wrong?" Okechukwu asked.

Oluomachukwu stopped, speechless. She opened her mouth after a couple of seconds and slurred some rather incomprehensible words.

"I don't understand what you just said," Okechukwu replied, sounding puzzled.

"Never mind." Oluomachukwu sat back and poured herself another drink, then the awkward silent moment returned.

"Anyway," Okechuwku said. "You'll need some things to take to camp."

She looked at him. "Really? I've been checking online for a while now and I haven't seen anything yet."

"Well, I think there are some things you'll really need, and the online updates might not be helpful. I doubt there will even be updates."

"Hmm." Oluomachukwu sighed. She was beginning to sense her cold feet return. "So what will be helpful?"

"I have someone I can call. She will be able to tell you what you will need."

The only thing Oluomachukwu heard was 'she' and she hoped Okechukwu wasn't talking about Akunna. That was the last person she wanted to talk to.

Okechukwu called his friend, Idara, who had served in the Lagos camp about two or three years ago, he was no longer sure. She was now based in Calabar, but if anyone knew the 'A' to 'Z' of the NYSC Lagos Orientation camp, it was Idara. She was also visiting Lagos for the week.

Okechukwu held the phone to his ear, then changed it to the other ear. Idara must not have answered the call, because he put his phone down briefly and complained for a little bit before redialling.

"Yes, hey, Idara," Okechukwu said abruptly. "How are you?"

Oluomachukwu obviously couldn't hear what Idara was saying. In fact, she completely blanked her mind, not wanting to listen to Okechukwu's side of the conversation until he was ready for her. But before she could completely zone out, Okechukwu called her name.

"Oluoma, she wants to talk to you."

Oluomachukwu scrunched her face, she actually didn't want to talk to anyone, but he kept gesticulating to her to take the phone. She sluggishly leaned forward, then took the phone from him.

"Hello," Oluomachukwu said.

"Hey, Oluoma. So how are you enjoying Lagos?" Idara asked.

"It's all right. I've not really done a lot, because I don't have friends here."

Idara laughed. "But with Okechukwu there, what other friend do you need?"

"What?" Oluomachukwu had blanked out for a few seconds, so she didn't hear the last thing Idara had said.

"I said, 'you have an amazing cousin, so you can't be bored.'"

"I'm not bored." Oluomachukwu's reply was so sharp it could cut through a massive chunk of beef in one strike. Even Okechukwu turned and looked at her, probably wondering what was going on.

"Anyway," Idara said. "Here's what you will need, but first just know that you don't really have to stay in camp."

"Really?" Oluomachukwu sounded excited for the first time in days.

"Yes. You can just go on the first day, once the second week, then maybe twice the last week."

"I didn't know that."

"Yeah, you don't have to stay put for the whole three

weeks. But I'll advise you to go, just for the experience."

Oluomachukwu almost said "Duh." Of course she was going to attend camp. That was the reason she came back to Nigeria in the first place. She might have been having cold feet, but she knew deep within that she was headed to camp eventually.

"Will they just allow me waltz in and out of camp like that?" Oluomachukwu asked.

"If it's the camp in Iyana-Ipaja, then you don't have a problem." Idara laughed before she continued. "I could waltz out whenever I wanted and needed. In fact, I actually did sometimes when Okechukwu came to rescue me."

Oluomachukwu refused to acknowledge the last part of Idara's sentence.

"But I don't think anything has changed since 2011," Idara added.

"Okay, things like what?"

"Umm, basically, just items to go with." Idara sighed. "White tennis shoes and white socks, black undergarments that won't embarrassingly display your body parts because you'll be wearing white shirt and white shorts all day, then toiletries and a blanket."

"That's a whole lot," Oluomachukwu protested. "And I still haven't seen anything on the website."

"They wouldn't put anything on there, because they usually provide white shirts and shorts, two each, both of really poor quality, with some footwear they call tennis shoes that wouldn't be your size."

Oluomachukwu was about to thank Idara for her time, but she couldn't because Idara didn't stop talking. She just wanted to go to camp and find out for herself, because Idara was starting to scare her.

"Aha, get green belts, too. They'll give you belts made of cloth. And you'll also be lucky if your khakis fit. They are the uniforms you use for parade and ceremonies. And there's also a camp market that people call *mami* market, where you can buy everything you need..."

Oluomachukwu yawned, but Idara didn't notice.

"Always lock your box and trust no one, even your so-called new friends," Idara continued. "They steal things. Be at alert when you sleep. Also make an easy hairstyle that will be easy to style, because you are required to be at the parade ground by 5:00am and expected to put on a cap. If your hair is too full or styled like a crown, the cap will not fit..."

Oluomachukwu didn't know if Idara was genuinely trying to be helpful or if it was because of Okechukwu. Either way, she was done listening to her. She was going to figure everything out in camp.

She thanked Idara, interrupting her, then hung up after their goodbyes and good night.

"What did she say?" Okechukwu asked.

"That I didn't need to get a lot of things," she replied reluctantly, which was obviously a lie. "And that I'll know all there is to know in camp."

***

Oluomachukwu couldn't wait to get to camp. This time it wasn't because she wanted to escape Okechukwu and his unspoken love for her, but because she wanted to get camp over with. Idara had called again to tell her how and where to hide in the mornings, so that she would avoid going to the parade ground for morning drills. Idara also told her that she could go to camp with mufti, because she would be able to put them on, especially on Sundays.

Idara also proposed to take her to the market to buy some of her basic needs and wears, some of which were going to be fairly used, because she wouldn't need them after camp. She didn't accept the offer. Okechukwu also proposed to take her to a proper clothes store and super market to buy every other thing she needed, and she also refused the offer.

On the night before Oluomachukwu was to leave for

camp, Okechukwu bought her drinks. Well, it was for both of them, but since he had to work the next day, he really didn't want to drink. And as they sat down on the couch, close to each other, almost glued together, Oluomachukwu wanted to tell him that they could never be together. She didn't know how to tell him, but she didn't have to worry herself too much, because Okechukwu had things he also wanted to tell her.

"Is something wrong?" he asked, then got up to serve them some red wine, a very dry one that Oluomachukwu didn't really like.

"Nothing is wrong," she replied. "Why?"

"Because you've been acting very strange since Abuja and I don't know if something happened there."

"Nothing happened there," she lied, because in reality, Kayode and Nnanna had happened, their wife and fiancée had also happened.

"So what is it?"

"Nothing really," Oluomachukwu replied, then in an attempt to talk about something else, she asked, "So who is Idara to you?"

"Just a friend," he replied, then laughed. "Don't tell me you are jealous."

"I'm not jealous. I only asked who she was." She took a gulp of the wine and swallowed it quickly so that the dry taste wouldn't settle in her mouth.

Okechukwu approached her, took the glass from her and placed it on the table, then held her hands. "Oluoma, I love you," he said.

"Please, no," Oluomachukwu replied. "You can't do this right now."

Okechukwu didn't reply. He had waited an eternity to say that and didn't know when the right time was going to be. Besides, she was going to camp, and many people were said to fall in love in camp. He didn't want her to go there and find someone else.

"I have waited for too long. Even after you blew me

off for my friend, I never stopped loving you."

"What about Idara?"

"So you are indeed jealous?" Okechukwu asked, leaned forward and tried to kiss her, but she turned away.

"No. I'm not jealous," she said. "I just find it very hard to believe that you haven't found anyone else since all that time."

"I'm worried."

Oluomachukwu found his reply very strange. "Worried about what?"

"That you would go to camp and find someone there. People tend to fall in love there."

Oluomachukwu laughed. "Never in this lifetime. If at all I was searching, it would never be in an NYSC camp."

"So you are currently not searching, right?" He wanted to confirm that he still had a chance with her.

Oluomachukwu had actually been searching. In fact, her coming back to Nigeria was to go back to her roots as well, and eventually find a partner. But her encounter with Kayode and Nnanna sort of changed her mind and also taught her not to be in a hurry. Her partner would come to her hassle-free, eventually.

She looked at Okechukwu with a 'not-interested' facial expression, and said, "I'm not searching for anyone. I'm only going there for the experience."

CHAPTER FOUR: DAY ONE

Tuesday, 5th August 2014

Oluomachukwu arrived at the NYSC Orientation camp quite late, even though she started off her journey early. While Okechukwu slept after their late-night drinking session, which she regretted at that moment, she had to pack her box. She had contemplated taking a hand luggage or even a regular box, but camping without having to worry about heavy boxes sounded like a better plan.

She had prepared her luggage with everything she had and thought would be suitable for the camp, whatever was left, she would have to buy at the camp market. So in the luggage, she put in her toiletries, which were in a small transparent bag, her underwear, sports bra, regular bras, night wears, a few tops, a dress, a scarf, hairbrush, make-up, two pairs of sandals, a pen, her international passport that had her Call-up letter in it and other necessities. She was sure she was missing something, if not a lot of things, but she didn't care. She wrote Okechukwu a note and left.

Flagging down a taxi shouldn't have been a problem, but when Oluomachukwu waved her hand, two taxis were coming from opposite sides of the road and almost had an accident in front of her. The taxi drivers put their heads out of the window to argue and rain insults on each other.

By the time the taxi drivers were done arguing about who Oluomachukwu had called first, who got to her first and who was going to finally drive her to her destination, she had already flagged down another taxi and found her way.

As Oluomachukwu drove off in the taxi, the two other fighters suddenly realised that they had lost their first business of the day to a random taxi man who came out of nowhere, then they diverted their insults towards him even though he couldn't hear them.

The road to Iyana-Ipaja was lengthy and unfamiliar, Oluomachukwu wouldn't have known if they were even driving out of Lagos. As she looked out of the window, she started reflecting on her life, especially on the last two weeks she had been in Nigeria. Even though she never wanted to admit it to herself, she had hoped to come back to Nigeria and find a life partner in the process. If she said she wasn't thinking about marriage, then she would have been lying to herself. She then realised that she was going about it the wrong way. She didn't have to jump into bed with the first guy that crossed her path. She had to be patient and wait for the right one, if he was ever going to come.

The thought of going to camp to look for a husband or anyone at that, as Okechukwu had pointed out, never crossed her mind, but if the opportunity came up, then she might consider it. She made a mental note to make friends with only serious-minded young men, preferably those who were already working and had ambition. She didn't want to waste her time making male friends that she wasn't going to end up with. Her ideal partner was going to be a tall, muscular, handsome and hardworking guy... one that would complement her light-skinned tone and her natural beauty. She smiled at the thought of that, but didn't relish in the thought for too long, because her phone started to vibrate in her hand. It was Nnanna calling.

Oluomachukwu hesitated before she picked up the call. "Yes, how can I help you?"

"I'm sorry for lying to you," Nnanna said. He knew Oluomachukwu was still mad with him and wasn't so sure she wanted to talk to him. So he had to pass his message immediately in case she decided to hang up after hearing what he had to say.

"You never lied to me," she replied. "You just didn't tell me you were engaged."

"And that I was the one at the airport."

"Before you came back to my hotel to…" She paused when she realised that the taxi driver might be listening. "To deceive me," she added.

Nnanna expected her to react to the airport confession, but was quite surprised when she didn't, so he didn't push it further. "I'm sorry," he said.

Before Oluomachukwu could respond, the taxi driver suddenly came to a stop. She darted her eyes to the street and the area looked very deserted. She actually hadn't been paying attention to the road all along.

"Nnanna, wait let me call you back, I don't know why the taxi guy has stopped or where we are." She hung up, not waiting for him to say "Okay" or whatever he was in the process of saying. She then leaned forward so that the taxi driver could hear her. "Is there a problem, sir?"

The man turned around. "No oh. No problem at all. I just want to go to the bank machine and collect money for fuel or if you have 500 naira, please, help me with it."

Oluomachukwu thought it was weird for a taxi driver not to have enough fuel, especially early in the morning. She also didn't know that taxi men used ATM cards, too, and didn't see any banks around. She somehow found it amusing. Instead of allowing the man to park in a remote area, she agreed to give him the money. And while she was fumbling in her handbag for her purse, he decided to make small talk with her.

"Auntie, I like your accent oh. From which country?"

he asked.

Oluomachukwu smiled at his curiosity and at his accent as well. "United Kingdom," she said proudly.

The man nodded, then manoeuvred the car and went into a lane where she could finally see people. And not too long afterwards, he diverted and went into a fuel station that had a rather unique name. Instead of the usual oil and gas companies, this one had a Yoruba name and surname that she couldn't pronounce. Oluomachukwu sat quietly and waited for the tank to get filled up, then they left.

The man drove for a while, then they got into serious traffic. He glanced back at Oluomachukwu, and then at the window by her side. He then looked at the window at the other side, then the one in front.

"Is everything okay?" Oluomachukwu asked.

"Please, help me wind up the windows behind and pin down the locks."

Oluomachukwu was confused. "What's going on?" she asked, as she was doing what he instructed, but left a little breathing space for cross ventilation. It was small enough for only the size of fingers to enter.

"Ah, this is Oshodi oh!" he exclaimed. "Bad boys are in this area a lot. They give too much trouble around here."

"Even in broad daylight?" Oluomachukwu smiled and raised an eyebrow.

"Ah, Auntie, thieves and bad boys don't have any time table."

Oluomachukwu was genuinely concerned. "How long has this been going on?"

"Ah, forever *nau*. This area is not good at all. Almost everyone here is a thief or a bad boy. If your car breaks down here, then there's big trouble. Many bags and things have been stolen in this area. Too many *area boys* are here."

"Hmm." Oluomachukwu sighed, still concerned. "So what are the police doing?"

"I don't know. I don't know who will ask them that. Until they are attacked and robbed once, they won't do anything. Maybe the thieves even settle them with some money, but I don't know oh."

Oluomachukwu didn't say anything anymore. She got carried away, then relaxed in her seat. The weather was hot and stuffy, and in no time, she slept off.

The sound of someone banging on the car window woke Oluomachukwu up. She opened her eyes and saw a rough-looking young man at the window. Believing that he was just one of the annoying hawkers trying to sell off their products, she closed her eyes again, but the young man kept banging on the window. She opened her eyes again immediately and saw the taxi driver winding up his own window very fast. She turned to look at the man by her side, who had started yelling.

"Give me money, *jor*, before I shoot you."

Oluomachukwu tried to wind up the window fully, but the tout put eight of his dirty fingers in the space and tried to force the window down, then rob her. She didn't know what to do. She wanted to wind up again, but the tout kept pressing it down and yelling at her to give him money. At that moment, she wished she had a knife on her to cut or slice off the tout's fingers, or pepper spray to give him a healthy dose in his eyes or even better a Taser to shock the living daylights out of him. She shook the feeling out of her head when the tout started calling out to someone.

Before she knew what was happening, another tout had gone to the other side of the car and was banging on the window, also trying to force it down. She looked at the taxi driver, confused, but he said nothing and kept his eyes to the road. He had already completely wound up his side. He had told her to do the same, so whatever the outcome of the encounter was, it was solely on her.

The other tout kept yelling too, and she couldn't stand the yelling. So she yelled at them too, telling them that she didn't have money.

One of the touts spoke in Yoruba, but Oluomachukwu

heard the word 'Oyibo' and knew that they were referring to her coming from abroad because of her accent, her nice British accent. She looked around at other cars, wondering why no one had offered her any help, but everyone had already wound up their windows, afraid that they would be attacked too. Some were even sweating in their cars and it was obvious that they had no air conditioning.

The touts kept yelling and banging on the window, asking for money, and Oluomachukwu told them that she was a Youth Corper.

"What kind of Youth Corper is that?" one of them asked in a weird accent and husky voice. "I will shoot you oh. Give us money now." The tout then looked around and started calling out in Yoruba and Oluomachukwu had a feeling he was calling more touts for back up and to feast on her fear.

"I said I'm a Youth Corper," Oluomachukwu repeated. This time, her voice was shaky. She was beginning to get really scared.

"Youth Corper no *dey* earn money?" the other tout, who had been quiet, asked.

"I don't know." Oluomachukwu almost started to cry. "I said I'm a Youth Corper. Why don't you ask the Federal Government if we earn money."

The touts looked furious, then both of them removed their fingers from the windows concurrently and probably went to look for other motorists to harass and frighten into giving them their money. The traffic had also started to move, so the touts would have had to leave either way.

Neither Oluomachukwu nor the taxi man said anything after the incident. There was an awkward silence in the taxi and the only thing Oluomachukwu could hear was a voice in her head, saying a little prayer of thanks to God.

By the time they approached Iyana-Ipaja area, she had cried out her eyeballs. She was still a bit shaken up by the incident and for a second she thought about calling it quits and going back to Ikoyi, and eventually to the UK.

TWENTY-ONE DAYS

Along the Iyana-Ipaja road, there was a small fast food restaurant that Oluomachukwu asked the taxi man to enter and stop for a while. She wanted to see if she would be able to calm herself down before entering the camp.

She called Okechukwu and told him what happened, and he panicked seriously, regretting why he didn't drive her to the camp instead. He didn't know the direction, but he could have asked around and found it if it would have prevented her from being harassed.

She sat in the restaurant for a few hours until she was relaxed and less traumatised, then had something to eat. Okechukwu had succeeded in making her laugh a little and cheer up. He made sure to point out that her accent had surely added to her plight, and if she was going to survive in Lagos, she had to let go of it. She called her parents and told them what happened. Her mother was the first to ask her to return to the UK so that she would be free from the rampant roadside robberies, which were tearing the city of Lagos down. With every nine out of ten men on the street a potential thief, it was not certain how she was going to cope.

After the roadside-tout incident, Oluomachukwu swore never to use her British accent in public again. There was no point. After all, she was in Nigeria, and she had learnt the best way. Back in the UK, she always used her British accent when speaking with British people, and whenever she met other Nigerians, she transformed to her Nigerian accent. Many British born Nigerians, who had never even stepped a foot in Nigeria did the same thing, so what made her any different? She thought. And the fun of Nigerians *selling* white people with their Nigerian accents and slangs was amusing, anyway.

So as Oluomachukwu approached the camp gate, she decided to check her British accent at the entrance, then walked in with an understandable Nigerian one.

***

Before Oluomachukwu crossed the gate of the camp, she decided to buy a few things. Since almost everything she could need seemed to be out there, she saw no reason to wait to buy them from the camp market later.

She waved her hand to a girl selling socks and every other seller in range rushed towards her, asking her to buy things she didn't even think she needed.

She ended up buying two pairs of white socks that had two green lines going round at the top and spaced in the centre. With the way the lines were separated, it formed the pattern of the Nigerian flag, but Oluomachukwu didn't know if they were going to be accepted in the camp. She also bought a bucket, a bathing bowl and a smaller bucket that had a lid. She looked around, checking if she needed any other thing. Nothing came to mind at that instant, so she turned around and left.

As she entered the camp, she didn't envy the Corps members she saw trying to drag along their boxes — some with just one box and others with two boxes, together with the other little things they had just bought outside the gate. She even saw some carrying pillows under their arms and wondered why they needed it.

Just a few meters from the main camp gate, there was a checkpoint. Oluomachukwu was asked to open her box, and it was searched thoroughly. She could understand why they needed to search her box, but what she didn't get was why she was asked to throw out her umbrella, which she carried along with her everywhere she went, thanks to her experience with the unique British weather. She asked the security officer, who had already flung the umbrella to a corner, and the woman simply replied "Under the sun and in the rain." Oluomachukwu didn't understand what the officer had said, but she hesitated before asking the officer again. And the officer simply said that umbrellas weren't allowed in the camp, then kept quiet.

As the security officer continued combing through her box, she looked around and saw other officers searching other boxes, seizing various items and sharp objects like razor blades and scissors. The officers also took extension cables from prospective Corps members, asking them indiscreetly for the cables before seizing them.

One officer had even asked, "Where are your extension cables?"

Those who didn't know that it was a trick question, produced their extension cables and the cables were seized and put in a corner. Oluomachukwu didn't know why they were seizing extension cables, but she felt that the officers were probably going to keep them for their own personal use.

However, what she did know and notice was that the officers weren't searching handbags. So if there was a next time, she would have kept her umbrella and other 'illegal' items in her handbag. But luckily, there was never going to be a next time.

When the officer was done searching the box, she did not even arrange it properly or zip it up, she simply pushed it away with her foot, allowing underneath it to scratch against the stony floor, then called for the next person to be searched. Oluomachukwu quickly rearranged her box and zipped it up. She then picked it up, along with the few things she had bought, and headed into the main camp, all the while murmuring insults at the security officer.

As she proceeded further into the camp, a group of photographers, both men and women, young and old, ran towards her, almost knocking themselves over. She didn't know what was going on. She wondered if they thought she was a star, but it was a ridiculous thought. It was when they approached her and surrounded her, she understood what was going on.

Some chorused in different accents and tones, "Auntie, your passport photograph here." Others asked, "Corper, do you have your red background passport photograph?" Another one even said, "Only passport photographs with red background are accepted in the camp."

Oluomachukwu stopped for a second. She had about twelve passport photographs, but not only were they on a different background colour — six were on white and the other six on blue background. She hadn't had the time to take new passport photographs, so she mixed and matched everything she had brought back to Nigeria with her.

She thought about it and didn't want to have to go for registration, only to be sent away just because of passport photographs. At the same time, photographers were still asking her if she had hers, urging her to make a decision or they would leave her. One even went ahead to add, "It's only 2,500 naira for six copies. It's not expensive, Corper."

Before she could make a decision, someone yelled from around her. She turned and saw another prospective Corps member enveloped by a swarm of photographers. The girl, who looked overwhelmed with the things she was carrying, was yelling, "Leave me alone, please. Why would I pay that much for only six copies, when I paid 800 naira for sixteen copies?"

"Is it on a red background?" one of the photographers asked the girl.

"No!" the girl yelled.

"Then you've wasted your money. You better get new pictures and save yourself the trouble and embarrassment during registration."

Oluomachukwu was amused at the conversation and even more amused at the fact that the other photographers around her left and went to look for other potential clients. Since she knew that the photographers were demanding exorbitant prices, she decided to take her chances and use the ones she had brought. Besides she didn't want to waste any money on things she wasn't sure she would need.

As she advanced into the main camp, she became a bit sceptical about being there. She had mixed feelings, being around too many people when she was already used to her 'staying alone' life. And while she was at the gate, she had heard rumours from two bucket sellers that camp officials kept about thirty girls in a room like refugees. She didn't want to believe that, but when she looked at the buildings in the camp and crossed them with the amount of people that trooped in, it started to seem possible.

Oluomachukwu asked the first person she saw for direction. The officers at the gate hadn't told her where to go next, so she didn't know what she was supposed to do. She was directed to a queue on the parade ground, which was by the left side of the camp. Up ahead led to the dining section and the right side was a large sand field that tripled as *mami* market, evening hangout area and football field.

The parade ground was empty, but the surrounding areas were filled with large canopies that could take over 3,000 people and had a lot of plastic chairs stacked up together. Some of the chairs had been arranged for people to use while waiting to register and some were already broken. Whether they were broken before camp started or on that same day, Oluomachukwu didn't know. She went to join the queue and her adventure started full time.

Oluomachukwu stood for about two hours straight on the queue before she was told that it was a queue to get accommodation. She had heard people say that normally, accommodation was given only after registration, and not before. Nobody knew why it changed this time, but they didn't think it mattered at the end of the day, as long as they all got a room to sleep.

During the second hour of the wait in line, it started to drizzle and Oluomachukwu heard people wish they hadn't come to camp during the raining season. They wished they had waited until the dry season.

Before long, the drizzle began to turn into heavy rain and an officer, who had 'Nigerian Civil Corps' written on his shoulder tag, moved everyone to sit under a canopy, which they did. But when the rain subsided and it was time to join the line again, everyone rushed to be in front, even though they had been behind before the rain started. Some girls fell over each other, and some landed in the puddles of dirty and muddy water that the rain had formed.

Oluomachukwu saw more girls trooping into the camp and coming to join the queue, and she wondered if it was an all-girls camp, because she was yet to see any guy. She knew that she would never survive in an all-girls camp, especially when they start with their trouble-making and fighting; she wondered if it was too late to leave.

The queue extended from the parade ground to inside the hostel ground where there was no canopy, just more rain, wet hair, wet clothes, wet bags and wet shoes. The hostel ground was opposite the parade ground, and had a two-way entrance with doors that could lock. By either side of the doors, there were games tables, for Ping-Pong and table soccer.

The walls had been turned into a notice board where information was posted. But then, when Oluomachukwu looked at the other side of the hostel camp, she saw a queue for male Corps members. It was a short queue, with about twenty people, but she was glad that there were guys around.

After another long hour of waiting, Oluomachukwu was finally assigned a room on the fourth floor. There was no elevator obviously, but she couldn't complain when she saw other girls who had come in with two or more heavy boxes, trying to carry them up all at once. When she got in front of room 45, the female Hostel Officer, who sounded more like a man, instructed them to enter, and one by one they did, until they were twenty-six of them in the room. Just then Oluomachukwu remembered the sellers who had said that there were thirty girls in a room; twenty-six wasn't so far from thirty.

There were thirteen bunk beds in the room, clamped up together, there was hardly any space to walk between them. The Hostel Officer assigned the girls to their beds in the order they entered. The first girl got the lower bed on the first bunk and the second got the top bed.

Oluomachukwu was number ten on the list so she was given the top bed on the fifth bunk and wasn't too pleased with it. The girl who got the bottom bed was called Ijeoma and she didn't look too pleased either.

Oluomachukwu had never slept in a bunk before and she knew she definitely couldn't stay on the top one. It had nothing to do with the fact that she was afraid of heights, she just felt that one day, she might roll off the bunk and fall or when climbing up or down the bunk, she would fall.

Oluomachukwu had chatted and made friends with Ijeoma and two other girls while they waited on the queue for the rooms, so she had no problem asking Ijeoma to swap bed space with her. Ijeoma seemed very happy to oblige, as she had spent all her life sleeping on bunk beds and her very long legs made it easy for her to climb up and down without stepping on the bottom bed.

The two other girls who were on the right side of her bunk were: Fadeke at the top and Ogo at the bottom. Ogo had a very small stature and looked like she could break if she even lifted herself unto her bed, so it was only natural she stayed on the lower bed. Fadeke, on the other hand, was quite bulky, and one could only hope that the top bed would take her weight and not break. So, all four of them happened to be the first set of friends in the room, as they didn't know any other person in the room at that moment.

Oluomachukwu was yet to chat with the girls on the bunk by her left side, but from the little she had heard, their names were Eternity, on the top bunk, and Oghene, on the lower bunk.

The girls directly opposite Oluomachukwu's bed didn't seem to be talking that much, so knowing who they were or their names was going to be for much later.

After Oluomachukwu had put her things on the bed, her luggage by the bed and her buckets under the bed, the Hostel Officer appointed a room leader and an assistant. They were the first two girls on the list who had the first bunk, and Oluomachukwu was somewhat glad that she hadn't been the first on the list, because the last thing she wanted was to be a room leader or an assistant.

Oluomachukwu couldn't see the faces of both the room leader and the assistant from where she stood and she didn't bother stretching her neck to check. The Hostel Officer mentioned their names — the room leader was called Dunsin Tijani, and the assistant, Foyin Olaolu. They were going to be responsible for locking the door when there was no one in the room early in the morning, and also for opening it whenever everyone got back. It meant that everyone had to participate fully in camp activities and the room leaders had to make sure they did.

As Oluomachukwu was leaving the room to go for registration, she looked towards her right and made an awkward eye contact with Dunsin. She assumed it was Dunsin, since she was on the bottom bunk. In order for it not to seem anymore awkward, Oluomachukwu said "Hi" to Dunsin and she responded. She then made a bold move to ask Oluomachukwu if she wanted to assume the role of room leader.

Oluomachukwu shook her head indicating "No," then made for the door. As she walked down the corridor, she heard Dunsin poaching other girls, asking them to take her place. Oluomachukwu assumed that she had asked all the girls and that they had all said "No," as no one would have wanted that sort of responsibility.

Something worried Oluomachukwu as she went down the stairs, handbag hanging loosely over her shoulder. She had seen Dunsin somewhere before, but she didn't know where, yet what she knew was that she wasn't supposed to like Dunsin — maybe it was in Abuja at the NYSC Head Office, where people insulted her, as she walked in with Kayode or at the Secretariat in Surulere when she went to pick up her Call-up letter, she didn't know where.

Oluomachukwu came out of the hostel and looked at the open space where the number of people had doubled since she arrived. With what was lying ahead of her, she had to keep the thought of remembering who Dunsin was and why she didn't like her for another time. It was now time to face registration proper.

C. M. OKONKWO

CHAPTER FIVE: THE RUSH

Registration was a total disaster, so poorly organised that Oluomachukwu wondered why it wasn't done online and why she had even bothered going all the way to Abuja for verification of documents. It looked as if she was going to redo the whole verification of documents there as well, because everyone came with folders packed with documents. Some even had pencil cases, staplers and every other thing a recent graduate would have.

Oluomachukwu had been out of all education systems for a while, so she had forgotten how to be a student, and the whole idea of that made her laugh. She had only come out with her handbag and a pen that had dried out when she tried to use it, so she knew she was going to have to borrow every other stationery she needed.

As she approached the parade ground, where she had been directed to go for her registration, she met a queue of people, and it was beginning to rain again. A Registration Officer asked everyone to sit under a canopy and collect blue and white forms, one each, and two green forms each. Oluomachukwu collected hers and when she went to sit down, she saw her roommates, Ijeoma, Ogo and Fadeke. They were not smiling.

Apparently they had wanted to go for the registration together as new friends, but Oluomachukwu had gone on without them. They didn't say anything to her at first, they just went to hustle to get their own forms. The rush was overwhelming, even though the NYSC official sharing the forms had confirmed that there was enough to go round everyone in the whole camp.

Eventually, the girls all got their forms. As soon as they sat down close to Oluomachukwu, they smiled, forgetting that they were angry with her, and started to chat away.

Oluomachukwu wasn't really interested in the chat. Her mind wandered as she sat there, looking at everyone and what they were doing. She thought that there were at least 2,000 people in the camp and only wondered if the hostels would accommodate everyone. She looked ahead and saw that people were still walking into the camp from the gate.

Oluomachukwu came back to reality when she heard people murmuring, laughing and gazing towards the left side of the camp. Two white boys sat at a corner amongst the crowd, looking lost and confused, and everyone stared at them, wondering if they knew what was going on in the camp, or if they even knew that they were going to be resident in a camp for three weeks. The boys answered the questions everyone probably had when they collected their own forms and sat back, waiting to fill them.

Just then, the Public Address System came on and one of the camp officials started to speak in a very coarse tone. She must have felt she was addressing primary school kids, because she wanted to teach everyone how to fill their forms. She began by reading every line on the forms, from the title to the last word, then taught everyone how to fill them and what to do with them later.

After that, there was scramble for registration and verification of documents, where Corps members rushed like termites, pushing each other in the rain and splashing muddy water everywhere. Insults rained everywhere and everyone seemed to be in a contest for what they were all going to get, no matter who went first or last.

Oluomachukwu didn't know where the tiny and tired-looking Ogo got the strength, but she ran to the front of the line, cutting every possible queue she could see.

She made it to the front line, surprisingly, then waited for Oluomachukwu, Ijeoma and Fadeke to join her.

Registration was taking place in the dining hall, which was spelt 'Dinning Hall,' and inside, there were also about ten queues for different things. At the beginning of each queue, there were 'seat queues' such that when one person moved, others would advance to the next chair.

Oluomachukwu and her new friends went to separate seat queues so that it would be faster for them to finish up their registration and meet at the exit. The guy in front of Oluomachukwu was a foreign-trained Nigerian student.

She figured it out because he didn't stop speaking to someone on the phone in an American accent that went on and off. He was asked to end his phone call and put his phone away when it was his turn to present his documents — certificate, transcript and statement of result. The boy didn't have any. He only had his international passport and Call-up letter.

He tried to explain to the Verification Officer — a man who didn't look like he knew how to smile, and who wore square dark glasses that hid his eyes — that he didn't think he needed to bring any documents since the verification had already been done in Abuja. The officer looked over the boy's shoulder and yelled "Next." The boy tried to explain again and the man also yelled "Next" again.

As the boy was getting up, the officer said something that sounded like, "You cannot read. The information is written behind your Call-up letter." He hissed afterwards, then shouted "Next" again, but Oluomachukwu didn't go. She didn't have the documents either and she hadn't read behind the Call-up letter. In fact, she didn't know that there was anything written behind the letter. She had just put the letter in the middle of her international passport on the day she received it and put it away.

Oluomachukwu went outside and called Okechukwu to ask for help, but he couldn't bring the documents to her all the way to Iyana-Ipaja. Besides, he didn't think he would make it in time, since he was still at work. And instead of proposing a solution to her, he decided to ask her why she had forgotten all her documents and ruled every reason she could possibly give as invalid. Nothing could explain why she would go to camp without all her documents, whether she had done verification in Abuja or not. He also had to get back to work, so he told her to decide what she wanted to do, then call him back later. He hung up after that.

Oluomachukwu started to get agitated. The only option she had then was to go home, get it and come back much later, or go home and come back the next day entirely.

It was a two-day registration process for Tuesday and Wednesday, so she could always come back the next day and meet up with the registration. She sat on a plastic chair under one canopy that was just outside the dining hall to think about what to do. She was about to start crying when Okechukwu called her with some good news — he could send someone to bring her documents to her.

After she had explained where she kept the documents, Okechukwu hung up and headed back home to help her out. He would do anything for love... Sadly, he felt that the opposite was the case for a typical girl or woman — they would *ask* anything for love, but not *do* anything for it.

Oluomachukwu looked for what to do as she waited, because she knew the wait was going to be long. She knew how long it had taken her to get to the camp, and coupled with the fact that Okechukwu would have to go home, look for the documents, then send someone; it was going to be a long wait. Instead of sitting outside, she went into the hostel, which was empty, because everyone was still outside trying to finish up all the paperwork, including her new friends. So she decided to lay her bed and rest her head for a while, and eventually slept off.

***

After waiting for more than three hours, the person Okechukwu had sent to the Orientation camp with the documents gave Oluomachukwu a call to say that he had finally gotten there. She ran outside as quickly as possible, and towards the front gate to meet him. She smiled when she saw him, not because he had just helped her out, but because she knew who he was — Okechukwu's security guard, and he shone so bright as if he had just been soaked in cooking oil. He gave her the envelope and left almost immediately. She was ecstatic, so she called Okechukwu to thank him, but he didn't pick up. She then composed a text message and sent it in case he was driving or he was in a meeting. He didn't reply either.

Oluomachukwu didn't bother trying to contact him any further. At least she was sure that he was going to see the missed call and text message.

Before she headed back inside, she saw some hawkers selling stationery, so she used the opportunity to become a student again. She got everything she thought she would need, including a plastic-like office file to put the envelope in and prevent rainwater from damaging it. She also put in all the other forms she had filled earlier. When she was done, she scuttled towards the dining hall, almost falling down twice because of the wet and muddy ground, to continue her registration.

When she entered the hall, the first queue with the unsmiling man who wore square-glasses was empty, so all her documents were verified within seconds, and she wondered why she hadn't initially waited until evening to get to the camp. After that, she had to join another queue for something she didn't know. When she saw people filling out forms, she asked a girl standing behind her why they were filling the forms and was told that the queue was for online registration and that she had to buy a form for 10 naira. Oluomachukwu grumbled, but went to buy one of the forms, and the supposed man or woman selling it was nowhere to be found. No one knew why the NYSC office couldn't provide the forms for all Corps members.

One male Corps member had decided to join the line even without the form. Finding the form to buy was close to impossible, so his intention was to ask the Registration Officer for a form, but before he got to her, the sound of a trumpet went off and they all wondered what it was. Then there was an announcement for everyone to report to the parade ground immediately.

None of the Corps members moved a muscle until all the registration officers immediately started logging out of their systems and standing up to leave the hall. One of the registration officers, who had a constant smile on her face, gave tally numbers, numbering 1 – 5 consecutively, to the first five people on the queue so that when they returned, they could get back in line to how they were before.

Oluomachukwu was the fifth person on that queue.

It took roughly twenty minutes for Corps members to gather on the wet parade ground, and some were still seen running around, some were still in *mami* market and some were still trooping into the camp from the gate. Soldiers moved around, yelling at people to leave everything they were doing and report to the parade ground.

When the parade ground was extensively full, so full that one could no longer see the white lines on the ground, a lady, who sounded like she was crying, got a microphone to address the crowd.

"Corpers, wii oh," she yelled.

Nobody answered her.

"Corpers, I said wii oh," she repeated.

Still, nobody answered.

The woman shook her head. "*Otondos*, I said wii oh, do you not know anything? Or don't you have older ones who have passed through the NYSC scheme?"

When there was still no answer, Oluomachukwu then wondered if and when the woman would realise that no one knew what she was talking about, and also how many more times she was going to embarrass herself.

"If I don't get an answer, no one will leave this parade ground today," the woman said, then in a high-pitched tone, she yelled again, "Corpers, I said wii oh."

Surprisingly, about ninety-five percent of the crowd shouted, "Wa oh."

"*Ehen*, that's better." The woman smiled. "So why were you all pretending before? Corpers wii, wii, wii."

"Wa, wa, wa." A chorus answer from nearly everyone, who in a short moment had gotten the gist that 'wa' always followed 'wii' or maybe they already knew that and purposely didn't want to give the woman the satisfaction she needed.

The woman didn't introduce herself, so Oluomachkwu didn't know who she was. She went straight ahead to introduce the NYSC Lagos State Coordinator, who gave an official welcome speech and shared some important information with everyone.

When the State Coordinator completed her speech, she dismissed everyone and allowed them to go and continue their registration or whatever activity they were engaged in before the call to gather. Oluomachukwu didn't think the gathering had been necessary. For one thing, she hadn't paid full attention during the whole speech, and secondly, Corps members were still trooping into the camp and had missed all the information.

***

Oluomachukwu already knew that she was the fifth person on the queue, so before she went back to continue her online registration, she stopped by at a stall in *mami* market where some men were scanning documents and making photocopies for people. They also sold the online registration forms, but at a hiked price of 20 naira, instead of 10 naira, because they knew that everyone needed the forms. Oluomachukwu paid 50 naira, but there was no change, which she found to be ridiculous, especially as a lot of people had been paying little change for the forms and other services they needed.

Instead of looking for change for Oluomachukwu, the man gave her three extra forms that she didn't need, and she left. She then ran back to the hall, filled out one of the forms immediately and gave out the rest to people who asked her where she had bought them from.

By the time she joined the queue, there was only one person in front of her, so her own registration was next, and it went fast. The Registration Officer, who had given out the slot numbers for the line smiled as Oluomachukwu approached her. Oluomachukwu smiled back at her and was told that she had a nice smile. They chatted briefly as the woman typed the contents of the 20 naira form that had been filled into the system.

When the woman was done filling it, she turned the screen towards Oluomachukwu to verify the details, and the information displayed was verified. After that step, the Registration Officer was supposed to give Oluomachukwu a four-digit identification code. She explained that there were ten platoons in the Orientation camp and a Corps member's platoon was determined by the last digit of the identification code, from zero to nine, and those ending with zero formed Platoon Ten.

There were going to be platoon activities and contests, and every platoon member had to work as a team. The Registration Officer started going through the cards on her table and Oluomachukwu wondered what she was doing.

As if the officer had heard Oluomachukwu's thoughts, she said, "I'm looking for a code that ends with seven."

"Why, ma?" Oluomachukwu asked.

"Because I know the Platoon Inspector and Assistant, and they are very nice women." Both Oluomachukwu and the officer smiled.

Oluomachukwu then thanked her, and before she left, the officer wrote her name and phone number on a small piece of paper, and asked Oluomachukwu to call if she ever needed anything. Oluomachukwu looked at the paper. The officer had written 'Mummy Dorcas' on it and her cell phone number below it. Oluomachukwu smiled and put the paper in her personal file.

Oluomachukwu stood on another short line to collect her temporary badge, which was just a plain paper, with the code printed boldly, that had been laminated. She was also given a paper file with two other forms to fill, with a space for passport photographs and a pin code for online verification. She couldn't understand why the registration had that many steps, forms and codes. She was already getting tired of it.

As she left the dining hall, she bumped into a couple of security officers, because she hadn't been paying attention. They had entered into the dining hall to arrest a girl posing as an NYSC official. The girl had one good eye and one bad eye. The bad eye had a film-like substance blocking it, so when Corps members described her, they said "The girl with one eye," and it was obviously because they were angry. The girl had been collecting 200 naira from Corps members to help them arrange their documents. Right at the entrance, she had told them that they wouldn't be attended to if their documents were not properly arranged in their files. So Corps members, as dumb as some of them were, paid the money to have their documents 'properly arranged' in their files. The girl was eventually discovered and arrested when word went round.

After that episode, Oluomachukwu went to an open space, which was behind the dining hall and saw about five more long queues. They didn't seem to be moving and noboby knew why. Oluomachukwu saw Ijeoma on one of the queues and was shocked. So instead of staying at the tail of any queue, she squeezed her way to the middle of the first queue and met up with Ijeoma.

"You are still here?" she asked, still shocked. "I even thought you would have already finished by now, and be back in the room, resting."

Ijeoma shook her head. "It's moving too slow for my liking. I've been standing here for a very long time. Did you get your documents?"

"Yes, someone eventually brought them not too long ago, and registration has gone rather fast since then." Oluomachukwu looked around. "Where are the others?"

"We sort of separated when we joined different queues, so I'm not sure where anyone is."

"Okay. So what is this queue for again?"

"It's for online registration."

"But didn't we just do online registration in the dining hall?"

"That one was to create an account and get a pin code. With the pin code, you are supposed to log in and start uploading documents."

"What documents?"

"Passport picture, personal data and others."

"That's just nonsense and a complete waste of time," Oluomachukwu said. She used her British accent this time, then immediately switched back to the Nigerian one. "Why can't we just do it by ourselves? I'm very sure that's what's taking time."

"You can, if you have everything." Ijeoma held up a slip that Oluomachukwu also had. "You can log on to this website, use your user name and pin to enter your account, then start filling it in."

"Have you tried it?"

"No."

Oluomachukwu raised an eyebrow. As she was about to ask Ijeoma why she hadn't even thought of trying it, someone interrupted them.

"Please, does any one of you have 200 naira?" It was Fadeke. She was the girl on the top bunk to the right side of Oluomachukwu and Ijeoma's bunk.

"Why, what's going on?" Oluomachukwu asked.

"It's almost my turn in front and they are asking for 200 naira to do the online thing."

Oluomachukwu exchanged glances with Ijeoma, then put her hand in her handbag and took out a 200 naira note. "Here you go."

"Thanks." Fadeke attempted to leave.

"Wait, please, can we come and join you in front?" Oluomachukwu asked. "It's getting late and I'm not sure we'll finish this up tonight."

Fadeke shook her head. "It'll look somehow. I can't just bring someone in front of me when there are a lot of people there."

"But there were a lot of people in the dining hall when you were brought in front."

"I can't. People are grumbling." Fadeke turned around to leave. "It's almost my turn. Thank you for the money, I'll give it back to you later."

"Can you believe that?" Ijeoma asked. "She can receive help, but she isn't willing to help."

"Well..." Oluomachukwu said, but didn't complete the sentence.

"Anyway, I'm not even able to jump from queue to queue. I'm not that fast, plus I'll feel people are judging me. It's fine. I'll just stay here."

Oluomachukwu laughed. "So let's see if we can do the online thing on our phones instead of wasting time on the queue."

Ijeoma didn't want to try, but Oluomachukwu did. She managed to open the account and fill in all the data. But she didn't have any passport photograph on her phone to upload. She had thought of taking a snapshot of one of her passport photographs and uploading it when she saw that her cell phone battery was already getting low. So she logged off, locked the screen, remained in line with Ijeoma and waited for her turn.

As they advanced gradually in the line, Oluomachukwu asked, "So what platoon are you in?"

"Platoon?"

"There are ten platoons. Corps members will be placed in different platoons and each platoon will participate in all the camp activities and contests." Oluomachukwu opened her palm. "Let me see your temporary badge."

Ijeoma showed her the four-digit pin.

"You are in Platoon Six, just next to my own platoon," she said. "It's determined with the fourth digit of your code. Mine is seven."

"Oh, okay," Ijeoma said, smiling. She kept looking at the badge as if something new had appeared on it since Oluomachukwu told her what the fourth digit signified. When she was done looking at it, she asked, "How did you know?"

Oluomachukwu smiled. "I have a new *mummy* in camp. She gave me all the information I needed."

***

After the online registration, there was another queue to get the paper file that had been given out earlier on, stamped, and Oluomachukwu wondered why the people collecting the 200 naira couldn't just stamp the file. The queue to stamp the file took another long hour for reasons unknown. So after the final verification and e-registration, some Corps members, who had agreed to snap passport photographs at the main camp gate, grumbled at the fact that passports with red background weren't a requirement for registration. Oluomachukwu had forgotten about that until someone mentioned it and complained about the money she had wasted. Oluomachukwu was glad she had not done the same, because all her passports with different colour backgrounds had been accepted.

The registration stress wasn't over for them after that, because after getting the file stamped, the next step was to get the NYSC kit — white tennis shoes; two pairs of white socks; two white tee shirts; two white shorts; orange jungle boots; khaki pants and jacket; a crested face-cap; a crested ceremonial white shirt with NYSC's logo printed in front and just 'NYSC' printed behind; and a khaki belt with an NYSC crest as the buckle.

Oluomachukwu was walking towards the front of the hostel when she heard the sound of the trumpet again and wondered why they were calling them for another speech, when they were yet to complete the registration exercise for the day. She reluctantly started heading towards the parade ground when she saw a soldier gesticulating at her. She turned around and there was no one behind her. In fact, everyone behind her had stopped moving, following an instruction from a soldier.

She stood there and watched as the whole camp stood still. She could see the main gate from where she stood and everyone was standing still. She listened to the sound of the trumpet, which was still being played, then realised that it was supposed to be the Nigerian national anthem. She smiled, because she was impressed at the uniformity of everyone. When the anthem finally ended, Oluomachukwu looked around her first to check if people had resumed movement before she continued her journey.

"*Otondo*," a coarse voice yelled.

She turned to the source of the word and saw a soldier looking at her. He waved her over to him. She looked at her wristwatch and it was 6:04pm. She wanted to answer the soldier, but she also wanted to go and finish up her registration since it was getting late.

"Corper, am I not calling you?" the soldier yelled as he approached Oluomachukwu. She started to walk towards him. When she was close enough, he added, "Don't you know you have to stand still when you hear the sound of the bugle?" He pronounced it as 'beegool.'

"Bugle?" Oluomachukwu repeated, pronouncing it the right way, as 'byooguhl.'

"Yes, that trumpet sound you were hearing. Apart from the 5:00am Wake-Up call, everyday at 6:00am and 6:00pm, the national anthem will be played, and you must stop whatever you are doing, stand up and stand still."

"Okay." Oluomachukwu's mind was under the canopy where she had been directed to for her kit.

"Okay, what?" The soldier sounded fierce.

"What?"

"You don't have respect?" The soldier raised his voice. "We will teach all you useless *olodo* youths something in this camp.

"Sorry, sir. I meant to say 'Okay, sir,'" Oluomachukwu said, but the man looked at her as if she was speaking in tongues. "I understand sir, and next time, I will stand still."

The soldier seemed to have calmed down a little bit. "Where are you off to?"

"I want to hand over my forms, sir." She looked at his badge and it had just 'Elijah' on it. She looked back at his face. "I believe that is the only thing left to do in order for me to collect my kit."

"Okay," the solider replied. He pointed towards a small canopy that wasn't situated on the parade ground. "That's where they are sharing the kit. Check the last digit of your code, then look for the number pinned on the canopy for your own platoon."

Oluomachukwu thanked him, then hurried off. She got under the small canopy that had the sign 'Platoon 7' taped to one of its rusty poles. It was already getting dark, as it was almost 6:15pm. The women she met there were extremely nice, as Mummy Dorcas had told her, and she wondered if she had been truly lucky to have 'seven' as the last digit of her identification code.

The Platoon Inspector was called Auntie Vera. She wore a big dress that looked oversized, and she had no hair at all. Her head was shinning, so it was obvious that she had just cut her hair. Even with that, her smile was still captivating and it appeared to be the reason why she felt comfortable with no hair. The Platoon Assistant was called Sister Mary, but she didn't do justice to the name. She wasn't dressed like a Sister. She wore a very tight pair of jeans that hugged her hips firmly, and a sleeveless shirt that was open in front to reveal some cleavage.

Oluomachukwu found it funny that the women would purposely add 'Mummy,' 'Auntie' or 'Sister' to their names as if it was normal.

After the chitchat and the laughing, Auntie Vera asked Oluomachukwu to hand over her paper file. The paper file was full, because all the documents were complete, which was a problem. Apparently, Oluomachukwu had to submit the blue and white forms for signing and collection before going to get her kit. If someone had thought about telling her that before, she would have felt a lot better. Everyone followed each other blindly in the camp, and sometimes people stood in queues for hours only to realise that they were in the wrong queue.

Oluomachukwu was asked to go under another canopy to get it done, then return to the Platoon Seven canopy immediately for her kit. So she left hurriedly. The queue to hand over the blue and white form had about 1,000 people standing in it, and she was sure that she wasn't going to meet Auntie Vera *immediately* for her kit.

She stood on her toes and looked in front only to see that just about four NYSC officials were attending to the crowd of frustrated Corps members. It was now 6:25pm and most of them had been there from as early as 6:00am, as they professed while on the line, standing, stressed and starved.

When Oluomachukwu asked someone on the queue, she was told that only two out of the four officials were attending to the Corps members. The other two were just sitting there, doing nothing. By the time an hour passed, Oluomachukwu wanted to call it a day and go back to her room to settle in, but she decided to hang on. She just wanted to get everything over with, collect her kit and call it a night.

There were not too many lights under the canopy, so it was very difficult to see anything or the faces of the Corps members that queued. But there was one bright light far off, positioned over where the four officials sat to sign and collect the forms. Oluomachukwu used the light as a guide. So the closer she got to the light, the closer she got to her mission.

Two Civil Service Corps officials had been trying to manage the traffic, because Corps members were rushing and pushing each other. But they later got irritated and left when it was evident that no one was listening to them. In fact, some people were listening, but simply refused to act as instructed. As soon as the officials left, there was chaos everywhere — seven queues were trying to converge and form two queues, and many people insulted others who tried to jump the queue. The registration officers even threatened to stop signing and collecting the forms if the Corps members didn't behave themselves. Another hour passed and Oluomachukwu was still not close to the light.

At about 9:00pm, two other officials came to help with the signing, and the crowd broke out into four additional queues. Oluomachukwu must have entered the wrong one, because everyone seemed to be moving around her, except for her queue. Even the new fourth queue that had been formed moved very fast, but soldiers had come to organise them and didn't allow people jump from queue to queue.

Even with the two extra hands that joined, it felt like things had gotten slower than they already were. Also, one of the registration officers kept reminding the crowd how long they had until they closed for the night.

"Thirty more minutes," the official stated, when it was 9:30pm, making everyone grumble. Tired Corps members wished the man would just concentrate on the task he had to do, and not on the time that was left, because each time he stopped working to make a needless announcement was enough time to sign one document and collect it.

When it was fifteen minutes to go, the official made his announcement again and the crowd yelled at him. He got annoyed, stood up and made the announcement again. He threatened to stop the process if anyone dared respond in an unruly manner to his announcement again. No one did. They had come too far to be sent away at the last minute.

When it was five minutes to go, the official yelled again, "Five more minutes to go and it'll be time for Lights Out."

Corps members started to mumble. They had all heard from one source to another that the NYSC camp observed Lights Out by 10:00pm each day, but they wanted to see, or hear it to believe.

"You all will have to come back tomorrow. Man must rest," the official added, making more people grumble at the time he was wasting.

"I'll take three more people," one of the officials said, and there was an uproar. Two other officials also said how many more people they were going to attend to. The one who announced all the time, said he was going to take ten more people, making everyone like him all of a sudden.

Oluomachukwu hadn't even noticed how far she had advanced. She looked directly above her and she saw the light. She had finally reached her destination in the nick of time. The girl who was standing in front of her presented her documents and was sent away, because the documents were rough and torn at some edges due to the heavy rain and drizzle during the day.

When the girl stepped aside, Oluomachukwu took her place. She brought out her documents and presented them. While the official was signing them, she looked at her wristwatch and it was 9:58pm. She closed her eyes and thanked her stars.

The signing was done in less than a minute, so the reason why it took that long for the queue to go down was not understandable. As Oluomachukwu ran off, she saw the number of pissed off Corps members who were going to be disappointed and angrier once it was Lights Out.

Oluomachukwu got to the small canopy for her kit, but the platoon stand was empty. They had already closed for the day. Before she could react, she heard the sound of the bugle — it was time for Lights Out and soldiers started moving round the camp, making sure that everyone went into their rooms. As Oluomachukwu went to her refugee camp of a room, she hoped that the next set of Corps members wouldn't have to suffer what she had suffered on her first day. She got to her room, didn't speak to her friends, who all successfully got their kits, and called it a night.

CHAPTER SIX: DAY TWO

Wednesday, 6th August 2014

Oluomachukwu had hardly even slept when her alarm went off. She had set it for 3:30am instead of 4:30am, as she wanted to have an early bath, then lay on her bed until 4:30am when it would be time for the Wake-Up call and Corps members would be expected to report to the parade ground for their morning exercise and drills.

Events from the night before were still blurry, as she had been drained from all the hassle. She remembered hearing some of her roommates talk about their eventful day — some had not yet completed their registration, like Oluomachukwu, and some had also complained about not eating anything the whole day. Oluomachukwu related to that, because after her stop at a restaurant the morning before, she hadn't tasted anything all through the day and she didn't know how she managed, given that she loved to eat a lot — an almost self-acclaimed foodie.

Even in her tired state, she had heard them say that the Wake-Up call was by 4:30am. Some people had argued about it and some confirmed that they had seen it on the notice board, which was just at the entrance of the hostel. Oluomachukwu had found the strength to set her alarm before finally nodding off.

Oluomachukwu's alarm rang a second time because she had hit the Snooze button, so she turned it off and tried to put it under her pillow when she realised that she had no pillow — the NYSC hadn't provided pillows, contrary to what she believed, and she regretted not buying one. She came to the camp with a duvet cover and wrapped herself in it, because she was afraid of being bit by mosquitoes and getting the dreaded malaria. And as she moved to the top of her bed, in a sitting position, to say a quick morning prayer, she sat on something small and solid. She touched it and noticed that it was a cell phone. She tried to pick it up and the charger followed.

Just then, she looked at her bed and saw about seven phones there, and three of them were charging. From the way things were looking, it seemed like the only charging port in the room was behind her bed. It wasn't going to be good. She glanced towards the bed directly opposite hers and saw a similar thing there. There was a port and it had been flooded with phones and chargers, kept on the bed of the girl who slept in front of it.

In the port behind Oluomachukwu's bed, there was a small white extension box that could charge three phones, and three phones were already being charged. She felt it was rude, and unhygienic, for people to place their phones on her bed without her permission. She wanted to ask the owners to take their phones or she would fling them, but everyone was still asleep. Instead, she moved the phones to the windowsill and some to the floor, hoping that the owners wouldn't put their phones on her bed anymore.

At the same time, she remembered that her phone needed to be charged, so she browsed through all the charges and found one that could charge her phone. She took off the phone it was connected to and plugged hers in. She then put the phone inside her duvet cover, hoping that she would still see it when she came back from having her bath. She had been told to trust no one, and just about anybody could steal her phone.

She picked up her bucket, bathing bowl, face towel, toilet bag, and left the room quietly, not wanting to wake anyone up. The room door opened from the inside, so it had been locked with a rusty nail that was put over it to prevent people from coming in to steal at night. But if the door was pushed open forcefully, there was no guarantee that the nail wouldn't snap.

When she entered the bathroom, which was two doors away from her room, she felt nauseous. Dirty water lay still on the dirty floor, ankle level. The drainage looked like it had been blocked for days, and the colour and thickness of the water was enough proof. The only thing was that the camp had been opened the day before, but if nearly one hundred girls had used the bath, then it was sure to have been misused and eventually gotten blocked. The worst part was that no one was obviously going to clean it. It was going to be a use-and-go policy.

As Oluomachukwu stood there wondering what to do, a bird cried not too far away, scaring her. It was still very dark and she appeared to be the only person awake at that hour. At that moment, she contemplated going back to the room until the Wake-Up call, and considered the cry of the bird as a warning.

Before she turned around, a girl, big in stature, walked out of the dirty, flooded bathroom, in a towel that barely covered her up. Oluomachukwu wondered what she had been doing there, because there hadn't been a single sound from anywhere around in the last three minutes.

There was no way on earth Oluomachukwu was going to use that bath, but when she turned around to go back to the room, she saw another girl quietly coming out of the room next to hers, in a wrapper, holding her bucket. The girl walked past the 'dirty-river-bath' and turned towards her right and walked down the hallway.

Oluomachukwu followed her and saw that there were two other baths facing each other, and surprisingly, they were not dirty. They weren't clean; they were just not dirty. At least they were cleaner than the first one and she was going to have rest of mind when it came to having a bath.

And with that, she knew she was ready to experience community life, because spending twenty-one days without having a bath wasn't an option.

Oluomachukwu suddenly became afraid of having her bath when she entered the bathroom, because she feared that the water was going to be cold. She wasn't used to bathing with cold water, but it was something that she was going to have to get used to. She filled the bucket up, and with a small bowl, she scooped up water and poured it on her body. The water was indeed freezing cold and she felt a sting. It was as if she was bathing with ice cubes. She wished she could have at least warm, if not hot water, so that bathing wouldn't be such a rather tough process for her. But unfortunately, there were no hot and cold outlets. It was just a single tap that brought out water, which was awfully cold. And as she continued her bath, she shivered with every drop that touched her body, from her face, to her breasts, to her legs and to her feet.

She managed to finish up, and got back to her room, trembling. She dressed normally, putting on a pair of jeans and a plain black top, then decided to catch some more sleep, at least until the Wake-Up call, but it didn't play out as she had thought. Most of her roommates had already woken up and the room light had been switched on. Some of the girls were already talking on their phones, some played music with their phones — although the volume was not too high — and the rest, who weren't disturbed, carried on snoring.

She darted her eyes around the room, trying to take in the faces of her roommates, most of whom she didn't remember seeing the day before. She stretched her neck and looked towards the door for Dunsin. She still didn't know why Dunsin looked so familiar. Dunsin had woken up and began to casually undress, and Oluomachukwu was surprised. She still hadn't gotten used to the fact that she was going to eventually get naked in front of random girls. The way Dunsin easily undressed, it was obvious that she had lived in a boarding house before. Oluomachukwu had not, and she assumed she was going to have to get used to that as well, as most people probably wouldn't notice her, unless she was going to have her bath fully dressed. She kept looking at Dunsin until Dunsin looked at her too, and their eyes met. Oluomachukwu looked away immediately.

At the same time, Ijeoma looked into Oluomachukwu's bed space from the top bunk and greeted her.

"Good morning," Ijeoma said.

"Hi," Oluomachukwu replied.

"Are you still angry about yesterday?"

Oluomachukwu shook her head. "No, I was just tired, and I didn't know that there could have been another way to get what I wanted done."

"So you stayed on the queue for hours just to sign and submit two forms? Hmm."

Before Oluomachukwu could reply, Fadeke woke up and interrupted, also poking her head in from her top bunk, "You should have joined my own line. There was another one close to the hostel that moved very fast."

"You should have called me," Oluomachukwu said.

"I didn't have your number... I don't even have it."

As they were talking, the girls on the other bunk by the right side also woke up — Oghene on the lower bunk and Eternity on the top bunk. Without saying anything to anyone, Oghene got her bucket and bath things, and left the room. Eternity, on the other hand, joined in on their discussion. Ogo was yet to wake up.

Gradually, Oluomachukwu looked round and saw her roommates, some of whom weren't prepared to have their baths, get dressed in their white shorts, white shirts, white socks that had two green lines resembling the pattern of the Nigerian flag — so the pairs she had bought outside the camp were going to be accepted — white tennis shoes,

NYSC cap and waist pouch. Oluomachukwu regretted not collecting her kit the night before. Not long afterwards, the sound of the bugle, very loud and annoying, filled the air, and people started to grumble. The almost monotonous sound went on and on, like an alarm that couldn't be turned off. Oluomachukwu didn't know whether or not she should go downstairs, as she hadn't finished her registration and gotten her kit. She interrupted Ijeoma as she spoke.

"Ijeoma, aren't you going to get ready?"

"Me, *keh*?" Ijeoma laughed. "I'm not going anywhere."

"Why not?" Oluomachukwu was confused. "I thought you said you got your kit already."

"Doesn't mean I'm going anywhere."

Eternity stretched towards Ijeoma and gave her a high-five. "I'm not going anywhere too. I even want to go back to bed now."

"So you don't want to know what it's like, the exercise and drills?" Oluomachukwu asked.

"Is there going to be an award for knowing what it's like?" Ijeoma laughed, and Eternity laughed too.

Before Oluomachukwu could respond to Ijeoma, the door flew open and Oghene walked in, not smiling. She was wrapped up in her towel, water dripping from her body, grumbling to herself.

"Is something wrong?" Ogo asked Oghene when she heard her grumbling, but she didn't answer. Ogo had woken up, but nobody noticed at first. She also spoke in an American accent that nobody knew she had. Everyone turned to look at her and she asked her next question to whoever thought to answer. "What time is it, please?"

Oluomachukwu replied after checking her phone. "It's 4:35am."

"4:35am?" Ogo repeated, only that she pronounced 'thirty' as 'thuhree.'

Everyone kept quiet.

Ogo then got up, and as she prepared herself to go and

have her bath, she looked at Oghene directly, and asked, in an American accent, "Sorry, how did the bathroom look?"

"Very dirty, I can't live here. I can't even manage here. Even pigs can't use those baths. I need to get out of here, because I cannot suffer here." Oghene's facial expression indicated disgust. "Plus, there are two other cleaner baths, but everyone is in there, and there's a queue. So you'll have to forget about the bathroom this morning and use it after the drill."

Ogo didn't say another word. She simply started getting kitted for the morning drill. She wasn't going to waste her time. As she got ready, she complained about everything, things she wasn't sure of, just hearsays. Oluomachukwu didn't know if the other girls were in her platoon, but they weren't yet ready, and she wasn't going to wait for people who didn't know if they wanted to go for the drill or not. She unplugged her phone, surprised that no one had come to ask her why she had removed their phone. She put it in her handbag, carried her file and headed out of the room. As she was leaving, she heard Oghene lament again. She murmured, "I can't suffer, not in this camp."

***

Corps members lined up in four lines for each platoon, starting with Platoon One on the far left end of the parade ground and Platoon Ten on the far right end, so Platoon Seven wasn't too far from the right side. Oluomachukwu had to count from the end to find her own platoon, and she also asked the people who stood in front of each line just to be sure. That was how she knew it was four lines per platoon. None of her new friends seemed to be in her platoon and she wondered what the odds were. She felt awkward coming out in mufti while others were kitted up, but she didn't feel too bad anymore when she saw about three hundred other people in her platoon and in other platoons in mufti as well.

One guy who came out of nowhere, also dressed in mufti, looking like he hadn't completely woken up, walked to the end of the four lines of Platoon Seven and said that all Corps members who hadn't gotten their kits were to go and sit under the large canopy and wait until the morning drill was over by 7:00am. Oluomachukwu smiled at the news, as she didn't want to do any exercise in tight jeans and ballerinas, so she walked happily to the canopy and sat down comfortably.

Only a couple of seconds after she sat down and before the drill began, the Drill Instructor, who looked more like a boxer than a workout instructor, grabbed a microphone and made an announcement. "I do not want to see any corper sitting under the canopy. Get up and join the others on the parade ground right now," he said.

His voice was coarse and threatening. So he didn't have to repeat himself. As soon as he completed his sentence, everyone stood up immediately and rushed back to the parade ground, looking confused, and not sure if to stand in front or behind. Oluomachukwu wanted to look for the guy that had given them the false information and give him a knock on the head, but she didn't.

The morning activity started with a prayer, which was the second stanza of the Nigerian anthem, recited instead of sang:

"*O God of all creation... Direct our noble cause... Guide our leaders right... Help our youth the truth to know... In love and honesty to grow... And living just and true... Great lofty heights attain... To build a nation where peace... And justice shall reign.*"

Right after the prayer, the Drill Instructor corrected everyone, saying, "It's '*where peace and justice reign*' and not '*where peace and justice shall reign.*'"

He repeated the correction since he had said it without using the microphone, and not everyone heard him. Only those standing in front, and closer to him, actually heard him. He was supposed to be standing in the middle, but he seemed to be closer to Platoons Seven to Ten, than to One to Six. Perhaps standing between Platoons Five and Six would have been his best bet. He didn't ask the crowd to recite the whole anthem again, or repeat the last sentence, he just assumed that everyone had taken the correction.

After that, the Nigerian national anthem was sung, and it was the first stanza of the national anthem only.

"Arise, O compatriots... Nigeria's call obey... To serve our Fatherland... With love and strength and faith... The labour of our heroes past... Shall never be in vain... To serve with heart and might... One nation bound in freedom, peace and unity."

"*Ajuwayah, Ajuwayah,*" the Drill Instructor yelled into the microphone, but everyone continued singing. He yelled it a few more times, before Corps members understood that he wanted them to stop singing.

"The next time I, or any other official, say '*ajuwayah*,' it means you should keep your mouths shut, whether you are singing, talking or reciting anything," he yelled, sounding very angry. "*Ajuwayah!*" he yelled again, and this time everyone kept quiet and listened. And the many other times they heard the command in the camp, they kept quiet and waited for an instruction.

The Drill Instructor eventually made everyone stop halfway and start all over again, and it was done about six times because he felt the Corps members were not adding life to the singing, or that they were still sleepy, or simply being lazy. He made sure he shared his thoughts with them.

The next thing was the NYSC Anthem. It was actually sung, and had a nice rhythm. Best of all, it was short, so it was easy to memorise. It was only the first stanza out of three.

"Youths obey the clarion call... Let us lift our nation high... Under the sun or in the rain... With dedication and selflessness... Nigeria is ours, Nigeria we serve."

After that, someone came out to read the Meditation for the day. Oluomachukwu could hear a voice, but she couldn't see the person. The Meditation was a compulsory activity, which came up every morning, except on Sundays. And during the period, a representative from the platoon on duty would recite a Meditation write-up usually centred on national development, and it was written and prepared under the supervision of the members of the Publicity and Protocol Committee.

The Camp Director had arrived at the moment when they had just finished singing the NYSC anthem, but after the Mediation, she took the microphone and introduced herself. Her voice was a bit husky, so it was difficult to put a face to it. And even at that, she sounded very pleasant and made everyone laugh. She called the Corps members her children, prayed for them, then blew them kisses, and that actually made them laugh.

After that fun part was over, she made them all recite the NYSC anthem again, platoon by platoon, because it was supposed to help them memorise it in a short time. She actually said each line, and each platoon repeated it one after the other, so it took quite a very long time for recitals to be over. After that exercise, she then asked them all to sing it together.

Someone in the platoon just beside Oluomachukwu's own said 'Selfishness' in lieu of 'Selflessness' and everyone roared in laughter. As Oluomachukwu recited the anthem with her platoon members, she said, "Under the sun or in the rain," then remembered the security officer at the gate who took her umbrella and told her those same words.

It started to rain shortly afterwards, but just mildly, and Oluomachukwu didn't know where to keep her file. She didn't want it to get damaged and she hadn't expected to be on the parade ground for long, especially as she was yet to complete her registration. So the girl standing behind her, who was also in mufti, offered to put the file in her big bag to prevent it from getting ruined. And in the rain, they all worked out and did their drills until it was 6:00am when the bugle blower came.

Every movement stopped until he was done playing the national anthem that sounded nothing like the national anthem. Everyone stayed silent, until it was over. Work out and drills resumed afterwards until 7:30am.

After the drill, there were a few more announcements on the programme for the day from the same lady who had introduced the State Coordinator the previous day. Oluomachukwu didn't know the woman's name or title, but she recognised her voice. After the announcement, the Camp Director assigned names to each platoon, ranging from Humility, to Teamwork to Selfless Service. Platoon Seven was named 'Unity.'

After that, she informed Platoon One that they were on duty for the whole day, which meant that they would help out with the security at the gate; sanitation at the hostels; cleaning of the environment and arranging chairs under the canopy if and when needed; and cooking in the kitchen, serving of food in the dining hall and washing dirty pots and cleaning up the kitchen afterwards. Platoon instructors were supposed to assign the Corps members to either of the duties and ensure that the duties were duly carried out.

The next day, Platoon Two was going to be on duty, then Platoon Three the day after and so on. Summarily, every platoon was going to be on duty twice during the twenty-one days in the camp.

When the session was over, the Corps members were told that it was time for their Bath and Breakfast, while the ones in mufti had to go and complete their registration.

Oluomachukwu and her new friend, who had offered to keep her file when it started raining and who she later knew to be Ekene, went to finish up their own registration and get their kits.

All the while, Oluomachukwu was starving. She hadn't eaten anything in almost one day, and didn't know at that time where to get any food. She didn't understand why the lady had stated that it was time for Bath and Breakfast when she had no clue of how to procure the breakfast.

As she waited to get her kit, she decided to play games on her cell phone. She had wanted to write about all her experiences in the camp so far, but she changed her mind. For one, she wasn't a writer, and secondly, she didn't have any writing paper, notebook, note pad, jotter, journal; she had nothing.

As she put her hand in her handbag for her phone, she realised she hadn't checked the phone in almost one day and didn't know if the sinister trio — Okechukwu, Kayode and Nnanna had called her or left her a message. She pulled out her phone and checked it, it was switched off.

She immediately turned it on. The battery life was full, as she had charged it for more than an hour before going out to the parade ground. And just as she thought, quite a number of notifications and voice messages that totalled almost fifty came in.

Oluomachukwu never knew that voice mails worked in Nigeria or were even used, so she didn't bother checking any. She didn't even know how to check them, either way, and she didn't care to know.

***

Oluomachukwu wasn't sure if team Unity — Platoon Seven, was a blessing or a curse. The Corps members in the team were all nice people, that is, the few people she had met and spoken to. The Platoon Instructor and the Assistant were also very nice; but the services they offered weren't really nice. They were always the last to arrive at their canopy for anything, and the Corps members were always the last to be attended to amongst other platoons.

The team Unity Corps members stood and watched as other platoons issued kits under their assigned canopies. It was one canopy per platoon, but Platoon Seven had taken two canopies — theirs and that of Platoon Eight, since it looked like Platoon Eight had finished giving out their kits or they had moved to somewhere else.

After almost thirty minutes had passed and nothing had happened, team Unity Corps members sat down and gave each other tally numbers as they came, deciding on who had arrived first and who was behind who. It had started to rain again, and the two canopies couldn't accommodate everyone, so some people migrated to other canopies. But all of that didn't amount to anything, because when Auntie Vera and Sister Mary came, they told everyone to go under the big canopy, that they were going to set up there.

All those who were behind the queue, who probably couldn't remember their numbers, ran quickly and were now in front, while the ones who were initially in front had to go behind. Oluomachukwu was now behind — from number four to a number she didn't even know. Auntie Vera had arranged chairs, so they were now all on a seat queue. Oluomachukwu complained to her, that they had all allocated numbers on a first-come basis, but she simply said "Don't worry, everyone will get their kit. You are all accounted for."

Auntie Vera pointed out that she had waited endlessly for Oluomachukwu the day before, until she got tired and left. Oluomachukwu also pointed out that her colleagues had taken their time to sign all their forms, and she finally finished just before the Lights Out call.

The wait for the kit was long and annoying, but after nearly thirty minutes, Oluomachukwu found herself close to getting her own kit. It looked like Auntie Vera, and her assistant Sister Mary had finally woken up, because things started to move very fast. They even asked other Platoon

Seven Corps members, who had completed registration the day before, to help them out.

After another ten minutes, Oluomachukwu got her kit, carried it in front of her like she was carrying a baby and was seriously smiling as though she had just won a lottery. She looked at all the items and saw that something might have been missing.

"Isn't there something missing?" Oluomachukwu asked herself, but loudly enough to make Auntie Vera turn and look at her.

"Something like what?" Auntie Vera asked.

"The waist pouch. Everyone has it." Oluomachukwu pointed at one Corps member who was already kitted and was helping to distribute a small rectangular booklet.

Everyone laughed, making Oluomachukwu feel slightly embarrassed, then Auntie Vera responded, "We don't give that here, but it's sold everywhere in *mami* market. People usually bring their own from home."

The only thing Oluomachukwu could say was "Oh."

Still carrying her kit in front of her as though she was carrying a baby, Oluomachukwu was given a small yellow card to fill in and sign, then she was to attach a passport picture to the card with an orange-coloured watery gum. She had to press the picture on for a few seconds for it to stick and stay on. It was going to be signed by the Director General of the NYSC later, laminated by camp officials and returned back to Oluomachukwu, like for every other Corps member.

Oluomachukwu got into another queue to collect her meal ticket. Apparently, breakfast, lunch and dinner were going to be made available for everyone. Oluomachukwu wasn't expecting that, but it was good to know. She only hoped that the quality and quantity of the food would also be good.

And that marked the end of her registration process. It had taken her one day plus a morning, but it felt like it had taken the whole week. Oluomachukwu hoped, for the sake of the next batch of Corps members to come, that things were going to be done differently.

Oluomachukwu dragged her feet and went up four floors, wanting to jump into bed and rest her head before the 4:00pm drill. When she got there, she didn't see all the phones on her bed as she had seen in the morning, instead she saw a girl, a strange girl, lying on the bed, eating. It wasn't certain if it was Oluomachukwu's shock, the look on her face or the way she shook her head that made the strange girl jump out of her bed, then sit on Oghene's bed instead.

Without saying any word and refusing to let that bother her, Oluomachukwu simply went to her bed, dusted off the crumbs of bread that was on it and lay down to rest when she felt four phones charging under her duvet cover. That didn't annoy her immediately. What annoyed her was that the phones she had seen charging the day before, and also that morning, were the same phones charging again. It just meant that a group of girls were bent on monopolising one of the charging ports in the room and Oluomachukwu wasn't going to let it happen.

She used the opportunity to check her phone, and there were a few missed calls and messages from the few people she knew in Nigeria. Some other calls had come in and she wasn't sure from whom exactly, but she knew they had to be from her new friends in the camp. Oluomachukwu got comfortable and closed her eyes, then slept off in no time.

The loud sound of the bugle woke her up not too long afterwards. She contemplated going to the parade ground to know what was happening, and she eventually did. The girls in her room didn't even bother going downstairs to check out what the announcement was for. They preferred to stay in the room, talk, laugh, and charge their phones. Oluomachukwu smiled when she was leaving, because power went off when she got towards the stairs. It meant that the girls were not going to have to charge their phones until whenever the power came on.

The State Coordinator addressed the Corps members, calling them 'prospective Corps members.' She told them about the Opening and Swearing-in Ceremony, which was going to hold the next day and after which they would pass from prospective Corps members to Corps members. She told them the dos and don'ts, and what else there was to know about the ceremony, including the dress code, which was the khaki pants, white NYSC crested tee shirt, NYSC cap, crested belt, white socks and jungle boots.

There was also some special marching, recital, saluting and other things they were all going to learn during the evening rehearsal on the parade ground.

As the Corps members stood there, listening to her, platoon instructors shared a white form, which was the declaration of oath to build a united, peaceful, prosperous, hate-free, great and egalitarian nation. The Corps members were to fill the form and sign it the next day, then present it to the Chief Judge. Once the information session was finally over, everyone returned to whatever it was they had been doing.

Oluomachukwu saw some people walking and eating as she was going back to the hostel. She realised she hadn't eaten since she got to the camp because she hadn't had the time. She didn't feel hungry yet, she just wanted to keep on sleeping until it was time to report to the parade ground, dressed in all white and her NYSC cap, to rehearse for the ceremony the next day.

Some Corps members who were going to march at the Opening Ceremony were already rehearsing. A group of drummers, who were Corps members from the previous and current year — Batch C 2013 and Batch A 2014 —, were also rehearsing for the ceremony. Some new Corps members had joined them to see what they were doing and how they were doing it in case they wanted to be a part of the team much later.

TWENTY-ONE DAYS

When Oluomachukwu got back to the room, she saw Ijeoma, Ogo and Fadeke, and the others, Eternity and Oghene, the serial phone charging girls, were also there, but Oluomachukwu wasn't really in friendly terms with them yet. The room leader, who she was still trying to remember, wasn't there. Other roommates were there, looking at their kit and comparing them.

"Hi Oluoma," Ijeoma said. "Have you finally collected your kit?"

Oluomachukwu nodded. "I've packed it up for now, but I'll bring it out and try it on before the end of the day."

"You better try it on now," Ijeoma said. "Mine was so baggy, I had to go and drop it off in *mami* market so that a tailor would trim it down for me."

Oluomachukwu stopped to think for a few seconds. She didn't think it was necessary or that she would need to go to the camp market.

"Babe, try it on oh," Fadeke chipped in as she struggled to climb her bed, stepping on Ogo's bed in the process.

Oluomachukwu looked at her.

"Mine, too, was baggy, even for a plus size like myself," Fadeke concluded. After a few seconds, she got on her bed and Oluomachukwu wondered why she hadn't just asked to swap beds with Ogo who was smaller and slimmer, and more athletic-looking.

Oluomachukwu unlocked her box that stood by her bed and brought out the kit she had kept carefully. She opened up the pants, and lo and behold, a bedspread was the only adjective she could use to describe what she was seeing.

When she wore the pants, she swam in them, and when she tried on the crested white shirt, it was oversized. She also sank into the khaki jacket when she wore it.

"I told you," Ijeoma said, but the words echoed into Oluomachukwu's ears. "You should have tried it on before now."

Oluomachukwu removed the kit and placed it on the

bed, staring intently at the extra-large balloon-looking sacs. She imagined herself in it for the Opening Ceremony and it didn't look so good. So she decided to go and mend it. As soon as she packed up the clothes to leave, she heard the sound of the bugle again, and it was time to go to the parade ground for rehearsals.

CHAPTER SEVEN: DAY THREE

Thursday, 7th August 2014

Oluomachukwu woke up before the Wake-Up call as her alarm sounded in her ear. She turned it off immediately and headed straight for the bathroom. There was a mirror along the corridor that led to the baths, and she stopped to look at herself. She was looking different. Camp activities from the past two days had been overly tedious and so time consuming that she didn't have the time to look presentable, to relax and to have a few drinks. Not that she was an excessive drinker, but once in a while she liked to sit back and have a few glasses of wine or anything that had alcohol in it. When the whole stress was over and she was finally settled in, she was going to get into the fun of the camp and enjoy her stay.

After taking her bath, Oluomachukwu walked back to her room, passing by a lot of girls on the corridor and in other rooms, talking and laughing happily. A lot of people were excited about the Opening Ceremony. There had been rehearsals for the key players of the parade — a parade commander: a Corps member who was going to command and lead all the other Corps members; some flag bearers; band players, who were going to drum and play some musical instruments all through the marching and presentation; two flag girls who were each to hold a flag up by both sides of the podium where the invited dignitaries were going to give speeches; and ten Corps members from each platoon who were to stand in front of their respective platoons for the general salute to the Governor of Lagos State.

Before Corps members went to line up in formation on the parade ground, it had been chaotic — chaotic because the swearing-in kit didn't fit everyone. If at all they fitted anyone, it would have been only two percent of the Corps members, and not even every item fit. Maybe the white shirt and the belt would fit, but nothing else. The rest were either too big or too small. Some didn't try on theirs the day before. Corps members were also expected to put on their NYSC caps for the rehearsal and the ceremony, and hang their badges over their neck in a transparent badge holder that could have been provided by the NYSC, but hawkers sold it for 100 naira. Some Corps members had to even buy extras due to its poor quality.

The evening before, there had been a rush to the tailors who were situated at the back of *mami* market. Male and female alike, with oversized khaki pants that could fit at least three fat people at once, trooped there after rehearsals to get their kit mended. The ones who had smaller sizes either exchanged with others or asked for the hems to be loosened and redone with a smaller margin to allow more space to fit their legs. Some ordered new kits to be sewn from scratch if the first two options weren't feasible.

Some of Oluomachukwu's roommates had gone to get their kit fitted and were asked to come back the following morning to collect them. The only problem was that the tailors had said that to almost every Corps member in the camp, so they only hoped that the kits were going to be ready in the morning.

Fitting the kit didn't cost anything less than 1,000 naira, and some Corps members felt that the NYSC coordinators had sewed oversized kits on purpose. It was also believed that the NYSC official team had something to gain from the tailors. After Oluomachukwu had tried her kit, she concurred to the belief. She initially didn't want to get hers fitted, because she thought she looked okay in it and also because she had heard that people had to leave their kit with tailors until the next day. And if the tailor ended up not coming to the camp the next morning, it was going to be a very big problem.

Ogo had also wanted to go to the tailor, but changed her mind for reasons only known to her. After rehearsals, Oluomachukwu came back to the room and tried on her baggy khaki pants again, then decided she was going to fix it. She managed to convince Ogo to go and get hers fitted as well. And luckily for them, they found tailors who could mend their kits the same evening, within thirty minutes, and also at a reduced price of 900 or 800 naira, depending on their bargaining power.

Oluomachukwu paid 800 naira and Ogo paid 900 naira. So all they had to do was get measured, wait and watch the kit get mended, try it on, then pay and leave if it was okay. It was mostly okay for those who waited.

The only mistake Oluomachukwu and Ogo made was to mend their khaki jackets, because it wasn't part of the dress code on the Swearing-in day. They got to find out when they went back to the room and heard people talking about it. If they had known, they wouldn't have spent that much money for what they didn't need. Oluomachukwu would have bought herself a waist pouch of good quality, but she had only 700 naira extra cash on her after paying the tailor. The cost of the pouch ranged from 500 naira to 1,500 naira, and that was exactly how the quality ranged. Oluomachukwu was able to get one for 700 naira. She had money in her box in the room, but she didn't want to go upstairs and come back down again. Ogo also didn't have extra cash on her. The pouch wasn't that excellent, but it looked like it was going to last all through the remaining days in the camp.

Oluomachukwu entered the room and started getting dressed, looking very smart, stylish and sexy. For a brief moment she thought of joining one of the armed forces, just to always put on a uniform. She looked around and heard people lamenting. Some girls, including Ijeoma, had gone to the camp market to look for the tailors that had their kit, but none of them had arrived, so it wasn't sure they were going to be ready in time for the ceremony.

Oluomachukwu wasn't in the same platoon as any of the girls she knew in the room, so she didn't waste any time with them. The dreaded sound of the bugle blasted around the camp annoyingly, which was supposed to be a warning call that everyone should report to the parade ground for final rehearsals before the arrival of the guests. Oluomachukwu wore her badge over her neck, put her phone in her pocket — since she also learnt that morning that the waist pouch wasn't part of the dress code, so no one was allowed to use it for the ceremony — and ran out of the room.

The ceremony was seriously delayed for almost two hours because it was raining. It rained as if the country hadn't seen rain in years. Corps members were supposed to report to the parade ground by 8:00am, then rehearse until 9:00am when the dignitaries were expected to arrive. Oluomachukwu couldn't wait to see them and everyone anticipated the arrival of the Lagos State Governor. Every time a car drove in, all attention was focused on it, until the car drove by or out with no one alighting from it. It felt as though it was the main motivation of the ceremony. Everyone wanted to see him, even from a distance. Some people had even gone to the parade ground quite early so that they would see him before other people did, as if there was a prize to be won.

Corps members stood under the canopies as the rain

poured, preventing them from going to the parade ground to rehearse. Oluomachukwu knew that the extra rehearsal was needed because the day before, her platoon members were seriously flopping when it was time to raise their caps and give three hearty cheers to the Governor.

The soldiers called the cap 'headrest.' At least, that was what Oluomachukwu heard.

A girl had been picked to represent the platoon and command the team. While she did, some other girls kept laughing at her, so a soldier assigned to the platoon asked the laughing girls to recite the command. Even after the soldier repeated the command to them, over and over again, one of the girls said, "Remove head-dress." Another girl said, "Remove head-gear." Oluomachukwu wasn't sure how the girl had heard 'head-gear' from 'headrest.' The last girl, who was still giggling, stupidly said, "Remove head-dresser." They, of course, got serious scolding and insults from the soldier. The soldier even questioned the degree certificates they had gotten and doubted the fact that they were truly graduates. Oluomachukwu hoped that the rain would stop so that they would rehearse a little more.

The rain continued to pour, and not wanting to get out of the excitement and good mood they felt earlier, some Corps members started taking photos of themselves and others. With the way they posed and smiled, one would have thought that they were having an excellent time in the camp. Oluomachukwu looked around the canopy; it was mostly her platoon members that were there. Some of them grumbled and hoped that the rain wouldn't stop so that the ceremony wouldn't hold, or that the dignitaries wouldn't show up and they wouldn't have to perform the little they had rehearsed. Many people still hadn't mastered taking off their caps to give three hearty cheers to the Governor. They needed to rehearse some more.

Oluomachukwu turned to her side and heard one girl complaining about how small her cap was. She had braided her hair up like she was a genie and it protruded like a fist on her head, so the hair couldn't fit into the cap. She hung it over the fist-like top knot of her hairdo and always had to hold it so that the wind wouldn't blow it off.

Oluomachukwu was happy she hadn't made any fancy hairstyle that would have embarrassed her in the camp.

Unfortunately for many of the complaining Corps members, the rain stopped and the sunshine that followed was hot enough to make one believe that the dry season had already come. Corps members were then asked to stand in line, but didn't have the time to rehearse before the dignitaries were to arrive. Before long, the Governor's entourage was seen coming in from the gate and everyone started to murmur, smiles gradually spreading across their cheeks.

The female MC, the same woman who made the camp announcements, and whose name Oluomachukwu still did not know, shushed everyone and told them that Corps members never applauded for any reason — if someone made a very moving speech, no applaud; if a dignitary was introduced, still no applaud. Some Corps members almost clapped, in fact, some did, when the representative of the Chief Judge and that of the Commissioner of Police were introduced. The MC yelled and reminded everyone not to, and they immediately stopped clapping.

The ceremony started off with both the National and NYSC Anthems, then an introductory speech by the Lagos State Coordinator and afterwards, the Chairman of the Lagos State NYSC governing Board. The flag bearers, each representing one platoon then marched in, supported by beautiful drumming by the band. Six of them held six sides of a large flag so that it was flat in the air, and four others marched behind them. The same flag bearers were meant to go before the dignitaries when it was time for the oath to be read. No one had wanted to take that position, either because they were afraid to fail or scared that they might forget their role.

One of the girls holding the flag almost fainted, and no

one knew if she was really feeling dizzy or if she had suddenly grown cold feet. A soldier immediately went to carry her away, and another Corps member, who hadn't rehearsed for the role replaced her, but it wasn't a disaster.

After all the marching, drumming and general salute from Corps members, the representative of the Chief Judge came forward and read the Oath of Allegiance, and with their right arms raised up, the prospective Corps members repeated each line of the one-page Oath. At the end, they were officially sworn in as Corps members, with their right arms aching, as if they had just worked on farms, from holding them up in the air. Many sighed as they put their hands down. The representative then went off the podium for the Governor to take the stage and address the Corps members.

Everyone stood on their toes to see the Governor as he walked towards his reserved seat. The only problem was that it wasn't the Governor. Just like the Chief Judge and the Commissioner of Police, the Governor had sent in his own representative. Corps members hissed when they saw the stranger climb up the podium to address them.

As he started speaking, a plane flew by, lower than all the other cargo planes that flew in on a regular basis. Since Oluomachukwu entered the camp, at least fifteen planes had flown over the parade ground. But this one was so low that it felt like it was aiming to land on the parade ground. Everyone looked towards the sky, staring intently at the plane until it passed and flew towards the international airport to land. The MC redirected everyone's attention to the Governor's representative, whom nobody wanted to continue listening to.

He said he had brought along the speech he was to give, which had been prepared by the Governor himself, but nobody believed the Governor would write anything that unexciting. And as if nature had heard the silent cries in the hearts of the Corps members, a fleet of five birds hovered above the parade ground; one left droppings that landed on the representative's forehead when he looked up to see what everyone on the parade ground was looking at.

Instead of waiting for someone to bring him a napkin or even using his own handkerchief, the man used his hand to wipe the poop off and it wasn't done properly. Then instead of only one person, three people went up to the podium to assist him — one with toilet paper, another with soap and water and the third person, just in case. Oluomachukwu wondered how they had been mobilised in only a matter of seconds, especially with soap and water.

As all four of them stood uncomfortably on the small stage, Oluomachukwu feared that it would shake out of balance, that the canopy would cave in and all the water on it would pour on them and also on the paper that had the speech, then the representative wouldn't have any speech to read. That didn't happen. However, the microphone stopped working and another was immediately taken to him. After a little while, the man stopped reading from the paper and continued the speech with an unexplicable ease. It felt like he had either memorised it or it was indeed his own speech.

When the speech was over, he declared the 2014 Batch B Orientation course open and Corps members gave three hearty cheers to him as they had been trained to do. Both the National and the NYSC anthems were sung again, and it marked the end of the Opening Ceremony. Dignitaries and guests proceeded to leave the parade ground in the reversed order they came and had been introduced.

After the event, the Camp Director mentioned that Platoon Two was going to be on duty and take on the various duties that had been assigned to Platoon One the previous day. Everyone was then permitted to leave the parade ground after the dignitaries left.

Corps members stood at different angles of the parade ground, posing for selfies and group photograps by camp photographers lingered around like predators. Some Corps members were using their phones to take their pictures, while others were taking pictures of the crowd.

Oluomachukwu took a few photos with her phone and some with the soldiers assigned to her platoon flanking her like bodyguards, after which she exchanged numbers with them and left to look around. She later went back to the room and came down later with her waist pouch.

While Corps members were scattered around the camp, the Camp Director made an announcement a few minutes later for Corps members to reassemble on the parade ground. Impulsively, they all started to grumble, but when she stated that it was to receive the sum of 1,500 naira, which was meant for their travel allowance into Lagos State, they ran immediately and got in line.

Camp officials were setting up under the canopies with cardboard papers stapled at the top of different sections of the canopy. Numbers were written on it for collection of the allowance. It wasn't going to be by platoon numbers, but by ranges of the four-digit State code — from codes 0001 to 0500; 0501 to 1000; 1001 to 1500, and so on. In addition to the State code number, locally-trained Nigerian students were asked to present their university ID cards to collect the allowance, while the foreign-trained ones were asked to bring along their international passports.

Oluomachukwu already had hers in her waist pouch, so she stood in the line that corresponded to her State code number.

As she waited in line, she looked around, searching for anyone she knew, from her room or platoon, she didn't see anyone, not even Ekene that was supposed to be in her platoon and in the same code range as she was. She then did a head count of her roommates to try and figure out where they might be. Ijeoma was always in the room reading one book or the other. Ogo spent long hours on the phone and used up to four power banks to charge her phone every day. Fadeke was almost invisible. She hardly spent time in the room and heaven only knew where she was. But whenever she came back, she would bring along plenty of things to eat... things that looked like they had been bought by guys or men. Sometimes, she would share them with some of her roommates, and other times, she wouldn't. Eternity was always reading her Bible and Oghene always lay in bed lamenting on how she could not suffer. Oluomachukwu jumped out of her thoughts when someone tapped her shoulder from behind. She turned her head around and saw a girl.

"Hi, Oluoma," the girl said.

Oluomachukwu turned around completely, feeling awkward, because she didn't know who the girl was, how the girl knew her name and if she was supposed to know who the girl was.

"Hey," Oluomachukwu replied, not sure if she should continue talking with her or turn around and continue on the line.

The girl looked at Oluomachukwu's hand and pointed at her international passport. "So you are a foreign-trained student?"

Oluomachukwu nodded. She had done a very good job hiding that fact from the general public. "I schooled in the UK... in the University of Essex. What about you?"

"I'm from the University of Liverpool."

"Oh, really?" Oluomachukwu felt somewhat relieved to see someone she could relate to. And not wanting their conversation to be any more awkward, she asked, "Sorry, what's your name?"

The girl laughed.

"What's funny?" Oluomachukwu asked.

"So we are in the same platoon and in the same room, and you don't know my name?"

Oluomachukwu felt too awkward. She wondered why she hadn't just waited until much later to collect the travel allowance — that way she wouldn't have met the girl and been in that rather weird situation.

"I'm sorry, I always leave early to the parade ground and stay at the back. Plus I hardly ever relate to everyone in the room. There are twenty-six of us in the room, so it is difficult to keep up with everyone."

"I stay just opposite your bed on the lower bunk," the girl replied. "I just observe people and their characters in the room. Plus we are actually twenty-seven in the room."

Oluomachukwu raised an eyebrow. "Twenty-seven?"

"Yes," she replied. "The girls by my side are annoying, plus they already have a squatter. They are three on the bunk, not two. The third one came from the second floor and has been in our room since the first day, squatting. They must really think they are in Uni-Lag... I mean the University of Lagos, and they are always on my bed. It's irritating."

Oluomachukwu laughed. "I haven't even noticed them yet, and I know what Uni-Lag is."

"Me, I have noticed them well. Plus they are serial 'phone chargers,' just like the girls by your own side. I haven't charged my phone since I arrived and there's a socket by my head." She overemphasised on the 'head.'

Oluomachukwu looked in front of her to check if the line had started moving. It hadn't. The camp officials were yet to start attending to Corps members. She turned back to look at the nameless girl. "So how have you been managing?"

"I have been going to the camp market to charge my phone for a fee, and it's depending on how many phones you have and how long you want to charge them for."

"Interesting," Oluomachukwu said. "I don't think I would spend a kobo charging my phone when there's a socket by my head and a lot of phones charging on my bed. I'd rather destroy the socket and no one else would use it."

The girl laughed. "Anyway, I'm Nkiru. And I'm glad to have found another foreign student in the room." She smiled.

"What about Ogo?" Oluomachukwu asked. "The girl on the bunk by my left side?"

"That one who forgets her American accent at times? That's if I can even call the thing an American accent."

Oluomachukwu laughed.

"She's from a school in the North, but wants people to believe that she went to an American university." Before Oluomachukwu could comment on that, Nkiru added, "When I went to collect my international passport from the room, she was bringing out her national student ID card and I stole a glimpse of it."

"Hmm." Oluomachukwu sighed. She then realised that the queue had started moving when one guy asked her if he could cut the line and stay in front of her, as she wasn't ready to move. She let the guy stay in front of her because she wasn't in a hurry. After a few minutes, the guy turned back and spoke to her.

"Excuse me."

Oluomachukwu looked at him.

"You look familiar," he said. "Did you go to Ife?"

Oluomachukwu didn't know what that meant, but she knew she didn't go there. "No."

"What of Uni-Lag?" he asked. "Did you go to Uni-Lag?"

Oluomachukwu knew what that was. "No, I didn't."

"Okay, it's Uni-Ben then?"

Oluomachukwu shook her head, and not wanting the guy to keep naming all the schools in Nigeria, she said, "I didn't school in Nigeria."

"Oh," he simply said. "My name is John. I'm in the platoon next to yours."

"Okay," Oluomachukwu replied. "Nice to meet you, I'm Oluoma."

"Can I please have your number?"

Oluomachukwu thought about it briefly. "I don't know my number."

"Okay, take mine and call me then." Without waiting for an answer from her, he started calling out his number. So she brought out her phone and took the number down, then promised to call him when she bought some airtime on her phone. He then smiled and turned around.

Oluomachukwu looked back at Nkiru. "As we were saying."

"Don't mind the guy that just spoke to you right now," Nkiru whispered.

Instinctively, Oluomachukwu turned back and looked at him, then turned back to look at Nkiru. "Why?"

"Because he has been going round camp and doing the same thing to everyone, asking them for their numbers at the end, hoping that someone will fall for him."

"How do you know?"

"Because he did the same thing with me just yesterday, but I'm sure he can't remember that he did."

Oluomachukwu laughed, but kept the information safely in a part of her brain to use later, if needed.

***

After Oluomachukwu had collected her money, she walked towards the camp market to buy airtime for her phone. She wanted to call her parents and tell them that everything was going well, then maybe call Okechukwu and know how he was doing, but she wasn't going to call Kayode or Nnanna, or even speak with any of them if they tried to call her.

When she got to the camp market, she was accosted by almost all the recharge card sellers at the entrance of the place and other random sellers, asking her to buy one thing or another. She tried to squirm herself out.

"Please, leave me alone," she said. "I don't want to buy anything. I don't have money." She rejected the statement in her mind, saying that she had money in the name of Jesus Christ, she then said an 'Amen.' It was a Nigerian culture that her mother and aunties had thought her.

One man, who Oluomachukwu wasn't sure what he sold, yelled, "Didn't they just give you 1,500 naira now? Or haven't you collected your own yet?"

Oluomachukwu looked at him, wondering how he knew about the money, but that wasn't her main concern. "So even if I collect my money today, does that mean I should use it all up today?"

Another woman selling white socks and handkerchiefs replied, "But they will still share another 1,000 naira very soon, so you will still have money."

Oluomachukwu looked at the woman, but before she could say anything, another woman spoke.

"Your *allawee* of 19,800 naira will also be ready before the end of camp, so you'll still have enough. Or you want to carry it back home?"

Oluomachukwu was surprised at how the camp market sellers were so informed. They probably knew a lot more than most of the Corps members. She would have thought that the NYSC Board gave all the money while in the camp so that Corps members could spend it *in* camp, and then the officials would have a cut from it. But it was just a thought. In reality, it was obvious that the market sellers had been there, year in, year out, and even knew more than most camp officials, who were newly appointed.

"Okay, so when exactly will they give us the money?" Oluomachukwu asked.

"Third week," one person yelled.

"Even before," another one said. "If you people cry for it."

Oluomachukwu nodded and forced herself out of the crowd. She then went to the person she initially wanted to go to; a skinny woman who sold recharge cards. The other sellers who had gathered around her, hissed and ran off to look for other preys when they realised that they were not going to get a piece of Oluomachukwu's money.

As she bought a recharge card of 1,000 naira and was scratching the black strip on it, a woman came up from behind to ask for a recharge card as well. It was when the same woman asked for it a second time that it seemed like she was addressing Oluomachukwu, and not the recharge card seller. Oluomachukwu turned around and looked at the person, a young-looking woman or rather, a girl, light in complexion, almost bleaching, with short hair.

"Excuse me," the girl said again. "Are you going to pay for my own recharge card?"

Oluomachukwu looked back, then turned back to the girl again. "Why? Didn't you get your own 1,500 naira?"

The young-looking, almost bleaching girl looked closely at Oluomachukwu, but didn't reply. Just then, a gush of wind swept through the camp market and rattled both Oluomachukwu's badge and that of the girl begging her for airtime. Her badge showed 'camp official' as it dangled around her neck. Between the other lady, the one that had one eye, who had been posing as an NYSC camp official and collecting 200 naira to arrange files, it was uncertain who was who in the camp. Either way, Oluomachukwu decided to show the camp official due respect.

"Ma, I'm sorry, I thought you were a corper."

The girl scoffed and looked away, but it was obvious that she still wanted the airtime, because she hung around there and even offered to help Oluomachukwu read out the numbers on the recharge card while she typed it in. Oluomachukwu also worried that the girl would steal the recharge code, but she remained calm.

After Oluomachukwu loaded the airtime, she pulled out the remaining 500 naira and reluctantly handed it over to the seller when someone snatched the money out of her hand.

Oluomachukwu turned around and saw Nkiru. "What are you doing?" she asked.

Nkiru pulled her aside, then whispered, "I overheard you with that girl and you were going to buy her airtime, weren't you?"

Oluomachukwu nodded. And all the while, the camp official stood there, looking away as if she was hiding her face or looking for other people to ask for airtime.

"Sister, are you still buying from me?" the seller asked, and Oluomachukwu shook her head, indicating "No." At least, until she had heard more from Nkiru.

"Well," Nkiru started. "She asked me to buy her fruits earlier today, and I did."

"Really?" Oluomachukwu asked.

"Yes. Just as she did with you, she came over to the woman over there that sells pawpaw and watermelon." Nkiru pointed to a woman not too far from where they stood who was trying to stop flies from perching on the watermelon she was cutting. "And after I bought mine, she asked me to pay for hers. I only did it because I thought she was a corper who couldn't afford it. But when she left, the fruit seller told me to be careful of her, and some other corpers also told me the same thing."

Oluomachukwu turned and looked at the camp official with looks that could kill, but she was gone. She looked around her, and Nkiru did the same, but the camp official was nowhere to be found. Oluomachukwu felt that she had probably gone to look for another willing prey to beg or bug.

As Oluomachukwu and Nkiru stood there chatting, a black car drove into the camp and down the road that separated the volleyball court from the camp market. The car slowed down a bit as it approached Oluomachukwu and Nkiru, but it didn't stop. The car windows were tinted, so it was difficult to tell who could have been in it.

As soon as the car passed by, Nkiru turned back to face Oluomachukwu, then spoke immediately and quickly.

"Oluoma, don't look, don't look."

Oluomachukwu almost turned around to look, but she stopped. "What is it?"

"That guy, whose number you collected, is in the camp market looking around as if he is searching for someone."

"So?"

"He might be searching for you."

Oluomachukwu shook her head and laughed. "I doubt

it. How would he know I was here?"

"Because he was tracking you, why else?"

Oluomachukwu laughed again. "He couldn't possibly be tracking me."

"He's coming this way. He's a tracker. He always tracks people down, and it's your turn."

John, who was from then known as Tracker, started to approach them, because he was indeed looking for Oluomachukwu. She, still refusing to look back, started to walk towards the hostel because she didn't want to talk to anyone. Nkiru turned around too, trying not to gain eye contact with Tracker. He started to jog towards them, but before he could reach either one of them, a soldier walked up to them and stopped them.

"Which of you *otondo* is Oluoma?" he asked, and both Oluomachukwu and Nkiru almost laughed. They found the word '*otondo*' to be funny, even though the word was used to describe an idiot, a stupid person or a learner. The soldier also didn't pronounce her name properly, but she knew he had come for her. She wasn't sure if to raise her hand up, salute or say "Me, sir."

"Are you deaf?" the soldier yelled.

Oluomachukwu saluted dramatically, even some Corps members who passed by and saw her, chuckled. She then put her hand up and said, "Me, sir."

The soldier turned to Nkiru. "You are dismissed, *otondo*. Leave this place now." Nkiru ran off without asking any questions. He turned back to Oluomachukwu, and without looking at her, he said, "Follow me."

Oluomachukwu obliged. She followed the soldier to the main building where the office of the Camp Director was. She wasn't sure what was going on, but she knew she had done nothing wrong. When they got in front of the office the soldier told her to wait outside while he knocked at the door and entered.

A few seconds later, the door swung open and Kayode stood in the doorway. Oluomachukwu's heart almost exploded in her chest at that instant, shocked to see him. She loathed him and wasn't sure if it was because she had slept with him the first day she met him, because he had a wife, because he had told her about Nnanna, just to ruin her happiness or all of the reasons combined.

They stood quietly and looked at each other until the soldier took the hint and walked out of the office. Kayode wasn't really sure if to hug her or not, but he had a feeling that she would have probably slapped him, pushed him away or even done nothing, since no one was around. He opened his hands as if asking for permission to hug her. She stepped aside.

"So did you need to send a soldier to go around camp looking for me?"

He shook his head. "No. I saw you talking with a girl when I drove in with a colleague. I had wanted to come down and call you, but the soldier who came in with us offered to call you for me."

"Okay, so what do you want?"

"I wanted to see you again."

Oluomachukwu hissed. She made an attempt to leave, but Kayode grabbed her arm. She tried to release her arm, but he held her firmly urging her to listen. When she was about to scream, Kayode let go off her, raising both hands up as though he was surrendering.

"I didn't mean any harm. I just wanted to tell you why I am here and also to apologise to you," he said.

It was too late. Oluomachukwu already left the office and slammed the door behind her.

CHAPTER EIGHT: DAY FOUR

Friday, 8th August 2014

The day after the Swearing-in Ceremony wasn't like the other days. The youths in the camp had passed from prospective Corps members to full Corps members. The Camp Director preferred the appropriate term, which was 'Corps member,' and not 'corper.' But it seemed like she was the only one in the whole of Nigeria who used the former. Corps members had sworn the Oath of Allegiance and vowed to abide by all NYSC rules, which included discipline at the highest level. Any form of insubordination or disobedience was punishable by being decamped and probably missing out on the whole NYSC programme and returning a year later if allowed.

After all the camp training — exercise, drills and man-o-war — Corps members were expected to receive, they were supposed to be able to invade the North, and if a war was to break out, they would be conscripted, male and female alike. Oluomachukwu laughed at the thought of it.

Oluomachukwu didn't want to get up that morning and report to the parade ground for anything. She was not feeling too well. In fact, she hadn't been feeling too well right from the second day in camp. She didn't know if it was the stress, the fact that she hadn't eaten, the dirt that enveloped the camp or the drinking water that was sold in the camp market. Something was making her sick and she hoped it wasn't malaria. Her surprise meeting with Kayode had also rattled a lot in her and given her mixed feelings of sadness, anger and guilt, which compounded the way she was feeling at that instant. She picked up the phone and called Okechukwu, but he didn't answer. She knew he was still in bed, so she sent him a message just to check up on him.

As she lay on her narrow and barely long mattress, she continued to think about Kayode and wondered why he was in the camp. She felt that she should have waited and heard him out, but the way he grabbed her arm scared her. If she had considered listening to him, she changed her mind instantly because of his gesture. When she was even coming back to her room, she had bumped into Dunsin who was going out, and didn't apologise to her. She didn't actually like Dunsin, and didn't still know why.

A few minutes later into her thoughts, Oluomachukwu heard the sound of the bugle, it got more annoying by each passing day. She covered her ears with her hands. About fifteen of the twenty-six girls in her room had already dressed in all white — whether they took their baths or not, Oluomachukwu didn't know. She just wished that they would shut their mouths and turn off the light, the only light in the room, so that she could go back to sleep.

Oluomachukwu managed to stay back in her bed while the others had already scuttled off, afraid of what would happen if the female soldiers found them in the room. She didn't care, she slept for another hour until she heard a loud voice. Someone had barged into the room, yelling like there was a fire or even a riot happening. It was a security officer from the Nigerian Police Force, dressed in a black skirt uniform, and welding an iron rod she used to hit the edges of the iron bedposts causing an unbearable noise.

"My friend, stand up," the woman yelled. "Before the

count of three I do not want to see anyone lying down on the bed."

Oluomachukwu sat up and tried to talk to the officer.

The officer raised her hand. "I do not want to hear anything. You have no business speaking to me dressed that way." She then looked up and saw Ijeoma climbing down from the bunk. "*Ehen*, she, I can talk to because she is properly dressed."

Oluomachukwu had her pyjamas on. She looked at Ijeoma. Ijeoma was dressed in her white shirt and shorts. She looked at the bunk opposite her and didn't see Nkiru. She hadn't seen Nkiru the night before and wondered if Nkiru was truly in her room or even in her platoon.

"I can listen to her, but it doesn't mean I'm interested in her reason for staying back when others are out on the parade ground," the security officer added.

Oluomachukwu tried to speak again, but she couldn't hear her voice. She was starting to get sore throat, so she knew it was definitely the water. She told the officer that she wasn't feeling too well, but the officer shook her head and asked her to get dressed and go to the clinic.

Some girls were still on their beds, probably waiting for the officer to leave so that they would continue to bask in their sweet sleep, but the officer used the iron rod to make louder and more annoying gong sounds on the bed. It was then that Oluomachukwu noticed Oghene.

Oghene hissed and repeated the same words she had said on the first day in camp, "I can't suffer here." She had the look of someone who had a plan and who was going to do everything to make the plan work.

The officer pulled out a whistle from her pocket and started blowing it. It was so noisy that everyone got up and left the room. Oluomachukwu rolled her legs over to the edge of the bed, wearing a sickly look on her face, then went to have her bath.

There was a very fat girl in the bathroom who had just gotten there and occupied all the space. If Oluomachukwu had been one second earlier, she wouldn't have had to wait for the girl. The girl stood in the shower space, not ready to have her bath yet, but also not prepared to step aside for anyone else. She took her time, washing her underwear, then her flip-flop. She didn't know how annoying it was to watch her do those.

Oluomachukwu looked at the girl — her body was fair, but it wasn't the colour of her face and arms. All the parts of her body that were exposed to constant sunlight were darkened. Her breasts were big, but flabby, falling down to her stomach like bananas, very fat bananas. Her stomach was bulky and served as a tray to receive the breasts.

Oluomachukwu did not want to look any lower than that; the stomach area was just fine. She watched the girl, angrily, as she washed just one slack underwear for almost five minutes. It was still early, and the weather could pass for an early European winter.

Oluomachukwu hadn't come to the camp with a towel. It had taken a lot of space in her box so she had to take it out and use a wrapper she had brought back from the UK instead. Had she known, she would have carried the towel along, because morning baths were always a torture. So at that moment she regretted her decision. The wrapper she tied around her body was so thin, it felt like she was totally naked. When she had had enough of waiting, she decided to tell the girl to move it.

"Do you mind hurrying up?" Oluomachukwu said.

The girl didn't respond. It even looked like she was getting slower by each passing second. There were other bathrooms that Oluomachukwu could have used, but some of them had stagnant dirty and soapy water in them due to blocked drainages. Some of the other good ones were occupied and the empty ones were difficult to get to because the whole baths were flooded. Oluomachukwu wanted to use that particular one where she was, because it seemed not to have any problems.

As she stood there, a girl entered, tiptoeing as she went

to use one of the toilets. She was dressed in white shirt and shorts, with her white tennis shoes that left sandy prints on the floor. The girl had a small piece of pink paper pinned to her shirt that read '3 ON DUTY.' Corps members on duty were allowed to go round the camp without being asked questions as long as they said they were going to do some work.

Oluomachukwu had been carried away in her thoughts that she didn't notice the fat girl was finally done washing her body, but she wasn't done monopolising the bath. She spoke to Oluomachukwu, snapping her out of her thinking session.

"There's a girl after me who wants to take her bath," the fat girl said as she wiped her flabby tummy.

Oluomachukwu looked around, indicating how silly the fat girl sounded.

"She is still in the room," the fat girl added. She didn't get Oluomachukwu's sarcastic hint.

"Well, I don't see anyone here," Oluomachukwu finally said something.

The fat girl might not have actually realised how silly she sounded at that moment, but she still went ahead to talk. "She is sleeping, but she would be here as soon as she wakes up or I wake her up."

Oluomachukwu didn't care. The fat girl then took her time to finish up, probably secretly praying that whomever she was trying to keep a spot for would show up. When she was done, she left the bathroom in a hurry, and Oluomachukwu figured that she had gone to wake the sleeping girl up, but that didn't matter. Once the shower space was empty, Oluomachukwu hopped in and started to have her bath immediately. And just as expected, one girl walked up to her and asked if the fat girl had just used the bath.

Oluomachukwu poured a small bowl of on her body, then yelled before she realise public. "Yes, there was a girl here before me," sounding sarcastic.

"I was meant to be after her," the sleeping friend said.

"Was I supposed to wait for you to wake up and come over here?" Oluomachukwu wasn't sure who was more ridiculous, the fat girl who had kept a bath space for a sleeping friend or the sleeping friend who had come to use the space.

The sleeping friend probably took some time to think about it, watching Oluomachukwu as she spoke and as she soaped her body with lather from her black sponge. When she had had enough of the show, she said, "Okay, can I be after you?"

Oluomachukwu could have said "Yes," and she could have also said "No," but she was in no place to say either. Between the times the fat girl had gone back to her room and the sleeping friend had come to the bathroom, some girls had come into the bathroom and joined the queue behind Oluomachukwu, also angry at the fact that the fat girl had wasted time. They wouldn't have been too pleased to know that someone else was coming to take their spot. They, too, would have loved an extra twenty minutes of sleep, while a friend saved them a spot.

With the words that came out of their mouths and the way they sounded, the sleeping girl knew she had only two options: join the queue or go to another bathroom.

As Oluomachukwu walked back to the prison ward she called a room, she heard a sound coming from a bathroom — it was the flooded bathroom that stood two doors away from her room. So she wondered why anyone would still want to use it in its state and why that anyone was also moaning in it. The noise was totally distracting.

Girls passed in front of the bathroom, looked at it with scrunched eyebrows and muttered words of bewilderment, before moving on to other things.

Oluomachukwu didn't move on. She had gone to camp to discover a lot of things and finding out what happened behind closed doors was one of them.

She stood by the entrance, which was a little elevated, wondering how she would enter and look around without getting her feet in the dirty water. More girls went back and forth, each time staring briefly at Oluomachukwu as she stood there calculating what might or might not be, and narrowing her eyes at the moaning sound.

Someone tapped Oluomachukwu on the shoulder from behind. She turned her head around and saw Nkiru.

"What are you doing?" Nkiru asked. "I hope you don't intend to use that bathroom."

Oluomachukwu looked at Nkiru and wondered why she had a badge pinned to her shirt when she wasn't on duty. She then doubted that Nkiru was really in Platoon Seven. "I thought you were in Platoon Seven?"

Before Nkiru could reply to the question, there was the moaning noise again, so instead, she exclaimed, "Oh my god, what is that noise?"

"That is what I want to find out, too," Oluomachukwu replied.

The rusty door of the bathroom swung open and both Oluomachukwu and Nkiru were shocked to see Ijeoma, Oluomachukwu's bunkmate walk out. Oluomachukwu was speechless and didn't want to imagine what had happened in there. She decided not to think too much about it and went about her business as if nothing had happened and she hadn't heard anything.

***

Oluomachukwu got dressed in her white shorts and white shirt. The shorts were too short for her and had been badly sewn. It packed between her legs and exposed the black tights she wore underneath, so she had to remove the tights. She then made a mental note to buy new shorts from the camp market later in the day. The shirt was transparent, so transparent that she had to wear a black camisole underneath it, happy that she had brought one.

She went down to the clinic to get herself checked. She felt embarrassed because she had gradually started to fall ill right from the second day in camp, and so, wondered how the remaining days were going to be for her.

The clinic was big and wide enough, but jam-packed. It looked like all the doctors in the camp, who were also Corps members, were cramped up in it; one could hardly even tell who the doctors or the patients were. Tables were arranged in lines by the wall and a cabinet that held drugs was by one of the tables. There were also a couple of beds farther into the clinic and Oluomachukwu could see some people sleeping on them. She felt then that she couldn't have been the first person to fall ill in the camp. The noise in the clinic from talking and laughing was also disturbing.

Oluomachukwu approached one of the tables there and spoke to a girl, but the girl simply waved her away with no explanation. Whether the girl was not on duty or not a doctor, Oluomachukwu didn't know, so she advanced and spoke to another girl. After she had told the corper-doctor what was wrong with her, which sounded unfamiliar, the corper-doctor gave her anti malaria drugs. Apparently the Lagos State NYSC office had provided anti malaria drugs for everyone in the camp, and it was going to be two pills, three times daily, for seven days.

Before Oluomachukwu left, another corper-doctor, a male, asked her to wait and fill a form. It was part of their protocol to keep count and record of anyone that visited. Oluomachukwu filled the form, and as she was filling in her phone number, the female doctor turned to the male doctor, and said, "Uchenna, you better not try to call her oh. Because that is your work."

Oluomachukwu stopped, not sure if to complete filling the form. The female doctor looked serious, but the male doctor was smiling.

"Don't mind Lola," Uchenna said. "You can fill in your

phone number on the form."

Oluomachukwu finished filling the form, noticing that the doctor, who had beautiful eyes, kept looking at her. When she was done, she smiled at him and didn't mind the idea of him calling her. Okechukwu had told her not to fall in love in camp, but some things couldn't be controlled. He had to understand. Oluomachukwu left the clinic and that was the last time she saw Uchenna. She never saw him again and he never called her for once.

By the time Oluomachukwu was going back to the hostel, the morning exercise and drills were over, and it was time for Bath and Breakfast according to the NYSC schedule. When she got closer to the hostel, she saw Kayode waiting by the entrance, but she wasn't sure he had seen her. She turned around immediately and tried to leave, but saw John, or rather Tracker, walking towards her direction. She was cornered. She made a quick decision and opted for dodging Tracker instead.

But before she could make a move, the strangest thing happened. She saw Dunsin walking out of the hostel, then she went to hug Kayode. She hugged Kayode so tight that Oluomachukwu didn't know what to think. After the hug, they both walked away, probably to go and have breakfast together, it was uncertain. Oluomachukwu waited for them to leave before she made her move, but someone tapped her on the shoulder just then. She turned around and saw Tracker.

"I've been waiting for your call, please." He sounded desperate.

Oluomachukwu frowned. "I'm sorry, I haven't bought airtime yet to call you," she lied.

"Why don't you just give me your number so that I can call you instead?" Oluomachukwu did not respond, so he added, "I have enough airtime to call, and I also want to invite you somewhere this evening after camp activities."

The two questions that came to Oluomachukwu's mind were: 'Somewhere?' and 'Evening?' and so she wondered where else someone could be invited to in the camp other than the camp market — the parade ground? Under the canopy? The dining hall or perhaps the volleyball court? And what did he mean by 'Evening?' Was it a one-on-one romantic stroll in the camp in the birth of the evening? But she did not ask any of those questions. Instead, she asked, "What camp activities?"

"Oh, you were not on the parade ground this morning. They shared an orientation-guide to us and gave us the schedule for the three weeks. There will be inter-platoon social and sports activities, and then contests."

"Interesting," Oluomachukwu said, but she knew that she wasn't going to participate in any. "I hope they aren't compulsory."

"Well, our platoon instructors are going to have proper discussions when platoons meet later this evening."

"This evening?" Oluomachukwu wasn't sure if it was the same evening he had been referring to when he wanted to ask her out.

"Yes." Tracker gave her his copy of the orientation-guide. "Here, this is my own Guide, you can keep it. I'll get another one later."

Oluomachukwu collected the Guide and started to go through it. "So what are these lectures about? They have security, EFCC, traditional and co."

"We'll find out when we get there."

"So how are we going to have the lectures when we have no classrooms? Or, please, what kind of lectures are we talking about?"

Tracker laughed. "It's just a general address or speech from people in specific government agencies. I'm guessing we will sit under the canopies. I saw Platoon Three *otondos* on duty arranging the chairs. It's after the evening drills that our respective platoon instructors will address us and tell us what we need to do."

There was a brief awkward silence that Oluomachukwu broke. "So, what are you up to?"

"I'm going for breakfast," Tracker replied. "It's bread, boiled egg and tea. Do you want to come?"

Oluomachukwu thought for a couple of seconds, then nodded. "Fine, let's go."

"Do you have your meal ticket with you? It is date stamped, so you'll need it each time."

Oluomachukwu shook her head. She hadn't looked at it since she got it and felt it was time to start eating proper food instead of just biscuits and crisps she had taken along with her to the camp. "No, I don't. I'll go and get it now, then meet you down here in two minutes." She finally gave him her phone number before she dashed off.

***

Everyone reassembled on the parade ground for the lectures, and contrary to what Tracker had said, the Corps members were supposed to 'sit' on the parade ground for the lectures. Why they did not sit on the chairs under the canopy remained a mystery.

Corps members refused to sit on the ground, especially with their white shorts, so as not to get them dirty. Some used the orientation-guide they had gotten earlier, while others used face towels and scarves. Some shared with others and some allowed others to sit on their lap: girl on girl or girl on boy. Boy on boy would have been a major problem and would have probably led to the boys being decamped or even worse, jailed.

Tracker sat beside Oluomachukwu. He had a flyer that he had received earlier in the morning, but he gave it to Oluomachukwu so that her shorts won't get dirty. He sat on the ground like that. He would do anything for her. He had come to camp to look for a potential wife, and one of the ways for him to get one, was to groom one until the end of camp.

The Security lecture was kind of interesting. A staff of the Nigerian Police Force came to speak and gave Corps members security guidelines and steps on how to be alert and survive in Lagos, using concrete examples. He started off by greeting Corps members with "Corpers, wii oh," to which Corps members responded "Wa oh." And that was how almost every lecture or speech started off in camp. The speaker got an excellent round of applause when he was done, but the female MC was there to remind Corps members not to applaud.

For the EFCC lecture, everyone was moved under the canopy. Apparently an important guest from the Federal Government was coming to address the camp, so sitting on the parade ground was not an option.

The EFCC Chairman spoke on economic and financial crime and corruption, and urged Corps members to be engaged in the right activities and encourage others to do the same. The Chairman left as quickly as he came, then it was time for the Traditional lecture.

Oluomachukwu wondered what it was about. An older citizen — a Yoruba man — came around to teach Corps members how to speak Yoruba language. Clearly, no one was interested. Everyone laughed and made noisy chatters, even when the female MC tried to calm the crowd down. Tracker sat beside Oluomachukwu, but they weren't saying anything. She got distracted looking around the camp. She then saw Kayode again, and he was speaking with Dunsin. Oluomachukwu didn't know what they were talking about, but she knew that something was going on between them.

Not too long afterwards, she saw Ijeoma approach, but wasn't sure if she should talk to her after the moaning-in-the-toilet incident. She dodged until Ijeoma walked past. When her mind came back to the Traditional lecture, she wondered why camp officials were finding it difficult to calm the crowd. It was too noisy, just like a market place.

The voices of the Corps members overshadowed that of the old man who was putting in more and more effort to speak into the microphone. When it was clear that the Corps members had taken it too far, a tall man, dressed in mufti, who was passing by, walked up to the older man and took the microphone from him.

"Please, can everyone be quiet?" he asked, but nobody replied. It wasn't sure that everyone had heard him and the ones who had heard him didn't keep quiet. He repeated himself, but nobody answered him, until he yelled, "When I tell you all to shut up, you shut up."

As he said that, everyone kept quiet, wondering who the man was and why he felt he could yell at everyone.

"The least you can do as Corps members is to show some respect. If you wouldn't respect this older man here talking to you, you will respect the Camp Commandant."

Everyone started to murmur. No one knew the Camp Commandant. Some people hadn't seen him before, some didn't even know he existed. Oluomachukwu even thought the Camp Commandant was someone else; a hefty-looking man who always dressed in his uniform and cap, and carried a rod or a stick the length of his whole leg. People stood up and stretched their necks to see who the Camp Commandant was.

The Camp Commandant was offended, but remained calm. He even went as far as menacing Corps members for their bad behaviour. He had a top rank in the military and had the power to put an end to all camp activities and send everyone home. He also had the power to prolong camp time and keep Corps members for an extra month.

As he spoke, everyone sucked in what he was saying, with utmost silence. When he was done with what he was saying, he gave the microphone back to the older man and walked away in style. From that day on, Corps members always listened when they were asked to keep quiet.

After the lecture, Corps members were asked to stay back because a special guest was coming to speak to them. It was a surprise, and a pleasant one at that, because it was a visit from the First Lady of Lagos State. If anyone was sleeping, they woke up immediately. Some even stood up to see her as she walked in, smiling graciously and waving like she was a superstar. She might not have been into showbiz, but she was capable of moving the crowd.

She gave a very beautiful speech, then talked about her works and the organisation she owned, which was focused on igniting a passion for learning. When she was done speaking, Corps members applauded her, gave her a long, standing ovation that even the female MC couldn't stop. She had told Corps members several times never to clap, but this time they were resolved to. A series of young comedians also presented after the First Lady, including MC Pashun who did a great job.

After the surprise visit was Personal Administration and everyone reported to the parade ground and formed in their respective platoons to be addressed by their platoon instructors. Attendance was taken, which involved Corps members writing down their code numbers on a piece of paper that was passed around. As the paper went round, Nkiru came out of nowhere, without her 'on duty' badge and put her number down. She told Oluomachukwu that she would see her much later in the room, then took off again.

The Platoon Instructor started to pick representatives. She wanted two platoon presidents, a male and a female, to act as relay between her and the assistant, and the Corps members. They were also to coordinate all Platoon Seven activities on camp. There was a mini-voting session and candidates presented a short speech on why they should be picked as president. Two people were eventually picked, but it looked as though people voted just to get it over with. The speeches had meant nothing to anyone. They all just wanted to move on to other things.

After that, there were nominations for both a sports and a socials representative. The Platoon Instructor also wanted someone for the OBS, which was the Orientation Broadcasting Service. Every platoon was to bring out a representative and between all ten of them, they would take shifts to make announcements to the whole camp. It was the only thing as loud as the sound of the bugle. Then there was nomination for someone, preferably a lawyer, to work in the Justice office. For each sports and socials activity, the Platoon Instructor put one or two Corps members in charge of it. The only challenging thing about the impending competitions was the fact that they were supposed to start in three days' time, and Corps members were expected to start training and rehearsing, while they were waiting to receive the schedule on Sunday.

Once Personal Administration time was over, there was a Jumat service, and all Muslim brothers and sisters took permission to leave. One Muslim girl, who covered her head with a hijab that got to her ankle level, was cautioned. She was asked to wear only a scarf and cover her head, at most, up to her shoulder level. One's hijab got to her knee and another one wore full-length trousers instead of shorts and they were both also cautioned. The remaining Corps members, who were not Muslims, were allowed to go and do other things until it was 2:00pm and time for lunch.

As Oluomachukwu turned around to go to her room, Tracker tapped her from behind.

"Hi, do you want to have lunch?" he asked.

Oluomachukwu thought briefly and remembered the breakfast she had had — bread so hard, it felt as though it had been baked three days ago. The egg was hard-boiled and it was tough peeling the shell. The tea was another story. It tasted nothing like tea and more like coloured water. The few drops of milk might have added to the colour, but definitely not to the taste. She didn't know if she wanted to try lunch. When Tracker cleared his throat, she looked at him and nodded. She was going to try lunch.

***

After Lunch and Siesta, Corps members were to report to the parade ground for drills, martial arts and marching. There was going to be an inter-platoon marching contest, so the soldiers assigned to each platoon wanted to make sure that their platoon won. The top four platoons were going to march on the final day of camp, which was the Closing Ceremony, and a winning team was going to be picked and awarded a prize.

Oluomachukwu joined her platoon and they were split into three teams, each led by a platoon soldier. They were to learn the basics in marching and all the commands necessary. Oluomachukwu thought it was interesting, but she had just had lunch, so it was somewhat difficult for her to move and do any form of activity without throwing up her lunch. They had served beans porridge for lunch. It was so watery that she thought she could swim in it. She had also bought herself a plastic reusable bowl with a cover and some cutlery. NYSC didn't provide plates, cups or anything like that. Corps members were meant to take care of that by themselves.

After marching by 5:30pm, it was time for Games and Sports. Corps members were supposed to participate in games and sporting activities for their own leisure and well-being, and also to practice and train for upcoming competitions. The sports representative for Platoon Seven had already received the schedule and activities from the NYSC admin office. Since it was ready, there was no point hoarding it until Sunday. He needed Corps members for football, athletics, female volleyball, table tennis, and then one more sport that Oluomachukwu couldn't remember.

Nobody wanted to play any sport, except for football, where there were more volunteers than needed. Also, for athletics, they got just enough as needed, likewise for table tennis. It was the female part that posed a big problem, because basically, all the girls in the platoon didn't want to do anything. Oluomachukwu wasn't surprised, because girls normally never wanted to jump or run around when they could just sit down, look and stay pretty all day.

By the time the evening sessions were over, the sports representative had managed to recruit enough guys for all the activities and was still begging some girls he felt could participate. He spoke to two girls, who seemed to be very close, and asked them if they could be standby athletes, just in case he wasn't able to get any other person to join in. They nodded and dispersed.

***

The camp market in the evening was very interesting. Oluomachukwu didn't want to go at first because she didn't know what to expect, but she was glad she did. She went with Ogo, Fadeke and Nkiru, and they met up with Tracker. She had already told Tracker that she was going to be there with her roommates, and he also invited some of the guys from his platoon.

There was a lot to eat in the camp market, from local to intercontinental dishes. There was chicken and chips, fish and chips, sharwarma, kebab, small chops, noodles, pasta, *asun* meat, *suya*, and other finger-licking food. There were also drinks — soft drinks and alcoholic drinks — ranging from wines, to cocktails, to beer to hard liquor. There was also music, interesting music that kept people on their feet.

There were these four particular songs: Shoki, Sekem, Shake Body and Dorobucci that were played back-to-back and in that order. The songs had also been played in the morning during exercise and drills, then in the afternoon during lunch break and siesta. In fact, when there was no official address or lecture, all that was heard was music and the same four songs played all the time. And each time the songs were played, people started to dance specific dance routines to them. Those were the songs in vogue in the country and almost everyone knew the dance steps. While Oluomachukwu sat and drank a bottle of Orijin, a boy passed by her table and started dancing when the Shoki song was played again.

Apparently the boy was in her platoon and had been nicknamed 'Shoki' from the first day in camp, because he was always dancing to the song no matter where he was and what he was doing, even on the parade ground while marching, he would add some Shoki steps.

The market was sectioned into different stalls, and each stall had their own loudspeaker and DJ. It was sometimes too noisy and distracting, but when all the stalls played similar songs, it got better. Oluomachukwu was chatting with Nkiru, who clearly wasn't comfortable hanging out with Tracker. So she pulled her up and went to dance in a corner while people watched them.

Just then, a tall light-skinned guy walked up to them and asked to talk to Oluomachukwu. He claimed to be in her platoon and also know exactly who she was, while she had never seen him before. Even while she was dancing with Nkiru, he kept hanging around her, begging her for a chance to dance with her. She found it odd.

Nkiru whispered into her ear, "Don't mind that boy, he is a player. I know him. His name is Ola."

Oluomachukwu laughed. "Let me guess, he tried to talk to you as well and ask you out?"

Nkiru nodded. "Not just me. He has tried to talk to everyone in our platoon already and they have all turned him down. I chat with a lot of them, so I know what is happening."

"Hmm," Oluomachukwu sighed. "So what do I have to do to get him to step aside? He is standing too close."

Since they both hadn't eaten, Nkiru proposed that they go towards the entrance of the camp market to buy fried potatoes and plantain. It didn't stop Ola, or Player, as he was from then on called, from following them. He stood there and waited for them to buy the food, then stood there and watched them eat, still begging for one dance. Oluomachukwu wished that he would go away, then she tried to focus on something else when she saw Kayode from afar. He had seen her, but didn't approach her or make an attempt to talk to her. Before she could wonder what exactly it was he was doing in camp instead of Abuja, she saw Dunsin walk up to him and sling a hand over his shoulder. It was the first time she noticed that Dunsin had a ring on her finger, an engagement ring, and she knew that Kayode was married. She suddenly felt very guilty and awkward knowing that she was staring at a young woman whose husband she had had something with.

Oluomachukwu looked at Nkiru. "Since you know about everything and everyone in this camp, who is that man, what is he doing here and what's his connection to the girl that has her hand over his shoulder?"

Nkiru turned around conspicuously, making it obvious to Kayode and Dunsin that they were talking about them. And after scrutinising the couple, she turned back to look at Oluomachukwu, and said, "The man is Mr. Kayode. He is the new Platoon Instructor of Platoon Four, but I don't know his relationship with that girl. But I can find that out tomorrow."

"Platoon Instructor?" Oluomachukwu repeated. She had no clue he could even be one since it appeared as though he had a good position in Abuja. "But how are you going to find out his relationship to the girl?"

Nkiru laughed. "Don't worry, I have my ways."

The sound of the bugle gingered the air at that moment, its very loud and piercing sound, so close that Oluomachukwu felt the man was playing it right in front of her. It was 10:00pm and time for Lights Out. Both Oluomachukwu and Nkiru hadn't noticed time go by so fast. They wondered why the Lights Out call was at 10:00pm, and not 10:30pm, as noted on the orientation-guide. It was probably a prepare-for-Lights-Out call, so that people would start making their way to their rooms, then turn the lights off by 10:30pm. No room light was to be seen still on by that time.

The time wasn't the only thing that Oluomachukwu and Nkiru hadn't noticed. Player had still been standing around them the entire time they were eating their dinner, drinking what was left of their alcoholic drinks and talking.

Oluomachukwu wondered what he was still doing there, because there was no way she could still dance with him. Stalls had started to turn their loud speakers off and the sound of the bugle was louder than any song that played at all.

Oluomachukwu and Nkiru started to walk away, but Player still wanted to take something back with him.

He moved up to Oluomachukwu quickly and tapped her shoulder. "You still owe me a dance," he said.

"No she doesn't," Nkiru replied. "How can you still dance when there's no music in the whole camp? Or didn't you hear the trumpet?" Nkiru always called the bugle a trumpet.

"There's always a next-time," Player said, then looked at Oluomachukwu. "Please, can I at least have your phone number?"

Oluomachukwu didn't know what to say. She could have given him her number if Nkiru hadn't mentioned that he was a player, but now she didn't want to anymore. Before she could say anything, some angry soldiers showed up out of nowhere, yelling and sending everyone to the hostel. Oluomachukwu used that as an opportunity to run off with Nkiru, without giving her number.

CHAPTER NINE: DAY FIVE

Saturday, 9th August 2014

The morning started with an argument that got quite physical. Two girls were arguing about who o wned a cap. Oluomachukwu didn't know who they were or their names. She had never seen either of them before, even though they were in her room. It was right after the Wake-Up call, just when people had started getting ready for the morning physical training, that the trouble started.

Oluomachukwu had woken up earlier than normal so that she would have an undisturbed bath and not have to run into the fat and annoying girl again. When she got back to the room, she wore just her underwear, tights, bra and camisole. She removed all the phones that were on her bed, not minding if some got disconnected from their chargers, then lay down to rest. She realised that she hadn't really touched her phone since she got to the camp, so she decided to check what was going on in the world.

Her battery was already getting too low, so she fished out her charger from her waist pouch, which she always kept with her inside her duvet cover. She removed one of the chargers on the small white box-extension, then she plugged her phone in. She didn't feel bad for doing that.

She believed she had the privilege of charging her phone whenever she wanted to.

She had a couple of text and WhatsApp messages from Tracker, and at that point, she regretted giving him her number. He started to profess his love to her and how his life had changed since he met her.

"Blah-blah-blah," Oluomachukwu said to herself as she scrolled through the other messages. She smiled when she saw that Okechukwu had sent her a couple of messages too. He hadn't called her yet, because he knew how busy it could be in camp, especially the first few days. But he was going to give her a call later in the day to catch up with her. He also hoped that she hadn't been deceived by any guy in the camp and started dating anyone, it would have been too early. She didn't know what he meant by 'too early,' because one day was enough for her to agree to date someone, speaking from experience.

Oluomachukwu was sending a reply when Oghene, the girl on the lower bunk by her right side woke up. Oghene started off by hissing, and Oluomachukwu wasn't sure it if was due to the fact that Eternity on the top bunk kept tossing and turning, and shaking the bunk in the process or that she resented each new day she spent in the camp.

And as usual, she said, "I can't suffer here."

Oluomachukwu concluded that it might be due to the dirty bathrooms. Oghene hissed again as she got up from the bed and hissed one more time when she saw her cell phone on the floor.

She cut Oluomachukwu a nasty glance, but didn't say anything. There was absolutely nothing to say. Nkiru woke up at that instant and went to say hello to Oluomachukwu. After they chatted and laughed briefly about the night before and how Player had been standing there all the while, Nkiru went on to have her bath before the crowd started to increase. By the time she came back to the room, everyone had woken up and some had started to get kitted without even taken their baths. Fadeke and Ogo got kitted without taking their baths. They were not in the mood for ice-cold water.

It was when the annoying sound of the bugle shook the walls of the hostel that the fight for the cap broke out. One girl stomped towards the bunk after Nkiru's own and snatched a cap from the bottom bed — so girl A was the snatcher and girl B was the snatchee.

The snatchee had been applying her make-up, but she stopped, very shocked. "*Ahn-ahn*, who is this mad woman, *nau*?"

"It's your mother that is a mad woman," the snatcher snarled.

"God punish your mouth there. If you know what is good for you, you better bring my cap back," the snatchee shot back. She too stomped towards the snatcher's bed, which was three beds away, and went to collect the cap back. Then both of them started to argue and pull both edges of the cap, almost tearing it apart.

Both Dunsin and Foyin, the room leader and assistant, who should have tried to sort out what was going on, kept their mouths shut and their eyes glued to the fight like every other person in the room. After a short while, Foyin intervened.

"Please, can both of you keep quiet? You are disturbing everyone," Foyin said.

Oluomachukwu wondered how the statement was even going to solve the problem at hand. They obviously didn't pay Foyin any attention. And while the argument went on, Oluomachukwu asked around for a permanent marker. No one had. She did not want to ask Ijeoma at first, but she knew that she really needed the marker. Besides, whatever Ijeoma did behind closed doors did not concern anyone, and if she liked to touch herself, it was her own business. Oluomachukwu had to stop feeling awkward about it. She stood up and looked at Ijeoma.

"Ijeoma, please do you have a black permanent marker that I can use real quick?"

Ijeoma nodded. "I thought you wouldn't ask me, but I have blue, not black."

"Okay, I don't mind," Oluomachukwu replied.

Ijeoma removed her blanket — she was already kitted in all white, except for her shoes — and Oluomachukwu wondered when she had gone for her bath, come back and gotten dressed. Ijeoma then rolled out of bed, came down easily with her long legs, not stepping on Oluomachukwu's bed, then got the marker from her bag, which she had locked with three different padlocks.

Oluomachukwu wrote 'Oluoma' on everything she had received from the camp, even flyers, booklets and guides. Once she had marked her name on all her kit, she started marking her name on her bucket, bathing bowl, plate, cup, toothbrush and toothpaste. She couldn't be too sure. After she was done writing her name on everything she owned, including her waist pouch, she passed the marker to other people who needed it — the fight between the two girls, for an unmarked cap was an eye opener for everyone.

Fast-forward to almost three minutes later, and the girls were still fighting. And since Dunsin didn't say anything, Ijeoma decided to. She tried to find out why the snatcher thought that the cap was hers, since she had invaded the snatchee's personal space. The snatcher argued that she had seen the snatchee come and collect the cap from her space very early in the morning. They went on and on until Ijeoma got frustrated and started to indirectly insult them.

"The two of you are adults, and one of you know that either one is the liar here. So instead of letting us argue and allowing the rest of our roommates endure this noise, why doesn't the liar just own up and confess that she has lost her cap. In fact, how can you even lose your cap in just four days? Was it too much partying in *mami* market or was it too much drinking or what else could it have been?"

Oluomachukwu didn't know which of the words struck a nerve, but both the snatcher and the snatchee verbally attacked Ijeoma.

"Please, who are you to judge us when your hands are dirty?" the snatchee asked.

Ijeoma didn't understand. She looked at Eternity, then looked at a few other girls in the room, then turned back to look at the fighting duo. "What does that mean?"

"You know what she means," the snatcher responded. "You're very filthy, so please, don't come and preach to us about partying, drinking or what have you."

Ijeoma kept quiet, not sure if she should keep talking or to shut up and leave quietly while she still could. But the hunger for trouble got the best of her. "Not everyone here is an angel."

"And not everyone here is a lesbian," the snatchee fired back, and the snatcher nodded.

Everyone gasped at the mention of that, some began to murmur, some shook their heads while some clapped their hands and sighed in disgust.

Eternity got irritated. "That's a disgusting thing to say."

"Then you had better feel disgusted about your dirty self, you Holy Mary wannabe. Always praying and reading your Bible like there's no tomorrow, but entering the toilet with this one to do nonsense." The snatcher pointed at Ijeoma when she said "With this one."

No one said a single word, the air was so stiff and the silence so sharp you that could hear an army of red ants marching across the room.

"That's not all," the snatcher added. "They never want to go to the parade ground in the morning, *forming* that they are very tired. Eternity will say that she was praying all night and Ijeoma will say that she was reading, in the dark oh, so they need to sleep in the morning. I came back the other day to collect something from the room, and they were both under one blanket. They stopped moving immediately they heard my voice and stayed still until I left. If I wanted to do them *strong thing*, I would have spent the whole day there, let me see if they would not come out from under the blanket."

"You better be careful and watch what you say," a girl, who Oluomachukwu had never seen before that day, said. "Accusations like this can lead to them being decamped and thrown into prison for fourteen years, like the new law against homosexuality holds. And if such accusations were not true, you would have yourself to blame."

"Why is this one speaking big English?" the snatcher asked. "That wasn't the first time of seeing them together. If there's anyone that should be careful, it's both of them, alright?" She got angry, hissed, then flung the cap on the snatchee's bed and walked out of the room.

And that was how the fight for the cap ended — with everyone convinced that both Eternity and Ijeoma were lesbians, and that the snatcher was a fat liar and a big thief for eventually returning the cap.

***

The usual morning ritual started just before the drill — Morning Prayer, both National and NYSC Anthems, and Meditation. After the Morning Prayer, the Drill Instructor corrected everyone again. "It is *'where peace and justice reign'* and not *'where peace and justice shall reign.'* I have corrected you all before," he said. He didn't ask the crowd to repeat the Morning Prayer again, because there was no time to do so. Corps members had taken their time to report to the parade ground, which meant that they had to tighten up the programme a bit.

Physical training, which started by jogging around the parade ground in circles, within each platoon, was quite interesting, and was led by someone from the man-o-war crew. Instead of using songs, probably the same four songs from the DJ, the instructor decided to sing his own songs, military style, while the Corps members repeated each line after him.

It had taken Oluomachukwu some time to understand what the instructor was saying, but she eventually grasped the first few lines and thought it was ridiculous, but funny. It went like this:

Early in the morning the rising sun... Early in the morning the rising sun,
This is my rifle, this is my gun... This is my rifle, this is my gun,
Papa and mama are sitting on the bed... Papa and m ama are sitting on the bed,
Mama said to papa your thing is dead... Mama said to papa your thing is dead.

The whole crowd exploded in laughter at the last line, but the Training Instructor carried on and kept singing. Oluomachukwu saw Ekene come out of nowhere, and wondered where she had been all the while. They chatted a bit, while they jogged, and caught up on a lot of things. By the time they had jogged round ten times, people started to retire to the back, tired, to lean against the wall.

Sometimes, soldiers would chase everyone back to the line to jog, but if they begged, the soldiers would let them be. Oluomachukwu saw two girls talking and laughing — the same two girls she had seen together when the sports representative was looking for people to sign up for sports activities.

A soldier was yelling at them and calling them *otondos* for not jogging, and Oluomachukwu immediately thought about Nkiru. She imagined what nickname Nkiru would have given to them if she was there. And speaking of Nkiru, Oluomachukwu had no clue where she was and wondered if she was in a different platoon, and not in Platoon Seven.

While they continued to jog, the instructor introduced some more interesting songs — at least Oluomachukwu found them to be interesting and took note of each of them as they came in cue. She and Ekene laughed each time, and as usual, Corps members repeated the line after them. In fact, it was as if some of the Corps members had served in the NYSC scheme before, because they knew most of the songs as soon as the instructor started singing them.

Out of all the songs, Oluomachukwu took note of two — they were going to be her two best physical training songs. The first was about giving birth to a *mumu*, an idiot.

They go born mumu, they go born mumu,
If corper marry corper, they go born mumu

Corps members were supposed to repeat the lines, but instead some people sang something different, replacing 'corper' with 'soldier.'

They go born mumu, they go born mumu,
If soldier marry soldier, they go born mumu.

The instructor didn't mind what they were singing, but some of the soldiers did, and started asking who the *otondo* Corps members were, singing that soldiers would give birth to *mumus*.

In the same spirit, the instructor changed a few words of the song and made it a bit better.

They go born better, they go born better,
If soldier marry corper, they go born better

Everyone started laughing and this time, the Corps members sang it properly, only changing it to replace 'soldier' with 'corper.' When the turn to use *mumu* came again, they changed it completely to 'soldier.' A soldier standing close by heard Ekene use 'soldier' and ran after her to punish her.

In between the physical training, drill and martial art, the bugle blower played the national anthem by 6:00am, and it still did not sound like the national anthem. Some people talked about it and laughed, while others were not interested, probably half asleep and could not wait to get back to their rooms. Oluomachukwu wondered if Ijeoma and Eternity had come out to the parade ground or if they were under their blankets again. She soon shook the dirty thought out of her head.

After the whole morning exercise, the Camp Director came to address the crowd and didn't appear to be happy. Her voice was still husky, but she didn't have that usual playfulness that she carried along; the one that dissolved the stiff air after a reprimand. She complained that Corps members hadn't observed Lights Out; that soldiers almost resulted to force to send some Corps members back to the hostel; that room lights were still on even when it was almost 11:00pm, especially in the female hostel, and worse of all, that some male Corps members had been so drunk they acted inappropriately.

The Camp Commandant had called an early morning meeting and together with some senior camp officials, they decided to decamp the three drunken Corps members that had caused problems the night before. The whole crowd gasped. They had heard threats about decamping Corps members, but they didn't know that it could ever happen, especially not on the fifth day, and not before several more verbal warnings were issued.

The Camp Director reminded the crowd that there was a strict NYSC policy against getting drunk in the camp and misbehaving. She then changed her tone to the pleasant one that she usually had and told the crowd how much she loved them, how they were her children and how God was going to guide, protect and bless them if they behaved rightly. Some people said 'Amen,' and others didn't.

"*Ahn-ahn*, won't you all say Amen?" the Camp Director looked surprised. "I am praying for all of you oh."

A long uniformed chorus of 'Amen' sounded from the parade ground, but the Camp Director was not satisfied.

"One Platoon are you sleeping?" she yelled, her voice

huskier than usual. She normally put the number of the platoon before the word 'platoon,' and not the other way round.

They chorused "No."

"Then say a proper Amen, *nau*."

"Amen," they chorused.

"The Lord will bless you."

"Amen."

"The Lord will protect you."

"Amen."

"The Lord will let His face to shine upon you now and forever."

"Amen." This time, it was stretched out and it sounded so loud it felt like the parade ground shook. The whole camp had replied. Everyone wanted a piece of the prayer and the blessing too.

Before the Corps members were dismissed for Bath and Breakfast, the Camp Director reminded them of the reason why she was there and made them all promise to behave themselves throughout the remaining days they were to stay in the camp, then they dispersed.

Oluomachukwu walked behind some girls who had marked their names or initials on their caps and behind their shoes. She laughed when she saw one had written 'ANUS' and another had written 'E.Bola.'

Oluomachukwu was very hungry, but didn't want to eat what was being served in the dining hall, because it was beans and yam. She feared the beans would be tasteless and watery like the last time. So instead, she walked to the camp market, bought two Gala sausage rolls, feeling each roll to make sure the dough that wrapped the beef was soft and the beef, not too pink. She also asked if the Gala had been prepared that same day, and the seller confirmed it had. She then bought a chilled Fanta in a plastic bottle and went back to the room to eat and rest.

When she got there, she saw some strange girls on her

bed again and got angry, wondering why people didn't just respect other people's personal spaces. It was either they didn't know who owned the bed space or they refused to acknowledge the fact that she did. She had to practically shoo them away, before they left. She then lay in bed and wanted to rest when Nkiru showed up and sat on the bed, shaking it in the process.

"Didn't you sleep last night?" Nkiru asked. "Your mates have gone to the farm and returned, and you are curled up in bed."

"Well, I have gone to the parade ground and returned, so that makes 'me' and 'my mates' even."

Nkiru laughed. Oluomachukwu also did, then sat up when she noticed Nkiru had a pink badge on, a badge that read '4 ON DUTY.'

"Wait, wait, wait, this isn't normal." Oluomachukwu pointed at the badge.

Nkiru titled her head backwards as she laughed. "My dear, I try to escape morning drills and all the plenty hassle as much as I can, so I join the platoons that are on duty and don't do anything. But I will be active when it's time for our own platoon to be on duty."

"I don't even know what nickname to call you."

"I'm the name giver, not the name collector, so nothing would stick." Nkiru laughed again.

"'Serial badgee' or 'Platoonier' or 'Hopper' or 'Miss-on-duty?'" Olumachuwu asked. There was a brief silence, then the two of them shook their heads. "You are right, it won't work," Olumachuwu added.

"I told you," Nkiru said proudly, as though she was in a contest.

"I just hope you are not discovered and reported, then get decamped."

"Just for this?" Nkiru shook her head. "They'll even be proud that I've been on duty for four days. I will be called a heroine and given an award. Besides, they'll never know unless they are told."

Oluomachukwu laughed, but deep down, she knew that Nkiru was giving her a warning, not to tell anyone about her platoon hopping, and she didn't plan to.

"Anyway, that's not why I'm here," Nkiru started to whisper. "I got the information for you about the girl you saw with Mr. Kayode."

Oluomachukwu's eyes lit up. "Really? You are very fast, though."

Nkiru smiled. "The girl is our room leader, can you believe it? I didn't even know that until I saw her this morning."

Oluomachukwu hissed. "Duh. Of course I know she is our room leader. I asked you about her relationship with Kayode, I mean Mr. Kayode." Oluomachukwu hoped that Nkiru didn't catch her error and wouldn't have to go and fish out why she hadn't used 'Mr.' at first.

"I know, I know." Nkiru laughed. "I was just joking. Mr. Kayode is married, and his wife is in Abuja. Our room leader is just his friend, maybe friend with benefit, I don't know, but she's engaged to be married sometime this year or maybe next year, it's uncertain. I heard that she had an argument with her fiancé before she came to camp, so only heaven knows if the wedding will still hold."

Oluomachukwu didn't say anything.

"Why were you asking?" Nkiru asked. "Why is their relationship of importance to you, by the way?"

"I was asking just out of curiosity," Oluomachukwu replied. "What is more important to me is how you got all that information."

"Well, I said Mr. Kayode was the new Instructor for Platoon Four." Nkiru stood up. "And I happened to be a member of Platoon Four today, plus I know just how to ask the right questions and get answers. Anyway, I want to go and get something to eat. I will see you later."

After Bath and Breakfast was observed, there was General Environmental Sanitation and Inspection. Camp officials went round all the rooms in both hostels to check that everything was in order. The hostel administrators made sure they asked female Corps members to take their clothes, shoes, shoe laces and even underwear hanging on the railings and in their room, to the general hanging space outside. Some, if not all the girls, refused to take anything outside. For one, they didn't want the guys to see their personal things, although the guys wouldn't have known who owned what, and secondly, they believed that their things would get stolen.

Oluomachukwu had bought some hangers in *mami* market to hang her things. She hung her underwear, shoe laces, face towel and wrapper, after washing or using, and wasn't ready to move them all the way to the ground floor to spread them. She hadn't washed her white tennis shoes yet, because those were the only ones she had, and they looked like they were going to fall apart if water touched them. She had seen some girls buy rubber trainers for a sum of 700 naira to 800 naira and she was going to buy one later. One of her roommates had even bought hers for 1,000 naira, because she had bought it on the first day of camp. The price naturally dropped as the day went by, since sellers wanted to sell off all the wares that they had, with the camp coming to an end.

By the time the inspection was over, everyone in the female hostel had taken all their wet or damp clothes to the clothes lines in the open space outside the hostel, and it was only natural that the line snapped and all the clothes dropped. At first, the lines had started to drop lower to the ground because they were too heavy, allowing all the clothes to sweep the ground. Also, there were only about ten long clothes lines for the whole female hostel, including female camp officials, so instead of hanging clothes directly on the line, people hung them on hangers first, then the hangers on the line... and that marked the fall of the lines. Even the metal rod-like pole that held the lines fell. Oluomachukwu didn't know how or if it got fixed, but once it was certain that the inspectors had left, she ran down to take her things back to her room, and many others did the same thing.

After the inspection was over, there was a Platoon Family Meeting, where platoon members were supposed to meet with their platoon instructors either on the parade ground or under the canopies. Members of Platoon Seven gathered at a corner of the parade ground and waited for Auntie Vera and Sister Mary — the Platoon Instructor and Assistant. As usual, they took time to arrive, when other platoons had almost finished with their meeting. One hour was allocated to the family meeting, and the instructors arrived when it was just twenty minutes left. Some platoon members had even left, tired of waiting endlessly.

Although the meeting time was short, it was effective. Auntie Vera had precise and concise information to pass along to everyone, which didn't even require up to fifteen minutes. But the difference with other platoons was that they had time to discuss and dialogue about each message passed along, as opposed to Platoon Seven, which was just a monologue; information was given and Corps members nodded that they understood, and that was it. Everyone was asked to sit on the floor for the meeting.

They grumbled and initially refused, but eventually did, because Auntie Vera threatened not to give out any information and keep everyone there until evening. With the remaining eight minutes of the meeting, Auntie Vera used it to ask why no one wanted to participate in any sports activities. She was referring to the females. She said she needed participants and was going to pick people randomly if she didn't have teams by the end of the week, which was on Sunday. She also needed people to head the socials events and start rehearsing.

There was the dance and drama event, cooking contest, Big, Bold and Beautiful — BBB — contest, Variety night, which was believed to feature Miss NYSC and Mr. Macho contests, and Camp Idol, then there was comedy night. Auntie Vera gave her platoon members until the next day to organise themselves and decide who was going to do what. She was about to leave when she noticed that Platoon Seven members were not complete. She then decided to take a random attendance, by passing along a plain sheet of paper for Corps members to write their code numbers on. It was at that moment that Nkiru came along and sat on the floor beside Oluomachukwu.

Auntie Vera looked at her. "My friend, what is your business here?" she asked, and people started to laugh.

"I'm in this platoon, ma," Nkiru replied, comfortably.

"C'mon stand up when you are talking to me," Auntie Vera spat out. "Why are you here, is this your platoon?"

Nkiru nodded. "Yes, ma."

"Even if it's your platoon, should you be coming by this time?" Auntie asked, but paused when Sister Mary whispered something into her ear. Auntie Vera looked at Nkiru again. "Come here."

Nkiru approached her.

"Let me see your badge."

Nkiru provided the badge.

"Okay, so you are in Platoon Seven, but why do you have a platoon four 'on duty' badge?"

Nkiru stood there speechless, not sure what to say. She looked back briefly and exchanged a worried glance with Oluomachukwu as if to say "Uh-oh."

Auntie Vera caused a small scene, then called Kayode to complain and made a big deal out of it. Normally he was meant to collect badges from all his platoon members, which meant that he was negligent. At the same time, even if he had collected her badge, he wouldn't have checked her code number, because nobody ever did, there were too many cards. Kayode, who had his eyes on Oluomachukwu the whole time, didn't say anything. He just lowered his head as if he was listening to what Auntie Vera was saying, but his mind was clearly elsewhere.

Even Nkiru noticed that he was staring fixatedly at Oluomachukwu and got suspicious, forgetting that she was in trouble. Oluomachukwu noticed that Nkiru had noticed, and hoped that she wouldn't go snooping around for answers. At the same time, she wondered if Kayode felt that Nkiru was a spy sent by her, and that was probably why he was staring at her. She had a couple of theories in her head, but managed to shake them off.

"Mr. Kayode, what do you have to say?" Auntie Vera woke him up from his gaze.

"We will punish her." He looked at Auntie Vera. "Since she wants to be on duty in another platoon, we will put her on duty until she leaves camp."

"Okay then, I will handle her." Auntie Vera took the attendance list, seized Nkiru's badge and put her on toilet cleaning duty for two weeks. She was to clean the toilet and give daily reports, then she would choose two socials events to participate in and one sports event too. When she was done handing the verdict, Auntie Vera dismissed everyone, because it was time for Personal Administration. Oluomachukwu didn't know what that meant, but she went back to her room to rest before it was lunchtime.

***

Oluomachukwu had actually enjoyed lunch. She went to eat with Nkiru, Ogo and Fadeke. For the first time in about two days, Oluomachukwu was seeing Fadeke during the day. Ekene also joined them to eat. The camp kitchen was serving yam porridge, but Oluomachukwu and her camp friends decided to eat in *mami* market instead.

They went to a stall that had 'Nwanyi Imo' written on it. Oluomachukwu's mother was from Imo State, so a stall with 'Imo woman' written on it was home. So they all lounged there, ate and talked about a lot of things.

On the discussion table was the topic of 'Guys,' camp guys — the ones they had seen and/or talked to so far; the pests; the cute ones; the ones they would never talk to and the ones they hoped to talk to. Male camp officials too and soldiers; they just wanted to admire the men. Whether they liked it or not, they had all come to camp for specific and different reasons, but some of them had come with the hope of getting hitched, whether they wanted to admit it or not.

Others, Nkiru had gathered from the little tour she had done in different platoons, had come for the money — probably the allowance they hoped to receive at the end of camp or from sugar daddy camp officials; some to look for husbands or boyfriends, first of all; some to look for professionals, those who were already working and were not going to depend on the allowance; and some for male camp officials that needed part-time girlfriends; some for second boyfriends in a different State, other than the State they were coming from, just in case they had to travel regularly; and others for boyfriends that didn't attend the same school as them. There was nothing Oluomachukwu didn't hear.

When they were done talking about what other people wanted, they asked each other the same question. What were they looking for in the camp, apart from the fact that it was a requirement to get some jobs in Nigeria, especially in the Federal Government offices and Ministries, and for government contracts.

"Just for the experience," Nkiru answered first.

"I just want this programme out of the way, so that I can travel to the US." Ogo went next, and both Nkiru and Oluomachukwu threw her a rather suspicious look. "My boyfriend moved to New York a few months ago and I don't want to be like all those girls in the village that keep saying "Dim noo abroad," "My husband is abroad." I want to hurry up and go there."

"So what's the point doing the whole year? Why didn't you just work it out and not even come to camp at all?" Ekene asked.

"Because I need inside contact first. Once I meet the right person, I'll work it out from here. Besides, I'm still waiting for my visa, so it beats staying at home and doing nothing."

"Me, I need to start working in high places oh, or doing business, *sha*. I want to start getting government contracts. I must eat out of the national cake one way or another," Ekene said.

"As for me," Fadeke started. "I am doing this to get work experience during the one-year, so that I can get a good job later."

Everyone burst into laughter, and Nkiru said, "Work experience from where? Teaching in one dead secondary school somewhere?" She hissed. "Please, wake up."

"True, *nau*. I don't care if it's in a school or in an office, I just want to make the best of the year and put something on my CV." Fadeke shrugged. " But why else would I be here?"

"Question for the gods," Ekene said, and all of them burst out laughing again. They laughed so hard that two girls who passed by the stall at that moment looked at each other, wondering if they were being laughed at.

"You that have been laughing since morning, why are you here in camp?" Fadeke asked. She was looking directly at Oluomachukwu.

Oluomachukwu suddenly stopped laughing. She forgot she hadn't answered the question yet. And since she was sure that all four of them had not been completely honest about why they were in the camp, she decided to play along. "I applied to work in a Federal Ministry and they asked me to get my NYSC certificate first, so here I am."

No one said another word after that. They kept quiet and finished up their lunch, as if they were thinking about their lives and why they were really in camp.

***

TWENTY-ONE DAYS

After Lunch and Siesta, the sound of the bugle echoed through the camp and Corps members were to go out for drills, man-o-war and martial arts training. Oluomachukwu did not want to go out for any, but the female security officers stormed into the room and asked everyone to get out. When the drills were over the Corps members, who wanted to compete stayed behind and practiced with the man-o-war and the martial arts instructors.

Oluomachukwu had joined them before, because she thought they were compulsory, but when she found out that only the best were picked for the competitions, she excused herself and never returned.

As Oluomachukwu was going back to the hostel, she heard an announcement from the OBS: Platoon Seven instructors were calling their platoon members for a brief meeting. Oluomachukwu knew that it was for games and sports, but she didn't go. Auntie Vera had given them a Sunday deadline to produce volunteers, so calling them out again didn't make any sense.

Oluomachukwu rested well and when it was time for dinner, she went to the camp kitchen to get food. They were serving *jollof* rice and fried chicken. There was no way *jollof* rice could ever be cooked the wrong way, so she carried her plate, along with Nkiru, Ogo and Ekene for the food. When they got back to the hostel, they sat together on Oluomachukwu's bed and talked as they ate. The food wasn't that bad, but it wasn't that good either — the rice was a little too hard, Oluomachukwu feared the grains would go straight to her appendix. She was also given the chicken bum and wasn't too happy about it. At least her own piece was the biggest of all of them, as Ekene got the neck that had only one side of the skin.

As they were eating, Oluomachukwu's phone beeped. She looked at it and saw that it was a text message from Tracker. He wanted them to go to *mami* market again for drinks later in the evening. He had enjoyed her company the last time they hung out and really wanted a repeat.

Oluomachukwu asked her friends and they were down for it. She smiled as she replied to him. She never thought she would ever have fun in camp, but everyday was beginning to look like fun to her.

When they were all done eating, they started getting dressed to go. By dressed, they wore their white shirt and shorts, did their hair properly and wore the NYSC cap just to pass the hostel security, because they were going to take it off once they were in the market. They also wore make-up, put on their tennis shoes and headed out to have fun. Oluomachukwu was getting much better health wise, and was talking without difficulty because she was getting her lost voice back. She could have stayed back and rested, but she couldn't think of missing out on *mami* market. It was the sacrifice she was willing to make in camp.

As they were leaving the room, Oluomachukwu's mind flashed to Ijeoma and Eternity. She didn't see them in the room and wondered where they were and what they were doing. She also wondered where Fadeke had disappeared to again. She thought about how Oghene had planned not to suffer, and eventually thought about Dunsin being engaged and Kayode being in camp.

CHAPTER TEN: DAY SIX

Sunday, 10th August 2014

For the first day in camp, nobody heard the sound of the bugle, because Sunday was meant to be for rest. There were no morning drills, physical training or the likes. Maybe the bugle had sounded at 6:00am for the national anthem or not, but Oluomachukwu didn't hear it either way. For one, she had had too many bottles of Orijin to drink the previous night and she had woken up with a hangover. She didn't even know if she could take the morning dose of her anti-malaria medication. It was the third day, she still had four more days to go and didn't know if she should continue taking them, because she seemed to be getting much better.

Instead of the usual morning rituals, Corps members had Personal Administration on their schedule, and Oluomachukwu still didn't know what that meant. She tossed and turned in bed until it was time for Religious Activities. She hadn't planned to go to church that morning. In fact, she hadn't even planned to go at all on any other Sunday morning for that matter. Some of her roommates kept talking about church, except for Eternity, and it didn't come as a surprise after what had transpired in the room. In fact, since that day, Ijeoma and Eternity hadn't spoken to each other, as they didn't want to arouse suspicions.

As Oluomachukwu lay on her bed, Nkiru went to join her. "Hi, sleepy head. You've been sleeping all morning."

Oluomachukwu stretched. "What time is it?" Before Nkiru could answer, she put her hand under the wrapped cloth she had used as her pillow to check for her phone, but felt about six other phones under it. She got furious and yelled, in the British accent she almost forgot about, "Who the hell has all these phones? I'm sick and tired of seeing phones on my bed all the time. I'll start flinging them any time I see them."

Nkiru laughed, and so did some other roommates, including Ogo. She too had woken up, but was not as hungover as Oluomachukwu was, she was just okay. She mentioned 'Church,' and Oluomachukwu looked away, towards the foot of her bed. She looked at Nkiru properly and was shocked. Nkiru was wearing a Red Cross vest.

"You this girl," Oluomachukwu said, and pointed at the vest. "What is this one again?"

Nkiru laughed. The same way she always laughed with her head tilted backwards and her mouth opened like she was smiling and choking. "My dear, I have to survive in this camp." She then lowered her voice to a whisper, and added, "I can't suffer here."

Oluomachukwu and Ogo laughed because they got the joke. Oghene was still fast asleep, so she could not have heard Nkiru.

"After that witch, Madam Vera put me on toilet cleaning duty, I thought I was going to die. I cleaned a lot of toilets yesterday and at the end of the day, I said no more."

Ogo laughed. "What happened?"

"Long story," Oluomachukwu replied, not willing to be drawn back into the gist. "So how did you handle it? Did you beg her?"

"She wishes." Nkiru rolled her eyes. "I hate morning drills and exercises, and also waking up very early in the morning. So once I get the 'on duty' badge, I just walk up to the hostel gate and the officers wouldn't ask me a single question and I'd go back to sleep. By that time, they would have already finished chasing people out."

"I know all of that." Oluomachukwu sounded rather impatient. "So how did you do it?"

"Isn't it evident?" Nkiru scoffed. "I joined the Red Cross Society. So I'll always be on duty with them, waiting for people to pass out on the parade ground or anywhere and help them to the clinic. I just assist people in general, the conscious or unconscious, the injured as well."

"Can you even carry anyone with those small arms?" Ogo teased.

"That's why there are a lot of us in the Red Cross Society. I wouldn't be the only one at all times. So I am off Auntie Vera's watch list, and she has given me back my badge now."

"I might want to join, too," Oluomachukwu said and laughed, although she was serious. But the idea of being on duty every day didn't sit too well with her. "Or not," she added.

"Well, new members are requested to pay 2, 500 naira to join.," Nkiru said.

"What for?" a voice asked out of nowhere.

Oluomachukwu and Nkiru looked up and saw Fadeke looking at them. They didn't even know she was in the room. Ogo also looked up, but she was staring at the bottom of the top bunk, because she was lying on her right side on her own bed, and obviously couldn't see Fadeke.

As if Fadeke had sensed that they were all surprised to see her, she said, "Hi, girls. I had so much fun yesterday with one guy, very handsome like this. I came back late at night after one soldier I know smuggled me in after begging the gate officers."

"Hmm." Oluomachukwu, Nkiru and Ogo sighed at the

same time.

"So about the Red Cross thing, is there really a joining fee?" Fadeke asked, interested.

Nkiru nodded. "A lot of people wanted to join, but didn't have the money, and coupled with the fact that they always have to be on duty, they gave up. It wasn't worth it for them. So the fee is to get only serious and genuine people to join, nothing more."

Fadeke didn't join. She didn't have that kind of money to waste and she definitely didn't want to be on duty all the time.

Ogo had convinced Oluomachukwu to go to church with her. Religious Activities were to run from 9:00am to 2:00pm when it would be time for Lunch and Siesta. Ogo was going to attend the Catholic Church mass, and it was to start at 11:00am at the dining hall, so there was still time. She got ready, and so did Oluomachukwu, then they both left the room. Nkiru went to report to her Red Cross duty, while Fadeke went to the Pentecostal Church service gathering on the parade ground.

Oluomachukwu attempted to leave the hostel in mufti, a pair of dark-blue jeans and a white top, for the church service, but she was sent back by a security officer. Corps members were expected to be dressed in their all-white kit at all times. They were only free to dress as they wanted in the hostel or in their rooms. Oluomachukwu frowned at that. It meant that she had packed clothes she was never going to wear, clothes that she didn't have to carry along with her. And had she known that fact earlier, before she packed for camp, she would not have bothered. Had Idara not told her that she could go to camp with mufti and wear them on Sundays, she would not have even thought about it. She reluctantly went back to her room and got kitted.

Also because of the bad weather and the rainy season, some of her shoes had gotten infested by moulds. One of her roommates had even told her to wash the shoes and leave them to dry out on the balcony, then reuse them. Oluomachukwu refused. She was never going to put on those infested shoes ever again, knowing that moulds once grew in them. She was then advised to give the shoes to charity instead of throwing them away, which she did.

As she and Ogo went towards the dining hall, they saw Platoon Five Corps members on duty, with their 'on duty' badge pinned to their white shirts. They had dark brown aprons on that were oversized, and were walking towards the kitchen to finish up what they were doing so that lunch would be ready on time. Oluomachukwu imagined Nkiru with the badge, then laughed when she remembered how Nkiru had been disgraced by Kayode and Auntie Vera.

A group of people sat outside the church, under a canopy just by the entrance of the dining hall, singing gospel songs and talking. Instead of going into the dining hall, Ogo diverted and went to join the singing group, and Oluomachukwu followed her. Ogo started speaking to the people there, as if she knew who they were, and asking them questions. Oluomachukwu went to the back to watch them. She then saw Ogo walk towards a girl that sat at an old desk. By the time Oluomachukwu looked away — at a group of girls that walked by, talking and laughing loudly — and looked back, Ogo had already gotten a white and green shirt and was putting it on.

The shirt was customised and had the imprints of the National Association of Catholic Corpers — NACC — on it. It was actually a big association, present in every State in the country and also supported by the Nigerian Catholic Mission. Oluomachukwu wanted the shirt just because it looked very nice and it also gave a sense of community, of family, of identity.

She went to the girl at the old desk and asked questions too. By that time, Ogo had already sat down with the others and was singing. Ogo knew that Oluomachukwu hadn't come by her own free will, so she wasn't going to force her to sit down or do anything unless she wanted to.

The girl told Oluomachukwu that the group outside was the Catholic Church choir. They were going to give support during the mass and also sing during offertory, and when needed. Secondly, the white and green shirt cost 1,500 naira, and it came with a cap. After thinking once about it, Oluomachukwu thanked the girl and walked to the back. She didn't want to join the choir, so there was no point buying the shirt.

She stayed there and watched the group practice until a white mini-bus drove towards the entrance of the dining hall. Everyone started to mobilise and the Priest came out of the bus. He had actually been running late due to traffic on a Sunday morning, and that was why the mass hadn't started at almost 11:30am. When all the officials entered through the front door, Oluomachukwu went in through the back and was shocked to see the dining hall was full. The congregation had been there all the while, disciplined, quiet, while they waited for the Priest to arrive.

Oluomachukwu walked quietly to the first empty seat she saw at the back and sat in it.

A young man, in mufti, was beside her. He looked at her and said "Hi." Oluomachukwu looked at him too, but briefly, and said "Hello."

"You are late," he started. "Why are you late?"

Oluomachukwu didn't think it was his business, but she answered anyway. "I didn't come late, I have been outside with the choristers."

"Do you sing?"

"No."

The young man smiled, then looked towards the altar. He didn't say any other thing.

Oluomachukwu studied him from the corner of her eye. He had to be a camp official since he was on mufti, and she didn't want to be seen being friendly with a camp official. She then wondered why she had sat next to him and how she could escape him and go to another seat.

Before she could figure that out, an usher came to her row and asked everyone to move two seats away, so that others, who were just coming could sit down without disturbing the mass. Oluomachukwu's attempt to leave that row was now impossible, as she was now sandwiched between the young guy she wanted to escape from and two other guys to her left side.

The mass went very well, and Oluomachukwu enjoyed it. She enjoyed it so much that she didn't know when she removed her thoughts from the guy beside her and escaping from him, until the mass was over and the Priest asked everyone to go in peace.

"So did you enjoy the mass?" the young guy asked.

Oluomachukwu looked at him, then looked away. "I did." She had turned her gaze towards the back door, where several crates of soft drinks and two cartons of biscuits were kept. An announcement was made and the congregation was told to wait for light refreshments before leaving. Oluomachukwu waited, and so did the guy.

"What do you want to drink?" he asked.

Oluomachukwu looked at him and shook her head. She wanted to drink something, but she didn't want the guy to ask her about it or get it for her. He took the hint and walked away only to come back with a cold bottle of Sprite and two packets of biscuits, crackers that were more milky than salty. Oluomachukwu collected them from him, and he opened the drink for her.

"I hope you drink Sprite. It was the only coldest one there."

Oluomachukwu nodded. She ate the milky crackers, then took down the Sprite, after which she pulled out her anti-malaria medication from her wasit pouch and took what would be her morning dose. She was going to take the afternoon dose after a late lunch.

"Are you ill?" he asked. " Oh, my name is Segun, by the way."

"No. It's just anti-malaria medication." She paused a

bit. "Preventive measures."

"Oh, okay. Can I have your number? I'll like to see you again."

Oluomachukwu almost choked on her saliva. That was the part she dreaded the most, being asked for her phone number, because she didn't know how to say no. She was looking for the best lie to tell, when Segun interrupted her thoughts.

"You know that today is Sunday, so don't lie and don't be mean."

Oluomachukwu was cornered, and just as she was about to start giving out her number, her phone vibrated in her waist pouch. She felt relieved, as if a bag of rice had just been pulled up from her chest. She took out the phone, looked at the screen, then turned to look at Segun, and said, "Sorry, it's my father, I have to answer. I'll see you later."

"Where are you going to see me later?" Segun sounded disappointed, with a tint of anger.

"Maybe if we cross paths again or meet in church next week."

Segun hissed.

Oluomachukwu stood up and picked up the call, as she walked away. She had no intention of seeing Segun later or of going to church the following week, and it wasn't her father on the phone, it was Okechukwu.

***

As Oluomachukwu was walking towards the hostel, holding her phone to one ear, she saw Tracker coming towards the dining hall, holding his cooler in his hand. She had no reason to dodge him, assuming he hadn't seen her yet, but she decided to go the other way. As she was turning to go the other way, she saw Kayode coming towards the dining hall. She wanted to turn back and take another route, the one closely beside the hostel along the volleyball court. She would hide behind some of the stalls until the coast was clear.

When she turned around, she saw Segun. He was walking slowly and talking to a girl, not minding anything around him. She looked closely at the girl, then at the girl's Red Cross vest. It was Nkiru. Oluomachukwu didn't waste any time, she started walking towards the volleyball court, ignoring Kayode as he was calling out her name.

"Are you there?" Okechukwu said over the phone. He had been talking and Oluomachukwu seemed distracted.

"I'm here." Oluomachukwu still sounded distracted. "I was just trying to jump over a nasty puddle of mud in my way."

"Hmm. Sounds more like you were trying to avoid the man that was calling your name."

Oluomachukwu froze for a second. She looked around, as if afraid that Okechukwu had come to camp and was watching her. "What man?"

"I heard someone shouting your name and it was a male voice."

"But female soldiers sound like men," Oluomachukwu joked. And just as she was about to start laughing someone tapped her shoulder and she jumped.

"Oluoma, I have been calling your name. Will you keep ignoring me?" It was Kayode.

Oluomachukwu still had the phone to her ear, and she heard Okechukwu say "Man."

"I can't speak right now, please," Oluomachukwu said to Kayode, then jumped over a small puddle that separated her from her destination, and walked away. She turned back to check if Nkiru had seen anything, but Nkiru wasn't in sight. "Hello, Oke. I'm here now."

"Who was the man?"

Oluomachukwu wanted to say whom it was, but the words didn't come out. In fact, she had wanted to talk to Okechukwu about Kayode and Dunsin, but she changed her mind. "No one."

"So 'no one' has been calling you since and you have been ignoring the 'no one?'"

She maintained her stand. "It was no one." She didn't think it was the right time to bring up Kayode. Instead, they spoke about every other thing — experiences so far, people she had met and friends she had made, then good, funny, interesting and bad stories.

***

Oluomachukwu didn't eat lunch that was served by the camp kitchen. She didn't know what was being served and didn't care. She wasn't interested. She had been dreaming of *jollof* rice and plantain, with beef. The beef was cut very small, but she liked the way it tasted and melted in her mouth. Open door eateries and food stands, also known as *mama put*, were known for their tasty stews and juicy pieces of beef, and Oluomachukwu confirmed it in the camp market. She went to Nwanyi Imo stall again with Nkiru.

Nwanyi Imo's food stall was almost empty. It was just Oluomachukwu, Nkiru, and then a table with three men, who definitely had to be camp officials. They were already eating pounded yam and soup, and talking, but mostly looking towards Oluomachukwu's table. Oluomachukwu noticed, but didn't put her mind to it.

Nkiru forced a full spoon of rice that had a bulky slice of plantain on top of it in her mouth. She chewed, and her cheeks inflated and deflated several times, after which she swallowed.

"Why are you eating that much at a time? Didn't they give you something to eat at your Red Cross meeting?" Oluomachukwu teased. "After paying the joining fee?"

Nkiru laughed. "I wish. I didn't have breakfast and they didn't want to release us for duties. They kept us there, talking nonsense and wasting our time. I was just thinking about food all the while, and then having a cold bottle of Orijin afterwards."

TWENTY-ONE DAYS

It was Oluomachukwu's turn to laugh.

"Also, I like when there's a lot of food in my mouth, it brings out the taste. If I could, I would have also forced a small piece of beef into my mouth."

Oluomachukwu turned her head slightly when she noticed the three men were leaving. They kept looking intently at her and Nkiru, but said nothing. In fact, one of them smiled, but that was it. They called the woman that ran the food stall, paid her and left. They walked towards the camp market, probably to have a couple of cold drinks where fresh breeze would blow across their sweaty faces.

Nkiru touched Oluomachukwu's shoulder and brought her back to reality. "Why are you looking at them like that? Do you know them?"

Oluomachukwu shook her head. At the same time, one of the girls working in the food stall brought two cold bottles of Orijin and placed them on the table.

Oluomachukwu raised both hands up, as if she was surrendering, and said, "We did not ask for those. Please, take them back."

The girl turned to look at the owner of the food stall. "Mummy, they said they don't want it oh." She spoke in Igbo, but both Oluomachukwu and Nkiru understood what she said.

The owner of the food stall, who was at the back of the stall mixing rice in a big pot, came out, wiping her hands on her already dirty apron, and said, "Ah, my sisters. Those *ogas* who just left said I should give the two of you those drinks. They also paid for your food and said you should meet later at the back for some snacks or drinks if you want."

Oluomachukwu and Nkiru remained speechless. They were so sure that the men had been listening to what they were saying. They exchanged glances, and strangely, they understood what each other was saying: they were not going to meet the men. However, they took the drinks and smiled as they drank it.

After a few seconds, Nkiru said, "I saw Mr. Kayode today towards the dining hall."

"Really?" Oluomachukwu pretended she didn't know he had been there.

"Yes, I saw him running after a girl, but I didn't see clearly, because I saw only her back view. He then left and went to the kitchen to meet with Dunsin. Her platoon is on duty today."

"Hmm" was all Oluomachukwu managed to produce.

"All these men in camp are so desperate." Nkiru then lowered her voice, and it was certain she wanted to say something she shouldn't be saying. She always did that. "I'm sure that Mr. Kayode was horny today and needed someone to *do*." She laughed. "After he unsuccessfully went after that girl at the volleyball court area, he went after Dunsin again, but she was busy and couldn't tend to his needs."

Oluomachukwu was slightly embarrassed. In fact, guilt and filth were what she felt, since she had also tended to Kayode's needs before. In order to get out of the awkward situation, she asked an unrelated question and got into another awkward situation. "So who was the guy you said you were with at the dining hall?"

"I never said I was with any guy."

Nkiru had actually not said that, but Oluomachukwu didn't know. She had only seen Nkiru with the guy.

"Oh, I thought you said you were walking with a guy towards the dining hall when you saw Ka... I mean, Mr. Kayode," Oluomachukwu said

Nkiru looked at her suspiciously. It was the second time she hadn't used 'Mr.' to address Kayode. "Hmm, are you sure you weren't watching me? I was indeed with a guy."

"I knew it." Oluomachukwu tried to change the stiff air, making a mental note to not omit 'Mr.' again when it came to addressing Kayode. "So who was it?"

"Just another desperate goat." Nkiru hissed. "They are

everywhere, asking me for my number and if I want to go out with them. I have to be careful. We have to be careful. Because if we are like some other useless girls in this camp, we will end up sleeping with all the guys and even getting pregnant for a corper." Nkiru pronounced corper as if it was a disease, as if it was the same Ebola virus that was already threatening to become an epidemic in Nigeria.

Oluomachukwu laughed. "Nkiru, you are very funny. Even if the girls want to sleep with camp officials, or corpers, there is absolutely nowhere for them to do it. Unless, of course, it's with camp officials who have private rooms."

"My friend, open your eyes," Nkiru said, and they both laughed. "*Mami* market is where everything happens. I hear that wonders happen at the back at night just beside where the tailors stay. People are getting down on the dirty floor. Some of those food stalls, saloons, shops or laundry places rent out their stalls for a fee depending on if it's a quickie or a longie."

"Oh shut up." Oluomachukwu wore a disgusted look. "Where do you even get all these stories from?"

"I have ears everywhere." Nkiru and Oluomachukwu stood up. They had finished eating and drinking, and were going to rest until it was time for Personal Administration again.

***

When it was time for Personal Administration on the schedule, Oluomachukwu decided to quickly go and buy rubber trainers against the next day. Her tennis shoes seemed delicate and she always feared that they would rip apart during morning drills. She had wanted to go with one of her friends, but everyone seemed to be occupied — Nkiru was on Red Cross duty, Ogo was on the phone, Fadeke was nowhere to be found and Ekene was in her own room, sleeping.

Oluomachukwu got to the market, but no one ran after her like they used to. It was either the sellers were getting tired of running each time, or they were already familiar with the faces of people who never bought anything. She went to the stalls at the far end of the market and saw the women selling shoes. About three or four of them called out to her, urging her to buy from them instead, saying "Corper, follow me buy, I will give you good price."

Oluomachukwu entered one of the shops, not because the owner had managed to convince her, but because the owner also sold clothes, white shorts and tee shirts. She wanted to buy a new complete kit, one that would hug her body perfectly.

"Madam, how much are you selling those trainers?" Oluomachukwu asked, and sat down on a bench so low it almost touched the sandy ground.

"One thousand."

"One thousand what? For what?" Oluomachukwu scrunched her eyebrows. "These rubber things? Hmm."

"That's the price, corper."

Oluomachukwu hated that market sellers kept calling her and other Corps members 'corper.' It was true that they were all corpers, in unofficial terms, but the sellers seemed to be abusing the use of the word.

"That is not the price," Oluomachukwu replied. "My friend bought it for 600 naira."

"Ah! It's not from here oh. Last-last, I can give you 800 naira."

Oluomachukwu shook her head. "Give it to me for 500 naira. I want to even buy two shorts too. Besides you had better sell off all your goods, or you will carry them back home when camp is over."

"Don't worry, stream 2 is coming next month. We will still sell market even if you don't buy from us."

"Please, which stream 2 is that?" Oluomachukwu rolled her eyes. "With the high threat of Ebola in Lagos? I doubt anyone would even come to camp. If I had my way, I wouldn't even stay here any longer. Imagine me falling sick from the second day in camp. It was too embarrassing. I thought I had caught something, malaria or the dreaded Ebola." She laughed.

The woman didn't laugh or smile. She didn't comment either, as she didn't understand what Oluomachukwu was talking about. The only thing she would have understood was if Oluomachukwu was going to buy something or not.

After much bargaining, Oluomachukwu bought the rubber trainers for 550 naira, and then bought two white shorts, which were slightly above her knee, for 550 naira each, and left.

When she walked out of the stall, she heard people laughing loudly. She turned her head to the right and saw Fadeke sitting on Player's lap. They were on a table with Tracker and a guy that she did n't know. She was surprised. She and Nkiru had only talked about Player and Tracker the other day, and Fadeke had already gone to hang out with them.

There was a lot of food and drinks on the table, and Oluomachukwu wasn't surprised. She shook her head and went on her way. As she made it back for the hostel, a DJ played 'Shoki.' Some people shouted and hailed whoever the DJ was, and some started to display their Shoki dance steps in public.

***

Oluomachukwu had barely gotten to the room when she heard the sound of the bugle. She looked at the time on her phone and it wasn't time for the next activity yet. She wasn't sure what the call was for, and the look on the faces of other girls in the hostel revealed the same thing. No one knew what was going on. Just then, there was an announcement from the OBS.

"Good morning gentlemen, Corps members. Please, report to the parade ground now..."

The speaker's voice was very slow and monotonous, it was hard to tell the nature of the call, whether it was an emergency or not. Some of the speaker's words were overly stretched out, and spoken with so much ease like someone who had been trained to speak.

No one might have gone out to the parade ground, because the bugle sounded again, fiercer this time, and the speaker at the OBS repeated the message in the same monotonous pattern. But added three extra lines that made people laugh.

"Good morning gentlemen, Corps members. Please, report to the parade ground now. If you are still in the hostel, you are wrong. If you are still in mami market, you are very wrong. If you are not on the parade ground, you are wrong. Please, report to the parade ground now."

It took the Corps members almost thirty minutes and threats from soldiers to mobilise themselves. Both the State Coordinator and Camp Director came to address them. The Camp Director, still with her usual husky voice, complained about the Lights Out period again. As a new rule, room leaders were going to be held responsible if the room lights were not switched off at the right time. They didn't care who entered the room last or who had forgotten to turn the light off, when it was time, the room leader was to switch it off. She also talked about discipline and drinking in the camp.

She concluded by telling girls to be careful and not open their legs for just any guy that asks them to. She told them to focus on their goals and stick to them. When she was done, she told them how much she loved them and how God would bless them abundantly if they behaved appropriately. There was a resounding "Amen," and she passed the microphone to the State Coordinator.

The State Coordinator came to talk about the status of the deadly Ebola virus in Nigeria, how it was spreading and what the government was doing to contain it. Prior to the high alert level, there was a possibility to leave camp and return, but the State Coordinator didn't want that to happen again because of health reasons. So far, there was no case of Ebola in the camp, and she wanted it to remain that way. If for any reason anyone wanted to leave camp, they would have to be examined before they would be let back in. If Oluomachukwu had ever dreamt of waltzing out of camp like Idara had told her, then she could have just forgotten about it. To leave, there had to be a serious excuse, one that would be able to bring the person back.

While the speech was still going on, Oluomachukwu spotted Nkiru at a corner, and signalled to her to come over. Nkiru walked around as though she was examining the area for people who needed help, then somehow ended up by Oluomachukwu's side. Oluomachukwu then looked around to check if there was any camp official in sight before she started talking.

"Did they need to call us down for this?" she asked. "They should have just given us some flyers."

Nkiru laughed. "Lazy. What were you up to before?"

"I went to buy rubber trainers." Immediately she said that, Nkiru looked down at her feet, so she added, "I will launch them tomorrow. I didn't even have time to write my name on them before I heard the call."

"Oh," Nkiru replied. "We should kidnap that trumpet blower. That way there wouldn't be any more trumpet calls."

Oluomachukwu wanted to tell Nkiru that it was a bugle and not a trumpet, but she didn't want to appear as a know-it-all. Besides it was written on the weekly schedule pinned on the notice board by the entrance of the hostel. "I also bought two white shorts."

"Really? I hope they didn't cheat you."

"Hmm, I hope so too." Oluomachukwu paused, then remembered why she had initially called Nkiru. "Hmm, I saw Fadeke sitting on Player's lap today."

"What?" Nkiru exclaimed, and everyone turned to look at her. She then lowered her voice. "Are you serious?"

"Yes. She was with Tracker as well, and one other guy in our platoon." Oluomachukwu looked around. "I can't see him anywhere, but I have seen him in our platoon before."

"How does he look?" Nkiru asked.

When Oluomachukwu was done describing the person, Nkiru knew who he was.

"Oh," she said. "I know who that is."

"Who is he?"

"Cleaner."

"You and all these your nicknames." Oluomachukwu laughed. "Is he a cleaner or what?"

"No, he is a clean freak." Nkiru rolled her eyes. "And vain too... checks himself out all the time, and if there's a single stain or spot on his shirt, shorts, socks or trainers, he will go and change it. In fact, I think he has twenty-one kits, socks and tennis shoes... if not twenty-two. I believe his name is Chinedu."

Oluomachukwu laughed out loud this time. "How do you know all these things?"

"Not only have I observed him, some guys in his room have said the same thing. I have run into a lot of desperate guys and everything is gist to them, as long as it makes me laugh."

As they were talking, Auntie Vera walked up to them, angry and fuming. It was a miracle that she didn't spit fire. "My friend, get out of there," she said to Nkiru. "Get out, now."

Nkiru did not argue. She had escaped Auntie Vera's toilet cleaning punishment by joining the Red Cross group and Auntie Vera knew it, so she didn't want to see Nkiru in the platoon again.

After the announcement, everyone was free to go back and do what it was they were doing before.

***

The next time the bugle was blown, it was for evening drills, man-o-war activities and martial arts training. Oluomachukwu went for all the activities, but didn't put her hundred percent into it. The only thing she thought about was going to have drinks and dance at *mami* market. She wasn't sure Tracker was still her friend, since she had seen Fadeke with him and Player. Only time would tell.

After the sessions, Auntie Vera showed up randomly, asking who was going to participate in what competition, because there was no time. Everything was going to be rushed. The competition was going to begin with the Comedy event. Each platoon was to provide a comedian to perform at the event the next day. The schedule for each presentation was out and Platoon Seven hardly had any volunteers. Even when she picked people, they refused. When she begged them, they still refused. She then got angry and left. But after she did, the two platoon presidents begged everyone to join in and support the platoon. In the end, a couple of them agreed to join, but it was just a small number compared to the rest of the platoon. And it was also the same people that volunteered for almost all the other activities.

After a busy day's work, Oluomachukwu went to the camp market with Nkiru, Ekene, and Ogo. A couple of food and drink hawkers surrounded them, trying to lead them to take a seat.

"Sisters, come this side and sit down, I will take your order, anything you want."

"Do you sell *suya*?" Oluomachukwu asked, sarcastically.

"No, but just sit down first, I will help you take your order."

Oluomachukwu eyed him from head to toe. He wasn't the only one trying to get them seats. Other guys were saying the same thing. She wasn't sure if they owned the seats, because that was what it looked like, as if they just wanted people to sit on their own seats. She didn't want to answer any of them at first, but at the same time, the camp market was getting filled up, so they needed to find seats before everything was taken up by other Corps members. They eventually sat at a table with six chairs, and without being asked, the owner said his name was Rasheed.

Oluomachukwu and her three friends settled in, and surprisingly, Tracker tracked them down and went to join them at their table. He came with some of his friends including Player, Cleaner and the guy nicknamed Shoki. A few other guys from Platoon Seven and Platoon Eight, which was Tracker's platoon, came to hang out as well.

Immediately they sat down, Rasheed hovered around them, asking them what they wanted to buy. He sold drinks too, so he was more interested in selling drinks than taking their order for food or small chops. They were not ready and kept telling him to come back until they were. The guys had hardly settled in, and were still talking, so they wanted to sit down and rest for a bit before the alcohol started pouring in.

When Oluomachukwu and her friends were ready to order, Rasheed wasn't there. He was probably troubling other people who had been tricked into sitting at one of his tables, so they ordered from someone else, and immediately the drinks arrived, Rasheed came back and wanted to cause a scene, claiming that he owned the table they were sitting on, so he was the only one allowed to sell to them.

He asked them to leave because they hadn't bought from him. They were all surprised, but they didn't leave. Instead, to make him happy, they bought drinks from him too... a lot. They also ordered a lot to eat. Eventually, there was more than enough to eat and drink. Even with that, Rasheed wasn't content. When he left their table, he went to argue with the guy who had initially come to sell to them, claiming that he was trying to steal his customers and business.

After that, the feasting and talking went into full swing, friends laughing dramatically as they talked, boosted by the alcohol that fuelled their blood streams. But at that point, the only odd thing that crossed Oluomachukwu's mind was where Fadeke was and what guy or guys she was trying to secure dinner with. That was something she was going to worry about later. A new song was played and everyone jumped up and started to dance. It wasn't Shoki, Sekem, Shake Body or Dorobucci. It was Skelewu by Davido.

It was obvious that Corps members just wanted a new song, so anything different from the regular quartet was accepted. They ate, drank, chatted and danced until the sound of the bugle filled the air and it was time for Lights Out.

CHAPTER ELEVEN: DAY SEVEN

Monday, 11th August 2014

The morning of the seventh day was incredibly cold. Oluomachukwu took note of each day as it went by, because she counted down the days to leaving the camp. She was still taking her anti-malaria medication and was already getting fed up of it. She was also now taking vitamin C and was buying warm bottles of water all the time to curb her sore throat. She had lost her voice again, like almost every other person, since there was always loud music playing, the same four songs, so everyone had to shout and strain their voice boxes to be heard.

She had her bath early, as always, and went down to the parade ground. The morning ritual started the same way. There was the Morning Prayer, both National and NYSC Anthems, and Meditation. After the Morning Prayer, the Drill Instructor corrected everyone, yet again. "It is '*where peace and justice reign*' and not ' *where peace and justice shall reign .*' I've corrected you all before." And like the last time, he didn't ask everyone to repeat the last line of the prayer. Maybe that was why they kept repeating the same mistake.

By the time Oluomachukwu had gotten to the parade ground, it was drizzling. She was very happy that she had bought rubber trainers, because she didn't know how the NYSC tennis shoes would have survived what the cloud was threatening to release on them. She also hoped that the Drill Instructor would allow them to go back to their rooms, and not work out.

The Drill Instructor didn't mind the weather, he, too, was standing in the open and was ready to receive the rain. He kept on saying "C'mon, line up, line up," but Corps members were feeling very reluctant. The drizzle then turned to mild rain and it was certain that it was going to start pouring very soon. The Drill Instructor kept saying "C'mon," and the crowd started to murmur and complain.

"Under the sun or in the rain, C'mon, C'mon," the Drill Instructor said, but no one was buying into it. Just because they sang it every morning, didn't mean it was true. The cold was tickling their bones, so there was no way on earth they were going to work out in the rain.

Some people even started saying "To serve Nigeria is not by force..." It was a doctored version of the national pledge, which normally read "To serve Nigeria with all my strength." After contemplating for a short while and when the raindrops started to get heavy and painful on the skin, the Drill Instructor permitted everyone to leave, and Corps members scampered off like a colony of ants that were scrambling to feast on a dead cockroach. They ran from different directions towards the hostel, and there was then a queue at the entrance to get in.

Oluomachukwu saw Nkiru just by the entrance of the hostel controlling the mini traffic, and she wasn't smiling. Oluomachukwu was sure that if there wasn't one other girl and two boys trying to control the traffic with Nkiru, she would have ditched her duty and gone upstairs to sleep.

Oluomachukwu didn't want to join the queue in the rain, so she jumped out of it, dodging all the mud puddles around, and went to stand under a canopy. She waited for about fifteen minutes, then went to meet Nkiru. By that time, the rain had stopped falling, but it was too late to start mobilising everyone again.

Before Nkiru and Oluomachukwu went back to their room, they went to look for hot water in the camp market to make tea. They met the owner of Nwanyi Imo, who sold them Pure Water, which was water in a square sachet. She boiled the water inside her large pot of white rice. When it was very hot, she pulled it out by the tip, then gave it to the girls. The writing on the sachet had already peeled off.

As Oluomachukwu and Nkiru sipped their hot tea, they talked about the night before and how they had had so much fun. They whispered, as they didn't want to disturb and wake up those who were asleep. Ogo had come back to the room right after the Drill Instructor had permitted them to return to their rooms, and slept off immediately. Fadeke was not in the room. Oluomachukwu guessed that she had a friend in another room, where she went to once in a while to spend the night. It was the only plausible explanation. And in addition to that, they had gotten some information about her, but they weren't sure if they should confront her with it.

Oluomachukwu looked around the room briefly — others were quiet, either playing Candy Crush or one of the King games on their phones, talking on the phone, reading or just staring into thin air. When she confirmed that everyone was minding their business, she then began to talk freely.

They talked about how Fadeke had come on to the guys one after the other. It was right after they had spoken about the guys during lunch that she wanted to have them. She saw no reason why the guys should be chasing after Oluomachukwu and Nkiru when she was available. And if Oluomachukwu and Nkiru weren't ready to have the guys, then they shouldn't be dragging the guys along like goats. She slept with Player in one of the stalls at the back that he had rented, and when they were done, he ditched her. She should have known that he was not given the nickname 'Player' for nothing. And as if she hadn't learnt, she went after Cleaner too and he slept with her in the same dirty stall, and ditched her. Oluomachukwu and Nkiru started to wonder if that was the reason why she hardly ever came back to the room.

Oluomachukwu and Nkiru also talked about the three men, the same three men who had bought their drinks and paid for their lunch the other day. They were buying *suya* when one of the men showed up and stood behind Nkiru. Oluomachukwu looked at him and recognised his face. He told them that he and his friends had waited for them that day and had been very disappointed. He said they had no ulterior motives. They just wanted to hang out with pretty girls and have a few drinks. The man ended up paying for their *suya* and dropping his business card with them, and when Oluomachukwu looked at his card, she realised that he was the Camp Commandant.

At that moment, Oghene woke up. Whether she had been sleeping or not, Oluomachukwu didn't know. But it felt as if the word 'camp commandant' had an invisible magnet attached to it. Whenever people heard those two words, they started to shake, especially girls.

"Sorry, did you just say that you spoke to the Camp Commandant?" Oghene asked. Some girls looked at her, then at Oluomachukwu and Nkiru, then continued with what they were doing.

Oluomachukwu noticed that someone was looking at her from close to the door and hadn't yet looked away. She looked at the person, and it was Dunsin. Dunsin looked at her from top to bottom, rolled her eyes and looked away. Oluomachukwu was shocked, but she had a feeling she knew what was going on, but she was going to have to deal with it later.

"Hello?" Oghene spoke again. "I asked a question."

"Yes, we spoke to the Camp Commandant, is there any problem?" Nkiru answered.

TWENTY-ONE DAYS

Oghene shook her head, then replied, "No." She then turned around, laid back on her bed and slept off.

***

Oluomachukwu stood on the balcony, leaning on the iron railing that had once been painted white, but had gradually turned to white and rust-colour, as a lot of the white parts had peeled off. She was on the phone with Okechukwu and didn't want to take the call inside the room. Nkiru had gone to report for her Red Cross duties, while Ogo was still sleeping. She held the phone to her ear and didn't say anything for a while. She didn't want to bring up the Kayode gist, but she felt that Kayode had said something to Dunsin, and that was why Dunsin was now acting rather hostile towards her. She wanted to get to the bottom of the story.

Okechukwu had been talking, but he didn't know that Oluomachukwu hadn't been there with him. In fact, she hadn't heard any word of what he said. As he kept on ranting about Lagos, about work, about Lagos traffic and about the deadly Ebola virus, Oluomachukwu interrupted him.

"Kayode is in camp," she said.

There was silence. Okechukwu hadn't expected that and didn't see the connection. "Okay," he replied.

"What is he doing in camp?" Oluomachukwu asked.

"How am I supposed to know?" Okechukwu paused, then as if he had just realised what was going on and what she was asking, he added, "Did something happen?"

She shook her head, even though he couldn't see her. "No. I was just wondering, because he works in Abuja, at the Head Office. So why would he want to be a Platoon Instructor?"

Okechukwu laughed. "That's Kayode for you. He likes women too much. He goes to camp where he can spend time with women and do all sorts of crap without his wife complaining. But now, I'm wondering why he is in Lagos as well."

"Could it be because of Dunsin?"

"What?" Okechukwu sounded indisputably surprised. "That's Nnanna's fiancée. I know he had applied for her to be in Abuja camp, but since they aren't married, the NYSC rejected the request. But now that you have mentioned it, maybe Kayode had a hand in the rejection."

"Hmm." Oluomachukwu sighed. She then figured out why Dunsin's face had been so familiar on the first day in camp. She remembered seeing her with Nnanna at the airport and resented her on the spot.

"Is he toasting you?" Okechukwu asked.

"What?"

"I mean, 'is he asking you out?'" Okechukwu used a more understandable term.

"No, he isn't. But Dunsin is in my room and has been giving me some bad looks. In fact, she is the room leader."

Okechukwu laughed. "Girl drama. But I don't think she would be annoyed with you if Kayode asks you out, though. She would only be annoyed if she knew that you dated Nnanna a long time ago."

Oluomachukwu had a feeling that Kayode had told Dunsin about herself and Nnanna — and not from a long time ago, but from Abuja. It had to be the only possible explanation. Just then, the bugle blower exploded the air with his annoying call to duty. It was time for 'Sensitisation on Skills Acquisition.' Oluomachukwu didn't know what it was, but she was going to find out. She finished up with Okechukwu and promised to call him back another time, because she had something important to discuss with him. She hung up and went back to the room, and as she was entering, Oghene was leaving. She then woke Ogo up for them to leave.

As Oluomachukwu was getting ready, she noticed a card on the floor close to her bed. She picked it up and saw that it was the Camp Commandant's card. She was certain that she had put the card inside her duvet cover. It could only mean that Oghene had searched her things for the card, after listening in on the conversation she was having with Nkiru, and probably copied down the Camp Commandant's name and number. Oghene had vowed that she couldn't suffer in camp, and with the new contact information she had, she sure wasn't going to suffer.

Oluomachukwu and Ogo snoozed all through the skills acquisition talk. In fact, they had taken turns to sleep on each other's shoulder and didn't feel bad about missing the speech. There had also been a short play to explain the goal, aim, purpose and usefulness of skills acquisition in a programme that was tagged 'SAED' — Skill Acquisition and Entrepreneurship Development. It sounded more like the name Saheed, than any other thing. But the play wasn't enough to keep them awake, though. In fact, half the camp was asleep.

The morning had been very cool with cold raindrops, but the sunshine that followed could bake a cake. Corps members started to rush for every flyer or booklet that was distributed, so that they could fan themselves with it. It was gradually becoming the second use of documents, the other being to sit on the parade ground with. The flyers and booklets provided hot air, which made people grow very restless and count down to the end of the day and the start of the evening... one that they would spend in *mami* market.

Oluomachukwu had just completed her own fifteen minutes snooze when she spotted Nkiru at a corner. Nkiru was looking intently at her, as if she had been watching her sleep. Nkiru then spoke to a Red Cross colleague of hers, then she walked over to where Oluomachukwu was sitting, half asleep, with Ogo sleeping on her shoulder.

"Oluoma." Nkiru stooped down. "I dug around and found out why Dunsin is acting strange towards you all of a sudden."

Oluomachukwu was more shocked than surprised. She hadn't asked Nkiru or anyone at all to dig around or find out anything. And before she could say anything to Nkiru, Nkiru continued.

"Hmm, I found out that Mr. Kayode, or should I say, Kayode, told Dunsin that he slept with you in Abuja." She understood why Oluomachukwu had called him Kayode once and almost did it again another time. There had to be history between them.

Oluomachukwu shook herself out of sleep and almost fell off the chair. Ogo almost fell off as well and woke up immediately. Oluomachukwu apologised to her, told her to rest her head on the chair instead, then turned to look at Nkiru. "I don't understand what you are saying."

"We'll get back to that, but the two things that worried me was why Kayode told Dunsin and why Dusin is upset when she's engaged to be married to someone else. Unless of course, there's something else."

Oluomachukwu hadn't been listening. She believed it was time to talk to Kayode and ask him what the hell was wrong with him for telling someone else about her. After the skills acquisition session, there was a short seminar on HIV/Aids Care and Prevention, which was equivalent to more sleep time for Oluomachukwu and Ogo.

As Oluomachukwu slept, she couldn't stop dreaming of Kayode — of him making an announcement on the parade ground of how he had slept with her on the first day they met in Abuja.

***

Lunch was yam porridge and Oluomachukwu decided to taste it. Luckily, it wasn't watery. It wasn't also soft. It was just perfect and tasted okay. She ate alone in the room, because she wanted to rest for a short while until it was time for evening drills, then sports and games activities, and eventually the comedy event. All the while she ate, her mind was not on the food, but on Kayode. She wondered how and where she would meet him, and how she would start what she wanted to say to him without getting angry.

As she lay in bed, trying not to fall asleep, Nkiru walked in, but she wasn't looking too happy. She went straight to her bed and stooped down. It was as if something had happened. Oluomachukwu sat up and looked at the time on her phone.

"You are back early, no duties today?" Oluomachukwu paused a bit, but Nkiru didn't reply. "Nkiru!"

Nkiru had been searching for something under her bed, then looked up at Oluomachukwu. "Oh, I'm sorry." She sounded distant, somewhat distracted. "What?"

"What?" Oluomachukwu repeated. She was confused. "Did something happen?"

Nkiru shook her head. "No, why would anything want to happen?"

"You are acting strange, almost giving me an attitude."

"Almost?" Nkiru looked at Oluomachukwu and raised an eyebrow.

"And you are also giving me that look. The same look you had when we heard that Fadeke had slept with Player and Cleaner," Oluomachukwu said in a low tone. "Are you judging me?"

"Of course not." Nkiru sighed. "I'm just getting tired of the unending duties."

Oluomachukwu looked at Nkiru, but it was clear that she was lying. It wasn't the duties. It had to be something else. It had to be the new knowledge she had of Kayode. And if at all there was something else, Oluomachukwu wouldn't be able to know, because Nkiru was the only one that knew how to get to the bottom of everything.

Nkiru found what she was looking for, which was nothing. It was evident that she had come to the room to rest, but was shocked to see Oluomachukwu there. So she had to pretend to be looking for something, then leave with the excuse of being on duty.

"So are we seeing later this evening?"

"I guess so," Nkiru replied, without even looking at Oluomachukwu. Then headed towards the door.

"No 'goodbye?'"

"Does it look like I'm travelling?" Nkiru laughed and left the room before Oluomachukwu could say any other thing.

***

By the time the bugle sounded, Oluomachukwu hadn't even slept. She had a lot to think about, as she had to add Nkiru to her list of worries. She went down to the parade ground for drills, man-o-war and martial arts training, but her mind wasn't on any of the activities. She joined the group that practised for marching and even made silly mistakes, making one of her platoon soldiers insult her. There was one soldier, who had bold tribal marks scattered across her cheeks, but still had an okay smile and a good heart. She was also very funny. She always used jokes to scold people who made silly mistakes, and Oluomachukwu didn't escape both the serious and the funny insults.

Oluomachukwu had done only about thirty minutes when she realised that marching wasn't for her. She decided she wasn't going to represent her platoon in March past. The earlier she let the soldiers know, the better for them and herself. But instead of coming clean, she took an excuse. She told them that she wanted to go and use the toilet and never went back there. She then went towards the back of the hostel to where some of her platoon members were rehearsing.

Rehearsals for drama had started. And those who had put their names down were asked to go and rehearse while the rest of the platoon marched. Oluomachukwu hadn't put her name down, but she went towards the back of the hostel where her platoon members were gathered. Some were in front of the dining hall doing drama rehearsals, while another group was by the side of the hall dancing.

Oluomachukwu could see from afar that there was an ongoing Platoon Seven volleyball training on one half of the court. Another platoon was using the other half to train, which was ridiculous, because no coach wanted to talk and give out thier tactical plan to a potential opponent.

Oluomachukwu returned her focus back to the dance and drama rehearsals. She saw the two girls who were always together, shuffling between the drama and dance groups. She didn't know them personally, but she heard that they were foreign-trained Nigerian students — one, Chioma, schooled in France, and the other one, Yetunde, schooled in America. Oluomachukwu wanted to nickname them 'Frenchie' and 'Americana,' but instead she gave them the nickname 'Two,' which was simpler.

There was a group of six drummers as well, playing for the dance and drama groups intermittently, as participants were expected to use local music and also sing a long to the beats of the drum. For the dance group, they were not allowed to use pre-recorded songs as they had hoped, so they all had to learn the lyrics of the song they had chosen, which was Omawumi's version of Onyeka Onwenu's song, 'Ekwe.'

Oluomachukwu watched the rehearsals for a while until it was over. Then she went back to the room when it was time for Games and Sports. People had come out to play both physical and intellectual games, while others just patrolled *mami* market looking for what to eat. The gate officials were refusing to allow people enter the hostel, but Oluomachukwu had put on a sickly face, and also bought the officers soft drinks, and they let her go into the hostel.

Other Corps members were in the hostel as she made her way upstairs. She wondered if the girls had bribed the officers at the gate, played sick or hadn't even gone out to the parade ground in the first place. Either way, she was glad to be inside.

When she approached the room, she saw that the door

had been locked from the outside with a padlock. Dunsin was in charge of locking it before any camp activity and opening it after each one. There was a spare key that Foyin held on to. Whoever left last, locked the door and whoever came back first opened it. Oluomachukwu was pissed off. There was nowhere for her to sleep, and she didn't want to go back to the parade ground or do anything else. As she was about to turn around, she saw movement.

She peered through the window and placed both her hands by the side of her face to get a clearer view. The movement was on Ijeoma's bed, and Oluomachukwu had a feeling that Ijeoma wasn't the only one on the bed. She couldn't see Ijeoma because of the duvet on the bed. In fact, the duvet had a duvet of its own. It was as if Ijeoma had used three or four duvets to shield anything she was doing from being visible.

Oluomachukwu didn't want to knock, she didn't want to interrupt and be caught up in an awkward situation, but she didn't want to stand outside either and wait. Dunsin and Foyin might have taken the keys with them, or not, but there was only one way to find out.

She knocked on the door and the movement on the bed suddenly stopped. No one even attempted to open the door. She knocked again, and again, and again, until she had knocked for three minutes straight, but no one stood up. She didn't know what to do, so she kept on knocking, oblivious to the fact that an officer was walking up to her.

"Hey, you, corper, what are you doing there? Aren't you supposed to be downstairs?" the officer asked and approached her.

She looked at the mean face of the officer, she wasn't part of the ones that had been bribed, so it meant that she either had to be bribed or Oluomachukwu would have to cook up a story as to why she was there. Oluomachukwu wasn't going to implicate the other officers that had let her enter, as she didn't know if the mean-looking one was 'bribeable.'

"I... I... I forgot my medication in the room, I wanted to collect it," Oluomachukwu lied. By the time the officer was getting to the door, Ijeoma had opened the duvet a bit to peep and the officer saw her. The officer started to bang on the door, urging her to get out of the bed and open the door.

Ijeoma didn't get up from the bed. She didn't open her duvet again either. She just stayed under there and hoped the woman would eventually get tired and turn away. Ijeoma was stubborn, but the officer was more stubborn. She turned to look at Oluomachukwu.

"I think they have been locked inside either by the room leader or the assistant. Go to the OBS and make an announcement. Tell them that the room leader or assistant for room forty-five is needed in the hostel immediately. Either or both of them should report to the fourth floor, in front of their room right now."

Oluomachukwu nodded and turned around to leave. She took a peek at Ijeoma's bed before she left, hoping that there wasn't going to be serious a scandal when the door was eventually opened.

Oluomachukwu took a few too many minutes to find where the OBS was located. She asked a few people and they, too, couldn't direct her. She then realised that the NYSC hadn't given them a tour of the facility upon arrival, and there was no access guide or map that Corps members could use to locate places. Oluomachukwu saw a soldier walking by, who was about to ask her why she wasn't on the parade ground or doing anything, when she said it was an emergency and a gate officer had sent her from the female hostel to make an announcement.

The OBS office was located on the ground floor of the male hostel. There were a couple of offices located just at the entrance of the hostel. The first office was the OBS, but it wasn't accessible to just anyone.

Oluomachukwu had to learn that there was a process to making announcements. She didn't know that as well, because they had not been informed, and she had never planned on making any announcements in the camp.

She went through a window that was situated at the other side of the OBS office. She had to leave the hostel completely and walk towards the canopy not too far from the volleyball court. She was to write her message and give it to the person at the window and her request would be looked into. Oluomachukwu wrote her message and the title was marked as 'Urgent.' And it was a good thing she did that, because her case was treated immediately.

By the time she got back to the hostel, Foyin was climbing up the stairs. She met the same officers she had met before, so she didn't have to bribe them again. If she met new ones, she was going to tell them that she had made the announcement and needed to be upstairs at that instant.

She got in front of the room a few seconds after Foyin did, and after another thirty seconds, Dunsin came running towards them, panting as though she had just run a 2,000 meter race. The mean-looking officer then asked where the key was, why there was still someone in the room and why the person was even locked in the room. She said it was against hostel and security policy, in case there was a fire or any other emergency, and that she was going to punish both Dunsin and Foyin.

After the lecture, which Ijeoma hadn't heard, because of the layers of duvet she had over her, Dunsin handed the key over to the officer. She then exchanged glances with Foyin and Oluomachukwu, and they all understood each other, unspoken quarrels aside. They didn't know what to expect, and they hoped it wasn't going to be crazy.

The officer opened the door, stormed into the room and yanked the duvet off, the first one, because there were indeed about four duvets. After the first one was yanked off, there was a scramble on the bed, as if the person there didn't want to be seen. The officer yanked the second one off, and the third one was tougher, because Ijeoma was pulling it back to the bed. The officer managed to yank the two remaining duvets off and stood in shock when she saw Ijeoma and Eternity totally naked.

She remained speechless, as she stood there watching them.

***

Oluomachukwu ate the dinner that had been prepared with the help of Platoon Six Corps members on Kitchen duty. It was white rice, stew and a small chunk of fish. She ate alone in the room. She didn't want to think of what had happened earlier on, she just wanted to think of what would happen later on.

When she was done eating, she took her anti-malaria medication and some vitamin C. She was on the fourth day of the medication and couldn't wait to finish it up, so that she would stop eating three times a day. One or two soft Gala sausage rolls and a bottle of cold drink were enough to keep her until dinnertime even.

After she had washed her plate and cutlery and kept them neatly in a plastic bag under her bed, she picked up her phone and called Kayode. Kayode picked up just after one ring, as though he had been waiting by his phone for someone to call.

"Oluoma, what a pleasant surprise." He sounded more mischievous than surprised.

"Can we see and talk?" She went straight to the point.

"Finally, you want to see me. Hmm. I hope all is well."

"I don't want to see you, I want to talk."

"So why don't we talk over the phone then?"

"Fine. When can I see you?"

"Let's meet at *mami* market entrance now, we can talk then."

"There's a comedy night event tonight until 10:00pm. Can we see and talk after that?"

"That's when they blow the bugle for Lights Out."

"Yes, but it's just for people to start clearing up and finish up with what they are doing. We are expected to be in our rooms, asleep by 10:30pm."

"Okay, then," Kayode said. "10:00pm in front of *mami* market will be fine." There was a brief silence and Kayode thought to use the opportunity to apologise to her again. "Oluoma, I'm really so—"

He couldn't complete his apology. He heard a click and when he looked at his phone screen, Oluomachukwu had already hung up.

When the Lagos State NYSC office set up the comedy night event a couple of years back, it was because they had hoped that the best comedians in Nigeria would be discovered in the Lagos camp, and so far it had worked. But the same couldn't be said for 2014 Batch B, Stream 1.

The ten comedians from each platoon came up, and one after the other, they made the crowd laugh... not at the jokes they made, but because they were the joke. There were eight guys and two girls — two girls that the crowd went crazy for when they first stepped on the stage, and almost booed off when they were not any better than the guys. None of the comedians wowed the crowd, which made it easy to vote. None of the comedians got a single vote. In fact, someone had shouted "Last place draw for all of them" from the crowd and everybody laughed. That was the first time the crowd genuinely laughed all night.

Because there was no vote, the judges had to pick five comedians at random, the ones that the crowd had hated less and tolerated more — the ones that the crowd had laughed at instead of booed. There was going to be a second round, where the five finalists would compete for the best comedian for the year. The second round never held.

Oluomachukwu sat down after the event, which had finished way earlier than planned. She had given Kayode a meeting time, so there was no point going to *mami* market earlier than planned. She had seen neither Nkiru nor Ogo at the comedy event, and it wasn't sure if either of them had come to watch it. Worse of all, she couldn't call them to ask where they were, because she hadn't collected their phone numbers yet. She made a mental note to collect the phone numbers later that evening or the next day.

As she sat there, she saw the Platoon Seven comedian walking towards 'Two' and sat down beside them. They weren't seated too far off from Oluomachukwu, so she could hear everything they were saying. He asked them how he had performed, and one said he had done okay and the other said he could do better. He smiled.

Miraculously, he had been picked for the second round, and was looking for who would help him write his material so that he would do a better job. 'Two' agreed to help him, and he said he was going to meet them the next day to collect it. Whether or not they wrote it for him, and whether or not he collected it from them, Oluomachukwu didn't know.

As soon as the comedian stood up and left, a guy that had been sitting close to 'Two' turned to them and said, "For the fact alone that the guy is looking for who to write his material for him, lets you know that comedy isn't for him."

***

The *mami* market meeting was brief. Oluomachukwu met Kayode at the entrance as promised. Because of how the comedy show had ended, she had left there before 10:00pm, so she still had some time to talk to Kayode before the bugle call. She got there ten minutes to the meeting time and he was already there.

"Hi, Oluoma," he said. He didn't attempt to hug her again, because he didn't know how she would react. She noticed that he was looking around suspiciously, as if he didn't want anyone to see him or see him with her.

"Thanks for meeting with me." She sounded serious. "I just wanted to know why you went to tell Dunsin about what happened between us."

Kayode didn't say a single thing at first, but when he opened his mouth to speak, Dunsin came out of nowhere and went to hug him. Dunsin then turned around and looked Oluomachukwu from head to toe. "What is this one doing here?" She then turned to look at Kayode. "I didn't know you were meeting with her too."

Oluomachukwu then realised why Kayode had been looking around suspiciously. He hadn't come to their meeting on time. He had come for another meeting before her own. She ignored Dunsin and looked at Kayode. "Why did you call her for a meeting? Did you want to keep her informed about our own meeting or what? Telling her about what happened between you and I wasn't enough for you, right?"

Kayode didn't answer any of the three questions.

"What if he told me?" Dunsin asked. "You were one of the people condemning those *lesbo* girls in our room with your eyes, when you are not better than any of them."

"What *lesbo* girls?" Kayode seemed to be instantly concerned about something else.

"That's not the point," Dunsin shot at him, then she turned back to Oluomachukwu. "What if he told me? And I'm happy he told me, so that I can know who is who in this camp."

Oluomachukwu thought Dunsin sounded ridiculous. "You know, I could have slept with him because I didn't know he was married. That was the part he forgot to mention to me. But you, what is your own excuse? I didn't know he was married, but you did."

Dunsin didn't say anything. It was as if the cat had just eaten her tongue.

"You have no excuse. You knew he was married and yet you slept with him. In fact, what is more disgusting is that you are engaged, to be married. You will soon be someone else's wife and you are still crawling over another man. Only heaven knows how many more men you are crawling over. In fact, I'm sorry for your husband-to-be, not you."

Dunsin was still very speechless. If she had a way to permanently shut Oluomachukwu up, she would have done it. She looked at Kayode, and they exchanged a brief glance, then looked back at Oluomachukwu.

"So, please, what's your excuse, you disgusting girl?" Oluomachukwu's Nigerian accent had left her tongue and she had already gone full British. She always did that when she was angry or if she was speaking very fast.

"The same excuse your friend had," Dunsin replied.

Oluomachukwu was suddenly speechless. She darted her eyes back and forth from Dunsin to Kayode, and back to Dunsin. "What do you mean?"

"I have the same excuse your friend had. So if I am disgusting for going after Kayode, then she is too."

"I don't understand what you are talking about."

Dunsin looked at Kayode. "What's the name of that her Red Cross friend again?"

Kayode didn't know the person's name, put on the spot like that, but Oluomachukwu already knew that it was Nkiru. She also didn't believe what Dunsin was saying. She started to think when, where and how it happened, if it happened. The only thing that came to her mind was the dirty stall behind the camp market.

"I don't believe you," Oluomachukwu finally said.

"Then you can ask her. She is just right there." Dunsin pointed behind Oluomachukwu to Nkiru who was just standing there and watching them.

Oluomachukwu turned around and saw Nkiru. Nkiru had that look, the same one she had in the room after she knew that Oluomachukwu had slept with Kayode... it wasn't a judgmental look as Oluomachukwu had thought, it was a look of guilt... it was a look of regret.

CHAPTER TWELVE: DAY EIGHT

Tuesday, 12th August 2014

When Oluomachukwu woke up, she was very tired because she had hardly slept. She didn't mind sleeping for a few more hours, but it was thirty minutes to the Wake-Up call, so she couldn't. After Lights Out, she had spent the night thinking about everything that had happened. Nkiru didn't say a single word to her back in the room. They had walked back together, but didn't say anything to each other. Oluomachukwu didn't want to ask her anything, yet. She felt that when it was the right time, Nkiru would open up naturally.

Oluomachukwu stood up lazily from her bed and came out of her duvet cover. She didn't have the mosquito net that some other people hung over their beds and covered themselves with, but her duvet cover did the job. Besides, she was yet to see one mosquito in the room, although the toilets and bathrooms were filled with dirty and stagnant water, the perfect breeding grounds for mosquitoes.

She walked sluggishly to the bathroom, half asleep, but when she got there, the sleep was immediately wiped out of her eyes. The fat girl she had once encountered was in the bath. In fact, if Oluomachukwu had gotten there just one minute earlier again, she would have entered the bath space before the fat girl. As usual, the fat girl was acting very slowly, as if her legs couldn't carry all the weight on her body. She wasn't ready to have her bath, but she stood in the bath space, trying to waste time, as usual.

It was as if the fat girl was slowly washing her things intentionally, so that Oluomachukwu would get pissed off and leave, or just so that she could show Oluomachukwu who the boss was by making her wait as punishment for their last encounter. Whatever the reason was, it worked. Oluomachukwu was pissed off.

"Hi, can I please have my bath real quick while you wash?" Oluomachukwu asked. "I will not take time. I'll be done before you know it."

The fat girl ignored Oluomachukwu and continued washing, even slower than she had been washing before. Oluomachukwu turned around and looked at two other girls who had come in to form a queue, they also looked shocked.

"Are you just going to ignore me?"

"Please, leave me alone," the fat girl said. Everyone was surprised and all exchanged quick glances.

"What did you just say?" Oluomachukwu asked, even though she had heard clearly.

"I said you should leave me alone. If you want to have your bath early, then you should be here early. Why do you keep disturbing me all the time? Every time, every time, you keep disturbing me, what is it?"

Oluomachukwu looked at the girl as saliva jumped out of her mouth, and was disgusted. The girl kept ranting and Oluomachukwu just felt like telling her to shut the hell up. "What do you mean by 'all the time?' Isn't this the second time I'm asking you?"

"Please, stop asking me. Just come early if you want to use the bathroom early."

The two girls who stood behind Oluomachukwu, and the other ones who hung around the bathroom brushing their teeth and reserving bath time slots, were not in the mood for any early morning drama, so some of them left the bathroom and went to queue up in other bath stalls. It was not worth the stress. Oluomachukwu did not want to go and queue up in any other place, especially as she was next in line where she was.

The fat girl eventually finished washing her things and started to have her bath. But instead of fetching water and moving her bucket aside, she left the water running and did not care that she was wasting it. The bucket filled up and water was running over, but the girl didn't care. What was more annoying was that there was limited supply of water in the camp during the day. Sometimes there would not be any water until evening. Therefore Oluomachukwu expected people to use their heads, and not their anuses to think when it came to conserving water.

Oluomachukwu didn't want to stand there and wait for the fat girl to finish her rituals, so she moved the fat girl's bucket aside and put hers under the tap to fetch water and have her bath in the open space, and that was when all hell broke loose.

The fat girl held on to Oluomachukwu's bucket and started dragging it, and Oluomachukwu was afraid the girl would slip and fall face down.

"This is my fucking space, I can do whatever I want in my fucking space," the fat girl yelled, and Oluomachukwu wondered where that was coming from. Which person in their right mind would want to secure a space in a public bathroom? She thought.

Every other person wanted to have a bath and leave the dirty bathrooms immediately but not the fat girl. If she had her way, she would have filled the dirty shallow tub with water and swam in it or even turned the bathroom into her bedroom. As the fat girl continued to rant her heart out, Oluomachukwu decided to nickname her 'Fucking Space.'

The fat girl emptied her already full bucket of water and placed the bucket back under the tap to fill up again, indicating that Oluomachukwu's presence or bucket had soiled her water.

Oluomachukwu eventually took her bucket away and waited for the fat girl to finish up. "I truly don't know why some girls act very stupid. What's the point yelling like a mad woman and using curse words this early morning, or using them at all? If you don't want to let me fetch water, you can just say it."

"Didn't I say it?" the fat girl shot back. "It's my fucking space, please, leave me alone."

Oluomachukwu had been trying to ignore the fat girl, but finally gave into the temptation, and said, "Then by all means, stay in your fucking space and have your fucking bath."

***

The usual morning ritual began right before the drill — Morning Prayer, National Anthem, NYSC Anthem and Meditation. This time, Corps members took to correction and didn't say '*where peace and justice shall reign*.' They said, '*where peace and justice reign*' so the Drill Instructor didn't have to make the correction again and so it was all through the remaining days in camp.

The Camp Director was on the parade ground that morning with her workout kit, and she had to interrupt the girl who was reading the Meditation. She was representing Platoon Seven. The Camp Director readily corrected her saying that it was 'Seven Platoon,' and not 'Platoon Seven.'

The girl took to the correction and repeated the line, that she was representing 'Seven Platoon.' Oluomachukwu wondered why the Camp Director always put the number before the platoon, because it didn't sound very pleasing to the ear.

After the girl had finished reading the Meditation and before the physical training started, the Camp Director came to talk about how disgusted she was to have heard about some things that happened in camp the previous day. That was why she had joined them on the parade ground that morning. It was not because she wanted to work out with them, it was because she wanted to scold them when the action was still very fresh in her memory. Oluomachukwu knew for sure what the Camp Director was referring to. She darted her eyes around the parade ground to check if Nkiru was there or any other person from her room who knew what was about to be said.

The Camp Director talked about the two girls that were caught in bed together, naked, and all the guys started to yell, catcall and applaud. Some said they wished they had been there, some asked if someone had had the sense to record it, while others asked if the girls could come on stage and repeat what they had done as their punishment. The Camp Director shut everyone up, stating how serious the case was, and how it was liable to punishment. The girls were liable to prison time, and whoever supported them, was also liable to the same thing. At the mention of that, everyone kept shut and listened. She told them that the girls had been decamped, their next-of-kin — their husbands in both cases, had been contacted, and that they had been sent to the authorities to handle their case.

After the serious talk, the Camp Director congratulated those who had made it so far in the camp for their good behaviour. Not everyone was of good behaviour, but only the ones that were caught were of bad behaviour. She then reminded them that one week had gone by, and two weeks were left to stay in the camp. So she pleaded with them to stay out of trouble and hold their sexual urges until it was time to leave the camp.

In an unrelated note, she also talked about how the NSYC had finally concluded registration for everybody including all latecomers, who were either pregnant women, nursing mothers or the disabled. In total, there were 2,031 Corps members registered for the Lagos State Batch B, of which 1,169 were female and 862 were male. There were

48 doctors, 35 pharmacists, 7 nurses, 157 nursing mothers and 77 pregnant women, but nothing was given on the disabled people who had tried to be present in the camp. Nkiru had had to assist a couple of visually impaired girls to go to the dining hall for their meals and go back to the hostel.

When the Camp Director was done, she prayed for everybody, and thanked Platoon Six for their work the previous day, as they had been on duty. She then handed the microphone over to the Drill Instructor and left the parade ground. Before the physical activity began, he dismissed Platoon Seven members to report for duties. He started singing one of his funny songs as soon as the last Platoon Seven member jogged out of the parade ground.

***

Oluomachukwu and her platoon members gathered on the volleyball court. Auntie Vera and Sister Mary were both there and actually early for the first time. And also for the first time, no one would have minded if they came late or didn't show up at all... anything that would stop them from being on duty was welcomed. Auntie Vera started by imploring everyone to take their duties seriously. She said that so far, no one had complained about other platoons and she didn't want Platoon Seven to be the first on the complain log.

She listed the four duty areas, which were — Security, Environmental, Sanitation and Kitchen duties. Naturally, everyone wanted to do the first two duty areas, and not the last two, but Sister Mary told them that the first two were more difficult because Corps members were expected to stand all day, at the gate for the security team and around the camp for the environmental team. But that didn't matter to anyone. In fact, it was almost like the warning had passed from one ear and gone out through the other without sticking. They reasoned that if the duties were that difficult, the NYSC wouldn't be asking Corps members to do them. And no matter how bad it was going to be, it would definitely be better than cooking food and cleaning the hostels.

Oluomachukwu kept quiet and watched. She did not have any preferences. Anywhere they put her was going to be fine with her. Auntie Vera asked people to volunteer into the last two duties, and if nobody did, she would have to pick people randomly. She pulled out an A4 size paper from a white notebook she had and handed it over to the platoon president to take attendance of everyone there by writing down their code numbers. At the same time, she was to collect all their ID cards, and in exchange, she was to give small pink paper cards with '7 ON DUTY' written on them. She wanted to use their code numbers to assign them to different duty posts.

Just then, one of the girls from 'Two' raised her hand, and said, "Ma, what about we, that are rehearsing for some competitions? We really don't have that much time and we would love to rehearse today."

"Very good," Auntie Vera said. "If you are rehearsing for dance or drama, please come out and stand at this corner." She pointed to her left side and half the crowd came out. "No, no, no, no." Auntie Vera shook her head. "You were not this much the last time. If you think you are not going to be on duty, then you are joking. Dance and drama participants would be on the Kitchen duty, and from the rest of you, I will pick people for the Sanitation duty." Half of the people that had come out before went back in.

While Auntie Vera was picking people for each duty, the paper came to Oluomachukwu and she wrote down her code, but didn't drop her ID card. She then somehow manoeuvred herself to the dance and drama group without writing her name down as one of their members. She just wanted to go round and see what the groups were doing without joining in. Support was the least she could give.

When Auntie Vera was done assigning people to the different duty areas, she split the kitchen group into three teams — one for breakfast, one for lunch and the third for dinner. Those who were to do the morning Kitchen duty were happy, because after that, they were going to be free until the next day. The afternoon group was going to be free in the morning and evening, and the evening group was going to be free until dinnertime. Oluomachukwu was put in the afternoon group together with 'Two' and some other people. She actually didn't mind helping out in the kitchen and knowing how they were expected to help or if Corps members actually did any form of cooking.

As Auntie Vera was about to dismiss everyone to their respective duties, one guy also raised his hand and spoke. Oluomachukwu couldn't remember who he was, but when he started talking, it was evident that he was the Platoon Seven representative for socials activity.

"Good morning, ma. Ma, the Big, Bold and Beautiful contest will hold tomorrow evening and we still don't have anyone to represent our platoon. I have been going round and asking eligible girls, but no one wants to do it. I need to get a name and give it to the NYSC official in charge at least one day before the contest, which is today. They gave me until this evening to provide the name." Some people laughed when he said 'eligible girls.'

Auntie Vera scrunched her face, then looked at the crowd. "*Ahn-ahn*, girls what's going on? Where are the big girls in this platoon? All of you come out right now. Don't you know we're supposed to be a team? We're team Unity for heaven's sake. Issues like this shouldn't even come to me. You should all take care of it within yourselves and only call Sister Mary, or I, when it's time for the contest. *Ehn*? Why *nau*?"

As Auntie Vera was speaking, some of the big girls in the platoon started coming out. Some girls didn't want to come out until they were pushed out by some guys. It was the first time Oluomachukwu noticed that 'Fucking Space' was in the same platoon as she was. Oluomachukwu could have proposed that 'Fucking Space' represent the platoon, but someone with a dirty heart and mouth was not worth representing anyone but her kind. She even scrunched her face when Auntie Vera asked her to represent the team, and Auntie Vera didn't bother trying to beg her.

Another dark and beautiful girl was asked. She wasn't really that big, but she was on the big side, somewhere in between very big and chubby. Auntie Vera asked her to represent the team, and without asking any questions, she nodded and agreed to do it. And that was how the case was closed. Auntie Vera then dismissed everyone and told them to make her proud. After that, she left with Sister Mary, and probably went back to her room to continue sleeping.

***

Oluomachukwu spent some time watching the dance group rehearse. In fact, everyone was watching them rehearse, including the guys who should have been training for table tennis and athletics. The dance group seemed to have advanced in their dance routine from the last time Oluomachukwu saw them.

The drama group, on the other hand, wasn't rehearsing. The problem was that they had no story to work with at that moment. They had been rehearsing before only to find out that their story didn't make any sense. Secondly, it was only that morning that the socials representative told them that the Drama Committee had given them a theme on Community Development Service — CDS.

The CDS was the third out of the four cardinal programmes of the NYSC scheme. The first was the Orientation programme in camp, which Corps members were now undergoing and which was supposed to prepare them physically and mentally for the service year and post service year challenges. The second was the Primary

Assignment, where Corps members would be posted to employers in the communities of their State of deployment for eleven months to render service to the nation. And the fourth was the Winding-up or Passing Out programme, where Corps members would be appraised and discharged from the NYSC scheme.

For the CDS, Corps members were expected to use their innate talent to improve on the lot of their host communities by rendering free and selfless services, and that was what the drama group was supposed to portray.

After the socials representative read out all that information to them, the drama group members sat down, some on chairs and others on the floor, to think. They didn't know how to draw up a story from what they had just heard, so their rehearsal was more of a think-tank session. They had until that afternoon to come up with a story and start rehearsing.

Oluomachukwu was bored after a while of watching the dance group, as they were doing the same thing over and over again. When they went on a break, the sports representative went to plead with some of them to volunteer for athletics and volleyball. There was no one for athletics and only five people for volleyball. He managed to convince the 'Two' girls to volunteer. One of them went in for volleyball and the other for athletics.

Not too long afterwards, the bugle's annoying sound filtered the air and it was time for Bath and Breakfast. Oluomachukwu didn't want to eat what the kitchen was serving: bread, boiled egg and probably watery tea like the last time. She went to *mami* market to get hot water for a cup of tea. She only wondered where Nkiru was. She bought four soft Gala sausage rolls and went up to the room. When she got there, she saw Nkiru lying on the bed sleeping, or rather pretending to be asleep.

She threw two of the four Gala sausage rolls on Nkiru's bed, then went to sit down on her own bed. Nkiru opened her eyes and looked at Oluomachukwu. "Hi Oluoma."

"First things first," Oluomachukwu said and pulled out her phone after she kept the torrid sachet of Pure Water on her bed. "What's your phone number?"

Nkiru laughed. "I even thought that something had happened." She started calling out her phone number as Oluomachukwu punched it into her own phone. She then pointed to Oluomachukwu's chest. "Are you enjoying your duty?"

Oluomachukwu bent her head and looked at her own chest. "Oh, we are on duty today, but I am not sure I'll do anything. I'll just go around and see how preparations for the competitions are going."

"What was for breakfast?" Nkiru opened one of the Gala sausage rolls and started to chew it up.

"Bread, boiled egg and tea."

Nkiru threw on an angry face. "I like boiled eggs. You should have taken one for me."

"Sorry, maybe next time." Oluomachukwu proceeded to make some tea for both of them.

"What of lunch?"

"*Amala* and *ewedu* soup," Oluomachukwu replied.

"I'll pass." Nkiru finished the Gala and picked up the second one. Oluomachukwu placed a hot cup of tea beside Nkiru, then there was silence.

"So, about yesterday, are you ready to talk about it?" Oluomachukwu asked.

Nkiru shrugged.

"I called Kayode and asked to meet him so that I could ask him why he would tell Dunsin about me, and now that I'm thinking about it, I'm even wondering why he told you," Oluomachukwu said.

Nkiru shook her head. "He wasn't actually telling me about you, he was saying what he told Dunsin and didn't realise he had told me about you. Either way, for me to have understood, he had to tell me what exactly it was he had told her."

"Okay, I see." Oluomachukwu shrugged. "I was rather

shocked when Dunsin showed up out of the blue and even more surprised when she said you had something with Kayode. I asked her what her excuse was for sleeping with Kayode and she said she had the same excuse my friend had, my Red Cross friend. She didn't even know your name, and neither did Kayode."

"I don't blame him." Nkiru focused on the Gala, opened it up and started eating all the beef in the middle. It was obvious that she would have preferred to talk about something else.

Oluomachukwu, on the other hand, didn't want to talk about anything else. "So what was the excuse?"

"Nothing."

"I'm sure you can tell me. We have already gone past that level."

"I mean the excuse is 'nothing.' There was no excuse, that's what she meant. We did what we did, and we have no excuse, no explanation, nothing."

"Oh."

"Yeah. I had gone to hang out with him in his room because he seemed kind of cool, but the 'cool' turned to something else. I shouldn't have been there in the first place. It was my fault, but I won't make that mistake again, with him or with any other guy for that matter, in this camp. In fact, after he told me what he had told Dunsin, I became afraid that he would speak about me too, if not to Dunsin, then to someone else, and he did. He is such a loud-mouthed idiot."

Oluomachukwu laughed. "Oh, so he actually gave you the information after the whole hook-up thing with him?"

Nkiru nodded. "He did. Can you imagine?" She asked, sounding too casual than normal.

"Oh, well. I just hope his behaviour doesn't put him in trouble."

There was a very brief silence as Oluomachukwu didn't know what else to say. She had gotten the information she needed and was somewhat satisfied.

"Hmm, did you notice that Dunsin didn't come back to the room last night?" Oluomachukwu broke the silence.

Nkiru nodded. "And I haven't seen her all morning. Maybe she has moved in with Kayode. He will just spoil her life for nothing." She stood up and threw on her Red Cross vest. "Let me go for my duty. Call me when you are going to have lunch in *mami* market."

Oluomachukwu nodded, and when Nkiru left, she finished up what was left of her Gala, then drank the tea, after which she took her anti-malaria medication. She was going to complete day five, and couldn't wait two more days for it to be over.

***

The afternoon session was on SAED — different entrepreneurs and small business owners brought their different craft to show to Corps members. They already had small stands prepared for them under the canopies. The whole place had been set up by Platoon Seven Corps members on Environmental duty, and Oluomachukwu didn't envy them. Kitchen duty was fine at the end of the day.

Oluomachukwu didn't know what SAED group to join. The options ranged from beads making, to sewing, to making of small chops and to creating things with 3D animation. There were a variety of SAED activities and she went from one SAED group to another, spending between ten to fifteen minutes in each. The session was to last for three hours, and she ended up in the small chops stall, learning how to make spring rolls, samosa and the likes.

After the session, there was a one-hour Sensitisation lecture on the Nigerian Millennium Development Goals project — the MDG. The chairs had been arranged per platoon under the canopy, so Oluomachukwu easily found Ekene sitting at the back, probably waiting to sleep like Oluomachukwu always did when any lecture started. She took Ekene's phone number down, so that she could call her whenever she wanted them to meet up.

They did a bit of catching up, because Ekene hadn't come down to the parade ground for some time, claiming that she was ill. Oluomachukwu knew that the only thing Ekene was doing was hiding when it was time for morning drills. To prove to Oluomachukwu that she had been really ill, Ekene mentioned that she had seen Fadeke in the clinic two days in a row and Fadeke had complained of pains, probably linked to tummy ache.

Oluomachukwu and Ekene chatted all through the lecture, and when it was over, it was then time for intra-platoon activities. Oluomachukwu missed the table tennis game, so she didn't know what platoon won, but she was certain that it wasn't Platoon Seven. She went to watch the athletics, both male and female. It was a sixty-meter race. The guy representing Platoon Seven went on to the next round, but the girl didn't. She shrugged and walked out of the field.

There was also a football match going on between two platoons, and Oluomachukwu didn't know what teams were playing, but she was sure it wasn't Platoon Seven so she didn't bother watching it. While there was still time, she ran back to the kitchen, as she was meant to be on afternoon duty to help with lunch. All she and the others had to do was help wrap the *amala* in small transparent plastic bags, then keep them in coolers until it was time to be served.

When it was lunchtime, another group of Kitchen duty Corps members collected tickets at the dining hall entrance and helped to serve the food. Oluomachukwu removed her apron, returned it and went to have lunch at *mami* market with Nkiru, Ogo and Ekene. When lunch was over, she went back to the kitchen to help with washing up the pots and coolers, and sweeping the floor.

***

TWENTY-ONE DAYS

The rest of the day went as planned, as usual. From 4:00pm until 5:30pm, there were drills, martial art training and man-o-war activities. After that, there were games and sports activities from 5:30pm to 6:30pm, which a lot of other platoons used to rehearse for either their sports or socials competitions. The bugle blower didn't forget to play the national anthem at exactly 6:00pm and also lower the national flag.

***

Oluomachukwu didn't know what was for dinner, and she didn't have it. She also didn't want to hang out in *mami* market, because that was all they had been doing for a while. She had gotten invitations from Tracker, Player, Cleaner and other guys she barely even knew, but didn't acknowledge any of them. Instead, she bought fried yams and plantains, enough for three, then bought three bottles of soft drinks, a big bottle of water for herself, and went back to the room to eat with Nkiru and Ogo.

While they ate, Oluomachukwu's mind kept wandering. It wandered to Okechukwu, then to Kayode, and finally to Nnanna and Dunsin. At that instant, she looked towards Dunsin's bed and noticed that there was no bedspread, pillow or anything to indicate that someone was still using the bed. It seemed as though Dunsin had moved out of the room and gone somewhere else. She could have either been asked to be moved to another room or she could have taken an exeat. Or maybe she could have moved in with Kayode.

Oluomachukwu shook the thoughts out of her head. What really interested her was how she was going to pay both Kayode and Nnanna back for what they had done, then move on with her life. By moving on with her life, she wanted to talk to Okechukwu first, so she made a mental note to give him a call the next day.

By the time they had finished eating, the bugle sounded

for everyone to prepare for Lights Out. Oluomachukwu and her friends hadn't noticed how long they had spent eating, talking and laughing together. They decided to go to bed early for the first time, and they did. Well, not all of them went to bed early. Oluomachukwu didn't. She still had an unfinished business to take care of. When Ekene left, Foyin turned off the light. Lights Out was supposed to start from 10:30pm, but Foyin thought it didn't make any difference.

So when everywhere was quiet and it was sure that everyone was asleep, Oluomachukwu took her phone and left the room. While she was going out, she glanced at Dunsin's bed again and saw that Dunsin was still not there. It was more or less certain that Dunsin wasn't going to return anytime soon.

Oluomachukwu unlocked her phone to call Nnanna. If there was a 'telling game' going on, she wanted to be a part of it. She dialled Nnanna's number and waited, and after just a few rings, Nnanna picked up the call.

"Oluoma." Nnanna sounded surprised. "You finally decided to call me after all this while."

Oluomachukwu sighed. "I'm in camp."

"What do you mean?"

"NYSC Orientation camp, in Lagos."

Nnanna didn't get the point. "Okay... is that why I have not heard from you or are you telling me this for another reason?"

"Kayode is in the camp too."

"What?" Nnanna exclaimed, then didn't say any other thing.

"Why are you shocked that he is here? Or is it because your fiancée, Dunsin is here too?"

Oluomachukwu heard a strange sound, like someone who had almost choked on saliva, or water that had gone through the wrong channel. After a few seconds, she heard Nnanna coughing.

"How do you know about Dunsin?" he asked, when he

could finally speak.

Oluomachukwu could have been nice, she could have painted the story in a nice way, but she wanted Nnanna to feel pain, the same type of pain she had felt once before in the UK and also after their Abuja fling.

"I was always seeing a girl with Kayode around camp, and others have also seen her inside his office and room. I figured she was his wife since it was very obvious that they were sleeping together. But when I asked a friend, I heard that she was not his wife. In fact, I heard that she was engaged, to be married. I didn't put two and two together until I spoke to Okechukwu and he told me that Dunsin was your fiancée."

Nnanna didn't say anything, but it didn't discourage Oluomachukwu from still talking.

"There was a little confrontation yesterday and it ended with a lot of secrets being revealed. I didn't see Dunsin all day and I haven't seen her tonight, so I'm guessing she is sleeping in Kayode's room tonight."

"She is not," Nnanna replied, sounding pissed off. "She told me she took an exeat to come back to Abuja because she was missing me and she wanted to do some wedding planning in the process, and that she would go back to camp on or before the Closing Ceremony."

"Well, I guess she lied to you, but don't be too upset about it. That's what you do, that's your thing. You also lie to her, so it's only natural that she plays the same game."

With that, Oluomachukwu hung up. She didn't even wait for Nnanna to comment on what she had said. She wasn't interested, but happy that she had spoken her mind and that she had made Nnanna feel bad as well. That was enough payback for her. She then went back to the room, climbed into bed and smiled as she slept off — she slept happy that night.

C. M. OKONKWO

CHAPTER THIRTEEN: DAY NINE

Wednesday, 13th August 2014

When Oluomachukwu woke up, she felt lighter and happier, and the air seemed fresher and smoother. It wasn't because of what had happened the night before, it was because they were short of three people in her room — Ijeoma, Eternity and Dunsin. Oluomachukwu had the whole bunk to herself, not that she would use it. She thought of using it sometimes, because the top bunk had its own perks.

Firstly, people on the top bunk were closer to the light bulb, the only light bulb in the room. They could read and do other things without straining their eyes. Secondly, they were close to the fans. There were two fans in the room and the cool air it produced touched people on the top bunk first before it circulated. And lastly, people on the top bunk didn't have to deal with strangers or random people sitting on their beds, or putting things on their beds. It was one of the many things that Oluomachukwu found annoying. Ijeoma had been a good bunkmate, but other bunkmates like Ogo and Fadeke was a different story. Fadeke always had to step on Ogo's bed to get to her own bed, which was another perk of staying on the top bunk — not having people step on the top bed to go anywhere.

Oluomachukwu dreaded going to the bathroom, as she didn't want to run into 'Fucking Space' and ruin her happy mood. She prayed as she went into the bathroom, and luckily for her, she didn't see her in there. She didn't even want to see her anywhere at all, and whenever they almost crossed paths on the parade ground or during their Platoon Family Meeting time, she would take another route or stand at another corner.

She got ready and went out to the parade ground with Nkiru and Ogo. When they got there, they went their separate ways; Oluomachukwu and Ogo to their respective platoons, and Nkiru to her Red Cross duty post.

It was the same process as the other days — Morning Prayer, National Anthem, NYSC Anthem and Meditation. Platoon Eight was on duty and they had repeated the same Meditation that Platoon Two had recited, word for word.

One of the coordinators came and apologised to the crowd. It was at that moment that everyone knew that the Meditations had already been prepared, typed and printed, then brought to the parade ground in the mornings. The coordinator must have picked an older script by error. And since it was already too late, she allowed the Platoon Eight representative to read what she had, then apologised again.

The drills started immediately after all Platoon Eight Corps members jogged out of the parade gound, and the Drill Instructor used more songs for the jogging that were also interesting. And just like the very first time during the drill, Oluomachukwu memorised two songs that she liked.

The first one was linked to their 'corper' status. The instructor sang the first line and Corps members repeated the next line, tweaking just one word from it. The song went like this:

This is the way you wanted to be... this is the way we wanted to be,

TWENTY-ONE DAYS

This is the way you wanted to be... this is the way we wanted to be,
Ehh, you want to be a corper... ehh, I want to be a corper,
Ehh-ehh-ehh you want to be a corper... this is the way we wanted to be.

Corps members sang enthusiastically. It was clear that they didn't want to be corpers, but they liked the way the song flowed as they sang it and jogged. They were even more enthusiastic about the second song, which was linked to the end of the month allowances that they were going to receive in the coming week. It meant that if there was no allowance, there was going to be serious trouble.

Yawa go gas oh... yawa go gas,
Yawa go gas oh... yawa go gas,
If allawee no dey... yawa go gas,
If allawee no dey... yawa go gas.

Out of nowhere, the Drill Instructor added a line and the whole camp went crazy, singing with so much passion and ease that Oluomachukwu couldn't shake the feeling that most of them had been to an NYSC camp before or at least to a man-o-war camp.

After each line, Corps members repeated the next line.

Oya, hold something... hold something,
Hold something... hold something,
Hold something... hold something.

During the 'Hold Something' fad, male Corps members ran behind female Corps members or the closest female Corps member they could see, to hold their waists, bums, hips or shoulders... anything they could hold. Some got a spanking, others had their hands pushed away and some were scolded. Oluomachukwu made sure that nobody held any part of her body by running around, with her hands over her bum, instead of jogging freely.

By 6:00am, the bugle blower came in front of the parade ground, just by the rusty pole that held the Nigerian flag, to play the national anthem.

For the first time, Oluomachukwu noticed that there was a flag, and that someone raised the flag as the bugle blower played the national anthem. Oluomachukwu always stood behind, but this time, she stood in front, because that was where she found herself when the bugle blower came out, and they were all supposed to stop what they were doing until the anthem was over. Also for the first time, Oluomachukwu listened intently to what the bugle blower was playing. It didn't sound exactly like the national anthem, but some parts of it actually did.

After that, the Drill Instructor continued with the workout, then they moved to martial arts training, after which he dismissed everyone for Bath and Breakfast.

***

Breakfast was *akara* and *akamu*, prepared in the camp kitchen with the help of Platoon Eight Corps members, and Oluomachukwu didn't eat it. It was not that she didn't like *akara* and *akamu*, or that she didn't eat that type of food, she didn't just like eating it if it wasn't prepared in her own home or in a home she knew. Some types of food, she believed, were only to be eaten at home, like beans porridge, all kinds of soups, *akara* and *akamu*. While rice, beans, pasta, plantain, yam or potatoes could be eaten anywhere.

Oluomachukwu went to buy two soft Gala sausage rolls, while Ogo and Nkiru went to the dining hall to get their breakfast. They were to reconvene in the room and eat before the bugle call for SAED activities.

Oluomachukwu took her anti-malaria medication and counted down until the next day when it was going to be all over. She had not really noticed, but she was already feeling well. The other thing that she had not noticed was that the contents of her bottled water had gone down tremendously. She knew she had drunk some the previous night before going to bed, but it seemed like someone else had drunk out of the bottle and she didn't like that.

Everyone could easily buy a bottle of water, and if they couldn't, there was always Pure Water at 5 naira or 10 naira a sachet to quench their thirsts and do whatever else they wanted.

Oluomachukwu and her friends didn't have the time to rest before they heard the sound of the bugle and had to go down to the parade ground for their activities. Ogo and Nkiru hadn't picked a SAED group yet, and just like Oluomachukwu the last time, they went through all the groups before ending up in beads making and 3D animation respectively. Neither enjoyed what they were doing and joined the groups just to have something to do until they picked one.

They had left the room kind of late, so by the time they got out of the hostel, they started running. Nkiru ran towards one direction at the end of the camp, in a section under the big canopy where the 3D animation table was, while Oluomachukwu and Ogo ran across the parade ground, where their SAED groups were, side by side. But before they got to their destination, Ogo stopped halfway, bent forward and vomited a squashed brownish-pink and watery mash of *akara*, *akamu* and Fanta.

Some people from the Red Cross and some NYSC officials ran towards her to offer help, but Oluomachukwu raised her hand, signalling to them that she had it under control. She then helped Ogo up by the arm and told the onlookers that she was going to help her to the clinic.

Ogo didn't realise it, but she had just helped and saved Oluomachukwu the stress of sitting down for three hours, frying springs rolls, samosa, meat on stick, chicken, *buns* and *puff-puff*, which the Corps members were not going to taste unless they paid 50 naira each.

As Oluomachukwu was leaving, she heard the female MC making an announcement to the Platoon Eight Corps members on Environmental duty, asking them to go and clean up the mess on the parade ground.

Oluomachukwu shook her head as she imagined who the unfortunate Corps member or rather Corps members from Platoon Eight would end up being.

Oluomachukwu got to the clinic, secretly hoping that she would see the cute doctor again. The one who could have called her, but never did. She remembered his name, it was Uchenna. She remembered everything about him, from the way he smiled, to the way he blinked, to the way he talked. She didn't see him, instead she saw Fadeke coming out of the clinic ward just next to the clinic. That was where she had been hiding or rather sleeping for the past couple of days.

Apparently corper-doctors, who were going to be on-call, were given rooms in the clinic ward. A Chief Medical Director — CMD — was constantly in the room. The title was given to the first corper-doctor to report to camp for registration. No one knew the current CMD, because he was always busy attending to the more serious cases, and sometimes he rode out of the camp with patients in the ambulance. This particular CMD had come to camp a day before registration, so there was no doubt he was going to be the first person present.

Out of curiosity, Oluomachukwu passed by the room after Fadeke left, while Ogo went into the clinic. Fadeke hadn't even noticed Oluomachukwu, she just walked away absentmindedly. Oluomachukwu looked inside the clinic ward and saw that the place looked quite good. There were about nine bunk beds, each covered with white or blue mosquito nets. The corper-doctors were well taken care of, she thought, even though the clinic ward was not really meant for them. There were only about three beds in the main clinic, so if more people were ill and needed to rest, they were taken to the clinic ward to sleep.

Oluomachukwu was going to meet with Nkiru much later and talk about Fadeke. If there was anyone that could get her information about what was happening in the clinic ward and what Fadeke was doing there, it was Nkiru.

There was no space in the main clinic. As usual it was overcrowded. Oluomachukwu remembered that there was a total of 90 medical practitioners — doctors, pharmacists and nurses alike, as the Camp Director had said, and all of them wanted to be in the clinic at the same time, just to escape going to the parade ground or being on duty. There was visibly nowhere for Oluomachukwu to sit or stand, so she went outside to wait for Ogo.

While she waited, she decided to call Okechukwu and have a talk with him. If she had any plans at all of finding a life partner in camp, it had gone down the drain, down the gutters that surrounded the volleyball court and the hostel. So instead of looking far, she decided to look close to home. She dialled Okechukwu's number and he picked up almost immediately.

"Oluoma, is everything okay?" he asked.

Oluomachukwu smiled. She smiled, glad that he always cared for her and wondered why she wanted to throw that away. "Everything is all right. I wasn't even expecting you to pick up the call, because I figured you would be at work."

"I work in an office, and not in a prison cell," he said and laughed. "So what's up?"

"Can you talk now?" Oluomachukwu asked.

"Sure, I'm on an hour break. I'm having lunch not too far from the office."

"Oh okay." Oluomachukwu hesitated. "I just had some things to discuss with you."

"Hmm, it has finally happened."

Oluomachukwu laughed. "What do you mean?"

"You have found love in camp, after I begged you not to. What happens to me now?"

Oluomachukwu was happy that Okechukwu brought it

up, that way she wouldn't sound too forward. She looked at her rubber trainers, as she said, "I haven't found love in camp, because I'm not searching. I want to make it work."

"Make what work?"

"Us."

There was utter silence. Only heavy breathing could be heard on both sides. Oluomachukwu looked up briefly and saw one guy from her platoon waving at her fervently. She ignored him and looked back at her rubber trainers.

"So what happened?" Okechukwu asked. "What made you say that all of a sudden?"

Oluomachukwu started to feel embarrassed and wished she hadn't said what she had said. But since it was too late, she wished the gutters would open up wider and swallow her instead.

"I've been doing a lot of thinking, so I felt it was time to make a decision and I've made one." She paused. She hadn't thought of a possibility. The possibility that maybe Okechukwu had given up on her and found someone else, so she added, "Unless, of course, you have already moved on to someone else."

Okechukwu laughed. "Don't be afraid, babe. I'm just surprised to hear you confess your love after all this while. I'm impressed."

He had a certain tone, and Oluomachukwu wasn't sure if it was that of mockery or amusement that she had finally succumbed. Either way she waited for him to continue talking. He paused a bit, then said, "How about we hang out this coming weekend, maybe on Friday or Saturday evening? I can take you back to camp the next day or on Sunday evening against Monday."

Oluomachukwu wished she could say "Yes," but she couldn't. It wasn't in her power despite what Idara had told her. "I don't think we are allowed to leave camp and come back in just like that because of the Ebola threat."

"Oh that's true. People have been calling you guys 'The Ebola Batch.'" Okechukwu laughed.

"They are not serious." Oluomachukwu also laughed. "It's Stream 2 that'll be 'The Ebola Batch, because I doubt they'll make it to camp."

"But seriously though, camp is almost over, can't they allow you leave for just two days?"

"I don't think so," Oluomachukwu replied. "I guess we will just have to count down until I come back or you come and pick me up."

"I guess so too."

There was another brief silence, and Ogo came out of the clinic at that instant holding a small bag that contained some medication. Oluomachukwu then said goodbye to Okechukwu and promised to call him back much later, and in the meantime, they were going to chat on WhatsApp. When she hung up, she turned to Ogo.

"What did they say is wrong with you?"

"I don't know what the doctor was talking about. She seemed to be more engrossed in one other guy that sat next to me."

Oluomachukwu pointed at the small paper bag. "So, what medication did they give to you?"

"Anti-malaria medication and vitamin C."

Oluomachukwu laughed, and they both walked away.

***

After the SAED activity, there was an NYSC lecture for one hour. Nobody knew exactly what topic had been prepared, but the Assistant Director for SAED came to speak about the SAED project group. They brought a discharged Corps member, Mubarak Tiamiyu, who was a former member of the SAED project team and who had developed the first ever NYSC Mobile App.

Everyone marvelled at him as he spoke about the app, how long it had taken him to build it, and how well it was doing so far. As he spoke, some people started to connect to the app store on their phones to look for the app. It was on all other platforms, but yet to be on iPhone. The app owner then assured iPhone users that it was going to be available to them in less than two weeks. Oluomachukwu wasn't affected by the information; she didn't use an iPhone, so she was able to look at the app in real time as Mubarak spoke.

When he was done, he advised the Corps members to make the most of their one-year, especially their CDS days, to achieve something meaningful, instead of doing nothing but complaining and wasting their time. Some people nodded as they digested the advice, while others hissed, rolled their eyes and grumbled as if they were tired of sitting on the hard ground and listening to him gloat about his achievement. After the word of advice, Mubarak thanked everyone, bowed his head, then left the parade ground.

After the lecture, there was a motivational talk, where some pastors and motivational speakers were invited to talk to the Corps members about life, its many challenges and how to overcome them.

They also talked about relationships with the opposite sex and self-preservation. The session lasted only an hour, but it seemed like three hours.

Oluomachukwu wished that they had sat under the canopy so that she would sleep. It wasn't that she was tired, but there seemed to be something about the lectures that made everybody fall asleep. Maybe it was the heat, even in the raining season; maybe it was the message that was being passed or maybe it was how the message was being passed and the voices of the speakers, she didn't know which. But she knew it had to be something, because it felt like sleeping dust had been spread around the camp.

In order not to fall asleep and make a fool of herself, she looked around the parade ground, observing everyone there. Some people had fallen asleep awkwardly with their heads dropping at intervals. Some of the camp officials and platoon instructors went round the parade ground, waking Corps members up, just like ushers normally did in churches. Some of them went back to sleep immediately after the officials walked away.

After a while, officials started asking Corps members who were caught sleeping to get up and stand at the back of the crowd, close to the walls. That way, they were not able to snooze again, and they felt like scapegoats because people turned around occasionally to look at them.

***

Lunchtime was right after the motivational talk, and Oluomachukwu went to Nwanyi Imo to eat with Ogo, and Nkiru met them there. All of them looked worn out, which was strange given that they weren't doing as much physical activities as they were sleeping.

As Nkiru dug into her heaped plate of rice, she shook her head, and said, "I'm tired of being in the Red Cross community."

Oluomachukwu and Ogo laughed.

"I thought you loved being on duty. What happened?" Oluomachukwu asked.

"I'm tired, that's what happened. I don't want to do anymore, please."

"It is by force oh. There's no going back for you." Ogo laughed. Oluomachukwu noticed that Ogo hadn't used her American accent in a while.

"Don't mind her," Oluomachukwu said. "She wanted to run away from the toilet cleaning duty, or rather, the punishment she got. She knows that if she leaves the Red Cross now, she will go back to her punishment."

Nkiru shook her head. "I'm sure that old witch has forgotten. I'll just be changing platoons like the last time, and I'll make sure I'm not caught this time."

There was a very brief silence. Oluomachukwu looked outside and watched people walk by. She saw a girl walking across the market with three guys, then remembered she had a job for Nkiru.

"That's true..." she said to Nkiru. "Guess who I saw today?"

"Who? Who? Who?" both Nkiru and Ogo asked, then Oluomachukwu remembered that Ogo hadn't been with her earlier on outside the clinic.

"I saw Fadeke, finally."

"What?" Nkiru exclaimed. "Wait, where?" Ogo asked, simultaneously.

"I saw her coming out of the clinic ward just beside the clinic and it looked like she had just woken up."

Before Oluomachukwu could say what it was that she wanted Nkiru to do for her, and why she had brought that information to the table, Nkiru spoke up.

"I'm on it," Nkiru stated. "I'll find out what she was doing there. There's always a small event there at night. I've been invited a couple of times, but I've never gone. Maybe I should."

Oluomachukwu was suddenly concerned. With what happened between Nkiru and Kayode, she didn't think that Nkiru should really be 'hanging out' to get any more information. "Do you actually have to attend the event or whatever it really is? Can't you just ask questions?"

"That's all I'll be doing, asking questions. You'll never see those medical people to ask any questions during the day. But at night, they would be happier, because there's always enough to drink there."

Oluomachukwu wanted to ask how she knew and if she had attended any of such events before. And if yes, she would have wanted to ask if she had seen any cute doctor by the name Uchenna, but she realised that she had just professed her love and allegiance to Okechukwu. "Just don't drink too much and forget your mission," she finally said.

"I won't. Let me even utilise my privileges of being in the Red Cross as access to the event for now until I finally sign out." Nkiru smiled and forced a spoon full of rice and plantain into her mouth and chewed it slowly.

***

Drills, man-o-war and martial arts training took place the same time as they always did each day. Oluomachukwu didn't participate in any, neither did Nkiru and Ogo. Nkiru went back to her Red Cross duty and Ogo went back to the hostel. Oluomachukwu escorted Ogo there, but the officials at the gate refused to let her enter, even after she told them she wasn't feeling too well and showed them her medication. It was just anti-malaria medication and vitamin C, so it wasn't real medication. Everyone was given that whether they were ill or not. It was when she mentioned that she was the girl who vomited, that they allowed her enter. Oluomachukwu made a mental note to nickname her 'Vomiting Corper,' because that was the gate code she had used to get into the hostel.

The officials didn't allow Oluomachukwu enter. She wasn't surprised and she didn't care. She wanted to go and watch her platoon members rehearse for the dance contest, check if the drama group had finally gotten a story and see how the representative for the Big, Bold and Beautiful contest was doing, anyway.

The dance group members were dancing away and looking good. Both Auntie Vera and Sister Mary were there, nodding their heads approvingly at what they were seeing. One of the guys in the drumming team went to whisper something into Auntie Vera's ear. She laughed and beat him on his back, but in a joking way. Sister Mary bent her head towards Auntie Vera and asked her what the boy had said, and she said the boy told her that he wanted to marry one of the girls in the dance group.

Oluomachukwu didn't know whose name the boy had mentioned, but she had a feeling that it was one of the girls from 'Two,' because they were both in front and they danced very well.

From there, Oluomachukwu moved to see the drama group. They had finally figured out a story that seemed to be interesting. Both Auntie Vera and Sister Mary also moved there to watch their first rehearsal and to check if it was in line with the NYSC requirements. It was, so they helped them develop the story, and the representative started giving everyone their lines. She didn't have the time to start writing a script. She gave everyone their role, then told them how and when they would appear, so it was left to them to write their own script.

With that done, Sister Mary went to help the Big, Bold and Beautiful contestant get ready. She checked if the girl had all the required outfits, and if she knew a lot about the NYSC scheme, because there was going to be a 'Question and Answer' session, and if she knew all the important names. Sister Mary vetted her and gave her a pass mark. The only thing left was the contest itself.

***

Oluomachukwu didn't know how she had managed to miss the whole BBB contest. She had stopped by at *mami* market with Nkiru and Ogo for just a few drinks and to buy bottled water, then got carried away with eating and drinking. They had seen Rasheed, the same guy who had given them grief for sitting at his table and buying drinks from someone else. Naturally, they didn't talk to him. Instead, they went to another table, where a young girl was standing close to. She seemed calm and said it was her auntie that owned the table, so Oluomachukwu and her friends camped there.

Tracker and some of his friends had tracked them down there, and he was asking Oluomachukwu why she never checked his messages on WhatsApp. She had no excuse, obviously, when the truth was that she wasn't interested in anyone again. In fact, the thought alone made her think of Okechukwu and think it was time for her to go back to the hostel and either talk or chat with him.

It was when she was going back to the hostel that she heard people screaming and clapping under the big canopy at the end of the parade ground. She then remembered that the competition was going on and she immediately felt bad, because she wanted to show some support.

"What is going on there?" Nkiru asked. She was in the camp, but it didn't feel like she really was.

"It's the Big, Bold and Beautiful competition, actually," Oluomachukwu said. "I totally forgot it was for tonight. Let's go and see what's happening real quick ."

Nkiru said "Okay" and followed her. Ogo didn't say anything, but she followed. She was glued to her phone, chatting away, not minding what Oluomachukwu or Nkiru were saying, but she still followed.

When they got there, they saw only three contestants on the stage, so it was clear that the judges were already pronouncing the winners. Oluomachukwu wanted to get up close, but it was difficult because almost the whole camp was there, watching. Well, the people who weren't in *mami* market drinking, were there, watching.

Oluomachukwu and her friends climbed chairs so that they could get a clearer view even from afar. It paid off because they had a better view. By the time they climbed up, the judges had already picked the second runner up, so it was Platoon Seven contestant and someone else left on the stage. Oluomachukwu didn't know what platoon the other girl represented, but she was really big. ... way bigger than the one for Platoon Seven. In fact, she was twice the size of the Platoon Seven contestant, so it was a miracle that the Platoon Seven contestant even got up to the last two slots.

The suspense didn't last that long before the judges pronounced the other girl winner, and the Platoon Seven contestant, the first runner up. Oluomachukwu was very impressed either way. She figured that both girls were bold and beautiful, but only one was really big.

Before they went back to the hostel, Oluomachukwu went behind the stage to congratulate the Platoon Seven contestant. The girl was very happy and smiled all through, proud that she had agreed to contest and that she had gone that far. She was given a microwave oven, which one guy helped her carry to the hostel gate.

Oluomachukwu re-joined Nkiru and Ogo, and then they went to the hostel together. Nkiru didn't stop talking about everything she had witnessed that day, and Ogo didn't get off her phone.

The only thing that was on Oluomachukwu's mind was Okechukwu. She couldn't wait to enter in side her duvet cover and start talking with him. And that was exactly what she did. At the end of the call and before she went to bed, she sent him a text message. "I love you."

CHAPTER FOURTEEN: DAY TEN

Thursday, 14 th August 2014

When Oluomachukwu woke up, she used her hand to feel around her bed for her bottle of water, and when she found it, she noticed that almost half of it was gone. She wasn't really sure of how much of the water she had taken down the previous night after she finished speaking with Okechukwu, but she knew it wasn't that much. She had a feeling that someone else was drinking her water, so she made a mental note to hide her bottles of water and another note to buy some more water after the morning drill.

Before she got out of her bed, she checked her phone to know if Okechukwu had replied to the last text message she sent to him after their call. He had. He told her that he loved her too, and that he couldn't wait to see her. He said he was also counting down to the end of camp so that they could be together. Oluomachukwu smiled, although she couldn't understand where the butterflies in her belly were coming from. A few days ago she hadn't considered him in that way and all of a sudden, she was glued to her phone.

At the same time, Okechukwu hadn't initiated any of the text messages, and every message he replied to her had either 'too,' 'as well,' or 'also' in it — I love you too, I miss you too, I can't wait to see you as well, I'm also happy that we will make this work. Oluomachukwu felt that she was the one pushing him and wondered if he was genuinely in love with her, or if he was just in love with the idea of being with her. As she thought about it, wondering if she should be worried, images of them together in the future, with kids, crossed her mind and it took all doubts away.

"Why is this one smiling like a chicken?" Nkiru asked, then approached Oluomachukwu's bed, pushed her legs aside and sat down at the foot of the bed. "Please, who is the man? Who is this man making you grin like this?"

"What do you mean?" Oluomachukwu blushed, but it obviously wasn't noticeable on her cheeks.

"What else would be making you smile before dawn? And it's not even 5:00am yet." Nkiru hissed, then leaned forward and slapped Ogo's buttocks. "My friend, wake up. *Sleep-sleep.*"

"Oh-ohh," Ogo protested and turned around. "What's wrong with you *nau*? Don't you know that I'm not feeling well?"

"Don't worry, the morning drill will make you feel well and strong." Oluomachukwu laughed.

Ogo got up, grumbling. She was indeed feeling well. Her throwing up was a one-time thing, probably because she had run down eight flights of stairs and ran to the parade ground right after eating. They then decided to go and have their baths at the same time, so that they would go down to the parade ground together. It worked well for Oluomachukwu, because she didn't want to see 'Fucking Space' again, at least not alone, and endure watching her wash just one underwear for eons. While they got ready to go to the bathroom, they started talking about everything, including the desperate guys in camp, then they diverted to the vomiting incident that happened and laughed about it. Oluomachukwu remembered the name she had given to Ogo, 'Vomiting Corper,' and was teasing her with it, then they talked about the unlucky person that had to clean up the mess.

Oghene woke up at that instant and hissed. It was clear that the laughing and early morning gist was disturbing her. "Do you girls not know when to shut up and when to talk? *Ehn*? Do you not know?" she asked.

All three of them kept their mouths shut, shocked. Even the other girls in the room, who had either started singing praise and worship hymns, or talking to each other also kept quiet, shocked.

"Early in the morning, you are already running your dirty mouths. Please, shut up. Shut up, and let us hear something else like the sound of the bugle when it is finally played this morning."

She had pronounced it as 'borgule' and Oluomachukwu almost laughed, but she didn't. That was an indirect insult, though, but none of them reacted or replied. Some other girls who were awake started to giggle. Some laughed out loud. It wasn't sure if they were laughing at the indirect insult or the pronunciation of 'borgule.' Oluomachukwu felt that it had to be the former.

One of the girls that laughed and was probably trying to understand Oghene's sudden rage sat up, and asked her, "Oghene, did you see any of them in your dream?"

"God forbid bad thing." Oghene raised her shoulders high and snapped her fingers on both hands, taking it over her head to demonstrate that God should really forbid it. "It would have been a nightmare."

The girl laughed even more. "So what is it?"

"Can you imagine what they are saying? So one of them vomited on the parade ground and they are laughing about it and also laughing at the person that cleaned it, calling the person an unfortunate person. Can you imagine?"

Oluomachukwu, Ogo and Nkiru scrunched their faces, and it was quite evident to them that either Oghene knew who the unfortunate Platoon Eight Corps member was or she was *the* unfortunate Platoon Eight Corps member that cleaned up the mess on the parade ground, and she was very upset about it.

"But how is it paining you *nau*?" the girl went ahead to ask Oghene again.

"Because I had to clean up the mess with someone in my platoon. My platoon was on duty and I had picked the Environmental duty just so that I wouldn't clean up after anyone. I was so angry as I cleaned it up, but then I started to feel sorry for the person, because the person must have been genuinely ill. But now they are laughing at me. They are laughing at their mothers."

With that, the girl asking all the questions kept quiet. Oluomachukwu, Ogo and Nkiru had been quiet the whole time. They then picked up their bath things and left the room quietly, and as they left, they heard Oghene use her favourite line again.

"I can't suffer here. I can't suffer for anybody."

Oluomachukwu wondered why Oghene still used that line, since she had stolen the Camp Commandant's contact information from her.

***

The morning exercise went as usual. After the Morning Prayer, the National Anthem, the NYSC Anthem and the Meditation, Platoon Nine members left the parade ground and filed away towards the volleyball court to organise themselves for their duties. When they left, the physical activities went on and by 6:00am, the bugle blower came to play the national anthem as the flag went up, and people remained still as it was played.

As usual, the anthem sounded nothing like the national anthem, only some parts did. Each day, just a little part sounded like the anthem, but before the anthem got to the end, it sounded different again.

After the morning drill, Corps members were dismissed for Bath and Breakfast. It was *akara* and *akamu* again, and

TWENTY-ONE DAYS

Oluomachukwu wondered why the camp kitchen would want to serve the same thing two days in a row. But this time she decided to eat it... just for eating sake. She had no reason for eating the food and no reason for not eating it. She just decided to eat it, hoping that it wouldn't be bad, as her friends had told her from the previous day that it had been good, quite edible.

Just as she had believed, the *akara* was very cold and tasteless. It lacked spices and it felt like the beans had been ground with fewer beans and plenty of water before being dumped into hot oil to fry. The *akamu*, on the other hand, wasn't sweet enough, because they hadn't added enough sugar, and it had large lumps in it that made it irritating to drink comfortably. The lumps were uncooked bits of the *akamu* paste, and after just a few spoons, Oluomachukwu wrapped it up. She was done with breakfast. She gave the remaining *akara* to Ogo, who wanted it, and poured the *akamu* away. Although she hadn't eaten a lot, she still took two pills of the anti-malaria medication and drank enough water to hold it down. It was going to be the final day for the medication and she was happy that she didn't have to eat every single morning anymore.

After Bath and Breakfast, the bugle call was made for everyone to come out to the parade ground. The bugle call was supported by the OBS speaker who kept saying that everyone should report to the parade ground immediately. If anyone wasn't on the parade ground, they were wrong. At a point, Corps members started mimicking whoever the speaker was and mouthing what he or she was saying as the person said it. It was difficult to tell if that particular person was male or female.

The call was for the SAED group meeting, and Corps members were meant to report to their various groups for the training. Oluomachukwu contemplated which group to go to, then ended up going to the beads making group, so that she would sit behind and chat with Ogo. Rectangular shaped SAED ID cards were shared on that day. It had

'SAED NYSC' boldly printed on it, with the full meaning written just below it. There was a white space for passport picture, and close to it was 'Participant' written in bold and green colour.

Oluomachukwu flipped the card over and it had some slots to fill in some information such as: skill area, name of facilitator, and name and State code of participant. There was also a table on the card that had the number of days attended, the signature of the facilitator, the dates attended and the facilitator's remark. Oluomachukwu did not know how her card was going to be signed, since she had been going from one SAED group to another. A facilitator had to confirm that the Corps member was active to be able to sign the card.

At the bottom of the card read 'SAED: Corps Member Creating Wealth.' Oluomachukwu looked at the beads that were being made in front of her and wondered how she would create wealth with them. It was probably possible to create wealth with them, but it just wasn't for her, neither was making small chops. She was going to find her own SAED group that would help her create wealth, whether it was in camp or outside camp.

It had also been announced that the NYSC office was going to collect the card at the end of the service year, and it was going to count towards being discharged and given the NYSC certificate. Oluomachukwu didn't know if it was true, but that information alone almost gave her a heart twist.

For some people, the SAED could serve as their CDS group, and a facilitator would be able to recommend them for the certificate if they were very active. Oluomachukwu didn't know what to do. Her only option was to become friendly with a facilitator, anyone at all, preferably a man, if they were going to sign her card without any question. She and Ogo decided to go round the SAED groups, and the first facilitator that looked her in the eye and smiled back at her when she smiled, was going to sign her card.

TWENTY-ONE DAYS

It didn't take her long to accomplish her mission. She passed by a SAED group with just a few people gathered around two tables and three young facilitators. All three of them looked at her and when she smiled, they smiled back. She went and sat down there with Ogo, not one little bit interested at first, but they were eventually interested in the SAED group and ended up staying till the end. Their cards were signed for three days until the present day.

After the SAED activity, there was a NIM/Red Cross lecture and everybody reported to the parade ground and sat on the floor, while the invited speaker walked around.

Oluomachukwu had contemplated going to watch her platoon's dance and drama groups rehearse, but decided to stay back for the lecture, so that she could sleep. Had she known that the lecture wouldn't hold under the canopy, but on the floor, she would have easily slid away through the back of the hostel, and gone to watch the rehearsals.

She sat down at the back with Ogo, who was not in her platoon and they hoped that neither Auntie Vera nor Sister Mary would show up out of nowhere and punish Ogo. Auntie Vera had seized the cap of one girl who had come to Platoon Seven uninvited, probably to gossip. The girl had a friend in Platoon Seven and enjoyed talking with her, but Auntie Vera had warned her a few times not to return to Platoon Seven, but she did, and that was when Auntie Vera seized her cap. Somehow, Auntie Vera had managed to memorise almost all the faces of Platoon Seven Corps members, even though she hardly spent time with them.

Oluomachukwu endured the lecture, which she liked eventually. In fact, she felt that if she gave most of the lectures a chance, she would actually enjoy them and have a complete and nice package in the camp... not just the fun part, but also the didactic part.

During the lecture, she looked at Nkiru from time to time, who stood like a bodyguard, flanking the Red Cross speaker. Nkiru always tried not to laugh whenever she crossed glances with either Oluomachukwu or Ogo.

Occasionally, the Red Cross team would walk around and check that everyone was okay, then walk back to the centre of the parade ground and offer some support to the invited speaker if she needed to demonstrate some safety and security tips.

Even though it was a NIM and Red Cross lecture — the NIM being the Nigerian Institute of Management — there was more Red Cross talk than NIM talk. In fact, the only thing the NIM did was to hand out flyers, which contained all the necessary information needed about their institute. There was also a contact phone number and an email address where Corps members could send all their questions and enquiries. Some Corps members used the flyers as sit-mats and sat on them, while others, who were already sitting on other flyers, booklets, newspapers and small towels, proceeded to read the contents of the NIM flyer.

Right after the NIM and Red Cross lecture, there was a programme on 'Collaborating Partners.' Oluomachukwu didn't know what it meant, and as usual, she didn't give it a try to know what it was about. She figured that it might be a session to introduce all NYSC partners or discuss various means of becoming an NYSC partner. Neither interested her at the moment, but she had a feeling that sometime in the future, both might. She shrugged and concluded that when she got to the bridge eventually, she would cross it.

Oluomachukwu snuck to the back of the hostel, using toilet-break as an excuse. She did want to use the toilet, but the security officers wouldn't have let her enter the hostel, either way. They would have directed her to the mobile toilets, the red mobile toilets that looked like UK telephone booths. The toilets stank and didn't have any water in them, so it was a no-go area for Oluomachukwu. Luckily for her, she went to the clinic ward, and there was a toilet just beside it, which she used. She then went to meet her platoon members as they rehearsed.

The dance group had already mastered their routines.

When the girls were done rehearsing, they went to watch the drama group. While they were watching the rehearsal, someone came to them and tried to persuade them to join the volleyball team. There were already six players, but the officials required at least nine girls in total — six on the first team with three substitutes. The self-appointed coach started begging everyone he saw to join them. He had even mistakenly asked a girl in Platoon Five to join the team, before she said that she was already in her own platoon's team.

The drama group seemed to have put their hearts into the rehearsal and it looked pretty good already. There were just a few forgotten lines, actions and scenes, but they kept repeating it. Oluomachukwu watched them rehearse for the whole one-hour, and each time, they got better. The competition was in the evening, so they had every reason to keep rehearsing until they were perfect.

When the bugle sounded, it was time for Lunch and Siesta, and at the same time, there was an announcement. The person at the OBS asked everyone to go to the parade ground and receive their second allowance. It was a local transport allowance of 1,000 naira, which was also known as Bicycle allowance. While the first allowance was to bring Corps members from out of State to Lagos State, the second one was to bring them from their points of entry into Lagos State to the Orientation Camp, and like the last time, locally-trained Corps members were asked to bring their university ID cards and foreign-trained students were expected to present their international passports.

Corps members appeared to be interested and pleased with the news, and like white ants, they rushed to collect their own share. They presented their student ID cards and international passports respectively, and then signed off collection of the allowance. Some went straight to *mami* market to spend the money as it came in. Maybe not some of them, but all of them. Oluomachukwu used 500 naira to buy top-up card for her phone and used the change to buy lunch in *mami* market. Instead of eating in Nwanyi Imo again, she and her friends decided to try out the Calabar Kitchen. They served all sorts of soups and dishes, but Oluomachukwu ate the usual *jollof* rice, plantain and small pieces of beef, and this time, she added *moimoi*, while Ogo and Nkiru ate pounded yam, vegetable soup and beef.

***

After having their heavy lunch, all three girls retired to the room to rest before the bugle call for evening drills and activities. Time always seemed very short, because barely a few minutes after the bugle sounded, it was time for them to go to the parade ground again. Nkiru did not go. She claimed to be tired since she was always on duty, and being always on duty meant that she had to stand most of the time when people were seated. It was going to be the same thing during the evening drills, martial arts and man-o-war activities, and she wasn't feeling up to it. She threatened to leave the community again and Oluomachukwu reminded her to leave only after she had gotten information about Fadeke — Fadeke still hadn't come back to the room.

Oluomachukwu went to watch the rehearsals again, and admitted that the drama group had greatly improved since the last time. In fact, she was impressed with the storyline. The dance group were already perfect with their routine and didn't feel the need to continue rehearsing and tiring themselves. They did a lot of bending, jumping, twisting, rolling and shaking, and doing it repeatedly was sure to wear them out. Oluomachukwu noticed that Ekene had joined both the dance and drama groups. It wasn't sure exactly what day she had joined them, but she blended in perfectly. It had to be because, like many others, she spent hours watching the rehearsals.

During the time Oluomachukwu watched the drama rehearsal, other sport competitions were going on — finals for athletics, first round matches for intellectual games like chess, Ludo, table soccer, and one football match between two other platoons. Platoon Seven was going to play their volleyball match after the dance contest and the volleyball coach was glad. He wasn't going to get any excuses from the dancers again that they had to rehearse. He begged them however to join the training later that evening, and the ones who weren't already worn out agreed.

After the drills, man-o-war and martial arts training, the time for Games and Sports came, and all the competitions continued in that light. Oluomachukwu should have gone to watch at least one of the games, but she didn't. As she was about to go back to the hostel to beg the gate officers to let her go in, she saw Segun, or was it Sola? She couldn't remember his name, but it was the young guy she had seen in church wearing mufti, whom she thought was an NYSC official. Only that this time, he was dressed in white shirt and shorts, and he had the same temporary badge that everyone had, with their four digit code written on it. He smiled at her and there was a certain depth in his eyes, one that Oluomachukwu couldn't explain. She didn't know if she should say hello to him, or just pretend that she didn't know who he was and walk away. She did the latter.

"Oluoma," he called.

Oluomachukwu paused, frozen. If she had just ignored him and continued walking, the guy would have thought that 'Oluoma' wasn't her name. And at the same time, she didn't remember telling him her name the last time they talked. She stared at him.

"Don't you remember me? I'm Segun. We met at the church."

Oluomachukwu nodded twice. Of course his name was Segun, she thought. "So you remembered my name?" She knew full well that she hadn't told him her name.

Segun laughed, but Oluomachukwu could tell that the laugh wasn't genuine. It was more of a mocking laugh. "Of course, I remembered your name. Only that it wasn't you that told me. I saw someone who happens to know you and I got your name off the person."

Oluomachukwu made a mental note to bite off Nkiru's head when she saw her much later.

"Also," Segun said, making Oluomachukwu come back to reality. "You promised to give me your number the next time we see."

Oluomachukwu did not need to be reminded of that promise. Either way, she was not going to honour it. She started to mumble some words that translated to, "I don't want to give you my number."

"So why did you now say you would give it to me the next time we see?"

Oluomachukwu didn't comprehend the young man's tenacity for the phone number of a girl who clearly didn't want to give it to him. "Yes, I said that, but you didn't say 'Okay.' You simply hissed and went your way."

Segun did not think her response was worth giving a reply to. He hissed again, then walked away, saying, "*Abeg*, eat your number. I don't want it. There are other finer girls in camp." As he walked away, Oluomachukwu shook her head and laughed.

Luckily for her and unluckily for Nkiru, she saw Nkiru coming out of the clinic and was prepared to orally attack her for telling Segun her name. Nkiru looked like she was going to pass out. She was fanning herself with her hand. There was no power in the camp, the clinic was overly packed as usual, and there was hardly any air to breathe in there. She saw Oluomachukwu and smiled, but got a raised eyebrow from Oluomachukwu.

"What?" Nkiru asked, defensively. She opened up her mouth and sucked up pockets of air and a fly almost found its way into her mouth before she closed it immediately. "What is it?"

"Why did you tell Segun or whatever his name is, my name? I hope you didn't give him my number too, because he didn't pester me for it even after I promised him that I would give it to him the next time we saw."

"Wait, I'm sorry, who is that?" Nkiru looked confused, whether it was genuine or not, it was not certain, but an unusual smile cut across her lips, as though she was trying to figure out who the Segun was.

"So now you are pretending like you don't know him right? The same guy you were with on the first Sunday of camp."

Nkiru thought briefly, and said, "Oh." She then hissed. "I haven't seen that desperate soul or spoken to him since Sunday. I gave him my number and he started calling me endlessly. I ignored all his phone calls and he didn't get the message until I sent him a text message and asked him not to call me again. He kept asking me out and was so rude and arrogant about it, asking me if I wanted him or not. So it couldn't have been me that told him your name, sorry."

"So how did he get to know it? He said someone who knew me told him."

"It might be that guy they call Shoki. The all-time Shoki dancer."

Oluomachukwu smiled. "Oh, I know him, but I have never spoken to him before. In fact, he hardly ever says anything to anyone, he just drinks and dances Shoki to every song. I doubt he knows my name."

"Let me think." Nkiru paused for a little bit. "Maybe it might be Tracker. I think they are in the same platoon."

"Please, riddle me this. Why does it seem like they are in a contest? They all know one another and they are all asking the same chain of girls out. It's just as if one says 'That girl did not agree to date me, maybe you should try your luck with her, while I go for her friend or another random girl."

Nkiru laughed. "It's no riddle, neither is it a contest. I have told you before that they are all desperate. Everyone came to this camp for a reason. Some for the experience, some to look for wives or girlfriends, some for quick flings and to count the number of cheap flings they can have in here. You know, all sorts of rubbish. My dear, if you have come to this camp looking for the one you will walk down the aisle with, then you are fishing in the wrong river."

Oluomachukwu shrugged. If Nkiru had said that to her earlier, it would have hurt her a lot, but now that she was trying to work something out with Okechukwu, camp guys didn't matter anymore to her. And after a brief silence, she asked the question that she had been meaning to ask all along. "Anyway, so what's up with Fadeke? Any news?"

Nkiru shut her eyes halfway and shook her head. "Not yet, but I am going for the small get-together, or is it party, in the clinic ward tonight. I will see what I can get out of them."

"Okay. Let's have dinner early today so that we can be early for the drama competition and get good seats."

"I'll meet you at the camp market entrance when they blow the trumpet."

Oluomachukwu shook her head and wondered when Nkiru would stop saying 'trumpet.' "Okay." She diverted to go towards the hostel, while Nkiru made to go towards the parade ground, but then Nkiru called her back.

"Oluoma, hold on."

Oluomachukwu turned around.

"Do you want to come for the party at the clinic ward? We can go together after the drama competition."

Oluomachukwu thought about it for a second, then gave a half nod-half headshake. "I will think about it."

"Okay, then. See you later."

***

Oluomachukwu didn't eat proper food in *mami* market. She was glad that by the time she got to there, the *Mallams* who sold *suya* by the left side of the market had already set up, so she bought enough beef to last her all night. She contemplated buying a soft drink too, but ended up buying a small bottle of Orijin. She also bought a bottle of water and took it up to the room to keep for the night. Alcohol

TWENTY-ONE DAYS

always made her very thirsty, so she needed to keep water around her all the time to quench the thirst.

The drama competition was somewhat disorganised to Oluomachukwu because the organising committee refused to allow the use of microphones. Only those in front could really hear what the actors were talking about, those at the back could see only lips moving and hear the songs that were being played by the camp DJ, coupled with the ones that were being played in *mami* market. In fact, it was more of noise than music. Oluomachukwu and her friends sat in front, so they didn't have any problems with hearing.

Each platoon came out to present, beginning from Platoon One to Platoon Ten. And one after the other, they did the same storyline. The only difference was the amount of actors in each play, the costumes, the acts and scenes, and the dialogue. It got very boring when it got to the fifth platoon.

In their story, there was always a community where a parent, always the father, didn't want one of his children, always a daughter, to get adequate education, either high school level or undergraduate level. The Corps members would visit the community and try to convince the parent to allow his daughter to go to school and learn, so that she would come back to develop their community. It went in line with the saying about educating a girl translating to educating a nation. Sometimes, they would use a Hausa girl for the role of the daughter who wasn't allowed to further her education, and alternatively, they would use an Igbo girl, but the storyline was the same.

Sometimes in the storyline, in order to influence the father, the Corps members always used the mother by convincing her into believing that her daughter was equal to her son, and that her daughter was capable of doing something with her life other than just cooking, cleaning, then becoming a wife to someone. Daughters could also bring positive changes to the community.

The only platoon that had a different and interesting

storyline was Platoon Seven. It was like a breath of fresh air to everyone because it was different. In their own story, Corps members had been posted to a community where there was no power and water. It was always very hot and Corps members had to always go to the stream to fetch water. Corps members identified a need and sought out a solution for it. So together with their Local Government Inspector — LGI, the Camp Director and the Lagos State Coordinator, the Corps members managed to convince the elders and residents of the community of the need to build a transformer in the community for power and also sink a borehole for clean and constant water supply.

In the presentation, the roles of the Camp Director and the State Coordinator were perfectly mimicked like the real ones, so much that people laughed at the genius in finding perfect matches. It was a fun story, but one of the actors took it seriously... way too seriously. He played the role of an elder, and was always yelling. He forgot one of his lines and walked off the stage, only for him to bring the elders and residents back for another unscripted awkward scene.

He also went ahead to mock the Nigerian government, and made a very silly joke about the Camp Commandant, shocking everyone. The joke was so disrespectful and was perceived as a direct insult to the Camp Commandant. In fact, it was so unexpected that silence swept through the air for a few seconds, then murmurings started to erupt everywhere.

Oluomachukwu was so disappointed. Even Ogo who wasn't in her platoon was asking what had happened and why the guy had insulted the Camp Commandant. She asked if it was really part of the story and if the Platoon Instructor had approved it and Oluomachukwu said "No." The guy had modified the lines all by himself.

Oluomachukwu looked at the faces of Auntie Vera and Sister Mary, and they were embarrassed. They sat in silence waiting for the verdict, as they knew what was coming.

After that play, the Head of the Socials Committee, a

camp official, came out to make an announcement. She used a microphone, so that everyone would hear. It wasn't one bit surprising that she condemned what the boy had said and urged Corps members to be careful with their use of words, and platoon instructors to be more attentive. It wasn't also surprising that Platoon Seven took the last place in the competition. That one mistake... the one silly unscripted joke turned their unique story into a disaster and Platoon Seven never won any socials competition in the camp from that evening onwards.

C. M. OKONKWO

CHAPTER FIFTEEN: DAY ELEVEN

Friday, 15 th August 2014
Oluomachukwu woke up thinking about what had happened the night before. She didn't even know why she was thinking about it. Whether her platoon won the competition or not, it wasn't her problem. Maybe it was the fact that her platoon member openly insulted the Camp Commandant — someone she had met before and talked to. Maybe it was the insult she was thinking about, and not the last position.

She remembered speaking with Okechukwu on the phone, then exchanging the photos she had taken inside her duvet cover with him. Okechukwu had also sent photos of himself working out and another one of himself about to take a shower. He had a black towel that hung loosely around his waist. She had smiled when she saw it, and unfortunately, she wasn't able to send him the same type of photos.

If she wanted to match the photos, she would have had to send him photos of herself doing the early morning drills in white shirt and shorts, then another one when she was about to take her bath in the shared bathroom with a print wrapper tied around her breasts. It wasn't a sexy image, so she just took a photo of herself inside the duvet cover, wearing a seductive smile. He liked the smile and told her to always keep smiling. They spoke for some more time, then diverted to chatting on WhatsApp before she eventually slept off.

Oluomachukwu felt around her bedside for her bottle of water from the previous night. She didn't remember to hydrate enough before sleeping off, especially as she had drank alcohol, so it was only natural that she woke up with an extremely dry throat and sounded croaky when she tried to speak to herself. She found the bottle and lifted it up, and it came up to her easily. It was strange, especially as she had just bought it. It was when she looked at it that she realised that the water had gone down almost half.

She sat up immediately, wanting to complain to Nkiru, but she didn't see Nkiru on her bed. She looked to her left side for Ogo, and Ogo wasn't there either. It couldn't have been rapture, she thought. The camp couldn't have already come to an end, or maybe it was still night and her friends were not yet back. She felt under her wrapped cloth-pillow for her phone, and as usual, there were other phones by it. Very angry, she pushed everything to the floor, not even minding if they scratched in the process.

She looked at her phone and saw that it was 4:13am. It was indeed morning, which meant that her friends could have already gone to have their baths. She looked under Nkiru's bed and her bucket was there, with water so full it was almost dripping. Just then, she noticed that there was a text message on her phone. It was from Nkiru and it had come in the night before. She opened it.

"Babe, you slept off after your phone call and didn't wake up even after trying to wake you up on several attempts. I went for the party in the clinic ward. So I will give you the gist later. Nkiru."

"Oh," Oluomachukwu croaked to herself. She then took a few gulps of her water, but didn't finish it. As she drank it, she eyed the rest of the girls in the room, wondering which of them was the water thief.

TWENTY-ONE DAYS

There was another text message that came in from Nkiru about one and a half hours after the first one came in.

"*Oh wow. You would not believe what I found out about Fadeke. This one is very hot. I will give you the story much later. Nkiru.*"

Oluomachukwu knew that she could have waited, but instead she replied to Nkiru's text message immediately. "*Please, what did you hear and when are you coming back? Or don't you want to come back again? I can't wait. Spill now, now, now. Oluoma.*"

A few seconds after Oluomachukwu hit Send on the message, and when she was sure that the message had been sent, she heard a beep by her bed side, as if she had sent the message to one of the phones she had pushed to the floor. She moved up quickly and checked the phones, then saw the light on one of them was just going off. She picked it up, and saw the message she had just sent on the screen. It was Nkiru's phone. She cleaned the phone and put it on her bed. It had privileges because it was Nkiru's phone.

Oluomachukwu wondered why Nkiru's phone was in the room, and as she was about to get up, the door opened and Nkiru walked in, her towel tied around her body and bucket in hand. Oluomachukwu's bucket actually. She smiled when she saw Oluomachukwu and went to sit on her bed.

"Rise and shine." Nkiru sounded excited. "You are finally awake."

"I just sent you a text and your phone beeped in the room." Oluomachukwu laughed.

"Oh, I hope you don't mind, I left my phone on your..." Nkiru paused and darted her eyes towards the wrapped cloth-pillow, and didn't see any phones at all. "Where's my phone?"

"It's under my wrapped cloth-pillow," Oluomachukwu replied.

"Where are the other phones? There were more than five phones when I plugged mine in."

"I pushed them down," Oluomachukwu whispered. "It's irritating."

Nkiru giggled. "Oh, sorry, I used your bucket. I soaked some things in my own, so I had to use yours."

Oluomachukwu glanced at Nkiru's bucket again. "No wonder it looks so full. I should even do my laundry too. I'll go to the laundry stall today. I'm tired of washing with my hands and I want to even see what that back area looks like."

"The famous back area," Nkiru complemented, and they both laughed.

Oluomachukwu nodded towards Ogo's bed. "Did you leave her in the bathroom? I want to quickly go and have my bath before the place gets too rowdy."

"Hmm. It's already getting crowded, so I suggest you go now, unless you want to take your bath much later. And by the way, Ogo followed me to the clinic ward party and didn't come back with me."

Oluomachukwu's eyes popped open. "She slept there?"

"That's if they even slept. The party was still on when I left about an hour ago, but she is still there."

"Okay, you'll give me her gist later, and that of Fadeke. I cannot wait for Fadeke's gist."

"Me neither. I can't wait to tell you Fadeke's gist... she's pregnant."

***

Oluomachukwu did not have her bath before going to the parade ground, but at least she brushed her teeth. After the two-word revelation she had heard from Nkiru, there was no way she could go and take her bath without getting the full gist. In fact, she didn't want to go to the parade ground anymore until the female soldiers came and chased her out, but they didn't chase Nkiru out.

TWENTY-ONE DAYS

Nkiru had started with Fadeke's gist — Fadeke was pregnant. She had gotten pregnant in camp, but it was still uncertain who was responsible. Nkiru could have gotten a name from one of the doctors, but Fadeke claimed that she didn't know who was responsible. She had spent the first few hours after receiving the news crying. She cried so much that she fell sick and said she wanted to stay in the clinic ward.

And even during her short stay in the clinic ward, she tried to seduce one of the doctors and lure him to bed. The corper-doctor would have probably yielded if Fadeke weren't pregnant. But it looked like Fadeke was trying to pin her pregnancy on someone and no one wanted to be that someone. Oluomachukwu thought the gist was quite interesting, but not knowing whom the father was put the gist on standby. She diverted to Ogo's own gist, because it sounded more exciting.

Nkiru had described the party so vividly. It felt like the day had just started by 11:00pm in the ward. Some of the corper-doctors were already drunk and some of them were staggering around, intoxicated. When Nkiru and Ogo got there, some of the corper-doctors cornered them, and one would think that the doctors hadn't seen or been with girls before.

One of the drunken doctors asked both Nkiru and Ogo for their numbers and promised to call them both later. They were amused and gave him their numbers knowing full well that he might be typing the wrong thing and that he was probably too drunk to remember anything the next day. He then went along to kiss both of them on the back of their hands, then staggered away, holding half a bottle of Hennessey. Nkiru said she was shocked and wondered how they had managed to smuggle a bottle, if not bottles of alcohol inside the clinic ward.

So as Nkiru and Ogo were standing there awkwardly, obviously feeling out of place, the CMD walked into the room, shocked to see two strange girls. Well, one strange girl, because when he looked again carefully, he recognised Nkiru. He then walked up and said hello to both of them and didn't take his eyes off Ogo. Ogo, too, didn't take her eyes off him. His badge had a bold 'CMD' written on it, then a four-digit code number. He was in her platoon... Platoon Ten. She smiled when she saw that.

He introduced himself as Martins and their handshake lasted longer than normal. He obviously liked Ogo in what appeared to be 'like at first sight.' Nkiru was wary of Ogo's countenance, since Ogo had a boyfriend, who she claimed lived abroad. But the hungry look in her eyes was one that someone who wanted to have fun had. Someone who didn't mind one day of fun, where she could let go and do whatever she liked, without reporting to anyone.

As they stood still there, awkwardly, a guy walked up to them — another drunken corper-doctor, and pulled Ogo away. He held a bottle of Johnnie Walker that was almost empty. He asked her if she wanted something to drink and she turned back to look at Nkiru, as if she was asking her permission or asking if it was safe. Nkiru nodded to her and Ogo went-a-drinking.

Nkiru then found out that Martins had signalled to the drunken doctor so that he could come and take Ogo away temporarily. It was then that he told Nkiru that he liked Ogo and asked if she could help make things work out. Nkiru used that as an excuse to get all the information she needed about Fadeke first, then proceeded to tell Ogo that Martins liked her.

By that time, Ogo was already laughing too much and at almost everything. She was just tipsy and it looked like she liked the feeling. She and Martins talked. They stood together — so close together that their bodies almost touched as they talked. From talking, he invited her to his bed for some more talking. He helped her take off her shoes and ignored that her white socks stank because she had them on all day. He then pulled her up on the bed and they got a bit too comfortable. Nkiru believed that it was at that moment that he professed his love or lust to her, because he talked directly into her ears, and sometimes, it looked like he was going to kiss her, but refrained because she was tipsy.

Nkiru hung around awkwardly, had a few drinks, and danced a little bit because nice music was playing from a speaker, but the volume had been moderately reduced to avoid making noise. By the time a few hours had passed, Nkiru wanted to go back to the hostel, but Ogo wasn't ready. She was curled up in Martins' bed, discussing so intently, Nkiru thought they were making plans to change the world. When she eventually got tired, she left the ward and went back to the hostel to have her bath and prepare for the long day ahead.

Just after hearing the gist, Oluomachukwu immediately thought about Uchenna and smiled. She was now with Okechukwu, but it didn't cost her anything to just admire another guy and even ask about him. So she asked Nkiru if she had seen the cute corper-doctor called Uchenna and she said "Yes." She had seen him kissing and smooching a pharmacist.

***

Oluomachukwu had been disappointed by the gist, all three of them — Fadeke being pregnant for an unknown fling; Ogo going to a party to have serious discussions was rather boring; and finally, Uchenna kissing and smooching another girl was no gist at all.

Oluomachukwu wondered why she had even endured listening to any of it, instead of just having her bath. And to make matters worse, she had been sent out of the room for morning drills, but not Nkiru. Nkiru told the female soldiers that she had stayed up all night in the clinic, so she needed to sleep. One of the soldiers asked for her badge and verified that she was with the Red Cross, and just like that, she was allowed to sleep.

It was when Oluomachukwu got to the parade ground that she realised she had wanted to talk to Nkiru about the serial water drinker in the room. She looked at the bottle of water in her hand, the one she had wanted to keep until she got back to the room, and started to wonder how she would solve the issue. She opened it again and took a gulp, then replaced the lid immediately and kept the bottle of water to stand by her feet.

Just then, a soldier walked up to her and stood so close that the bottle between them touched both their legs with no free space.

"*Ehn*? Coming to the parade ground with a bottle of water?" the soldier asked, although it sounded more like a remark to her. Apparently she wasn't supposed to bring a bottle of water, or any other thing to the parade ground "Turn that bottle in your pocket."

Oluomachukwu could have asked the soldier what he meant, but she felt intimidated, so she started to put the bottle in her pocket and it obviously didn't enter.

"What is this one doing?" The soldier's voice increased. "I said you should turn the bottle in your pocket."

Oluomachukwu looked around herself for support, and someone whispered to her, "He means you should empty the contents of the bottle in your pocket."

"Oh," she gasped, then immediately swung her head to the direction of the soldier, about to attack him with her eyes, when she eventually calmed down. It was nothing more than just water in her pocket. There was no need for her to get upset, and additionally, he was a nice and funny person. She looked at his badge and it read 'Elijah.' She then realised he was the same soldier that had spoken to her and directed her on her first day in the camp when she was looking to get kitted. How time flies, she thought to herself. She had eleven days to go till the end of the camp.

She had to gulp down all that was left of the water and throw the bottle away before the soldier left her alone. She saw him as he strolled away and went to harass another girl who was chewing a bubble gum with her mouth very wide-open and lower lip sticking out. He asked her to remove the bubble gum and stick it on her head. Oluomachukwu thought it was a ridiculous request, liable to be condemned by NYSC officials. But she kept quiet when the girl took the bubble gum out of her mouth and put it on her head. The solider asked her to press the bubble gum harder into her scalp and the girl did it, probably unfazed, because she either had a wig or a weave on. The soldier then moved on to disturb another person, a girl who wore Adidas trainers. He accused her of feeling too rich and asked her to go and roll her trainers in a dirty puddle of water that was at the back of the parade ground. Without arguing, the girl went to roll her trainers in the dirty puddle and was asked never to put them on again.

It must have been Discipline Day, because everywhere Oluomachukwu looked, someone was getting reproached. From the person that was wearing a Nike shirt; to the one that didn't come to the parade ground with her cap; to the person that tied her khaki jacket around her waist like it was a wrapper; to the Muslim girl who wore white trousers instead of shorts, the ones who turned their khaki pants to skirts, and those who covered their heads with hijabs that reached their ankles.

The Camp Director saw some of them as they jogged to the parade ground, then she took the microphone and let the Corps members know that improper dressing and indiscipline weren't tolerated in the camp and wasn't going to be overlooked.

The morning drill and physical exercise began the usual way after the Camp Director was done with her speech, and handed over the microphone to the Drill Instructor. It started off with the Morning Prayer, National and NYSC Anthems, and Meditation. After that, Platoon Ten Corps members left the parade ground, as they were supposed to be on duty. Oluomachukwu watched them file out, then after a few seconds, the DJ played a song and the workout session began.

***

Lunch was *eba* and soup. Oluomachukwu didn't know what type of soup it was, but she was not going to eat. *Eba*, or the likes, and any type of soup were on her list of food she could not eat outside of a home. She decided to go to the camp market to eat instead. She called Nkiru to ask her for her plans. Nkiru didn't have anything planned, so she said she was going to meet her in *mami* market.

Oluomachukwu did not want to eat rice again. She was hungry for something else, maybe pasta. That wasn't a bad idea, maybe she could eat pasta, she thought, but she did not know where pasta was being sold. She was going to have to look around *mami* market for it with Nkiru.

While she was waiting, her phone vibrated in her hand. She looked at the screen and she saw that it was Tracker calling her. He hadn't called her in quite a while. She didn't know if she should pick up the call or not. She didn't pick it up. Tracker called back, and he called about three more times until she finally picked it up.

"Hi, Tra..." She stopped immediately when she realised what she was about to say. But before she could correct herself, Tracker cut in.

"Tra what?" He laughed. "Hmm. It's John. Or have you forgotten me already?"

Oluomachukwu laughed. *If only he knew,* she thought to herself. "I haven't forgotten you at all. I was going to say something else." After a brief pause, she added, "So what's up with you?"

"I was just checking on you since you never call, text or even reply to my WhatsApp messages."

There was another brief pause, but it almost started to get too long and awkward.

"Anyway, I'm going to collect lunch from the kitchen, do you want to come too?" he asked.

"I don't eat *eba*, so I'll pass."

"Hmm. What would you rather eat?"

"Pasta. That's what I'm actually hungry for."

"I know a woman who sells pasta at the back of *mami* market, we can go there now."

"Nah, don't worry. I'm meeting up with my friends much later, so we'll figure out what we would eat then."

"Okay then..." Tracker sighed. "Enjoy your lunch, and see you later, maybe? We can go to *mami* market for drinks if you want."

"Yeah, maybe later," Oluomachukwu replied, then said goodbye and hung up.

Oluomachukwu met Nkiru at the entrance of the camp market and was surprised to see that she didn't have her Red Cross vest on. Instead, she had a badge, the small pink cardboard badge that was normally pinned to the shirt of people on duty. It had '10 ON DUTY' written on it.

Oluomachukwu shook her head. "Oh, so you are back to your platoon hopping again, right? Hopper. Don't let Auntie Vera catch you."

Nkiru hissed and rolled her eyes. "That's if she sees me. I'll be staying at the back now if I ever come to the parade ground. We're supposed to have fun in this camp, and not suffer."

Oluomachukwu laughed. "And speaking of fun, please, where's Ogo? Doesn't she want to come back again? She should better not get pregnant like Fadeke."

"Who is getting pregnant?" Ogo asked from behind, startling both Oluomachukwu and Nkiru.

They both turned around instantly, shocked. Ogo had approached from the back, and that was why they didn't notice her at first.

"Where are you coming from?" Nkiru asked. "Or were you already in the camp market?"

Ogo shook her head. "No. I was in the room. I went to have my bath quickly, and luckily there was water. Then I changed and came downstairs. I saw both of you talking so seriously, so I passed through the other entrance to turn around and scare you. And good thing I did." She laughed, and then she looked at Oluomachukwu. "Because I'm not pregnant. I'm just here to have fun."

"Ah. What about that your boyfriend in New York?" Oluomachukwu asked.

"What is this one saying?" Ogo asked, making Nkiru laugh. "I can bet he's out there now, having more fun than I am, so don't worry. He'll be fine. Besides, I'm not doing anything really crazy. I'm just having drinks and chilling."

"Yeah, chilling with the CMD on his bed and drinking his saliva," Nkiru said.

"Eww." Ogo slapped Nkiru on the shoulder. "Please, stop, before I lose my appetite."

Three of them then proceeded to the heart of the camp market, looking at the entrance post of each stall to know their name and what they sold. They finally found a pasta stall that wasn't too far from where the tailors sat and entered there. They had barely even ordered their food when Oluomachukwu saw Tracker walking around the back area, looking as if he was searching for someone, probably her. She looked away and he passed by. After they had ordered their food, Oluomachukwu saw Tracker again, and this time, he also saw her. It was an eye-to-eye contact, him in relief, Oluomachukwu in exasperation. He walked immediately to the table and sat down as he sighed.

Ogo and Nkiru looked at him, then at Oluomachukwu, but she looked away and it meant that she also had no idea what he was doing there.

"I have been looking for you since. I went round *mami* market. I even passed by here before and didn't see you. I thought you would be in the other pasta place."

Oluomachukwu looked at Ogo and Nkiru, and they had a certain look, an accusing one, like 'how does he know you were looking for a pasta place?' She then looked back at Tracker, and asked, "Why?"

"Why, what?"

"Why have you been looking for me since?"

"So that we can eat together. You said you wanted to eat pasta."

"And I also said I wanted to eat with my friends, while you said you wanted to eat *eba* and soup from the camp kitchen."

"I changed my mind." He stood up and went to order his own pasta.

Oluomachukwu, Nkiru and Ogo attempted to use sign language, but it was no use. They didn't know each other that well to understand each other's sign or eye language, so they sat down there, quiet, as Tracker joined them for lunch. And because of him, they were not going to be able to eat and gossip as freely as they would have wanted to. Oluomachukwu's phone vibrated in her hand as her plate of food arrived. It was a text message.

She opened it and smiled softly, shaking her head as she read it. "*Tracker has put a tracking device on you. We need to find it and get rid of it. Nkiru.*"

As if that was not enough, Tracker started to eat some pasta out of her plate, claiming that he was starving, when in reality, he wanted whoever that cared to know that he was sharing a plate of food with her, and that it could be the beginning of something for them.

***

After lunch, there was the usual SAED activity that Oluomachukwu didn't miss. It wasn't because she wanted to get her card signed, but because she actually enjoyed the activity from the last time. Maybe it was fifty-fifty; she liked it and also wanted her card signed. She also hoped that the card would be useful after camp, because if not, it would have been a wasted effort. She was sleepy as usual, but she needed to get her card signed... eventually. So it was twenty-eighty — twenty for liking the SAED lecture and eighty for getting the card signed.

When the SAED group activities were over, Personal Administration commenced from 12:00pm to 1:00pm and Oluomachukwu still didn't know what it was for. But she found time to go and watch those that were rehearsing and also training for the sports contests. She didn't know who had won all the sports contests they had done so far, but she knew that the football team of Platoon Seven had won their first match and was going to move to the next round; and that the volleyball team had also won their own match. They were going to play the next round of competition as well.

After Personal Administration, there was Jumat service for the Muslim brothers and sisters. Some of them were rehearsing and training, but had to stop halfway and leave, while every other activity went on as planned.

The camp kitchen served rice and stew with fish for dinner and Oluomachukwu didn't eat it. Her friends didn't eat it either. They went to *mami* market to eat. Ogo bought pounded yam and okra soup with goat meat, while Nkiru bought chicken and chips. Oluomachukwu, on the other hand, bought a sharwarma. She wasn't in the mood to eat any serious food. They sat at the same spot they normally sat at after the Rasheed-incident, and the young girl, whose auntie owned the table, ordered the food. That was where they now preferred to sit whenever they went to chill and have drinks in the camp market.

When they were done eating, they asked the girl to also place an order for pepper soup. Nkiru and Ogo ordered fresh fish pepper soup, but Oluomachukwu didn't. She had never considered it before, but that evening, she added pepper soup to the list of food she could only eat inside of a home. The young girl who helped them order the pepper soup said her name was Blessing, and her auntie sold the pepper soup. So to show appreciation, she gave them an extra piece of fish in each bowl of pepper soup and gave Oluomachukwu a small bottle of Orijin. They ate, drank and laughed until Oluomachukwu looked up suddenly and saw Tracker. He had tracked them to where they sat, yet again.

Tracker noticed that all three of them scrunched their faces when he pulled a chair. "Don't worry, I'm not here for long. I just wanted to ask you girls if you are going for the concert."

"What concert?" Oluomachukwu asked.

"*Ahn-ahn*, you didn't hear that Tu Face is coming today to perform?"

"What?" all three of them screamed in unison.

At the same time, young Blessing ran out of nowhere to take Tracker's order, but he waved her away.

"It's quite strange that none of you girls heard about it. Everyone is talking about it. I think he has just arrived and he'll soon perform. That's where I'm going to right now. Are you girls coming?"

There was silence. They wanted to go, but certainly not with him, so they shook their heads in very awkward ways. Then Oluomachukwu spoke up. "Maybe when we're done eating, we'll come there. But let's not keep you here. You should go."

Tracker did not get the message at first. He considered waiting for them, but eventually left.

Apparently, the concert was organised by Beat FM radio station and Tu Face's appearance was supposed to be a surprise. Camp officials, together with Beat FM officials had planned to surprise everyone, but Tu Face took to his Twitter page and mentioned it — how he couldn't wait to be there—, forgetting that Corps members were all over social media. That was how the secret leaked and that was why everyone was talking about it.

The concert went well. It started with some cool music to warm up the atmosphere, then there was a mini dance contest sponsored by Palmchat app. Organisers asked five dancers to go on stage for a chance to win a smart phone.

The criterion was that they had to have the app installed on their phone, so five Palmchat app users were asked to go on stage. One girl ran up the stage and when she was asked to show her phone and the app on it, she didn't... simply because she didn't have the app.

Oluomachukwu didn't have the app and didn't intend to compete, but she went to download it on her phone just to know what it was. She looked at the description of the app quickly — a free social software integrating chatting and dating. She filtered through the description very fast, scrolling down in a speedy fashion. When she was done, she deleted the app. It didn't interest her, although she re-contemplated going on stage to dance. By the time she looked up, five contestants were already on stage and their phones were being verified.

After the verification was over, the MC announced the terms of the dance competition. The contestants were to dance to Shoki — the same Shoki that was played every single day in camp. Oluomachukwu was glad she hadn't attempted to climb the stage after she had downloaded the app, because Shoki was the last thing she knew how to dance to.

In the first round, one girl, who wasn't really dancing, was kicked out. Oluomachukwu thought that she could have been that girl, one who would go on stage and fool herself. In the second round, another girl was kicked out, then a boy. It was now left to a guy and a girl, and they both danced very well. It was difficult to tell who had won, but the guy was voted winner by popular demand and he got the smart phone.

When the dance contest was over, Tu Face made his guest appearance and the crowd went up in a roar that lasted too long that when he spoke to the crowd, no one heard him. Two soldiers, who hardly smiled, stood on the stage to protect him from any Corps member who would try to jump on the stage or do anything funny, but nothing happened. There was no incident, just a nice show. He did a very amazing job and everyone clapped and sang along as he sang his songs. Oluomachukwu didn't know most of his songs, but the few she knew, she sang along to. He also made some jokes pertaining to hooking up with girls and getting them pregnant, but he ended the jokes by stating that he was only joking. He kept repeating the line, "*Na* joke oh. I *dey* joke oh, make *una* no put me for trouble. I am a married man now."

When the show was over, he thanked everyone, shared a word of advice, bowed down and bowed out in style. The crowd stood up cheering and clapping until the MC took the stage, asking everyone to calm down so that he could be heard. No one listened to what else he had to say. Tu Face had opened the concert and had also closed it.

Oluomachukwu and her friends decided to quickly go to the camp market after the concert to buy some oranges and apples, and to restock on bottled water when they ran into the Camp Commandant and his friends. He waved Oluomachukwu over and she was quite surprised that he still remembered her.

"Good evening, sir," Oluomachukwu greeted him as she approached him, and her friends also greeted him.

He was standing with two of his friends, so naturally, one started to talk to Nkiru and the other started to talk to Ogo. Oluomachukwu just looked at them briefly, then she took her focus back to the Camp Commandant.

"Did you like the concert?" he asked.

Oluomachukwu nodded. "It was very nice, thank you." She didn't know why she thanked him.

"You have been trying to call me. I didn't think you would call me, and not so many times too. I saw all your missed calls, but I couldn't call you back."

Oluomachukwu looked at him without blinking.

"And don't you sleep?"

Oluomachukwu still said nothing.

"Because you only call me late at night and very early in

the morning."

It looked like the Camp Commandant was a little bit disappointed in her. He thought she was intelligent, smart and different, and now it felt like she was just one of those girls, looking to befriend older men for money or favours.

"Hmm," Oluomachukwu sighed, after a brief pause.

"What is it?"

"It hasn't been me calling you."

"What do you mean?" The Camp Commandant looked confused. "You are the only one I have given that number to so far. So who else would be calling it?"

"One of my roommates."

"And why would you give one of your roommates my number?"

"I didn't." Oluomachukwu paused. "She stole it."

The Camp Commandant heard the words clearly, but didn't just understand. "Why did she steal it? Why would she even want to steal it?"

Oluomachukwu laughed. In fact, she kept cracking up, making the Camp Commandant a bit uncomfortable.

"Are you going to tell me why you are laughing?"

"The girl that stole the number, her name is Oghene. She overheard me and my friends..." She pointed at Nkiru and Ogo. "...Talking about you and how we didn't know it was you until you gave me your card. She asked if we knew you, then didn't say any other thing. After that, I left the room and when I got back, she had searched my things for your card and didn't even bother to keep it back where she took it from. It was obvious she wanted your number."

The Camp Commandant seemed to be more disgusted than disappointed.

"But what was making me laugh is the fact that she keeps saying that she can't suffer in camp. Maybe she is looking for an easy way, but I don't see the point, since camp is almost over, unless of course she needs an easy way out of camp, too, and an even easier way after camp and beyond NYSC."

TWENTY-ONE DAYS

Oluomachukwu realised that she was talking too much, so she shut up immediately. The Camp Commandant was clearly not listening to her anymore. Believing him to be a tactical man by profession and by rank, she felt that he was calculating something in his head. And at that instant, the sound of the bugle exploded in the air and she knew that it wouldn't be long before the soldiers came to disturb Corps members, but she also knew that they wouldn't give her grief especially if she was with the Camp Commandant... their superior officer in rank.

Oluomachukwu glanced at Nkiru. Nkiru and the man she had been talking to were looking at everything else but at each other. It looked as though they were waiting for Oluomachukwu and Ogo to be done, so that they could both move on to other things. They had probably talked about everything in so little time that they had nothing else to talk about. She then glanced at Ogo.

Ogo had suddenly remembered the American accent she had buried someplace and it surprised Oluomachukwu. She shouldn't have been that surprised, though, because it looked like Ogo spoke with the unusual American accent when she talked to people she didn't know or... guys. But she did speak typical American, not pronouncing her 'Ts,' and Oluomachukwu felt she might have learnt it from her New York boyfriend. There was nothing more annoying to hear than not pronouncing a 'T.' Oluomachukwu found it annoying.

When the bugle sounded, Ogo had asked the man she was talking to for the time.

He looked at his wristwatch, and said, "It's ten thirty."

"Oh, ten thirty?" Ogo repeated or maybe she corrected him, Oluomachukwu didn't know which, because she had pronounced the thirty as 'thuhree' as usual.

The man didn't say any other thing, and suddenly they became like Nkiru and the other man, quiet like mutes, looking around each other, but not at each other, and now waiting for Oluomachukwu to be done.

After a moment of thinking and calculating, the Camp Commandant looked at Oluomachukwu, and said, "You should go to your hostel now before you get punished. It's already time for Lights Out."

Oluomachukwu nodded and ran off with her friends, after saying good night to the three men.

***

"It's so hot in here," Ogo said, as soon as they entered the room. She pronounced hot as 'hoh' instead of 'hot.'

"And who are you speaking that one for?" Nkiru asked. "Do we look like guys?"

"What do you mean?" Ogo was slightly embarrassed.

"You resurrected your American accent with that old man, so you better bury it back now, and please pronounce your 'Ts.'" Because of that, Oluomachukwu made sure she pronounced and emphasised on her 'Ts' whenever she saw such foreign students with accents.

"Wait, what?" Ogo said, although she pronounced her words as 'Wai, wha?'

Oluomachukwu shook her head and went to her bed, and Ogo laughed, and very contagiously, which made both Oluomachukwu and Nkiru eventually laugh.

Even though they didn't fall asleep immediately, Nkiru and Ogo went to their beds just after briefly talking about what each man had said to them. The men who spoke to both Nkiru and Ogo were rather boring, but they found the Camp Commandant's chat very interesting, because he was a handsome Camp Commandant and it seemed like he was waiting for Oghene to call him again, so that he would embarrass her.

Once everywhere was very quiet and the light had been switched off for the night, Oluomachukwu decided to call Okechukwu. The only voices she heard were faint and they were of girls who were chatting in a whisper; who were on their phones; and who were reading aloud or praying.

Oluomachukwu turned on the flashlight on her phone when she heard a mosquito buzz by her ear. She followed the sound and saw one mosquito hovering around her corner, as though it had been sent by the community of mosquitoes to look for the presence of humans. It was the only one she had seen since she got to the camp. She sat up and swung at the mosquito until she squashed it. Her roommates, the ones who were still awake didn't know what was going on and looked at her in a bizarre way. She saw their confused gazes even in the dark, but she didn't mind. She had done all of them a favour and the mosquito spy wasn't going to give feedback on the amount of blood filled bodies that they could come and suck on.

She then called Okechukwu and had a very sweet chat with him. In fact, it was so sweet that she felt she could tell him just anything and everything... and everything included Kayode and Nnanna, in Abuja. She thought about it and decided that she would pick the right moment to tell him before the end of camp.

When she was done with the phone call, she took a few gulps of her water, then hid the bottle in her bucket and covered it up so that no one would drink out of it before she woke up in the morning. She then slept off afterwards, exhausted, mentally and physically.

CHAPTER SIXTEEN: DAY TWELVE

Saturday, 16 th August 2014

Oluomachukwu almost choked when she woke up, with tears dripping from just her left eye. She felt around her bed quickly for her bottle of water and didn't find it. It was just when she was about to throw a tantrum that she realised she had hidden the bottle in her bucket. She reached for it immediately and pulled the bottle out — the water was almost half gone, again.

Before she grumbled to herself, she opened the bottle and gulped down everything that was left. When she had successfully emptied the water into her stomach, she said to herself that "enough was enough." Whoever the water-drinking culprit was, the person had to stop. She only had to look for a way to handle the situation.

She looked at Nkiru and Ogo, they were still sleeping. She looked at her phone and it was not even 4:00am yet, which meant that she had woken up too early. Maybe that was why the room was very quiet, she thought. Instead of going back to bed, she decided to take her bath then go back and catch some more sleep before the Wake-Up call; anything that would keep her away from running into 'Fucking Space' in the bathroom.

She had an idea when she was going to the bathroom and carried her bucket with the empty water bottle in it. She looked around and saw some other old empty bottles and carried them as well. The idea she had was to fill the bottles with tap water. The evil person, or perhaps people, who were always drinking her water, or doing whatever it was that they were doing with it, were going to pay. She didn't fill just one bottle, but three bottles. When she got to the room, she put them by her bed where she normally kept her bottles whenever she got back to the room.

Nkiru woke up shortly after Oluomachukwu got back to the room. Her alarm had gone off by 4:15am, and a good number of her roommates woke up, excluding Ogo. Nkiru went and sat on Oluomachukwu's bed.

"You woke up quite early today," she said. She had her toothbrush and toothpaste with her, and she placed them on the bed beside her.

"Yes, I did. I was choking and thought I was going to die. That was what woke me up. I had to drink water."

"Oh, I see." Nkiru leaned forward and smacked Ogo mildly on her buttocks, twice. "Wake up, Americana."

Ogo grumbled, kicked her legs around, then turned to look at Nkiru. "Please, stop waking me up in the morning, this woman. Did someone send you?" She hissed.

"Wake up, my friend. Go and take your bath before the rush starts or even before that fat girl locks the bathroom down." Nkiru laughed, while Oluomachukwu just made a laughing sound, but didn't laugh.

"Have you bathed?" Ogo asked Nkiru.

"I haven't."

"So why are you disturbing me?" Ogo hissed. "I don't care about the fat girl. If she likes she can sleep in the bath space, I will go somewhere else or have my bath after the morning drills."

Nkiru picked up her toothbrush and toothpaste, then put a peanut size of the paste on her brush, and started to brush her teeth. Both Oluomachukwu and Ogo looked at her, then Ogo turned to look at Oluomachukwu.

"Why do you look so angry this morning and why were you talking to yourself?"

Oluomachukwu was shocked. "I look angry and I was talking to myself?"

Ogo nodded. "You were talking to yourself while you were watching Nkiru prepare to brush her teeth. What is the matter?"

Oluomachukwu knew that she was still upset about her half-empty bottle of water event, but she didn't know that she was showing it, or that it was quite obvious. "Someone keeps taking my drinking water all the time and it's very annoying. In fact, what is more annoying is that I don't know what the person is doing with the water. Maybe they are drinking it, and drinking it directly from the bottle with their dirty mouths or maybe brushing their dirty teeth with it. Or maybe they are even rinsing their dirty hands, plates, cups or cutlery with it. I don't know."

"You are really angry," Ogo said, and laughed. Nkiru also laughed and some toothpaste almost escaped from her mouth.

Oluomachukwu knew she sounded angry, but that was the only way she could vent.

"So what are you going to do about it?" Ogo asked.

Oluomachukwu whispered, "I have put tap water from the bathroom in it. So whoever is drinking it will pay."

Ogo laughed. "I just hope you won't forget and drink it yourself. You better keep it in a different place from your own."

"I will keep them together, but I will use a marker to write something on it to differentiate the tap water from my own water."

"That's fine then. As long as you don't drink it." Ogo turned to look at Nkiru. "*Ahn-ahn*, are you still brushing your teeth? It's been almost five minutes now."

"That's what she does everyday," Oluomachukwu said. "She's a world class brusher."

Nkiru laughed, and ran out of the room immediately, carrying her bucket, bathing bowl and toiletries.

***

The bugle call sounded not once, not twice, not three times, and for some reason Corps members were feeling overly lazy to report to the parade ground, forgetting that Saturday wasn't a rest day in camp. A lot of them had hung out in *mami* market after the concert and had likely taken up alcoholic drinks in water or soda bottles to continue the drinking in their rooms.

The parade ground was empty when Oluomachukwu and her friends went out, almost ghost like. The OBS had to make an announcement to ask everyone to report to the parade ground, and as usual, the speaker, in a monotonous voice, added the signature line, "*If you are still in your room... You. Are. Wrong. If you are not on the parade ground... You. Are. Wrong.*"

Even after the announcement, people didn't really go out. If they had not heard the bugle call three times, then they were not going to hear an OBS announcement either. Soldiers actually went into the hostels to bring people out. It took them about thirty minutes to mobilise everybody and bring them all out.

By the time they all came out and finished the morning usual, Morning Prayer, National and NYSC Anthems, and Meditation, it was already 6:00am, and the bugle blower came to play the national anthem. It still sounded nothing like the national anthem to Oluomachukwu. In fact, at a point in the song, one part sounded like he was playing "*Hold something, hold something, hold something...; Hold something, hold something, hold something....*" The first part sounded base, and the second part, went an octave higher, like a soprano singer's voice.

Oluomachukwu wasn't the only one that was thinking about it, because some of the guys who stood at the back were whispering the 'Hold something' line. They caused a stream of laughter around the parade ground, and the Drill Instructor spoke into the microphone, asking them to shut up and show some respect. But Oluomachukwu knew that from then on, everyone would recite the 'Hold something' line once the bugle blower got to that part; and they always did.

After the ritual, the Drill Instructor commented again on the people who were singing while the bugle blower was playing, and told them not to repeat such again. He also commented on them not coming out to the parade ground on time. He told them that henceforth, latecomers or those who remained in the hostels after the bugle call would have their badges seized. When he was done, he asked Platoon One Corps members to file out, since they were on duty again. The platoon duty cycle started again and the platoon members filed out before the drill started.

The Drill Instructor introduced new songs to the Corps members. This time, it was songs aimed directly at Corps members, and that was what made it funny. The first one was talking about how ugly the Corps members were, and used the slang *wor-wor*, which stood for something that was very ugly. And as usual, the Corps members sang along, repeating *wor-wor* after every line that the instructor said, as if they already knew the song.

Wor, wor, wor... wor-wor,
Wor, wor, wor... wor-wor,
Mosquito leg... wor-wor,
Grasshopper waist... wor-wor,
Okpolo eye... wor-wor,
Wor, wor, wor... wor-wor.

Everyone sang along happily. They had been tired from all the drinking from the previous night, but somehow the singing and the jogging around was giving them all some unexplainable strength.

The *wor-wor* song naturally transitioned into the next one, which was a direct insult, but a funny one, to Corps members. It said that some Corps members were monkeys and some were gorillas in their thousands.

All these corpers, some of them na monkey... All these corpers, some of them na monkey,
All these corpers, some of them na gorilla... All these corpers, some of them na gorilla,
One thousand, two thousand, three thousand, four oh... One thousand, two thousand, three thousand, four oh,
One thousand, two thousand, three thousand, four oh... One thousand, two thousand, three thousand, four oh.

As usual, the Corps members replaced 'corpers' with 'soldiers' and some soldiers went after, and probably even punished those who did that. Once that song was over, the instructor said, "*Oya hold something...*" and the whole crowd of Corps members were in disarray, looking for what to hold.

***

Breakfast was the usual bread, boiled egg and tea, and Oluomachukwu wondered why they kept giving the same meal all the time, but in reality, what else was there to be served for breakfast. She didn't know if any of her friends were interested, but she went to buy two soft Gala sausage rolls and also bought coffee from a Nescafé coffee stand. She thought it was a total rip off. The tiny cup of coffee was sold for 150 naira and she could take it down in just one gulp. It was also too concentrated and needed at least one cup of water to dilute it. Before she went back to the hostel, she bought a bottle of Coke, then went to have her breakfast in the room. It had started to drizzle when she was going upstairs, but she hoped it would rain seriously so that there wouldn't be anymore outdoor activity for the rest of the day.

Ogo came upstairs later with the bread, boiled egg and tea. She bought sachets of Peak milk and emptied about three inside her tea to make it creamy. She also bought two tubes of Blue Band margarine and squeezed them over the bread that she had cut into two parts with her hands, then scattered the egg in between and made an egg sandwich. Nkiru came into the room shortly afterwards with her own breakfast; bread, boiled eggs and tea.

"Two eggs?" Ogo asked immediately she saw Nkiru peeling the eggs.

"I took Oluoma's own." Nkiru said and laughed. "I felt like eating two eggs, so they gave it to me."

"Just like that?" Ogo was surprised.

Nkiru shook her head. "No." She then tilted her left shoulder backwards and her right one forward to reveal the pink badge she had on: '1 ON DUTY.' "My adopted platoon is on duty today," she added.

Ogo laughed. "That's true, no wonder. I didn't notice that you didn't have your Red Cross vest on today. Did you quit?"

Nkiru nodded.

"But why should you even quit when we don't have the concluding part of the Fadeke gist yet?" Oluomachukwu lowered her tone as she asked that.

"You don't need me when you already have Ogo here who chills with the CMD. She can get us any gist we want now. And like I said before, I'm tired of being on duty."

"And like I asked before, I thought you liked being on duty?"

"I like the idea of being on duty, but I don't want to do any work. Please, I'm tired of the unending standing and walking around. I'll just be avoiding Platoon Four because of Kayode."

"Who is Kayode?" Ogo asked.

There was utter silence. Neither Oluomachukwu nor Nkiru said anything, or even blinked. The only sound that was heard was that of the mild rain drops that hit against the walls.

"Hmm, this silence is suspicious." Ogo looked back and forth at them as she took a tiny bite out of her egg and margarine sandwich. "Is he someone I should know?"

Nkiru shook her head. "Nope. He is no one you should know."

Ogo shrugged. It was obvious that she felt upset and left out, because Oluomachukwu and Nkiru were keeping something from her, but she didn't say anything. She just pretended as if all was okay and smiled with them.

There was another brief wave of silence, and in order to avoid things from getting too awkward, Oluomachukwu decided to break the silence. "But why do you girls keep eating this horrible bread, boiled egg and tea all the time?"

"The same reason why you eat two Gala sausage rolls and one bottle of Fanta all the time," Ogo replied, and all three of them laughed as they continued eating.

***

The bugle call sounded across the whole camp after breakfast for Environmental Sanitation and Inspection, it went the same way as it had gone the week before. Camp officials went round all the rooms in both hostels to check that everything was in order, and just like the last time, the hostel administrators made sure that they went round, asking girls to take everything they owned that was either hanging on the railings or in their rooms, to the general hanging space outside the hostel.

Almost all the girls refused to take their things outside. It wasn't because they didn't want the guys to see their personal effects like before, or because they were afraid their things would get stolen. This time, they worried that the clothes line would collapse again and all their things would fall into the muddy wet floor that sat outside in patches. The rain had already stopped, and it had left its souvenirs on the ground and no one wanted to have to wash their clothes again if they fell into the mud.

The hostel administrators and the inspection officers didn't care to know. They threatened to throw things from over the railings, if they met anything there. So the girls folded their wet and damp clothing and kept them on, or in some cases, under their beds for a few hours. And after the inspection was over, they took their things back to the corridor railings and also on the lines that went across their bedposts to spread.

Oluomachukwu was one of them. For one, she didn't have the energy to go outside; two, she didn't want to risk paying anything to wash her things again; and three, she didn't understand the purpose of the inspection, if there wasn't going to be a follow-up or even regular checks.

After the inspection, there was Platoon Family Meeting for an hour. Oluomachukwu went for it, but Nkiru didn't. She didn't want Auntie Vera to see her, and then suddenly remember that she had given her a punishment, especially as she was no longer in the Red Cross community. She had told Oluomachukwu her four-digit code number, just in case there was going to be an attendance list going round.

During the family meeting, Auntie Vera wanted to have a dialogue where people would talk about anything, but it ended up being a monologue as no one wanted to speak or contribute to anything that was being said. The people that eventually contributed and spoke were only the sports and socials representatives respectively.

The sports representative spoke about all the games they had played so far, what their positions had been, what was outstanding and what areas needed more volunteers. He also complained about how there was lack of support in Platoon Seven. Other platoons had a Supporters' club, and that was why most of them won.

The crowd was always cheering for their favourite team or contestant, and it sort of helped judges with their final decision. But it was never the same for Platoon Seven, as any group or person contesting was going to have to cheer themselves by themselves.

Auntie Vera and Sister Mary then begged everyone to give a supporting hand to all the participants, at least since they themselves weren't participating. It was the least they could do. The socials representative also talked about how there were no volunteers for both the Miss NYSC and Mr. Macho competitions. Auntie Vera scrunched her face and darted her eyes round the group looking for who would do it.

"I expect all of you to behave like the name the Camp Director gave to you 'Unity...' 'team Unity,' but yet I have to do everything for you," Auntie Vera started to lament.

"That's why you are the Platoon Instructor," someone yelled from the behind.

"Who said that?" Auntie Vera asked, breathing heavily, furious, like someone had just stolen from her.

Nobody answered.

"I'm going to seize everybody's badge and put you all on duty until we leave this camp if you don't produce the person."

There was still silence. Oluomachukwu did not know who the person was, but she was sure that someone at the back, especially the people who stood close to the culprit knew who the culprit was, but wasn't going to provide the person. When it was imminent that Auntie Vera was going to start seizing badges and thinking up punishments, one of the girls from 'Two' raised her hand.

"I don't want to hear what you have to say unless you know who made that silly comment," Auntie Vera said.

Everyone laughed, but the girl didn't.

"But what was said is true," the girl still said. Whether Auntie Vera liked it or not, she was going to say what she thought.

"I have not asked for your opinion," Auntie Vera fired back.

"Ma, I—"

"I said, I haven't asked for your opinion, so please, shut up unless you know who the person is."

The female platoon president decided to speak. "Ma, I think she—"

"Are you deaf?" Auntie Vera asked, interrupting her. "I don't want to know what anyone thinks unless it's to tell me who made that stupid statement." While still looking at the female platoon president, she ordered, "In fact, start collecting all the badges now."

At that instant, Oluomachukwu noticed that Auntie Vera looked towards the back of the crowd immediately, as if she had seen something shocking. Everyone followed her gaze and looked back as well, only to see that someone had raised his hand. He was the tallest guy in the platoon and was nicely built and fit — it was sure that he had to contest for Mr. Macho. Oluomachukwu wondered why the socials representative hadn't gone to ask him yet.

"If you don't know who made that comment, then put your hand down."

"I made the comment, ma," the guy said. "And I don't think it was silly or stupid. It was the truth."

Auntie Vera kept quiet. It wasn't sure if it was because she was in shock or because the guy was making sense, but she kept quiet.

"We're a team and the team comprises of you and Mrs. Mary. So if we need you to be a part of our activities, or if you eventually join us, I don't think there's anything wrong with that."

A guy in the crowd yelled, "Mr. Macho for President," and everyone laughed, cooling off the hot atmosphere that they were in while the culprit spoke.

Auntie Vera thought about it briefly, then asked the culprit, "What's your name?"

"Kelenna is my name, ma."

Auntie Vera then turned to the socials representative. "Please, put his name down for Mr. Macho. All we have to do now is to look for someone for Miss NYSC."

***

The search for Miss NYSC had ended inconclusively, and after the Platoon Family Meeting, there was Personal Administration. Auntie Vera used up that time to persuade the girls to participate in the Miss NYSC contest. She had tried to force some of them, but they all gave silly excuses and she got fed up. It was when she was about to give up on the platoon that Nkiru decided to walk by. And as luck would have it, Auntie Vera remembered her and called her over.

Nkiru was not fast enough to take off the 'on duty' badge and Auntie Vera saw it. She didn't give Nkiru the chance to explain, but told her that she risked being taken to the disciplinary committee for jumping platoons and the only way she could redeem herself was if she agreed to represent Platoon Seven for Miss NYSC. Naturally, Nkiru refused, but she soon found out that it was an order, and not a request, so she accepted it.

Oluomachukwu didn't think it was a bad idea, because Nkiru fitted the profile; she was smart, funny, slim, and tall with long legs, and had a very nice smile. Oluomachukwu hadn't even noticed before, but Nkiru had nice dimples that flattered her face when she smiled, and it was sure that Nkiru was going to win if she contested. Oluomachukwu, like every other person in Platoon Seven, endorsed Nkiru and her grooming was to start from the next day, because there wasn't much time left before the contest.

***

Lunchtime followed immediately after the session on Personal Administration. It was instant noodles and it was free in *mami* market. Golden Penny had been giving out free lunch packs to respective platoons on different days for a couple of days. It was Platoon Seven's turn, so all they had to do was to go to the Golden Penny stall in *mami* market, present their badges with the their four-digit code, then take the food pack.

The camp kitchen was serving *eba* and okra soup, and Oluomachukwu wasn't interested in that. She had never eaten Golden Penny noodles or any other type of noodles for that matter outside her home, so she didn't know if she should add it to her list or not. She was going to find out after eating it at the Golden Penny stall.

Oluomachukwu saw people running, rushing for the food as if someone had told them that there was a limited offer of it. Someone ran past her and almost knocked her down, just so that he could be in front of the queue, just in case there wasn't enough food to go round almost three hundred people.

"Are you blind?" Oluomachukwu yelled. "Haven't you eaten noodles before or seen free food?"

The boy didn't even acknowledge or answer her. He just joined the line in front, where one of his friends was standing, and smiled victoriously. Oluomachukwu shook her head, and as she was about to lament, Nkiru came to join her. She had wanted to insult the guy at first, but since Nkiru had also jumped the line, she let him go and focused her attention on Nkiru.

"So Miss NYSC, how are you?" Oluomachukwu smiled mischievously.

Nkiru hissed. "That Platoon Instructor is a big witch. I have been saying this since. I don't know if she sees me in her dreams."

"You are funny," Oluomachukwu said and laughed. "I was wondering what you were doing strolling by casually when you knew they were having Platoon Family Meetings in the camp."

"I didn't realise where I was until our eyes met and she called me over. I don't like this one bit. I don't want to do any stupid Miss NYSC. I'm so not interested."

"But you are very pretty. I only just really noticed your dimples today. You were blushing when Auntie Vera asked you to represent our platoon."

"You are not serious," Nkiru said. "So that's even her name. I didn't know. I better learn all these things before the contest."

Oluomachukwu continued with teasing Nkiru. "Ah, no wonder all those guys are always on your neck, asking you for your number. It's your dimples."

"Leave me alone, Oluoma. I'm talking about something else. What happens if I'm asked to say the Nigerian States and Capitals? I'll disgrace myself."

"Don't worry, we'll rehearse all the possible questions together. I've got you covered."

***

After lunch, there were drills, martial arts and man-o-war activities. Before this particular day, Oluomachukwu didn't know that there was actually a man-o-war activity that everybody participated in, two platoons at a time. She thought it was just training or simple practice for a contest much later, but it was more than that. Every platoon had to get accustomed to the main activity before the idea of contest was even going to come up.

It was Platoons Seven and Eight's turn to know what exactly man-o-war was all about. They were to go to the man-o-war village, which was at the rear end of the camp, behind the kitchen, for physical activities that included wall and tree climbing, with twists, climbing up widely knitted nets and jumping over it to the other side, walking on ropes that went from one high pole to another, walking on planks, crawling under barbed wires, and swinging over puddles of mud... same things one would see in a military training camp. They actually sounded interesting.

Before they went to the man-o-war village, the man-o-war instructors divided the two platoons into two groups

— male and female instead of Seven and Eight. As they went towards the village, they sang songs, the same songs that were used during drills. When they got to the village and before they started the activity, both teams sang a special number taught and led by the instructors.

The girls sang a doctored version of a nursery rhyme that was normally cheerful.

We are H-A-P-P-Y.... We are H-A-P-P-Y,
We know we are... We are sure we are,
We are H-A-P-P-Y, Happy!

So instead, they sang it another way, as they pointed at the boys.

They are H.I.V Positive... They are H.I.V Positive,
We know they are... we are sure they are,
They are H.I.V Positive, Positive!

The guys opened their mouths, shocked at the song the girls had sung and at the wordings, then gathered together. They conversed with their own instructor and he came up with their own song. It was the chorus of the late Father U-Turn's 'Shakara,' which was actually nice.

This girl, you think say you fine, I get another girl wey fine pass you.
This girl, you think say you fine, I get another girl wey fine pass you.

They laughed out loud at their own song when they were done singing it. Not only was the song very funny, it brought back memories for some people who knew the artist well in the 90s. After all the singing, the man-o-war village director, a chubby woman, who liked to make jokes and laugh, gave Corps members the guidelines and safety procedures to follow. She also told them that the real idea behind 'Hold something' was from man-o-war activities. Whenever someone missed a footing or was about to fall down, they were to try and hold on to something, and not to someone, like they did on the parade ground.

After that, Corps members commenced participation in the different tasks and missions, guided by a man-o-war instructor. Some girls, who were too scared to participate, climbed some of the planks and trees to take pictures. It was one amazing experience for Oluomachukwu and she made a mental note to visit a man-o-war camp during her one-year service period.

***

That evening, Corps members were given their real ID cards, which they had filled on the first and second days in camp depending on the day they collected their kit. The card was the size of a normal ID card and was yellow in colour. They stood in long queues to collect them. When Oluomachukwu collected her own card, she looked at the front side and frowned at the photo she had used for it. She had taken it in a haste, and it made her look like a refugee that was applying for allowances and benefits in a foreign country.

The card was filled with diverse, personal information, including the State code and Call-up number, Name, Sex, Date of birth, Blood group, State of origin and the State of deployment, that is, the State where they were posted to for the NYSC. There were two signature slots — one for the Corps member and the other for the Director General of the NYSC. At the last line of the card, there was the validity period for the card.

Oluomachukwu flipped the card over. It had some statements about impersonating the card owner and where to return the card to if it was lost and found. There was also the Name, Address and Phone number of the Corps member's next-of-kin.

Oluomachukwu wondered why the ID card had taken so long to be prepared, but she heard someone asking a soldier, and he said that there had been a lot of errors in some of the cards. Platoon inspectors had to go through the cards, one after the other, and verify that nothing was incorrect on them. And some cards did have errors on them, so the owners had to be called back to correct them.

Some people had filled in only the four-digit number of their State code, forgetting to start it with 'LA/14B.' Some people put in their genotype, instead of their blood group, especially when 'Blood Group' was clearly written on the card. Some people had mixed up the validity period of the card, making it two or three years valid, maybe to use it after the NYSC service year. Some people had even signed for themselves and for the Director General of the NYSC. When everything was rectified on the cards, they were then signed on behalf of the Director General and distributed.

Oluomachukwu, like others, pulled out the temporary white paper that held their four-digit code numbers, and replaced it with the new card. Auntie Vera asked everyone to wait behind after sharing the card, as she wanted to talk to them about the competitions. There was going to be the dance competition that evening and she wanted people to go and support the group. It was a plea, and not an order, and she sincerely hoped that they would all go.

Standing behind Oluomachukwu, was a girl who kept complaining to whoever cared to listen about how they were all feeling overwhelmed, because there was no time for anything. With all the lectures and activities, there was no time at all to rehearse properly. Oluomachukwu turned slightly to the back and saw that it was one of the girls from 'Two' that was complaining. She was obviously going to feel overwhelmed. In fact, both of them were, because they participated in almost every activity in the camp, and were standbys for the ones that they didn't participate in.

***

Dinner followed immediately after Games and Sports at 6:30pm and was supposed to be ongoing until 8:20pm, but the dance competition started earlier. People could either eat and miss the show or get their food and keep it until later, whichever that worked for them.

Oluomachukwu had escorted Nkiru and Ogo to the dining hall to collect their food, but she didn't eat with them. The camp kitchen was serving beans porridge and she wasn't interested at all. The last time she ate it, it was as watery as a plate of soup for eating *eba*. She went to the camp market and ordered a take away pack of small chops and decided to have that for dinner. They then went to the parade ground, under the canopies where the competition was going on and sat there to eat, not minding if people were staring at them.

The contestants came out platoon by platoon, starting from Platoon One to Platoon Ten. Some came out and danced horribly, but still got a standing ovation from their platoon members, which boosted their scores. Some did some spectacular displays with fire, some lifted people on their shoulders, some did acrobatics, while some displayed candles all over the stage to support their presentation — some were simply beautiful and some were not.

Platoon Seven was one of the platoons that didn't really have a spectacular addition. They did a little drama before the dance started just to add flavour to their presentation, but the guys who played in the drama overdid it and got a negative marking. Oluomachukwu thought for a second that the guys were going to fight. She wondered why her platoon members had problems sticking to scripts. They did way more than they had rehearsed and made it look disorganised. And not only was their dance presentation ordinary, they didn't get the support they needed, because more than half of the platoon didn't show up. Even the clapping and cheering from the few supporters who came were overshadowed by the mimicking silence of other platoons.

Only four platoons were picked for the next round, including Platoons Five and Nine. Platoon Seven didn't make the cut. In fact, Platoon Seven took the last place and Oluomachukwu wasn't surprised. After the very silly drama-joke-insult, their platoon was already destined for the last place.

After the dance competition, Oluomachukwu went to *mami* market to hang out with Nkiru and Ogo, and have some cold drinks at least before the Lights Out bugle call. She also bought a bottle of water that would complement her throughout the night and the next morning, as all she had under her bed were the tap water traps. After their hangout, they went back to the room and called it a night. Well Nkiru and Ogo did, but Oluomachukwu didn't. She spent a bulk part of the night talking to Okechukwu, and she slept happy.

CHAPTER SEVENTEEN: DAY THIRTEEN

Sunday, 17 th August 2014

Oluomachukwu woke up very early, earlier than her alarm clock that was set for 4:30am. She felt a bit happy due to the fact that she had had a rather nice chat with Okechukwu before going to bed. They talked about their pasts and the things they had done so far, but not their recent pasts. It was probably easier to talk about what had happened a long while back and had somewhat been forgotten than what had happened just a few weeks back, especially after there had been a huge decision to get into a relationship. It wasn't yet time to start getting into all that detail. Oluomachukwu wanted to give it some time first before she spilled the beans.

Oluomachukwu reached around her bed for her water, remembering that it was tap water, and it was full. In fact all three bottles hadn't been touched. She shrugged, as she didn't care. Her clean water had been kept inside her duvet cover, so no one would have used it, and it was just as she had left it before she went to bed.

As a habit, she felt the top of her bed and under her

cloth-pillow and pushed down all the phones. Just then, she dialled Nkiru's phone to check if she had pushed it down as well, but the phone started ringing mildly from Nkiru's bed. She ended the call immediately, then took a few gulps of water and got up to go to the bathroom, still praying that she would not run into 'Fucking Space' in the process.

There were not a lot of people in the bathroom and it looked like an apocalypse. For the ten minutes she spent there, only three people came in and left. She wondered what was going on and if everyone was being lazy, then she realised that it was probably too early. She had woken up too early like the other days and there was no one else there.

She had her bath, did all her underwear washing, every other thing that needed washing, then cleaned her rubber trainers. The good thing about the rubber trainers was that stains cleaned off easily, so she was happy to have bought them. The first time she had attempted to wash her NYSC tennis shoes, the 'N' and 'Y' peeled off the right foot and the logo was peeled off completely on the left one. So the shoes had been locked up in her box ever since it got dried from washing.

Oluomachukwu took her things and left the bathroom, and she didn't run into anyone until she got to the room, entered and locked the door. She didn't run into 'Fucking Space,' thankfully. In fact, she felt that 'Fucking Space' had either changed her bath time, changed bathrooms or even stopped bathing altogether. The last option didn't really seem possible, since 'Fucking Space' loved her bath time and space so much that she was never going to stop trying to monopolise it.

Everyone was still asleep when Oluomachukwu locked the room door and turned around. Everywhere was dark and quiet, and only the ceiling fan swirled round and made noise. There were two ceiling fans in the room and only one was functional, but nobody complained about it. The room leader, Dunsin had still not come back to the room since the confrontation. Whether she was still in the camp or she had already gone home, nobody knew.

Oluomachukwu put on her underwear, a pair of navy blue leggings and a black top, then she entered into her duvet cover and decided to sleep for just a short while before the sound of the bugle, whenever that was. She checked her time and it was 3:45am, so she still had at least forty-five minutes to sleep. She got comfortable and slept off.

The next time she opened her eyes, it was bright. The sun had already come up and it was fighting to make its way through the torn mosquito net and constantly open windows by her bedside. She looked up at the springs of the bed on top of hers and thought briefly about Ijeoma and what she would be doing at the moment, if she would be in prison or be at home with her boyfriend or girlfriend. Oluomachukwu couldn't recall if it was Ijeoma or Eternity, or both that were married.

She turned to the side and Ogo was still sleeping. She turned to her other side and Oghene was also asleep. She lifted her upper body and looked just opposite her bunk and Nkiru was sleeping peacefully. She then looked out of the window and didn't see anyone walking by. Well, it was normal that no one walked by aimlessly because her room was the last on the fourth floor. So unless they wanted to jump down from the fourth floor, no one went beyond her room.

Oluomachukwu leaned to the side and woke Ogo up, but she didn't smack her on the bum like Nkiru normally did. Ogo turned around and smiled.

"Morning." Ogo stretched. "Why are you always up so early, and looking very unhappy? Did someone drink your water again?"

Oluomachukwu had not been unhappy, but the three questions irritated her. "It's just my body clock. It's getting used to the camp life. I'm not unhappy and no one drank my water."

"Good, then cheer up." Ogo immediately got up from the bed when she saw that Nkiru was still asleep. She went towards her bed and smacked her buttocks twice and very hard. "Wake up."

"Ogo, I will kill you, leave me alone," Nkiru croaked, then cleared her throat. "Leave me alone. I didn't sleep on time."

"Yes, you did," Oluomachukwu said. "I watched both of you fall asleep, so if anything, I should be the one still sleeping."

"I hear you." Nkiru finally woke up and went to sit at the foot of Oluomachukwu's bed, carrying her toothbrush and toothpaste in the process.

"Was there an announcement in the camp yesterday? Where's everyone?" Oluomachukwu asked.

"Probably still sleeping, why?"

"Because everywhere seems quiet and the bugle blower hasn't made the morning call."

"Well, it's because today is Sunday. Did you forget? No morning drills on Sunday."

"Oh right." Oluomachukwu rolled her eyes. "That's my mistake."

***

Ogo had a speedy bath and got ready for church. She asked Oluomachukwu to accompany her like the last time, but Oluomachukwu didn't. She couldn't remember what she had learnt the last time, and she really didn't want to deceive herself by going there again. Plus anything that would keep her away from Segun was fine by her. Unable to convince Oluomachukwu, Ogo decided to go alone.

When Ogo left, Nkiru went to lie on Ogo's bed in the meantime, so that she would be close to Oluomachukwu, and they could talk.

She stretched and yawned, tucking herself into Ogo's bed, after which she looked at Oluomachukwu. "So did anyone drink the tap water?" she asked, whispering.

Oluomachukwu shook her head and laughed. "No. It's almost like they knew it was from a tap in the toilet. I don't mind though, as long as they leave me and my water alone, I will be fine."

Nkiru laughed, then started to close her eyes gradually to continue sleeping.

"Oh by the way, you platoon hopper," Oluomachukwu said and Nkiru immediately opened her eyes to look at her. "Are you not supposed to be on duty today? It is Platoon Two on duty today, right?"

Nkiru nodded. "Please, I cannot do any type of work on Sundays, I'd rather sleep, so Platoon Two is safe from a very lazy drone like me. Besides, we have Miss NYSC to work on and that wicked woman didn't give me an option. Shouldn't we go and look for my outfit and shoes, and also which hairdresser would do my hair, and then practice for the contest? How to walk, talk, dance, and so on. "

Oluomachukwu smiled. "You are right. We should go and check out dresses and shoes. Whenever you are ready, we can go."

***

Oluomachukwu went to *mami* market with Nkiru to check out some things after Nkiru had taken her bath and gotten dressed. Oluomachukwu had wanted to go out in mufti, but when she recalled being sent back the previous week, she changed her mind. When she got to the hostel gate that morning, she even saw the officers sending back people who were on mufti.

She smiled as she walked past the gate and went out. She would have been very mad if she had come downstairs with mufti only to be sent back all eight flights of stairs just to put on white shorts, shirt, socks and rubber shoes.

The hostel gate officers kept repeating that mufti wasn't allowed anywhere on camp except inside the hostel... not even on Sundays.

As Oluomachukwu and Nkiru walked towards *mami* market, they saw Shoki, and for the first time, he wasn't doing the Shoki dance. He was with two other guys from Platoon Seven, and they were all dressed in mufti, and Oluomachukwu wondered why girls were not allowed to wear mufti as well. She was so tempted to know why, so she asked one of the guys what it was about their hostel that guys could wear mufti, and not girls.

There was no security post, or gate officers, and the rear gate was opened, unlike the female hostel, which was always bolted and padlocked. And because of the liberty given to the guys, not so many of them came out to the parade ground during the day or came out at all. Some of them didn't even know what the parade ground looked like after the Opening Ceremony.

The stalls where clothes were sold were at the far right side of the camp market, and neither Oluomachukwu nor Nkiru had been to those specific stalls before. The only one Oluomachukwu had been to sold white shorts and shirts, but not dresses and high-heeled shoes. There was a variety of dinner dresses, casual dresses, evening dresses and work dresses, but none of them looked elegant. They looked like what one roadside tailor had put together in a hurry. Nkiru didn't think that any would do her or the platoon justice. She hadn't brought any evening dresses back from the UK, because she never expected to be in any kind of pageant, and neither did Oluomachukwu. All they had were simple dresses to hang out with friends, or go partying or go for simple events. Their only option was to send someone, probably a family member or friend, to buy from a boutique, then bring it to the camp. And if all else failed, they were going to buy an ugly dress from *mami* market.

Nkiru tried on some of the dresses and the shoes, while

Oluomachukwu took photos of her. They didn't want to pick anything just yet, so they decided to show the pictures to their platoon members and instructors, then together they would pick. All the dresses cost 8,000 naira, while the shoes cost something between 5,000 naira and 6,000 naira. Oluomachukwu and Nkiru exchanged glances. It was clear that they had done mental calculations of how much they would cost in pounds sterling, and they concluded that the ugly-looking dresses and shoes were overpriced.

They wanted to reserve or book the dresses; whatever it was that people did with dresses when they weren't ready to buy, but the seller refused to allow them. She said that they had to pay an advance sum first, and it wasn't sure if she was going to refund the advance sum.

Both Oluomachukwu and Nkiru didn't understand the system or how things worked in Nigeria. The seller said that if she reserved the dress and other people came to buy it, then she would have missed opportunities if she didn't sell it. And if Oluomachukwu and Nkiru didn't eventually buy the dress, then she would have lost out . And refunds were only possible if nobody came to ask for the dress during the reservation period. And knowing how dubious some sellers were, Oluomachukwu and Nkiru knew that this particular seller wasn't going to give them any refunds whether someone asked to buy the dress or not.

As they stood and talked, Nkiru pulled Oluomachukwu to the corner. "So what do you think?"

"Hmm. I want to reserve it, but I don't want to pay for it right now, just in case. Plus all the dresses are very ugly." Oluomachukwu glanced at the seller who was looking at them closely. "And I don't trust that woman."

Nkiru laughed. "Same here. I think we should show the others the pictures of the dresses and the shoes first. Then whatever they pick, we will buy."

"What if we don't find the dresses here again?"

"Nobody is buying any ugly thing from that woman, so I doubt the dresses would be gone by the time we return."

Both of them laughed, then they turned and looked at the woman, and Oluomachukwu said, "Sorry madam, we'll come back and buy the dress and shoes very soon."

"You might not meet them again. My things come and go very fast, and everybody will soon start looking for their own dress for Miss NYSC." The woman still felt the need to say that.

"Don't worry we will come back."

Oluomachukwu and Nkiru exchanged brief glances one more time before they left the stall. It meant that they were not going back to that particular woman. Her clothes were too ugly.

***

Oluomachukwu didn't eat any breakfast, so it was only natural that she felt very hungry when it was lunchtime. And the good thing was that the kitchen was serving *jollof* rice and fried chicken, very tiny pieces of fried chicken that Oluomachukwu felt it was birds that had been cooked and fried instead. Nkiru and Ogo were also hungry, so three of them went to collect their food. They ate quietly in the room, not talking too much, and it was obvious that they were already getting tired of camp, tired of doing the same things day in, day out. Inasmuch as they liked the evening life, everything was redundant. The only other thing that kept them going was talking about other people, assigning nicknames to people and looking for other people's gist.

After lunch, there was one hour dedicated to Personal Administration and Oluomachukwu still didn't know what it corresponded to. Nkiru and Ogo slept off immediately after having lunch, and just as Oluomachukwu was about to sleep, she heard an announcement from the OBS.

"*Good morning, gentlemen, Corps members. All Platoon Seven Corps members are requested by their Platoon Instructor on the parade ground now.*"

The speaker made the grating announcement again and

Oluomachukwu frowned. She didn't want to go anywhere, but her conscience would not let her stay back and miss whatever it was they were going to talk about. She got up, went to Nkiru's bed and plonked herself down on it.

Nkiru woke up and looked at her, confused. "What?"

Before Oluomachukwu could respond, there was the announcement again. "Listen," she said, as she placed her index finger over her lips to tell Nkiru not to talk.

When the announcement was over, Nkiru turned over. "I'm not going."

"Yes, you are," Oluomachukwu said, then pulled off the wrapper Nkiru had used to cover up herself. "You are contesting for Miss NYSC. The gathering might concern you."

Nkiru sighed. And at that moment, she wished she had remained with the Red Cross community and was seriously reconsidering it.

Platoon Seven was the only platoon officially gathered under one canopy by the parade ground. There were other Corps members around, doing one thing or the other. A TV screen had been mounted in one section of the parade ground under the canopy and guys had gathered around it, watching intently, then jumping and shouting in unison at intervals, while some grumbled.

Oluomachukwu could tell that they were watching a football match, but didn't know what teams were playing. It was certainly the English Premier League, since Nigerian guys always watched the league games as though it was the World Cup.

At the same time, there was music playing all over the camp, and it sounded more like noise. If they had thought of turning off the music once in a while, people would not have been having sore throat or wearing headphones over their ears all the time.

The camp DJ also played the usual selection of Shoki, Sekem, Shake Body and Dorobucci more than five times already on that same day, and Oluomachukwu was almost tempted to go and give him her cell phone to download all the songs she had on it.

The emergency platoon meeting had been proposed by the socials representative and everyone began to grumble, wondering why he was always disturbing their peace. He stated that the Camp Idol contest was the next day and they didn't have anyone to represent Platoon Seven. So he wanted a volunteer, and wanted Auntie Vera to help him pick someone, since no one ever listened to him or agreed to help him.

"Yet again, we are here trying to unite you all and pick just one candidate for the Camp Idol contest, why *nau*?" Auntie Vera asked and no one answered her. "I thought that by now you all would be able to organise yourselves. Other platoons plan these things and surprise their platoon instructors. In fact, it was so embarrassing when the socials representative called me, and I told one platoon instructor resting on the bed beside mine that I had to go and help to pick a candidate for the Camp Idol. She laughed and said that she had never participated in such things, and that her platoon members always pleasantly surprised her."

Oluomachukwu wondered why Auntie Vera was even giving a long lecture. The bottom line was that all platoons were different. Just because another platoon instructor sat down and did nothing, it didn't mean that she could do the same. Also, her lecture wasn't going to miraculously pick a volunteer for the competition or make anyone change their passive attitude. Oluomachukwu felt like telling her to get to the point, so that they could wrap up the meeting, and she could go back to bed.

Surprisingly, five people volunteered to compete when Auntie Vera asked. She then held a spontaneous audition session and told them to sing any song. All five of them sang over the noise that the DJ was making, then Auntie Vera asked the platoon members that had heard to pick one representative. They eventually picked a guy who was introduced as Olufemi, and he was to start rehearsing for the next day.

***

After the Personal Administration session was over, the bugle was blown to let everybody know that dinner was served, and the OBS completed it with an announcement. The speaker announced that dinner was *amala* and *ewedu*. And as usual, Oluomachukwu and her friends were not interested. She, Ogo and Nkiru went to have dinner in *mami* market and sat where they usually sat, at Blessing's auntie's table. That way, nobody would come and force them to buy drinks or ask them to leave if they were not buying drinks. Ekene, who Oluomachukwu hadn't seen in a while, also joined them, surprising all of them.

"Ekene, where have you been? Are you even still in this camp?" Ogo asked, as Ekene pulled out a chair and sat in it.

"That's true. I haven't seen you since after one of the contests. Was it dance or drama?" Nkiru asked.

"Hmm." Ekene shook her head. "I only rehearsed, but I didn't eventually participate. I had to request for an exeat to leave camp. None of you looked for me."

"Really?" Oluomachukwu exclaimed. She wasn't really interested in the reason why Ekene had left, but in the fact that she could leave and come back.

"Yes oh. I wasn't feeling too well, so I wrote a letter to Auntie Vera, she signed it, and then let me leave after the Camp Director or State Coordinator approved it. She said I could come back to camp, but only with a doctor's report stating that I was now feeling well and I didn't have Ebola, or didn't get in contact with anyone that had Ebola while I was in the hospital."

Ogo laughed. "That's serious. Your Platoon Instructor sounds too serious. But the doctor wouldn't know if you had gotten in contact with anyone that had Ebola outside the hospital."

"My dear, it's airborne," Nkiru said. "It can be gotten from anywhere, whether the doctor gives a report or not."

Oluomachukwu had been quiet the entire time, and she already started thinking of how she would leave camp to meet Okechukwu then come back. She wondered if they would just let her go or if she had to be sick or something.

"Oluoma, you are very quiet," Nkiru pointed out, and Oluomachukwu looked up at her.

"Hmm, who are you thinking about? Him, right?" Ogo asked.

"What 'him' are you talking about?" Oluomachukwu was glad she couldn't blush.

"The one you are always talking to at night," Ogo said. "Sometimes when I wake up briefly, I hear you or see you on the phone. Don't deny it."

"Please, there's no 'him,' Ogo. I just want to know how I can leave camp and come back." Oluomachukwu turned to look at Ekene. "Do I have to be sick to be allowed to leave?"

"I don't know. Maybe disabled, pregnant, married, I'm not sure. You should ask your—"

"Oluoma wants to go and see a man and you are here calling all these things for her," Ogo interrupted, making everyone laugh.

Oluomachukwu didn't continue with the conversation. She simply called Blessing to take their orders, and they all ordered chicken and chips, and bottles of Orijin to drive the food down. By the time they were done eating, Tracker showed up with a couple of his friends and bought a lot of *suya* and more drinks for the table. He had eaten *amala* and *ewedu* and wanted dessert, so *suya* and Orijin were the best bet. So they ate, drank and talked until the annoying sound of the bugle cut the cheerful atmosphere off.

***

It was 10:20pm and the light in Oluomachukwu's room was still on. Soldiers had already started moving round and asking people to turn the lights off. Nkiru and Ogo both sat at the foot of Oluomachukwu's bed, talking about how their evening had gone, and it was more of drunk talk as they weren't making that much sense. They then regretted having had so much to drink, as they were going to have to wake up quite early for the morning drills.

Oluomachukwu heard whispering as they chatted and laughed, and turned to her right side to see Oghene talking into her cell phone. Oluomachukwu couldn't make out the words that Oghene was saying, but it was obvious that she was talking with a guy. A couple of seconds later, a female soldier walked up to their room and flogged the door twice with an iron rod, startling everyone.

"Off this light, now!" the female soldier yelled, but she sounded like a man.

Foyin had already slept off, but she jumped up instantly and turned the light off, then went back to sleep as fast as she had woken up, as if nothing had happened. Nkiru and Ogo retired to their beds, and Oluomachukwu got into her duvet cover. She wanted to call and gist with Okechukwu, but she decided to wait until Ogo went to bed, at least, so that she wouldn't talk about her late-night calls the next morning.

Oluomachukwu didn't know how long she had been waiting, but she slept off. She woke up all of a sudden and looked around her. Ogo's breathing was soft and steady, so it was sure that she was fast asleep. She looked over at Nkiru, she was covered up and probably in dreamland. She then looked at Oghene, and Oghene wasn't moving. Not that it mattered if Oghene was asleep or awake, but she was by Oluomachukwu's right side, so it was only natural that she checked.

Oluomachukwu pulled her cell phone from under her cloth-pillow to check what time it was... it was 11:14pm.

She hadn't slept for too long. She felt around her bed and there were phones there, charging, as usual, and also, she got very irritated, as usual. Instead of thinking of a way to destroy the socket, she decided to count down to leaving the camp.

She didn't fling the phones down this time, because it was extremely quiet and she didn't want the noise to wake anybody up. So she picked the phones up, one after the other, and placed them on the floor. As she was picking up a Nokia phone, the screen came on and a call immediately followed from a name stored as 'CMDT.' Oluomachukwu didn't know why she was staring at the caller-ID, probably lost, wondering what it meant when it was clearly none of her business. Oghene woke up at that instant and snatched the phone from Oluomachukwu.

"What are you doing with my phone?" Oghene barked.

Oluomachukwu looked around quickly and no one else had woken up. "It was ringing," she replied.

"So you wanted to know who was calling me?" Oghene asked. "Is it your phone? *Amebo*."

"When something rings under my pillow won't I bring it out and check what it is?"

Oghene said nothing.

"And since I know it's your phone now, I don't want to ever see it under my pillow, because if I do, I'll break it. It's disgusting."

"Break it now, you'll see."

"Put it under my pillow again and you'll see."

"Whose fault is it that the socket is behind your bed?"

"I don't care, you can put your phone on the floor or on the windowsill, but not on my bed or under my pillow."

"What are you now feeling like?"

"I don't know where your phone has been, and in what hands. I don't even want to think about it, just don't put it here again."

Some girls in the room woke up at that instant, because Oluomachukwu and Oghene had been raising their voices, but unintentionally, then urged them to keep their voices down and settle the issue in the morning. Oluomachukwu kept quiet, but Oghene continued mumbling. It was clear that something else was bothering her, maybe a bad dream, Oluomachukwu thought.

Oghene's phone rang again. She looked at the screen, got comfortable in her bed, facing the other side, then she picked up. And judging by the way she spoke, it was sure that she was speaking with someone she ought not to be. Although she spoke lower than a whisper, Oluomachukwu could still make out the words in the almost grave-like quiet room. Oghene was talking about posting, probably where she would be posted to at the end of camp. She was asking if she had been posted to the private firm, where she could earn good pay. The person must have said 'No,' because Oghene then asked when it would happen.

Oluomachukwu got tired of listening to her talk, so she then decided to call Okechukwu and have a chat with him. Okechukwu didn't pick up. Oluomachukwu felt he had already slept off and decided to go back to sleep as well. She got comfortable in her bed, then nodded off.

***

One hour passed by after Oghene's phone call and she hadn't slept yet. She didn't know if anyone was still awake, and she hoped not. She had been waiting for everyone to fall asleep so that she could leave the room. It was actually Oluomachukwu that she had been waiting for to sleep off, because it felt like Oluomachukwu had been spying on her. When it sounded like the whole room was in dreamland, she got up, slowly and quietly. She darted her eyes round the room and didn't see any rectangular light from phone screens. She then opened the door quietly and slid out. She obviously couldn't lock it, so she hoped no strange person or thief would enter the room in her absence.

She managed to go out without waking anyone up. She

then ran to the ground floor, and when she got there, she saw two female hostel gate officials keeping watch, a police officer and a soldier.

"Where is this one going to?" the police officer asked. "My friend, run back to your room, right now."

"Ma," Oghene started. "I just—"

"Ah, are you deaf?" the soldier interrupted. "If I knock something on your big head, you will faint here. Run back to your room."

"But," Oghene said, then paused. She was going to say that she had an invitation from the Camp Commandant, but she thought twice about it. So instead, she said "Good night," then she went back upstairs, but stopped when she climbed the first flight of stairs. She took out her phone and called the Camp Commandant back to update him. The phone rang just once and he picked it up.

"Ogo, where are you now?" he asked. Oghene had lied to him that her name was Ogo so that he would agree to speak to her the first time.

"Sir, I have a problem oh," Oghene whispered.

"Why are you whispering? Can't you talk?" he asked.

"I was not allowed to leave the hostel. The guards here are so strict, they even yelled at me."

"Hmm." The Camp Commandant sighed. "Is there any other way?"

Oghene didn't say anything. She hoped that he would tell her that he would personally deal with the guards, but he didn't. He didn't even propose another way.

"Hello," he said. "Are you still there?"

"Yes, I am," Oghene retorted. "But I don't know any other way to come out."

"Tell them you are not feeling too well, and that you want to go to the clinic."

"They won't allow me, sir." Oghene was disappointed. "Maybe next time then. It's way past midnight even."

"Wait, hold on and hang on, but not too far from the entrance. I'll send someone to come and get you out of there."

Oghene smiled. That was more like it, she thought. She had indirectly threatened the Camp Commandant, because she knew that he would do something about her situation if she did. The Camp Commandant seemed very desperate to spend some time with her, and she was going to use it to her advantage.

A few minutes later, Oghene heard voices at the gate, and heard a male soldier asking about her from the hostel officers. She quickly ran down the stairs, almost missing a step and tumbling over. She heaved a sigh of relief when the thought of her falling and hurting herself flashed in her head. She went to the gate, and smiled at the male soldier who had come for her.

The police officer opened the gate and allowed Oghene leave. She said nothing to them, but she could have sworn that she heard the word '*ashawo*' as she left.

***

Ogo got up in the middle of the night to use the toilet. She had drunk a lot of water, and coupled with the amount of Orijin she had also drunk, her bladder was overloaded. She went towards the door with her eyes closed, since she already knew her way around and the lights were also off. She knew where the bolt was, and she could open it in the dark, so she didn't need her eyes open. She stretched forth her hands as she reached the door, not noticing the fresh air that was cooling her face, until she tripped over and fell to the floor. She screamed, waking everyone in the room up. Foyin got up and turned the light on. She went outside and saw Ogo on the floor, wincing and holding her right ankle. Oluomachukwu and Nkiru sat up on their beds.

"What happened?" Foyin asked.

Ogo hissed. "Someone left the door wide open. They should have at least closed it."

Foyin gave Ogo a hand and pulled her up. Her ankle

appeared to be fine. And as they stood by the door, Foyin asked Ogo again, "Who went out? Do you know?"

"I don't know." Ogo shrugged. She then went towards the toilet, while Foyin went into the room. Everyone was now awake, obviously wondering what had happened.

"What happened?" one girl asked, not able to take the suspense anymore.

"Somebody went out and left the door wide open, so Ogo tripped over the elevated entrance," Foyin replied.

"Hmm, so Oghene isn't back yet?" Nkiru asked out of nowhere. Everyone turned to look at her. "I saw her about an hour ago leaving the room, and she's still not back yet." Nkiru then pointed at Oghene's bed, which was just beside Oluomachukwu's bed, and it was empty.

They all looked at one another, wondering what was going on. Oluomachukwu and Nkiru exchanged glances at that instant, and they both had an idea of what might be going on. Everyone went back to bed a little after Nkiru mentioned that Oghene had left the room. It was not like they did not care, but Oghene could not have been in any form of danger while in the camp. And anywhere she had gone, it would have definitely been on her own free will. They, especially Foyin, only wanted to know who exactly had left the door open. Whether the person left the room an hour ago or the person was not yet back didn't concern any of them. Foyin just wanted to know whom she would query the next morning.

CHAPTER EIGHTEEN: DAY FOURTEEN

Monday, 18 th August 2014

Oluomachukwu woke up quite early, as usual. She checked her phone and it was 4:05am. She was not actually checking her phone for the time, she wanted to know if Okechukwu had sent her a message... he hadn't, and she got upset.

She then decided to calm down a bit, because if he was asleep by past 11:00pm, then he definitely would still be asleep by 4:00am she reasoned with herself. She put the phone inside her duvet cover, then went to have her bath.

Nkiru had her bath after Oluomachukwu, because she had soaked some things in her bucket and wanted to use Oluomachukwu's own. Ogo, on the other hand, could not get up to go and have her bath. Her right leg was hurting her badly and the ankle she thought was fine, looked like it was swelling up. Nkiru had to escort her to the bathroom, and instead of going to the parade ground, she was going to divert to the clinic.

Half the room woke up on time and got ready for the morning drill early. It was right after the bugle Wake-Up call sounded that the room door opened and Oghene came in, limping as if she had been busy all night, using her legs. It was obvious that different thoughts crossed everyone's mind as they wondered what might have happened. It was also obvious that they all had the same one thought: that Oghene had definitely had coitus all night, but they didn't know with whom. It was clear that they weren't going to know, except Oluomachukwu, Nkiru and Ogo, who could snoop around and ask questions to find out.

Oghene didn't bother going to take a shower or going to the parade ground. She didn't know which was more embarrassing, the fact that her roommates were looking at her suspiciously or what had actually happened with the Camp Commandant. She glanced at Oluomachukwu and frowned at her angrily, then lay in her bed and started to think about what had really happened:

After the soldier had come to get her from the hostel, both of them walked to the Camp Commandant's sleeping quarters, and the walk was a short, but awkward one. The soldier didn't say a single thing to her, and she felt that he was probably angry at the fact that he was woken up just to go and get her out of the hostel. And after a two-minute quiet walk across the hostel, they got to their destination. The soldier knocked on the door, then left without waiting for an answer.

"Please, come in," a strange voice ordered, but Oghene could tell it was the Camp Commandant.

Oghene smiled, opened the door, entered and closed it behind her. She had gone there to ask him for favours, and was ready to give him anything he wanted. But when she got in, she met three other men there. She wasn't sure how to proceed or if the men had all come for the show, as participants or as observers, but if they asked anything of her, she was willing to take her chances. So she stood at a corner waiting. She had smiled and entered the room, but the Camp Commandant told her to stand by the door, while he was talking on the phone. She couldn't make out what he was saying, because he was whispering, the same way she had whispered when she was talking to him from the hostel room.

The Camp Commandant watched her closely. She was wearing her white shorts, shirt, socks and rubber trainers. It was almost as if she hadn't changed from the day before or she was already prepared for the following morning. He looked at her chest, and he noticed something underneath her shirt. Oghene stood there awkwardly, wondering what the Camp Commandant was looking at and why he didn't take his eyes off her.

"Take off your shirt," he ordered. His voice sounded strict, like he was giving war orders.

Oghene did not waste any time. She had just started to take off her shirt when one of the other men in the room with the Camp Commandant raised a hand, stopping her.

Oghene had her white shirt on her neck already; it was revealing the black tank top that the Camp Commandant had noticed when he told her to take her shirt off.

She turned and looked at the Camp Commandant, then asked, "Sir? Should I stop?"

"Shouldn't you be ashamed of yourself?" the man, who had stopped her, asked.

Oghene didn't say anything. She looked at the Camp Commandant, but he was glued to his cell phone, probably reading a message or an email, acting as though he wasn't interested in what was going on or as though it wasn't his business when it was him that had invited her over.

"I just asked you a question, my friend," the same man yelled. "Shouldn't you be ashamed of yourself?"

Oghene put her shirt back down.

"What type of image do you want to give of corpers and of young girls like youself? *Ehn*? What type of image do you want to give of camp officials and of government officials in general?"

Oghene was still speechless. She looked down. At that instant, there was a loud knock at the door and the Camp

Commandant asked the person to come in, the same way he had also asked Oghene to come in, "Please, come in." The door opened and a female soldier walked in. She was the same soldier who was at the gate when Oghene tried to leave earlier on. Oghene recognised her and she recognised Oghene as well. She eyed Oghene from head to toe, then looked at the Camp Commandant.

"Sir, you called me," the female soldier said, sounding like a man.

The Camp Commandant finally looked up, but didn't exchange glances with Oghene. "Yes. Please, discipline this young girl."

"Sir?" the female soldier was not sure of what she had heard.

"I said you should discipline her. She stole my number off someone, lied she was someone else, then came here to ask me for favours and was willing to give me anything in return. Punish her appropriately."

Oghene was very shocked. She wasn't shocked about the 'favours' and 'willing to give anything in return' parts; she was shocked at the 'stole my number' and 'lied she was someone else' parts. It simply meant that Oluomachukwu, and maybe Nkiru and Ogo were aware of what was going on. And even if she didn't tell them what had happened, they could easily find out.

"*Oya, oya, oya,*" the female soldier said, shaking Oghene out of her thoughts. Oghene looked up at her. "Start doing frog jumps now."

Oghene did not argue. She did the frog jumps all night and even almost passed out. At times she would stop to rest her legs that already started to shake, but the soldier would yell at her to keep going. The Camp Commandant and his friends left the room, so it was only Oghene and the female soldier left in the room. She ordered Oghene to keep doing the frog jumps, while she watched a show on TV, probably glad to be off gate duties that night... thanks to Oghene.

TWENTY-ONE DAYS

As Oghene continued to do the weakening frog jumps, her legs very tired and shaky, the female soldier said, "This punishment is a warning to never repeat what you've done, ever again..."

When Oghene was done thinking about her extremely embarrassing night, she swore never to look at any soldier again, never to ask for favours and never to use herself to get whatever she wanted wherever she found herself. She laid on her bed and slept off, hoping that no one would come and disturb her and ask her to go out to the parade ground, especially the female soldier that had punished her all night.

***

Morning activities started on time. There was the usual Morning Prayer, National and NYSC Anthems, then the Meditation. There were no announcements that morning before the drills and workout. Oluomachukwu knew that something had happened the night before with the Camp Commandant, and although she didn't know exactly what it was, she wondered why there were no announcements.

The only way she could know what had happened was to ask from the sources, which were Oghene and also the Camp Commandant — the Camp Commandant, she could attempt to ask, but Oghene was out of the question, plus Oghene started acting hostile towards her.

Before the drills started, Platoon Three Corps members filed out of the parade ground and to the volleyball court to meet with their platoon instructors for the division of labour. The rest of the platoons then closed up the gap that Platoon Three had left on the parade ground and they were good to go for the morning.

The drills started and the DJ played songs this time. He made sure he overplayed the usual selection of songs, and Oluomachukwu saw herself singing along to all four songs. She couldn't believe that she had learnt all the lyrics in so short a time. She felt that if she stayed longer in the camp, she would also learn the dance moves.

At 6:00am, the bugle blower came out and played the national anthem and Oluomachukwu still thought he could do better. It sounded nothing like the anthem, and when he got towards the end, the naughty male Corps members started to sing in a low tone, "*Hold something, hold something, hold something... Hold something, hold something, hold something.*" Funny enough, female Corps members joined in this time and sang with them. And just like the last time, they had sung the first line in a base-like tone, then went an octave higher for the next line. The Drill Instructor didn't caution anyone this time. And it was obvious that he also found it amusing.

The morning activity finished by 7:25am and there was still no announcement, no notice of decamping; nothing. Oluomachukwu then had to let go of the thought that the Camp Commandant would have sex with a Corps member and then decamp the Corps member. There would have to be punishments, for all parties involved. So with that, she reckoned that there would not be any announcements or decamping. If anything, the Camp Director would come and address everyone, pray for them and ask them not to receive any favours in exchange for their bodies, as it was the temple of the Lord.

Before they went for Bath and Breakfast, Auntie Vera and Sister Mary showed up. They had received yet another distress call from the socials representative and wanted to sort things out while there was still time. Apparently, the socials representative had gone to give Olufemi's name to the Socials Committe as the Platoon Seven representative for Camp Idol, but was told that not only would Olufemi sing, he would have to dance as well. The only problem was that Olufemi couldn't dance to save his own life.

So basically, the socials representative wanted a dancer, or even dancers, to accompany Olufemi on stage, because

Olufemi had to be there compulsorily. Once Auntie Vera finished speaking and the socials representative finished explaining, they waited for volunteers, preferably girls, but no one came forward. Neither Auntie Vera nor Sister Mary was shocked, they already knew how Platoon Seven Corps members operated.

Oluomachukwu felt that it was too early to make that kind of request, especially as it was time for breakfast and they were also using up the time for something that didn't interest anyone. But in order not to waste anytime, Ekene volunteered to dance and Oluomachukwu volunteered to coach her. And since Olufemi couldn't dance, a guy from the platoon that claimed he could dance also volunteered to coach him.

Once all that was decided, Auntie Vera dismissed the crowd, and they ran off in different directions like a colony of ants that had been scattered around with a stick.

Breakfast was the usual bread, boiled egg and tea, and Oluomachukwu wasn't interested, as usual. She didn't buy Gala either, as she wasn't feeling hungry, instead she went to check on Ogo in the clinic.

Ogo's ankle had been massaged and bandaged, pending recovery. She had also been cleared to leave the clinic and go about her daily activities, but with not much stress to her right leg. She wondered how she would go about her daily activities without using one of her legs.

When Oluomachukwu saw her, she was in the clinic ward, resting on the CMD's bed. It was Ogo that told her that it was the CMD's bed. The CMD had also personally taken care of her leg, making sure to do the massaging and the bandaging. They sat there and talked for a short while before Nkiru joined them. They were to go back to their hostel room together, but before they did, Ogo held them back and looked around.

"What is it?" Nkiru asked. "Why are you scouting the area?"

"I finally got some more information about Fadeke," Ogo whispered.

"Really?" Oluomachukwu exclaimed, not noticing that she had raised her voice. When she felt a lot of eyes gazing at her, she whispered, "Really?"

Ogo nodded. "Yes, and keep your voice down."

"So what is the gist?" Nkiru asked. "So what are you waiting for?" Oluomachukwu asked simultaneously.

Ogo shook her head. "Fadeke is pregnant... for a camp official."

***

Oluomachukwu and Nkiru escorted Ogo back to the room, supporting her under each arm as she limped. They were both speechless after the revelation. Oluomachukwu wondered what was going on and why people couldn't just hold themselves until after the twenty-one days. Ijeoma and Eternity had already been decamped, because they just couldn't control themselves, and she wondered where they were at that moment. She also wondered if there were also scandals in the male hostel. If there were, then they were good at hiding them, because there had not been any male Corps member decamped yet for scandalous reasons. The only thing they had had were three drunken guys.

Oluomachukwu and Nkiru took Ogo upstairs, and then went back downstairs. Neither wanted to comment on the Fadeke story, even though they were both dying inside to know who exactly the 'responsible' camp official was and what the consequences were going to be. All they could do was to wait until the State Coordinator decided on what to do — either to release the information or not.

Ogo said that Fadeke had confided in the CMD. She told him that she wasn't going to give out the name of the camp official until she had spoken to him about it and also spoken to the State Coordinator. The State Coordinator had travelled to Abuja, and was to return the next day, so

Oluomachukwu and Nkiru were willing to wait. Until then, they had to worry about other important things like getting prepared for the Miss NYSC contest, the Camp Idol dance and SAED activities for that afternoon. Oluomachukwu was already getting tired of the camp activities.

SAED activities followed after Bath and Breakfast, and Oluomachukwu couldn't attend. The activities were to run for two hours, so she decided to coach Ekene for an hour and thirty minutes, then go and give an excuse to the team instuctor and also sign her card during the remaining thirty minutes. Nkiru accompanied her to the dining hall to give support; she, too, didn't want to attend any SAED activity.

Olufemi was there, singing instead of dancing. He had written a song and he was rehearsing it. His voice was soft and sweet... very melodious. Oluomachukwu didn't know the song, but the delivery was soothing to the ears, even though she thought he was better off rehearsing the dance, because his voice was good to go. Afam was the guy who had volunteered to coach Olufemi, but he was on his cell phone, probably watching videos online, and was laughing. Oluomachukwu felt that he had taken the role just to be away from the parade ground and other camp activities — Corps members would do anything just to stay away from the parade ground.

Oluomachukwu and Ekene spent almost one long hour dancing and trying to create a proper routine, but it didn't look like anything was sticking. Olufemi was still singing over the song that played from Oluomachukwu's phone, while Afam kept looking at them at intervals and laughing. It wasn't sure if he was still watching videos online or if he was laughing at their inability to put a simple dance routine together. They had changed songs like five times and still couldn't get anything good.

Nkiru had been watching them quietly all the while, and like a light bulb that had just been flicked on, her eyes lit up. "I think I know what the problem is," she said. She sat on a plastic table and was swinging her legs casually, rhythmically, left to right, back and front. She looked back and forth at Oluomachukwu, Ekene, Olufemi and Afam.

"Okay, what is the problem?" Oluomachukwu sighed and folded her arms under her breasts.

"Well, all your songs suck, and you are just twisting and rolling your waists. That's chick dance." Everyone turned and looked at Afam as he said that.

Oluomachukwu was offended. "What do you mean by that?" she shot back at him, sounding angry. "You've been sitting over there for more than an hour, laughing instead of contributing. Now you say our songs suck and that we are doing a chick dance. Should we be doing a dick dance then?"

Nkiru, Ekene and Olufemi muffled a laugh, then Nkiru said, "That was actually the problem I noticed, but I would not have put it that way. Olufemi and Ekene are meant to be dancing. So they should both be on their feet and do something that blends. Ekene can do a chick dance around Olufemi, while Olufemi... well, he can do the dick dance." Nkiru laughed.

Afam gazed at Oluomachukwu, giving her a sour look, as if she had just wounded his ego. She noticed, but didn't react to it.

Nkiru continued, "I think all four of you should pick a song, then contribute to the moves. While Oluomachukwu is teaching Ekene a routine, Afam should also be teaching Olufemi one as well."

Both Ekene and Olufemi nodded.

Oluomachukwu looked at the time on her phone and it was twenty minutes left to the end of SAED activities, so she took an excuse to quickly go and explain to the group instructor and also have her card signed. Before she left, she asked Ekene, Olufemi and Afam to pick a song with Nkiru, who represented her. She then told them to start rehearsing a dance routine, and once she was done with signing her SAED card, she would rejoin them and add to the dance routine. They all agreed and she ran off.

Giving an excuse and signing her SAED card was easy, in fact, too easy. Oluomachukwu didn't even have to stay the whole twenty minutes. When she got there, they were already in a Question and Answer session, and since she had missed the whole session, she obviously couldn't ask any questions or understand the answers. There were two instructors unlike the last time when there were three, so it was now just the lead instructor and an assistant.

When the assistant instructor started answering one of the questions, Oluomachukwu went to the lead instructor and whispered into his ear. She knew how inappropriate it looked and felt, but she believed it was the right time to get what she wanted. She explained to him that she was needed to help with rehearsals for a competition for that evening and he nodded. She also asked him if he could sign her card. He stretched forth his hand, took the card and signed it.

Oluomachukwu smiled and ran off, using the left side of the hostel that led to the back of the camp so that soldiers wouldn't see her and send her back to the parade ground. There was a CBN — Central Bank of Nigeria — lecture after SAED activities and she wasn't sure what it was going to be about, but like every other lecture, that one too was compulsory. She would have loved to sit back and listen, but platoon duties called.

As Oluomachukwu was coming out from the corner of the hostel where some red mobile toilets stood, she saw someone running towards the rear entrance of the hostel from the dining hall. It took her a few seconds to realise who it was.

"Nkiru... Nkiru..." Oluomachukwu yelled, but her voice faded into the noise or music that was playing. Even with all the SAED instructors speaking over their voices, music still blasted out in the camp, especially in the camp market. Oluomachukwu started running towards the rear entrance of the hostel and called Nkiru again. Nkiru looked at her and stopped.

When she finally got to Nkiru, almost out of breath, she asked, "Nkiru, what's wrong? Did something happen?"

Nkiru was also out of breath. "No." She panted. "But I just saw Cleaner, right now. He came to watch us rehearse behind the dining hall."

"So what?" Oluomachukwu raised her eyebrows.

"He told me that I was stained. Can you help me check, please?"

"He said that?" Oluomachukwu was surprised.

"Yes, he did. And he said it casually, as if it was normal. Everyone looked at me, then at my shorts, and it was very embarrassing, so I had to run off."

Oluomachukwu laughed. The idea of Nkiru running off was actually funny. "Turn around, let me see."

Nkiru turned around and Oluomachukwu didn't say a thing. After a few long seconds, she turned her head back slightly and looked at Oluomachukwu. "So?"

"I can't see anything." Oluomachukwu pursed her lips. "Okay, open up your legs a bit and bend." Nkiru did it and Oluomachukwu saw some stains. "Hmm."

"What does 'hmm' mean?" Nkiru asked, then turned around completely.

"I'm just wondering how Cleaner's eyes got there. I had to bend down to see it. What exactly was he looking at, or rather, looking for down there?" Oluomachukwu raised an eyebrow.

"I don't know. But it's funny that I'm stained, because I'm not on my period." Nkiru started making her way to the hostel to change her shorts. "Please, follow me."

Oluomachukwu laughed and followed her. "So what's the stain then, if it's not from your period?"

"I think I might know what it is, but you won't believe it."

"What?" Oluomachukwu couldn't handle the suspense. "What is it?"

"I used the toilet today, but I decided to use water to wash up for the first time instead of using toilet paper..."

Oluomachukwu immediately started laughing, holding her stomach and tilting her head backwards, the same way Nkiru always laughed.

"It's not funny *nau*." Nkiru also laughed. "I think as I washed my bum, the *poopoo* water poured on my shorts and coloured it dark brown, like stale blood. I'm sure it's a dark brown patch."

"Eww." Oluomachukwu could not contain her laughter anymore. "That's the funniest thing I've heard so far. But the main question is how Cleaner's eyes got there."

"I told you that he is a clean freak. And I'm never using water to wash up again. Ever."

They got to the hostel entrance, but the hostel security officials didn't want to allow them to enter, not until Nkiru showed them that she was stained.

"But do you not know how to take care of yourself or what?" one of the officials asked. "Do you not know when your period starts?"

Nkiru wanted to say that she wasn't on her period, but if she had, they wouldn't have let her enter. She kept quiet and looked at them until they allowed her go inside, but Oluomachukwu was blocked off at the gate. They didn't allow her to enter, so she waited there for Nkiru.

About ten minutes later, Nkiru came back downstairs in another pair of white shorts, not the very tight ones she normally wore. She probably didn't want the shorts to hug her legs anymore so that Cleaner's eyes wouldn't wander there anymore. She then apologised to Oluomachukwu for wasting her time and said that she had to soak the stained shorts in soapy water first before coming downstairs. As she was escorting Oluomachukwu back to the dining hall, they saw Cleaner, and Nkiru didn't know where to run to.

Cleaner jogged up to them, then looked at Nkiru, and asked, "How are you feeling now?"

Nkiru wanted to say that she was okay and that it was not her period, but the *poopoo* water story was even more embarrassing than actually being on her period. So she opened her mouth, and said, "I don't even know what that stain was. It wasn't there this morning. So maybe I sat on something."

"Right," Cleaner said. He had a look — a 'why-are-you-ashamed-to-be-on-your-period?' look. But if only he knew the real story, he would be ashamed for her. Nkiru could not stop thinking about the incident even after several days and so she dodged Cleaner every chance she got.

***

The CBN lecture ended by 1:00pm, and after that there were inter-platoon activities and language studies. In fact, it was more inter-platoon activities than language studies. The older man, who had come to teach Yoruba the last time didn't come again. Oluomachukwu felt that he had gotten the message the last time and didn't want to waste his time again. So there were more sports activities and contests, and more teams being kicked out of contests.

Oluomachukwu wasn't aware of all the other sports, but information had it that Platoon Seven's football team was going to play the finals with Platoon Nine's team the following week. Platoon Seven's team had been kicked out of volleyball, so it was just social activities left for them. And after the silly Camp-Commandant-joke, there were no guaranteed first place prizes for Platoon Seven.

Ekene and Olufemi practiced until it was 2:00pm, and time for Lunch and Siesta. They all agreed to reconvene by 4:00pm and do more rehearsals until it was time for the event. The camp kitchen served yam porridge and fish for lunch, and Oluomachukwu wasn't interested. She went to *mami* market to eat *jollof* rice, plantain and fried beef with Nkiru and Ogo. Nkiru almost choked when Cleaner saw them in *mami* market and asked to join them for lunch. The more she tried to be away from him, the more he was just there; everywhere.

Cleaner had lunch with them, quietly. They didn't say any word until he finished eating and left.

***

After lunch, there was an NYSC lecture until 4:45pm, which Oluomachukwu didn't go for, because she hadn't bothered to find out what it was about. Instead she met with Ekene, Olufemi and Afam. Nkiru didn't join them, because Cleaner had come around to watch them. They rehearsed for a few more hours, while drills, martial arts, man-o-war and sports activities went on. Dinner was then announced by 6:30pm and Oluomachukwu didn't bother eating anything. Her lunch had barely even digested, so she wasn't going to refill her stomach again.

Nkiru had gone back to the hostel after she put on her 'on duty' badge and hung out with Ogo. They were going to stay there until it was time to come out for the idols event. When it was thirty minutes to the start of the event, Ekene went upstairs to get dressed. She stayed on the third floor, so Oluomachukwu followed her to her room to help her out.

Ekene wore pink and black horizontal stripped leggings that hugged her buttocks and made her hips appear larger than normal. She then wore a black tank top and a short pink jacket that matched her leggings. She held her hair in a bun, applied nice make-up and was good to go.

Oluomachukwu went to call Nkiru to accompany her to the show, then they met Ekene by the stairs and went downstairs together. Ogo, on the other hand, stayed back in the room, confined to her bed, and had her phone glued to her ear. Whether she was speaking with her New York boyfriend or the CMD, Oluomachukwu didn't know, but Ogo seemed to be happy and it reminded Oluomachukwu that she also had to speak with Okechukwu. She checked her phone and Okechukwu still hadn't sent her a message.

The event went well. One after the other, as usual, each contestant came out and sang. Some people sang popular songs and got standing ovations, while some people, not too popular, but they still got amazing support from their platoon members. Olufemi sang, but the passion he had while he was still rehearsing wasn't there anymore. It was as if he was shy, uncomfortable or afraid of the crowd. He had his head bent down as he sang and his voice could be barely heard. He also played a musical instrument, a guitar, which was a surprise to many people.

When he was done, he didn't get any loud cheers or loud clapping. In fact, Oluomachukwu didn't know he was done until the contestant for Platoon Eight was called out. And as usual, and even after being begged, Platoon Seven members didn't come out to support their own.

After the singing round was over, the dancing round started. Each contestant had to come out with their dance partner or partners to present. Some danced to very simple songs, while some did dance dramas. Olufemi and Ekene danced to 'Show Me' by Yung Stet featuring Chris Brown.

They were in sync with the dance when it started and Oluomachukwu was impressed by the work that Nkiru and Afam had done with them.

The only problem was that Olufemi forgot his dance steps about ten seconds later and started doing something else. He kept on looking at Ekene and repeating her steps a few seconds after she did them.

They had barely finished their display when the DJ cut the song. He said that all contestants were given only two minutes, so their time was already up. And surprisingly the crowd applauded them, and Oluomachukwu was sure that the claps were more for Ekene than for Olufemi.

Shortly after Platoon Ten's performance, the judges conferred, and in less than five minutes the results were ready. The Socials Committee's Head gave a speech before she called out the result. She reminded everyone that the ten contestants had been judged by their ability to sing and dance, and that no additional scores were added because of their dance partner or partners. Oluomachukwu and Nkiru knew exactly where that talk was going.

When the woman was done with the speech, she called the result starting from the tenth place. And it was Platoon Seven. Olufemi was given one carton of Indomie noodles and he left the stage. Oluomachukwu and Nkiru also left immediately after that.

Oluomachukwu, Nkiru and Ekene laughed out loud as they went back to the hostel. Ekene admitted that she had a lot of fun notwithstanding the result. They also laughed at how Olufemi had forgotten the dance steps and done whatever he liked on stage. He had laughed about it as well while he was still on stage. Ekene had even seen some of the judges laughing while they danced. But in all, she had so much fun. And to show appreciation, Olufemi gave her the whole carton of Indomie noodles.

Ekene left Oluomachukwu and Nkiru when she got to the third floor, so they continued up to the fourth floor together. Ogo was already asleep when they entered the room, so both of them also eased into their beds to sleep. It had been a long day so it was just sleep on their minds.

As Oluomachukwu got very comfortable to sleep, she glanced at Oghene, who was looking at her with her lips tightened up. Oghene hissed and turned around to face the other side of the room just as her and Oluomachukwu's eyes met. It was as if she was irritated by the mere sight of Oluomachukwu. But Oluomachukwu did not care, as she knew that sooner or later, she would find out why Oghene was so angry.

Oluomachukwu dialled Okechukwu's number and he picked up immediately.

"Hi," she said. "Where have you been? What happened to you?"

"Baby, I am very sorry," he replied. "Work has been so demanding, and I went to Ghana over the weekend for an emergency programme, and I wasn't roaming with my cell phone."

"Ghana, hmm." She sighed.

"Yeah," he said, through his breath. "So how have you been?"

"I've been fine and a lot has been happening. It can be fun at times, but it's too repetitive other times and it gets tiring as well. There's always one lecture or the other, and an activity everyday. No time to rest between rehearsals. I can't wait to get home."

Okechukwu laughed. "Don't be such a lazy bum, babe. I went through it too."

"I can bet you never went to the parade ground once."

"Okay, I actually never did," he replied, and they both laughed. After a brief pause he said, "I miss you so much."

"I miss you too, so very much," she replied, happy that for once, he hadn't waited for her to say it first.

There was a sudden silent moment and it felt intimate. They could hear each other breathe and it sounded close. Then they started to talk about everything and nothing — their fears, their hopes, their dreams, their future and their past, their recent past. And that was when Oluomachukwu told Okechuwku that she had slept with Kayode in Abuja. And before he could react to that, she threw the Nnanna bomb. He didn't say anything again... in fact, he refused to say anything until she ended the call. And she went to bed, regretting her decision and her confession.

CHAPTER NINETEEN: DAY FIFTEEN

Tuesday, 19 th August 2014

Oluomachukwu woke up feeling very moody. She had hardly slept, as all that crossed her mind was Okechukwu — what she had said to him and how he had reacted, by not saying anything. It was as though a knot had been tied in her belly. She didn't know why she was feeling that way. She checked her phone, there was no text message from him, at least to talk about what she had told him. They had both agreed to talk about everything, so she trusted him and that was why she was able to open up to him.

She felt around her bed and her tap water bottles were still full. She had taken them out of the bucket for a few days now and they still hadn't gone down. It was getting suspicious. She had her own drinking water, which she hid inside her duvet cover, and she made sure not to drink it when people were looking at her.

She reluctantly got up and went to have her bath, tying her wrapper around her breasts and carrying her bucket with her toiletries. She dragged her feet and got to the bathroom, and fortunately for her, 'Fucking Space' wasn't there. She felt that 'Fucking Space' had definitely gone to use a new bathroom, where she could monopolise the bath space without being disturbed by anyone.

The bathroom was full that morning. It wasn't even 4:00am yet, and Oluomachukwu wondered why everyone was up early and already in the bathroom. There was one girl taking her bath, and Oluomachukwu eyed the girl from head to toe. She washed up very fast and poured water on herself with unexplainable speed and shivered each time. She was cold and it was because she was skinny. She had a very lean body and her breasts stood like large nipples on her chest. She finished in less than two minutes, and the next person went in.

There were about five people waiting in the line before Oluomachukwu, but she didn't mind. She used the time to brush her teeth, all the while thinking about Okechukwu. She didn't know how long she had the toothbrush in her mouth, but she was carried away when someone screamed dramatically, startling her.

She jumped to the side and looked towards the source of the screaming. A girl was standing in the middle of the bathroom, looking at her toothbrush that had fallen from her mouth and was now on the floor, in dirty water. The girl awkwardly looked at it for a couple more seconds, then walked away. Oluomachukwu thought the screaming and drama weren't necessary.

"That girl must be an idiot," a girl, who looked older than everyone in the bathroom, said, as she washed her kit in a bucket of heavily soapy water. "She lacks proper home training. How can she drop her toothbrush on the floor and leave it there. I wonder whom she is waiting for to pick it up and put it in the bin for her. *Tufiakwa!*" The girl exclaimed, then raised her shoulders to show her disgust.

Nobody said anything. They just looked at the girl who spoke, then looked at the toothbrush again like they hadn't seen it the first time. Oluomachukwu finished brushing her teeth, then waited until it was her turn to have her bath. As she was about to leave, she saw Nkiru and Ogo, who was limping, come into the bathroom, both looking half asleep. Oluomachukwu dropped her bucket for Nkiru to use, then left.

By the time Oluomachukwu was getting back to the room, the sound of the bugle echoed through the rooms in the hostel, waking most of the girls up. Oluomachukwu sighed — for once, she wasn't ready on time, and it was because she had been distracted all morning. She checked her phone again before she got kitted and checked it again before she was ready to leave; nothing new. She didn't wait for Nkiru and Ogo to come back to the room, she just put her cap on, buckled her waist pouch loosely around her waist, then left for the parade ground.

Morning activities went as usual and she was already getting bored by it. Maybe she wasn't really getting bored, it was just her bad mood taking the best of her. Before the drills started, Platoon Four Corps members filed out to the volleyball court to report to their platoon instructors for their duties. Oluomachukwu did not participate in any of the morning activity. She just went to stand by the wall and watched as Corps members jogged around, singing along with the Drill Instructor.

One of Platoon Seven's female soldiers, who had the bold tribal marks scattered across her cheeks, went to meet Oluomachukwu. "Wetin you dey do for there? You no fit jog, *abi* your leg don break?"

Oluomachukwu looked at her, then at her tribal marks. They were very distracting. She then deciphered what the woman had said to be '*What are you doing there, can't you jog or is your leg broken?*' Oluomachukwu replied, "I'm not feeling well, ma. Good morning, ma."

"Wetin *dey* do you?" She looked at Oluomachukwu's face, then at her belly as if menstrual period or probably, pregnancy were the only things that could ever be wrong with a girl who wasn't feeling too well.

Oluomachukwu took a few seconds to decipher the question again: '*What's wrong with you?*' then she replied, "I don't know, ma. I don't just feel too well this morning, ma. Please, ma, can I stand here? Just for today, ma?"

"Which one be all this 'ma-ma-ma?' *Abi* you no know *wetin* my name be?"

Oluomachukwu deciphered — *'What's with all the 'ma-ma-ma?' Or don't you know what my name is?'* But before she could reply, the soldier pressed further.

"*Wetin* be my name?" she asked, and it sounded more like a threat than a question.

Oluomachukwu looked around and people had already started looking at her, laughing at the whole scenario.

"Na so dey ask one girl for my name oh, and instead, she go describe me. She come say 'the soldier woman wey get mark everywhere for face.'" The soldier then turned to someone else, and asked, "Na that be my name? My name na tribal mark?"

Oluomachukwu shook her head. She wasn't used to Pidgin English, so she acted fast in her decoding — *'That was how one girl was asked for my name, and instead, she described me by saying, 'that lady soldier with marks all over my face.' When she turned to someone else, she asked, 'Is that my name? Is my name 'tribal marks?'"*

While Oluomachukwu was deciphering the final part of the conversation, the tribal-marked soldier already started talking to some other Corps members who replied to her questions. She was making more jokes and walking away, when Oluomachukwu stopped her.

"Ma, please, what is your name?"

"My name *na* Antonia Igose. Lance-Corporal A. Igose. L.C.P.L, na so dem dey write am."

"Thank you, ma," Oluomachukwu responded, then she deciphered the last bit — *'My name is Antonia Igose. Lance-Corporal A. Igose. L.C.P.L, that's how it is written.'*

The soldier then walked away and went around to see what everyone else was doing, forgetting that she initially wanted Oluomachukwu to join in on the jogging and leave the wall area where she was standing. The Corps members jogged until it was 6:00am when the bugle blower came and played what he liked. He must have still been sleepy or might have woken up on the wrong side of the bed, but the sound was nothing like the other ones he had played. It was completely off tune, and the naughty Corps members couldn't even sing their "Hold something" line to it.

After the morning drill was over, Corps members were to go for Bath and Breakfast between 7:30am and 8:55am. But before all Platoon Seven Corps members left, Auntie Vera and Sister Mary came out of nowhere and told them to wait behind just for a very brief meeting. Everybody grumbled since the instructors were taking their breakfast time, again.

"Please, listen. I have just been informed that there will be a Business Plan lecture this afternoon, and after that, there'll be a contest in three days. So three representatives would be expected from each platoon. I need the names of three people, now. Who studied Business Administration, Management or any course in a related field?"

Nobody replied.

"Please, let us not do this again. Please," Auntie Vera pleaded. "I just need three people to go for the lecture, but everyone will participate in preparing the business plan."

At that instant, someone tapped Oluomachukwu at the back. She turned around and saw Nkiru, then she smiled a weak smile at her.

"Is something the matter?" Nkiru asked. But before Oluomachukwu replied to her, Nkiru winced. "Ouch."

Oluomachukwu looked at Nkiru's hand and saw that there was a little pink card in it with a pin. It was a '4 ON DUTY' card and the pin that had been used to hold the card pierced her thumb. "I see you are fully back on your platoon hopping," Oluomachukwu said.

Nkiru smiled. "I guess I am. So what's wrong with you? You have been acting odd. You were also acting funny this morning, and you left us to go to the parade ground alone. Now, you are not smiling."

Oluomachukwu shrugged her shoulders. "Just having a bad day, I guess. I believe I woke up on the wrong side of the bed."

"I know what you mean," Nkiru replied, then tilted her head to the side. "What's that witch talking about now? Is it every morning that they have meetings?"

Oluomachukwu laughed. It was the first time she was laughing that morning. "She said that there'll be a Business Plan lecture today, and also a competition afterwards, and she needs three representatives."

"This woman is so demanding. In fact, the whole camp is demanding. All the activities are so packed up together."

Oluomachukwu wanted to reply, but stopped when she realised that everyone was staring at her and Nkiru. Before she knew what was happening, Auntie Vera was already in front of her, and she hit her on the shoulder. She also hit Nkiru on the shoulder.

"Are you girls deaf?" Auntie Vera asked. "Didn't you hear me tell both of you to shut up?"

Oluomachukwu and Nkiru glanced at each other. They hadn't heard anything that Auntie Vera had said earlier on. They glanced back at Auntie Vera, but didn't say anything.

"In fact, the two of you should go and register for the Business Plan lecture and competition." She looked behind her and spoke to the platoon president. "My dear, take a piece of paper and write down their names. Then we need one more person to add to the list."

One guy raised his hand to join the group and Auntie Vera asked him what he had studied. He said he studied Engineering for his Bachelors degree, then Engineering Management for his Masters. Everyone stared at him as if he was a mini god.

"What is your name?" Auntie Vera asked.

"Juachi, ma."

Auntie Vera looked at the platoon president again. "Put Juachi's name and code down."

"Ma," Nkiru raised her hand, not the one that held the

card and the pin, the other one. "I'm already preparing for Miss NYSC. I won't be able to do this one too."

"Oh, that's true." Auntie Vera looked at her from head to toe, as if she was checking to see if she was still the right candidate. "Please, who else wants to join the team?"

One other girl raised her hand. "Me, ma. I want to join the team and I studied Creative Arts."

"What can you even do with it?" Auntie Vera raised an eyebrow. "Can you manage a business?"

"I can add to the creativity of the business plan."

"Okay, what is your name?" Auntie Vera didn't sound convinced, but relieved to have gotten someone.

"Anita, ma."

Auntie Vera looked at the platoon president yet again. "Please, add her name and code number too to the list."

As Auntie Vera was about to dismiss the team, one girl raised her hand and everyone complained loudly. Auntie Vera asked them all to keep quiet, then looked at the girl.

"Who are you? Are you in this platoon?" Auntie Vera asked.

"Yes, ma. I am."

"Platoon Seven?" Auntie Vera was doubtful.

The girl nodded. "Yes, ma."

"So why haven't I seen you before now?" Before the girl could answer, Auntie Vera turned to look at the female platoon president, and asked, "Do you know her?"

The female platoon president shook her head. "No."

Auntie Vera then turned to the male platoon president and repeated the question. He said "No" as well. She went ahead and asked other platoon members, and one by one, they said "No."

Auntie Vera looked back at the girl. "Nobody knows you here. Let me see your badge."

The girl gave her badge to Auntie Vera. Auntie Vera scrutinised it, then gave it back to the girl. The four-digit code number ended in seven. She was definitely in Platoon Seven.

"So where have you been all this while?" Auntie Vera asked.

"Partly in my room, partly in the clinic ward. I have not been feeling too well."

"Since we got to this camp?" Auntie Vera snapped her fingers several times to indicate 'a long time ago.'

"Yes, ma," the girl replied.

There was absolute silence within the platoon, but not in the camp.

"Okay, so what is it?"

"I want to contest for Miss NYSC, ma."

Everyone remained silent and stared at her, wondering if she had been sitting under a rock the whole time.

"Where were you when we were seriously searching for a representative?"

"I didn't know when they started looking for someone, until they mentioned it in my room."

Auntie Vera looked at the girl, then looked at Nkiru, then looked back at the girl who really wanted to represent the platoon, but didn't look like she would be in the first five positions, let alone win.

"What is your name?" Auntie Vera asked. She hadn't checked it on the girl's badge.

"Eugenia, ma," she replied. "My name is Eugenia."

***

Oluomachukwu didn't know how she forgot about her sorrow. Since the morning activity and impromptu Platoon Family Meeting, she had long forgotten that she was upset with Okechukwu. She didn't have breakfast, but she went to the clinic ward with Nkiru to see Ogo briefly. Ogo had gotten another massage and re-bandaging. It seemed like her leg was getting better, so it meant that she just wanted the CMD to touch and rub her leg.

That was what Oluomachukwu and Nkiru concluded, making Ogo blush, even on her dark skin.

TWENTY-ONE DAYS

As they left the clinic ward, Oluomachukwu and Nkiru went to *mami* market to get a dress for Nkiru. They didn't go to the woman they had visited the first time. They went to another one, which was just opposite the first one. They didn't feel bad, because they didn't owe the first woman anything. They also didn't think the woman would even recognise them. And besides, only two stalls sold dresses. So it was either one or the other.

As Nkiru was trying on dresses, Oluomachukwu waited outside. She pulled her phone out of her waist pouch and dialled Okechukwu's number. He didn't pick. She dialled it at least three more times when a text message came in.

"In a meeting, please. Would call back."

It was from Okechukwu, and Oluomachukwu knew he wasn't in any meeting. He was obviously avoiding her. She contemplated replying, but before she did, she heard her name from behind, from a very firm and mature voice. She turned around, and saw who had called her.

"Good morning, sir." She grinned. It was the Camp Commandant.

"What are you doing here?" he asked.

"I came with a friend to get a dress for the Miss NYSC contest."

"Okay, I know you will win."

Oluomachukwu smiled, or blushed. It wasn't sure. "It's not me contesting."

"Oh. Who is then? The person should better win or let you do it."

Oluomachukwu smiled, or blushed, again. It still wasn't sure. "It's my friend, Nkiru, doing it."

"Which one is Nkiru again?"

"The slim and tall one. She is inside the stall. You'll see her when she comes out."

The Camp Commandant kept quiet for a second, then looked at Oluomachukwu. "That other girl called me, the one who stole my number. And I called her back."

Oluomachukwu already knew that, but she still nodded,

wearing a surprised look on her face.

"I told her to come to my room after Lights Out and she made it possible, even with the security officers in the female hostel," he continued.

Oluomachukwu liked where the conversation seemed to be going, but suddenly wasn't sure why he was telling her, since it would be awkward to mention that he had sex with a Corps member.

"She is a very useless girl. She was ready to do anything to get favours for posting to a private company. Can you imagine?"

Oluomachukwu kept quiet. She felt the awkward part was coming and wasn't prepared to hear it.

"She even attempted to take off her shirt when I asked her to, but then one of my friends scolded her."

Oluomachukwu popped her eyes open, shocked. The word 'friends' had thrown her off balance. So there were more than two men... and just Oghene. Could that have caused her to limp? Oluomachukwu wondered to herself. She obviously couldn't ask that.

"I just got on my phone and made a few calls until one of the female gate officers came and I asked her to punish the useless girl. I heard the girl did frog jumps all night." The Camp Commandant laughed. "I made sure I told her that I knew she had stolen my phone number and that she was impersonating someone else."

Oluomachukwu's jaw dropped at the frog jumps and at him revealing that he knew her secrets. It then explained why Oghene was looking at her very funny since that day. Anyway, it was Oghene's problem. She got herself into the mess, so it was her own problem. Oluomachukwu finally laughed, even though it was eons later. She took some time to process all the information and laughed even more.

The Camp Commandant had a satisfied look on his face as if his mission had been to make Oluomachukwu laugh. Shortly afterwards, he told her to enjoy the rest of the day and went on his own way. Oluomachukwu ran into the stall immediately after and halted when she saw Nkiru standing there, looking at her.

"Have you found something?" Oluomachukwu asked. "I thought you would come out. The Camp Commandant was here and I wanted you to see him."

"I have found a dress," Nkiru said.

Oluomachukwu hadn't noticed before. She looked at the dress and it was beautiful; a pale-green alter-neck dress with glitters. It looked like what Agbani Darego had worn for the 2001 Miss World beauty pageant, which she won. Oluomachukwu was surprised that *mami* market had such a beautiful dress. It cost 8,000 naira and Nkiru paid for it. They also got a pair of silver high-heeled shoes for 5,000 naira, which Oluomachukwu paid for — they were then ready for the contest. Nkiru was going to do her hair on the day of the contest, so her work was almost done.

They put the dress and shoes in different plastic bags, then left. For some strange reason, they glanced at the woman who sat in front of the other clothes' stall, and she looked at them from head to toe, and hissed. She definitely remembered them.

As they walked towards the hostel, Oluomachukwu said, "Oh that's true, you can not believe what I heard. The Camp Commandant told me what really happened with Oghene. They didn't have sex."

"I know, I know," Nkiru replied, smiling. " I listened to everything from inside the stall."

***

Oluomachukwu went for her SAED activity and sat through it. She counted each second as it went by, because she was sleepy, very sleepy. She was also starting to feel hungry and then regretted why she skipped breakfast. She could have bought one Gala sauge roll to hold her until it was lunchtime, but she couldn't go to *mami* market at that time. No one was supposed to be there and the soldiers were making sure it remained that way.

Sometimes, hawkers walked round the parade ground during lectures, bending down as they carried their basins of biscuits, sweets, snacks, sodas and water. If they got caught, their goods were seized, so they came only during specific lectures. SAED group time was too dangerous, as it could expose them, since Corps members were in small groups.

Oluomachukwu had to sit and wait, hungry, tired and sleepy, her head bouncing from left to right at intervals, when she drifted in and out of sleep. To keep busy, she played games on her phone. She had recently downloaded Smash Hit on her phone, and spent the rest of the time playing it. She stopped sometimes to check if Okechukwu had sent her a message or called her back. She didn't know why she did that, as she would have gotten notifications, either way. When the SAED activity was over, her card was signed and she ran off to buy herself one Gala and a plastic bottle of Fanta.

After that, she strolled casually to the dining hall, where the Business Plan lecture was to be held. Apart from the representatives, who were thirty in number, other Corps members were to sit at the parade ground for a lecture on Professional Orientation and the topic was on Education, Engineering and Law. The Platoon Four Corps members on Environmental duties had arranged the chairs under the canopy for the lecture. Oluomachukwu wished she could know what the lecture was about, but she supposed that learning to write a business plan was also a professional orientation.

She entered the dining hall and saw Juachi and Anita who were already seated and had saved a spot for her. The lecture was very concise. The instructor explained what the course was about and also the terms of the competition. With the guidelines he was going to give, each team was to design a business plan for a made-up company.

He started the lecture by giving a business quote from

Christopher Williams: *Every great business begins with a creative idea and tedious planning.*

At that moment, Anita looked at both Oluomachukwu and Juachi, and they understood what she was trying to say — Auntie Vera had thought she was useless, but creativity was one of the key points to success.

The instructor then continued by stating the common mistakes that people make and there were ten of them: Selling to the wrong person; Not having a niche for your ... — Oluomachukwu had slept off a bit and when she woke up, she had scribbled something incomprehensible at the end of that point. She missed the main idea, but was able to work something out; — Poor and inadequate market research; Hiring the wrong people; Failing to focus on the creation of value; Not understanding your strength and weaknesses; Weak financial planning; Taking your eyes off the competition; Spending too little or too much money.

By the time Oluomachukwu finished scribbling down everything the instructor was saying, or rather reading out of his PowerPoint presentation slides, she looked up and saw Juachi taking snapshots of each slide with his phone. At that instant, she ditched the small notebook she had, pulled out her phone — still no text message or call from Okechukwu — and started taking snapshots of the other slides that followed.

The instructor went ahead to define a business plan — a road map — then listed out three purposes of a business plan. He also listed five importances of a business plan and concluded with the ten main elements of a business plan. Oluomachukwu had slept almost all through, but when it came to the end, she woke up. The ten elements were the most important parts of the business plan and the contest. All representatives were supposed to use the elements as a guide in drawing up the business plan.

Oluomachukwu had taken snapshots of each slide that had one element and an explanatory text. They were, and in order of appearance: the Executive Summary; About the company; Products and Services; Target market; Marketing strategy; Competitors; Management team; Operations; Financial forecast; and the Conclusion. Oluomachukwu added 'With Risk management' after the conclusion as an addition to the elements. She had learnt that part in the university and felt it was going to give them an extra point.

When the class was over, she staggered out, but before leaving, she made arrangements to meet Juachi and Anita after Lunch and Siesta to decide on a business idea, and then start working on the business plan. It was actually due in two days' time, but could be submitted anytime before then. Then for the competition, when they would present the plan, was on the third day, so they had a lot of work to do... with so little time, of course.

***

Oluomachukwu, Nkiru and Ogo didn't know what the camp kitchen was serving for lunch and they didn't bother checking. They went to *mami* market to eat lunch — the usual for Oluomachukwu, *jollof* rice, fried plantain and chunks of beef. They didn't go to Nwanyi Imo or the Calabar kitchen this time, they decided to try another stall and they regretted it.

The amount of flies that hovered around where the women cooked, where they served the food and where people ate was alarming. Oluomachukwu and her friends had even thought of leaving, but the food had already been dished out. They complained bitterly and endlessly to the owner of the place about the flies and how they were not going to return there. They then wondered if that was why the place was empty.

"Oh, by the way, the State Coordinator is back from Abuja," Ogo said, casually.

Oluomachukwu and Nkiru looked up, removing their eyes briefly from their plates while swinging their hands fervently at the flies.

"Oh, I didn't know you and the State Coordinator were friends," Oluomachukwu said.

"Or rather, I didn't know you were her PA and that you were keeping tabs on her travels," Nkiru added.

Ogo laughed. "You silly girls. You have forgotten how desperately we were all waiting for her return."

"Oh," both Oluomachukwu and Nkiru said in unison, then Oluomachukwu added, "So?"

"Okay, according to the CMD, they all talked about it. Fadeke has confronted the man that is responsible, and he went before the State Coordinator to explain himself. They had a very long and serious conversation, but it's uncertain what the State Coordinator would eventually do."

That extra piece of information did not really interest either Oluomachukwu or Nkiru. They wanted to know the main information.

"Okay, so who's responsible for the pregnancy?" Nkiru asked.

"A certain Mr. Smith is responsible for it."

Oluomachukwu and Nkiru looked quizzically at Ogo as if they had been expecting someone in particular. And as if Ogo had read their minds, she asked, "Were you expecting someone in particular?" She looked at Oluomachukwu and Oluomachukwu shook her head, indicating 'No.' She also looked at Nkiru, and Nkiru did the same thing.

"Well," Ogo continued. "I didn't know who Mr. Smith was, so the CMD told me that his first name was Kayode, the Platoon Four Instructor."

Oluomachukwu and Nkiru kept quiet and immediately wore straight faces, as if that was the name they had been expecting. Ogo noticed.

"I'm sure that was the name you were expecting," Ogo said, sounding very suspicious. "And I'm guessing it's the same person that Nkiru had said I shouldn't know, or that I was better off not knowing, the other day."

Oluomachukwu and Nkiru still kept quiet. And just like conjoined twins, sharing internal organs, both their hearts thundered in their chests at the same time and at the same frequency. They believed that Ogo was going to ask them why Nkiru had said what she said the other time, and also if either of them had had anything to do with him.

"And just for the record," Ogo said, startling the two of them. "He wouldn't have seduced me. I know that was what you were afraid of."

Oluomachukwu looked at Nkiru, and they exchanged brief glances, hoping that each would understand what it meant: "*If only she knew.*"

They were done having their lunch shortly afterwards and left in a hurry. It was not the sound of the bugle that drove them out, but the disgusting clusters and hovering of flies that did.

***

Drills, man-o-war and martial arts contests held that evening, and Oluomachukwu didn't even know who had represented Platoon Seven or what positions they had all taken. The sports representative was not like the socials representative who needed to call the whole platoon out each time he needed one volunteer. She, Nkiru and Ogo went to the camp market to hang out until it was time for dinner, which they didn't eat in the kitchen. They ordered small chops, *asun* meat and cold bottles of Orijin, then sat to enjoy life.

Oluomachukwu had been thinking too much about Okechukwu and decided it was time to stop it for the day. She was going to have fun and worry about him the next day. As they sat there eating, drinking and talking, Nkiru suddenly wanted to run under the table and hide, and that was when Oluomachukwu turned around and saw Cleaner approaching. Oluomachukwu then remembered the *poopoo* water and couldn't stop laughing.

Cleaner tapped her and Ogo on the shoulders as a form of greeting, and then went to hug Nkiru. "You girls were talking about me," he said, then pulled a chair and sat next to Nkiru.

Oluomachukwu and Nkiru laughed, because they had been thinking the same thing, but not saying it. Ogo was a little bit lost, so Oluomachukwu explained the scenario to her while Cleaner spoke to Nkiru.

After the explanation, Oluomachukwu and Ogo stayed quiet, waiting for Cleaner to be done with whatever he was saying, so that he could leave the table.

Before Cleaner left, he looked at Oluomachukwu, and asked, "What of John? How is he doing?"

"Who?" Oluomachukwu asked. It took her a couple of seconds to register who John was. That was Tracker's real name. "Oh. He is fine, I guess."

"You guess?"

Oluomachukwu wondered what Cleaner's issue was. "I haven't seen him all day."

"Okay." Cleaner shrugged. "I always used to see both of you together, so I thought you were a handle."

"We are not a handle," Oluomachukwu said, sounding defensive. "And I don't know where he is."

Cleaner smiled, stood up and left. A few minutes later, Player stopped by and almost the same thing happened. He had greeted the three of them, but instead of going to sit on the chair that Cleaner had used, he sat down briefly on the table and talked to them.

When there was nothing else to talk about, he looked at Oluomachukwu, and asked, "How is that your guy?"

Oluomachukwu was offended. "I don't have a guy."

"Oh, sorry. Calm down." Player raised both hands. "I always see you two together here, so I thought there was something going on."

"There's nothing."

"Okay. I just wanted to stop by and say hi." He saluted them, then left, probably to go and catch up with some other interesting and interested girls.

Oluomachukwu, Nkiru and Ogo drank and danced a

lot when it was just the three of them at the table. The multiple DJs played the four usual songs and some other songs too, but they didn't move the crowd as much as the main four. Ekene joined them later, and there was more fun, more drinking and more dancing. They continued that way until the sound of the bugle cut through the exciting moment. Oluomachukwu and her friends went up stairs, prepared themselves for bed and tucked themselves in to sleep. Before Oluomachukwu went to bed, she looked at her phone again — no text message or phone call from Okechukwu. Strange.

CHAPTER TWENTY: DAY SIXTEEN

Wednesday, 20 th August 2014

Oluomachukwu woke up very early in the morning. In fact, she wondered why she woke up that early and why she wasn't feeling hung over. She had a lot to drink the previous night, and had had barely three hours of sleep. She looked around the room, and although it was as dark as night, she knew that everyone was fast asleep. The only functional ceiling fan twirled with so much force that she feared it was going to fall off. She shook her head, wondering if and when the NYSC would get anything right. The only good thing so far was that she had seen just one mosquito, and she killed it. That was most important.

She felt around her cloth-pillow for her phone and as usual, there were other phones there, which she pushed down. She made a mental note to tell everybody that she didn't want any cell phones on her bed anymore. She took her phone out and noticed two things — the battery was quite low, so she removed one of the chargers there and plugged hers in, and secondly she had a text message.

She opened the message immediately and it was from Okechukwu. It came in just a few minutes after she went to bed the previous night, and she wished she had stayed up just a little longer and waited for it.

"*Hey, how are you doing?*"

That was it. Oluomachukwu hissed, but she still smiled. At least he had contacted her. And it was late at night. Maybe he couldn't sleep and was thinking about her, and that was why he sent her the message, Oluomachukwu consoled herself. She wanted to reply, but she didn't know what to write. After some time, she composed something and sent to him.

"*I'm fine, thanks. How have you been?*"

"*Okay.*" His reply came in instantly, Oluomachukwu's hand shook and the phone almost fell out of it. "*I'm also doing well.*" Another one came in again.

"*You didn't call me back yesterday.*"

"*Sorry about that. Finished the meeting late and I got carried away.*"

"*Are you sure, or are you ignoring me because of what I told you two days ago?*"

"*No.*"

Oluomachukwu didn't know what he meant by 'No.' She bit her lower lip, as she thought briefly, then replied. "*No, what?*"

"*No, I'm not ignoring you.*"

Oluomachukwu noticed that he hadn't mentioned the part about what she had told him, so it was sure that her revelation had seriously upset him and was still upsetting him. She composed another text and sent it.

"*Okay, prove it to me.*"

"*How?*"

"*Call me.*"

Oluomachukwu waited for the call, but there was none, which meant that he was still upset. She waited for at least a text message to say that he was not going to call and that didn't come in either. She decided to text him after waiting for five extra minutes.

"*Are you still there? Or was I right?*"

He still didn't reply and she didn't bother herself. She

locked her screen and put her phone under her cloth-pillow for it to charge properly. She felt around inside her duvet cover for her bottle of water. She found it and gulped it down, leaving only very little in it. She then felt around her bedside and saw that the bottles she had filled with tap water were still in tact.

In fact, she stopped to wonder if everyone in the room knew that she had filled the bottles with tap water and did not want to use them anymore. She then wondered if it had been both Nkiru and Ogo using her water all along. They were her closest friends, and it was only after she had told them her tap water plans that her water never went down again.

But whether they had been using the water or not, or they had warned the others, she didn't care anymore, all she cared about now was that she could start putting her own fresh bottles of water by her bedside again without worry.

She carried her bath things, putting the bottles of water in her bucket. She had her wrapper tied round her breasts, shivering as she went to the bathroom. The air felt very cool and wet outside as if it had rained all night and into the morning. She feared that the water was going to be freezing cold, and even after sixteen days in camp, she was still not accustomed to the cold water.

As she fetched her bath water, she emptied the bottles of water into the sink and put the bottles in a bin that was beside the bathroom door. It was a recycle bin, but when she tried to put her bottle in, she saw all sorts of things in it — food, hair extensions, underwear, shoes; garbage.

When she got back to the bathroom, her bucket was already full and was overflowing. She turned off the tap, then took a few minutes to brush her teeth. She didn't feel like she was in hurry. For the first time, there was not a single soul in the bathroom, so she took her bath and went back to the room. She entered and locked the door firmly behind her, hoping that no one had stepped out since she left, because she was about to go back to sleep and didn't want to wake up and open the door for anyone. She arranged her things under her bed, then wore her panties, bra, tight and vest, then she slid back into her bed. She checked her phone again, there was no text message from Okechukwu... she snoozed off.

The sound of the bugle woke her up with a fright and she was disoriented for a couple of seconds, seeing people running around and some dressed in all white. She finally calmed down when she remembered that she was in camp, the bugle sound was the Wake-Up call, and the white and white was part of the NYSC kit.

She looked around and saw Nkiru and Ogo getting ready. In fact, they were already kitted and were applying their make-up. She jumped out of bed and started to open her box to take out her kit.

"None of you woke me up," she said. "What if I hadn't taken my bath?"

"I woke you up, but you didn't move," Ogo replied. "Plus, all your things were wet, which meant that you had already bathed."

"I was about to wake you up again when the trumpet sounded," Nkiru added.

"Which trumpet again, *biko*?" Ogo said, as if she had just read Oluomachukwu's mind. Had Ogo not said that, Oluomachukwu would have.

"Please leave me alone, the thing sounds like a trumpet, so it's a trumpet to me." They all laughed.

Oluomachukwu immediately got ready, then as she was rushing to lace her rubber shoes, one of the lace holes tore open.

"Cheap crap," she said to herself as she devised a way of knotting the lace with the remaining holes and without tearing any other one up. She was tempted to buy another pair, but they had barely five days to go in the camp. She smiled at the thought of just five days left. Inasmuch as she couldn't wait to leave, she was gradually enjoying some little fun moments she was having with her new friends, and in *mami* market.

Everyone doubled up to the parade ground. They saw Ekene by the hostel entrance and she joined them to run down to the parade ground. The parade ground wasn't too crowded, but it wasn't too empty either. It was evident that people were getting either fatigued or nonchalant, because camp life was coming to an end and they were going to leave soon.

The OBS speaker made several announcements asking everyone to report to the parade ground. And as usual, if they were still in their rooms, they were wrong, and if they were not on the parade ground, they were very wrong.

Everyone on the parade ground mimicked the speaker as the announcements were made, and they all laughed afterwards.

The parade ground filled up after about ten minutes, thanks to some of the soldiers who went to bring out the Corps members. Almost half the male population had still been in bed, sleepy, as they were the highest buyers and consumers of alcoholic drinks. They dragged their feet to the parade ground even though the Drill Instructor kept telling them to double up.

Oluomachukwu went to stand at the back with Nkiru and Ekene, talking, then got carried away thinking about Okechukwu. She pulled out her phone to check again and there was still no text or missed call, although she would have known if a call came in. Because she was glued to her phone, Nkiru and Ekene naturally faced each other and carried on with what they were chatting about — Miss NYSC, camp life, *mami* market — she had heard it all.

Just then, she felt a pair of heavy eyes looking at her. She turned to her right side, and even in the dark, she saw Sola, or was it Segun, the guy from church, staring at her. He didn't blink even when she turned to look at him.

He felt bold and started walking up to her. But she

looked around, checking if there was still time for her to run and hide. There wasn't. By the time she looked to her side again, he was standing beside her.

"Hi, Oluoma."

She looked at him blankly.

"I'm Segun, remember me?" He laughed, trying to joke, not knowing that she had truly forgotten his name. "We met in church, two weeks ago." He overemphasised on the 'Two,' since she had missed church the last week.

"Of course, I remember you." She rolled her eyes. "Hi, Segun." She made a mental note not to forget his name again or confuse it with 'Sola.'

"I saw you dancing yesterday in *mami* market. I like the way you dance. No, in fact, I love the way you dance." He smiled widely, as if he was waiting for Oluomachukwu to blush and thank him.

She blinked.

"I also didn't know you drank, because you drank a lot. I counted every bottle that landed on your table."

"Really?" Oluomachukwu was shocked.

"Yeah, you even looked my way a couple of times and I waved at you, but you didn't see me. I'm sure the alcohol was too much for you." He laughed, but Oluomachukwu didn't find it funny.

"Well, it's nice to relax and have fun sometimes."

"I guess so." He sighed. There was a brief pause, then he asked, "I would like to have fun with you some time, so can I have your number?"

Oluomachukwu did not want to disappoint him again, but she shook her head. "Sorry."

"Who do you think you are?" he snapped.

"Why do you keep asking for my number all the time and getting upset when I don't give it to you, and you still ask me for it the next time you see me?" Oluomachukwu sighed, offended.

"You think it's because you are a fine girl that you can just treat me anyhow." He hissed. "I don't know why I'm wasting my time on a silly girl like you."

Oluomachukwu was surprised, and before she could respond to his insult, he walked away.

"Clown," she said, shook her head and laughed.

She focused her attention back to Ekene and Nkiru, who were still chatting away until the MC, whom no one knew her name still, came to address the Corps members. She told them they were late and that camp officials would start punishing people who were caught in the hostel after each bugle call. After that, she led the Morning Prayer, the National Anthem and NYSC Anthem, then a Platoon Five representative recited the Meditation.

Once that was over, all Platoon Five members left the parade ground to meet with their platoon instructors to be assigned for their duties.

When Platoon Four had closed the gap left by Platoon Five, the Drill Instructor retrieved the microphone, then spoke into it.

"Are we good to go?" he yelled.

"Good to go, good to go, good to go, sir!"

Oluomachukwu was amazed. She hadn't heard that line before. She looked at Nkiru, and she was also as clueless. Oluomachukwu was then convinced that all locally-trained Nigerian students had gone through a pre-training camp in order for them to know the response to a lot of things.

"Corpers, I repeat... Are-We-Good-To-Go?" The Drill Instructor's voice was even louder.

"Good to go, good to go, good to go, sir!" The whole place shook with the reply, because it was even louder than the first time. Oluomachukwu and Nkiru had replied too, grinning from ear to ear like little kids that had just learnt something new.

After that, the Drill Instructor asked the DJ to play some music. He didn't play the same four songs back-to-back, but a playlist that contained all four of them, and they started their drills.

***

After the morning drills and activities, Corps members were dismissed to go for Bath and Breakfast. It was *akara* and *akamu* for breakfast. Nkiru and Ogo went to take their portion from the dining hall, and complained all through as they ate it. Oluomachukwu didn't want to have anything heavy for breakfast, so she took just an energy drink with some fruits and was good to go for the morning.

They went back to the room to eat, and while they ate, they heard the OBS speaker make an announcement. It was a bit muffled, but they could hear that it was about the Miss NYSC and Mr. Macho contests that were to hold the next day.

Neither Oluomachukwu nor Nkiru reacted to it. They knew that in no time, the socials representative would call Auntie Vera and Sister Mary again to help him pass along any message that he wanted to share with the rest of the platoon.

Nkiru realised that she hadn't done any other kind of preparation for Miss NYSC since they bought the dress and shoes, so together with Oluomachukwu, they decided to meet later in the day, preferably during the SAED group meeting and have a Question and Answer session.

***

When the bugle was blown for SAED group meetings, Oluomachukwu, Nkiru and Ogo dashed off to the parade ground to their respective groups. Oluomachukwu took permission from her SAED group instructor to be absent that morning and for the whole two hours. She then got her SAED card signed and went to meet with Nkiru at the open space behind the dining hall to practice for the Miss NYSC contest by doing some Questions and Answers.

Oluomachukwu made sure she covered all areas with Nkiru, starting from the names and roles of all the NYSC officials, to the names and positions of all the camp guests so far, to NYSC's core values, to SAED and CDS groups, to the topic of all the lectures they had had so far in camp. She didn't forget to test Nkiru on important dates of the NYSC, and when Nkiru was all set, they heard the sound of the bugle for the next programme.

Just like the previous day, there was another lecture on Professional Orientation, and the main areas this time were on Education and Medicine. During that period, Auntie Vera called thirty Platoon Seven Corps members, including Oluomachukwu, Nkiru, Juachi and Anita to work on the business plan, which was due the next day. They were to benchmark on creating and developing the business plan, and so they spent the whole two hours of the Professional Orientation time working on it.

Auntie Vera further divided the group into sub-groups of threes, and each group was to work on one item of the business plan.

It made the work easier and faster for all of them, and when they were done, the three main representatives — Oluomachukwu, Juachi and Anita agreed to meet up later to consolidate the ten parts, then rent a laptop from one of the photographers that sat under canopies in *mami* market, to type up the business plan. A couple of platoons were going to give out handwritten business plans, but Platoon Seven was ready to do whatever it took to stand out.

During the end of the session, Auntie Vera's cell phone rang in her hand. It was a small regular and archaic looking phone that seemed like it had been bought specifically for the Orientation camp. So whoever called that number had to be in the camp.

Auntie Vera looked at the phone screen, sighed, then picked up the call. "Hello?" she said, then waited. "Yes, good afternoon... I know who it is... I can hear you... I said I can hear you."

Oluomachukwu wondered how Auntie Vera could hear anything, and how whoever it was on the other end could hear too. The camp was noisy as usual, and even they, had been having problems communicating around the business plan, as they had to shout a lot.

Everyone was looking at Auntie Vera as she spoke on the phone, and Oluomachukwu used the opportunity to look at her own phone — still nothing from Okechukwu.

"When?" Auntie Vera continued with her call, bringing Oluomachukwu's attention back to her. "Okay, I'm beside the hostel, on the right side if you come from the back, or left side if you come from the front... Okay... Okay, I'll be here. Bye-bye."

Auntie Vera hung up and was giving a final address on the business plan, and after a couple of minutes, the socials representative showed up. He greeted everyone, then went to whisper into Auntie Vera's ear... a very long whisper that people started to get worried. Auntie Vera sat there and listened without even blinking. Her eyes were focused directly ahead of her and her left hand was on her chin.

When she was done listening, she turned to look at the socials representative. "What is the matter with that girl? Please, go and call her for me."

The socials representative ran off, and after about five minutes, he returned with Eugenia. They all looked at her, wondering what was going on. Oluomachukwu and Nkiru knew what it was. Eugenia was the same girl that wanted to represent Platoon Seven for the Miss NYSC contest, and she wasn't going to rest until she did. Eugenia stood beside Auntie Vera, wearing a serious look.

"Why would you go and write your name on the list for Miss NYSC participants when you know full well that we already have someone?"

Everyone exchanged glances, shocked, bemused. Nkiru was somewhere between shocked and relieved, but mostly shocked.

Eugenia did not answer the question. She had a rather victorious and arrogant look that meant she could not be touched, reprimanded, challenged or removed.

"Are you deaf?" Auntie Vera asked her. "I asked you a question."

"I heard an announcement from the OBS that platoons had to give the names of their representatives for the two contests before noon. So I went there by 11:50am and our part was not yet filled. I didn't know our representative's name for Miss NYSC, so I put mine."

Everyone kept quiet and digested the information, then the socials representative's voice cut through the pensive air. "But is it your business if our part is empty? Are you the one who is supposed to go there in the first place?" he asked, angry.

"But I waited for you for almost one hour and I didn't see you there. And I also didn't want us to miss out on the opportunity," Eugenia said, attempting to sound innocent and caring.

"But that's not the point," Auntie Vera replied. "Was it your business in the first place?"

"Don't mind her," the socials representative added. "So why didn't she fill in a name for the Mr. Macho as well? Or she didn't mind us missing out on that opportunity too?"

Everyone looked back and forth between Auntie Vera, the socials representative and Eugenia, as they debated. It was somewhat amusing, but no one was laughing.

The socials representative continued. "In fact, I went to the office at about 11:55am to fill the names, because I was getting the full names from the platoon president, and I was shocked to see that she had already filled hers, feeling smart with herself. I had enough time to do it. I know my role as a socials representative, and also what it entails. I wouldn't have left the spot blank and I wouldn't have been late, either."

At that moment, someone yelled, "Chiji for President," referring to the socials representative and it made everyone laugh.

Oluomachukwu never knew the socials representative's name and was prepared to call him by his title until the end of the camp. She then took note of 'Chiji,' but memorising names was becoming too difficult for her.

"It's not funny *nau*," Chiji said. "We had already picked someone, so why would she come and cause confusion?"

Eugenia stood there all the while not saying anything, but she still had a smirk on her face, and Oluomachukwu couldn't understand why. It was as if she was enjoying the attention.

Nkiru sighed. "It's not that serious. If she wants to do it so badly, then let her do it."

Auntie Vera shook her head. "No, it can't be that easy. Chiji, please, go back to the office and change the name to the initial person's name we had picked."

"Ma, if I could change it, I wouldn't be here. They said it was too late to change it when I got there, and that was why I was so angry."

Everyone instantly threw Eugenia an angry stare, and Oluomachukwu immediately understood why she had that smirk, that victorious smile that was plastered on her face.

Nkiru spoke. "I don't really mind her doing it, but it's annoying that she had to wait for me to buy my dress and shoes." She pulled out her cell phone, opened the picture of the dress and shoes and passed it around. "I have even over-prepared, rehearsed and done a Question and Answer session with Oluoma." Nkiru pointed at Oluomachukwu with her thumb.

Eugenia finally got her voice, but before she spoke, she also pulled out her phone and opened photos that she had taken of her dress and shoes. "I have also bought my dress and shoes for the contest, prepared, rehearsed and done Question and Answer sessions." She then looked at Auntie Vera, and then at Nkiru. "I heard that you were picked for the contest as a punishment, but I want to do this from my heart. You shouldn't be forced to do what you don't want to do."

The same person that yelled before when the socials representative spoke, yelled again, "Eugenia for Madam

President," and everybody laughed, softening the already stiff atmosphere.

***

Oluomachukwu, Nkiru and Ogo took lunch from the dining hall. They were serving *jollof* rice and beef, the size of Knorr cubes. At least some people got more than three pieces, while some got only one. Oluomachukwu and Ogo might have been served by a very angry person, because they got one piece each, but Nkiru got five. Maybe it was because she had the 'on duty' badge pinned to her shirt, and the Corps members on duty thought she was one of them.

Nkiru ended up giving a piece each to Oluomachukwu and Ogo, making theirs two each and hers three.

They ate up their lunch quickly, because they wanted to take a nap before it was time for the next programme. It was not like they were going to participate, but if soldiers came and sent them out after the bugle call, they wanted to be well rested, at least. After washing up their plates and cutlery, and after drinking water, Nkiru and Ogo slept off naturally, but Oluomachukwu didn't. She tried to, but she couldn't. She glanced at her cell phone and there was still nothing from Okechukwu. She was tempted to call or text him, and her inner mind told her not to, but she did. She called him and he didn't pick up, so she locked her phone screen and lay in her bed, preparing to sleep off.

By the time the bugle call was made, Oluomachukwu hadn't slept for a second yet. She had spent the whole time thinking of what she would do with her situation, then she gave herself an ultimatum. The ultimatum was more for Okechukwu, than for herself. If he didn't call her by the end of the next day, then she would assume that he wasn't interested in their relationship anymore, and she would be in the market again. An image of her being in the centre of *mami* market flashed through her mind and she shook it off. She knew that Nkiru wouldn't approve, since she said all the guys in the camp were desperate.

The sound of the bugle blasted through the air again, and this time it woke both Nkiru and Ogo up.

Nkiru sighed. "This stupid trumpet again. I can't wait to go back to my father's house and to my own bed."

Ogo had just woken up, but she was already laughing, just like Oluomachukwu. "Nkiru, you need to stop calling that thing a trumpet. It's a bugle."

"I hate the way it is pronounced." Nkiru shrugged as she got up from her bed. "So I'd rather stick to trumpet." She flashed her teeth.

They got ready and left the hostel before soldiers came to give them grief. Ogo went to join her platoon members, while Oluomachukwu and Nkiru went to meet with their business plan teammates. It was supposed to be only the representing trio, but there was no harm in allowing Nkiru to join in. And the good thing was that when she joined, she proposed that they add a logo to their business plan to make it stand out even more, and they all bought the idea. So Nkiru called her older brother, and he agreed to help them make one.

Juachi did the typing on the laptop they had rented, while Oluomachukwu and Anita read out from the paper they had written on, taking turns. They stayed behind the dining hall, away from prying eyes... from other platoons and from NYSC officials. Corps members weren't allowed to have laptops in the camp, so their rented laptop might have been seized if found.

By the time the bugle call was made for dinner about two hours later, Juachi hadn't finished with the typing, so he proposed to take the laptop up to his room to finish it up. Oluomachukwu knew that he was surely going to have difficulties typing on his own, as some of the handwritings were spidery, very illegible. Oluomachukwu even had to go through some of the texts and rewrite anything that would look difficult for Juachi to understand. So once that was done, they exchanged phones numbers to keep each other updated, then they were good to go for the evening.

Oluomachukwu and Nkiru made their way directly to *mami* market without going to the hostel first to rest or to eat. Hanging out was becoming more fun by the day. After every long day, bottles of Orijin were what they needed to cool down. Oluomachukwu called Ogo and Ekene to join them there, as they were going to have dinner first before having drinks.

They went to the table where they normally sat, and where Blessing served them drinks and took their orders for dinner. Nkiru, Ogo and Ekene ordered three bowls of fresh fish pepper soup, while Oluomachukwu went for *suya* and *asun* meat, which had a lot of pepper in it. As they were eating, Blessing brought the drinks. Ogo and Ekene wanted to start with soft drinks first, so they ordered malt drinks. Oluomachukwu and Nkiru started off directly with Orijin. Ever since they discovered the drink in the camp, they couldn't stop drinking it.

As Blessing was opening the drink for Oluomachukwu, she smiled sheepishly as she asked, "Auntie, how's Brother doing?"

Oluomachukwu gazed at her. "What did you just say?" She had heard her, even though the music was very loud, but she didn't want to believe what the girl was asking.

"I asked you 'how is Brother doing?' He did not come with you today?" Blessing's tone was firmer.

Oluomachukwu knew that she was referring to Tracker and she shook her head. Corps members weren't the only ones noticing that Tracker was always around her, but the people serving her too. She looked at Blessing and smiled at her, then said, "He is fine. He will be here soon."

The girl smiled back at Oluomachukwu and ran off. If Oluomachukwu didn't know any better, she would have thought that the young girl liked Tracker... or maybe she really did.

Oluomachukwu immediately pulled Nkiru closer, and whispered into her ear, "Please, we aren't hanging out with Tracker or any other guy again in this *mami* market for that matter."

Nkiru looked at her, shocked. "Why?"

"Well, because everyone thinks we are together and I don't want that. If they see me talking with any other guy now, they'll assume I'm cheating."

"Who cares?" Nkiru asked and rolled her eyes.

"I do," Oluomachukwu replied. "And also, that young Blessing of a seller just asked me 'how brother is doing and that he didn't come today.'" Nkiru wore a rather doubtful look, and Oluomachukwu added, "Her exact words."

Nkiru muffled a laugh and was about to say something, then quickly bent her head until she was almost under the table. Oluomachukwu was confused, but when she looked around, she saw Cleaner coming their way.

"What is she doing?" Ogo asked. She had been talking to Ekene, because they sat closer to each other and were opposite Oluomachukwu and Nkiru.

Oluomachukwu leaned forward. "Hiding from Cleaner. Ever since he told her that she was stained, but it wasn't from her period, she has been feeling uncomfortable."

"I don't understand," Ekene said.

Oluomachukwu wasn't sure if she knew the story, but as she was about to explain it to her, Cleaner showed up and greeted them. He then went straight to Nkiru, tapped her shoulder and asked her if she had dropped something when she looked up. Oluomachukwu saw the horror on Nkiru's face when she eventually sat up. Cleaner then bent down and was talking into her ear, as it was too noisy to have a conversation without being too close together.

At the same time, Oluomachukwu went to the other side of the table, stooped down beside Ogo and Ekene and gave them the *poopoo* water gist, and they laughed out loud, briefly getting the attention of both Nkiru and Cleaner.

Once Cleaner was done talking about whatever it was

he was saying, he stood up, patted Nkiru on the back, bade everyone else goodbye and left. Oluomachukwu also stood up and was going back to sit down when she saw Chiji, the socials representative approaching her.

"Thank God," he said to Oluomachukwu. "I have been looking for you everywhere."

Oluomachukwu tilted her upper body backwards, then glanced briefly at Nkiru. "Why have you been looking for me?" She sat on the chair, then he came and bent down beside her, but between her and Nkiru, just like she had done when she went to talk to Ogo and Ekene.

He started to reply, "I wanted to ask if you would be interested in the cooking competition..."

Oluomachukwu started shaking her head just as he was talking. She was not interested in any more competitions and did not want to even be on standby for it. She then continued to shake her head as he continued to talk about the competition and its specifics, when Nkiru spoke.

"I want to do it," she said.

Both Oluomachukwu and Chiji looked at her.

As if they had not heard her, she repeated what she had said, "I said I want to do it."

Chiji pulled out his cell phone and passed it on to her. "Please, can you type in your phone number, so that I can be calling you for updates?"

Nkiru took the phone, and as she typed in her number, she said, "I hope no one else will come and tell me that they want to cook 'from their heart' or preach to me on how devoted or more interested they are in it than I am."

Chiji laughed. "Don't worry, it won't happen again. I am going to give them the names now."

"Names?" both Oluomachukwu and Nkiru asked.

"Yes, names. Every platoon is supposed to have five representatives each."

Nkiru handed him back his cell phone. He saved the number, then told them to enjoy their evening and he left. Before they could start enjoying their evening, Tracker and one of his friends showed up out of nowhere. Nkiru gazed at Oluomachukwu, and she could tell that the look meant to allow him to hang out with them for one more night before she started avoiding him.

Even before he was invited to sit down, he pulled two chairs from a table that was beside them, then sat in the one that he put very close to Oluomachukwu. As if on cue, Blessing ran out from nowhere, greeted him and took his order: a lot of small chops and more bottles of drinks for everyone.

Oluomachukwu looked at her phone — still nothing from Okechukwu. She locked her phone screen, dumped the phone in her waist pouch and prepared herself to drink away her worries.

She was going to spend her night without feeling guilty. She drank as much as she wanted and danced as much as she wanted, and with whomever she wanted, without a care in the world... until, of course, the sound of the bugle ended the moment.

CHAPTER TWENTY-ONE: DAY SEVENTEEN

Thursday, 21 st August 2014

Oluomachukwu woke up feeling groggy. For the first time, she didn't wake up early. Her internal clock had failed her, and even her alarm clock didn't help her in anyway. It was the sound of the bugle that woke her up. She sat up and looked around the room, most of her roommates were already up, but Nkiru and Ogo were still in dream world.

Oluomachukwu knew that she could go to the parade ground and work out without having her bath, then come back after two hours and bath when there wouldn't be a rush. She went and tapped Nkiru on the leg, but Nkiru refused to wake up. Oluomachukwu tugged at her feet again, and Nkiru got up rather dramatically, kicking around angrily as if she had been fighting in her dream.

"Why are you waking me up *nau*?" Nkiru sounded upset, stretching out the '*nau*,' as she said it.

"At least now you know how it feels," Ogo said, and Oluomachukwu looked back. Ogo had woken up even before Oluomachukwu thought of going to wake her up.

"My friend, c'mon wake up. In fact, let me come there and spank your buttocks."

"Don't even try it," Nkiru said. She rolled her feet over her bed and was now sitting on it, her head tilted to one side, resting in her left palm, and her eyes half closed. "I'm not drinking anymore until I leave this camp."

"Me neither," Oluomachukwu added, as she prepared her things to go to the bathroom.

"Yeah, right." Ogo laughed. "But you girls are drunks. Thank God Ekene and I were there and sober. Those guys would have pressed the hell out of your boobs yesterday all in the name of dance. They even proposed to carry you both to the hostel, but Ekene and I insisted otherwise."

Oluomachukwu couldn't remember everything that had happened, but she was glad that she had had some fun, especially as it helped her to forget about Okechukwu. As soon as her mind went to him, she strolled towards her cloth-pillow, raised it up and there were no phones. She didn't recall telling everyone not to put their phones under the cloth-pillow again, but she felt that because it was morning, everyone naturally retrieved their phones from the charging port. She checked her phone and still nothing from Okechukwu. Her ultimatum was that day, and she was gradually beginning to feel agitated, wondering if she would really let him go. She carried her bath things and started to brush her teeth when Ogo spoke to her.

"That thing you are doing is dangerous," Ogo said.

Oluomachukwu stopped and looked at Ogo, but didn't talk, because she couldn't.

"What if there's no water in the bathroom? It has happened to me once and I didn't have any water to use. I had to beg someone."

Oluomachukwu rolled her eyes and walked out of the room. That definitely couldn't be classified as 'dangerous' to her. If at all she really needed some water, her bottle of drinking water would suffice.

There was a crowd and two queues in the bathroom for

either sides of the bath stall. Some girls were even bathing in the toilets, some in front of the bath stalls and others by the sink. Oluomachukwu contemplated going back and having her bath much later, but she didn't want to go out feeling dirty and smelly. Some people even came to the parade ground at times with stinking mouths, and she wondered why they couldn't at least brush their teeth. It was one of the reasons why she hardly spoke to anyone on the parade ground.

She stood there and waited until a spot close to the sink was free. She fetched water into her bucket, then took it to the spot and started to have a rushed and uncomfortable bath. She had to squeeze her wrapper and underwear into her smaller bucket that already had her toilet bag inside it. Normally, if she were using the bath stall, she would have put all her things on a hanger and hung it over the shower pipe until she was done bathing.

When she was eventually done, she hopped over the stagnant water that was gradually flooding the bathroom, then left, feeling irritated. She didn't want to have to be in a similar situation again.

She got to the room and Nkiru was back in bed, while Ogo was applying make-up. Ogo didn't have the energy to queue up or fight for a bath stall, so she simply brushed her teeth in the other bathroom that was so dirty, it had fewer people there. Then she dressed up to have her bath much later after the drills.

Oluomachukwu got ready quickly, then made to leave with Ogo. They woke Nkiru up one more time before they left, and she shrugged their hands off.

By the time they got to the hostel entrance, they saw hostel security officers punishing Corps members, seizing their badges and asking them to get on their knees. Some Corps members were retaliating, especially male Corps members, claiming that they were graduates, and the last time they had been punished was in high school. The gate officers had to call other male soldiers to help with the rebellion and the male Corps members eventually got on their knees.

The Corps members that had come downstairs during that period saw what was happening from the corner of the main hostel door. Some of them ran back into the hostel, while others ran to the parade ground, passing through the hostel inner space to the back, then via the left side of the hostel. Oluomachukwu and Ogo used the inner space to escape. When they got to the parade ground, they were lucky that a few soldiers were there, so they crept to their respective platoons unnoticed, while a Platoon Six representative recited the Meditation.

After the Meditation, there were a few announcements that all sounded like complaints, and were linked to the bad behaviour of the Corps members. The female MC, who Oluomachukwu had then nicknamed 'Madam MC,' since she didn't know her name, made the announcements. She warned the Corps members, especially the male Corps members that if they kept up with their bad attitude, they would have themselves to blame.

When the announcements were over, all Platoon Six Corps members filed out and went to report for their duties. The drills and physical exercises started immediately and surprisingly the DJ didn't play any songs by Nigerian artists. All were from a mix of foreign artists.

***

When Oluomachukwu went back to the room, Nkiru was still asleep, and she wondered just how much alcohol she had consumed the previous night. She tried to wake her up again, but she didn't budge. She then tried to tempt her with breakfast, but she didn't get up either. The camp kitchen was serving bread, boiled egg and tea. She knew how much Nkiru liked boiled eggs. She even proposed her own portion of boiled egg to Nkiru, but Nkiru didn't want to wake up. She was prepared to sleep for another day or two if possible.

Oluomachukwu didn't collect breakfast though because she didn't like that particular choice of meal. She didn't buy Gala either. She wasn't that hungry, and although she was complaining about Nkiru refusing to wake up, she, too, wanted to sleep for a while longer. She took off her rubber trainers and got into her bed, inside her duvet cover and slept off immediately.

While she was in bed, dreaming about being at *mami* market and drinking all the bottles of Orijin there, she got jolted from sleep by the OBS speaker's announcement. She opened her eyes, as if she could listen with her eyes. She had heard something concerning the business plans, submission and 2:00pm, but she couldn't connect the dots. She wanted to go back to sleep. As she closed her eyes, her phone vibrated in her waist pouch. She wanted to shrug it off when she realised that it might be Okechukwu. The phone continued to vibrate, which meant that it was a call, and not a simple text message.

She pulled out the phone and checked it. It was a call from a number she didn't know. She picked up either way to find out.

"Hello?" she said, her voice sounding very croaky. She didn't bother to clear it.

"Are you still sleeping? Did you even go to the parade ground this morning?" a male voice asked her, and she couldn't tell who it was. And as if the person knew that she was lost, he added, "It's Juachi."

"Oh." She hadn't saved his number on her phone. She had simply dialled both his number and Anita's, but didn't save any, and she didn't know what number belonged to whom. Also, she wasn't sure why he was calling her or if there was any problem. "So have you finished typing the business plan?" she asked.

"I have finally completed it, thank God. It's just left for us to review it before we print it out and return the laptop to the photographer. We also have to submit it before

2:00pm today, so I think we should meet now in front of the hostel to finalise it. Anita is here with me now."

Oluomachukwu scrunched her face, because she didn't want to leave the room, and wished that Juachi and Anita would just handle the entire thing. Instinctively, she looked at Nkiru, feeling jealous, and Nkiru was still enjoying her sleep. "Okay. I'll come down now."

Juachi hung up immediately, not even responding or waiting for her to say goodbye, as if he didn't want to use up his airtime for unnecessary talk.

Oluomachukwu got out of bed and put on her rubber trainers, then hurried off downstairs. She met Juachi and Anita talking when she got in front of the hostel. They exchanged brief pleasantries, then walked to *mami* market to the man that had rented the laptop to them.

They asked him if he could print the business plan out and he laughed. He said that no photographer in the camp could print, because there were no A4 format printers or any plain sheet type of printer. They all had small printers for printing photographs only.

Towards the end of where the photographers sat, one man with a printer the size of a small travelling bag was making photocopies. Juachi asked him if he could print out the business plan and he said that he could only make photocopies. It was an old machine, so there was no USB cord to connect a laptop or even use a flash drive. There was only one option left.

"I think we should call Auntie Vera and ask her if she can print in the NYSC office," Anita suggested.

"Do you have her number?" Juachi asked.

"I do," both Oluomachukwu and Anita responded at the same time.

Anita didn't attempt to bring out her phone and it was obvious that she wasn't going to make the call, as she too didn't want to use her airtime. Oluomachukwu took the cue, pulled out her phone from her waist pouch, looked at the screen — still nothing from Okechukwu — and called

Auntie Vera.

"Hello, good afternoon?" Auntie Vera sounded even croakier than Oluomachukwu had sounded earlier on.

"Sorry to disturb you, ma. We want to print out our business plan, but all the printers in the camp market can only print picture sizes and pictures."

"So what do you want me to do?"

Oluomachukwu thought the question was ridiculous. "I wanted to ask if you could help us print it out from any of the admin offices."

"I don't think I can do that. We are on a budget here, so I can't print for you."

"We can buy paper from the camp market and give it to you, if you want." Oluomachukwu wanted to put the phone on speaker so that Juachi and Anita would hear, but the place was too noisy.

"I'm not sure I can print. Other platoon instructors are not printing for their Corps members, so why should I be different? You are not babies. You don't expect me to do everything for you."

Oluomachukwu almost laughed, because she didn't understand why Auntie Vera was saying that. Before she could thank Auntie Vera and hang up, Auntie Vera had a suggestion.

"You can go outside the camp to print it. There's a cyber café just opposite the gate. I know the lady in charge at the main gate. When you get there, call me and I would speak to her."

"Okay, thank you, ma," Oluomachukwu said, then she hung up.

She looked at both Juachi and Anita, who were anxious to know what had been discussed. "Do any of you have a flash drive?" Oluomachukwu asked. "Auntie Vera said that I can go outside to print the document now."

They both shook their heads, indicating 'No.' So she called Nkiru to ask her, but she didn't pick up. She figured that Nkiru was still sleeping. She then called Ogo, and Ogo didn't have. She decided to call Ekene before calling the guys in her platoon to ask and surprisingly Ekene had one. Oluomachukwu then asked Juachi and Anita to wait for her in the camp market entrance with the laptop, while she went to collect the flash drive.

She went to Ekene's room for the second time — the first time, she was in a hurry during the Idol contest. There was nothing really different about the room. It looked as jam-packed as her own, and even worse, because everyone was complete. No one had been decamped from her room yet and no one had taken an exeat. Even though the place was full, it was not stuffy.

The ceiling fans were functioning properly and cooled the whole place, plus they looked new. Ekene noticed that Oluomachukwu was looking at the fans lustfully and told her that they had just been installed, because the old ones had stopped working. She then gave Oluomachukwu the flash drive, and Oluomachukwu went on her way. When she got outside, she saw Foyin, her room assistant and told her about the new ceiling fans in Ekene's room and asked her to go to the welfare office and see about getting a new fan installed in their own room as well.

Oluomachukwu remet Juachi and Anita a few minutes later. They saved the business plan on the flash drive, then returned the laptop to the photographer. Going to the gate was difficult, because soldiers guarded it as if they were guarding the President. Oluomachukwu had to ask one of the soldiers assigned to her platoon to walk with her until she got to the gate. She met the lady in charge, then called Auntie Vera to speak with her. Auntie Vera managed to convince the woman to allow Oluomachukwu to leave the camp briefly, and Oluomachukwu was cleared.

When she got to the main gate, an officer called her back and asked if he was invisible, because she had walked past him without telling him where she was going to, even though she had been cleared by the woman in charge. She then explained what it was that she wanted to do, then he walked her to the gate, and took her badge, pending the time she came back. He stood there and watched her cross the road, making sure she didn't get hit by buses or bikes. He then pointed out where the Internet café was.

The Internet café was made of wood and was the size of a small kiosk. The young girl there had to be sure that Oluomachukwu was going to print a lot of pages before she turned on her small generator, because there was no power. It took her some time to power up the computer system, then the printer, which tripled as a scanner and a photocopying machine. She printed one copy, then made three photocopies of it. She then spiral-bound them in blue colour for the front cover and black for the back, and gave them to Oluomachukwu.

Oluomachukwu paid her almost 1,000 naira, thanked her and went on her way. As she got outside the Internet cafe, her phone started ringing. She pulled it out and saw that it was Nkiru calling.

"Madam, you are finally awake," Oluomachukwu said.

Nkiru laughed. "Yes oh, and for a reason. I'm meeting with the cooking team today to talk about the contest."

"Oh, okay," Oluomachukwu said. She left the Internet café and was making her way back to the camp.

"Why is it sounding noisy in a strange way? It's like you are on the road. Where are you?" Nkiru asked.

"I'm on my way home."

"What?" Nkiru exclaimed.

"I'm just joking." Oluomachukwu laughed. "I went to print out our business plan in an Internet café opposite the camp. Outside feels so nice. I just feel like running away and going home."

"Where do you think you are running away to? Better come back right here and suffer with the rest of us." Nkiru laughed again, then after a brief pause, she added, "Oh, shoot. My brother sent me the logos for the business plan last night and I forgot to tell you. He even sent me three different versions to pick from and I'm sure you would like them. But it's too late."

"Yes, it is," Oluomachukwu replied. "Let me call you back, or I'll see you later. I want to get back into the camp now."

"Okay, no problem," Nkiru said, then they both hung up, and Oluomachukwu replaced her phone in her waist pouch.

When Oluomachukwu got back, the officer asked her what she had printed and asked her to explain it to him, which she did. Before she got to the second security check, another officer asked her where she was coming from and she told him she had gone to print out a document. He, too, asked her what she had printed and told her to explain it. They seemed to be fascinated at the way she explained the business plan passionately to them, its purpose and its usefulness, and the competition.

And when she was leaving there, another officer, who looked very tired in his oversized uniform wished her luck in the competition and told her that she, and others like her, are the change that Nigeria was hoping for. She smiled and left.

She had crossed the second camp security checkpoint when her phone rang in her waist pouch. She pulled it out and almost tumbled when she saw that it was Okechukwu calling her. He made it before the ultimatum, although she was still quite angry with him. It was a bittersweet feeling for her.

"Hello," she croaked. Her voice sounded like someone was beating local drums. She had shouted, because she was close to *mami* market and there was music playing from left, right and centre.

"Hi." His reply was curt, and sounded official, way too official for Oluomachukwu's liking.

"What happened to you yesterday morning?" she asked as she walked towards the SAED office in the hostel. The office was just at the entrance of the male hostel.

"I was sleep-texting actually, then eventually slept off," he replied.

Oluomachukwu felt that he was lying. How convenient it was that he would sleep off just when she had asked him to call her. It was obvious that he wasn't ready to speak to her then, but why was he ready to speak to her now, she wondered.

"Okay," she said reluctantly. "So about three days ago."

"What about it?"

"Please, Oke. You know what I'm talking about."

"I know what you are talking about, but I don't know what you want me to say about it."

"Are you upset?"

"No, I'm not, and I wasn't either."

"So why were you quiet?"

"Because you threw me two very unexpected blows. I had to take a step back and treat the wounds. I actually had to think."

The comment on blows, wounds and treatment was meant to be funny, but she didn't laugh. "What were you thinking about? If you could still be with me?"

Okechukwu didn't reply.

"Okechukwu?" She lowered her voice. She had gotten to the SAED office and there wasn't much music there, so she could hear and be heard properly. She stood outside.

"I'm here." Okechukwu sounded very distracted and as though he was moving around. "And like I said, I was not upset, I was just surprised."

"But that was not what I asked you, though. What were you thinking about, and are *we*, you and I, still going to work? Did I make a mistake telling you what I told you?"

"Or did you make a mistake doing what you did?" he complemented.

She said nothing immediately. She was annoyed. And after thinking a little, she commented, "But it has already happened. I have already made the *mistake*, as you called it."

"And you have already told me the mistake." He was trying to make a point, but she wasn't sure exactly what it was. After a brief awkward silence, he added, "I just mean that you have already done it and you have already told me, so there's no going back now. And don't worry about me, it doesn't change anything between us. I don't like you any less."

She noticed that he was now whispering and that he didn't use 'love.' Well, he never used 'love' until she used it first.

After speaking to her, he reassured her that everything was okay and that he had to go for another meeting, then he hung up. She didn't know how to react, because she was sure that he wasn't being completely honest. He was still quite upset and reconsidering their relationship, but she decided to give him the benefit of the doubt. She then went into the SAED office and submitted the business plan on behalf of her platoon, making sure to tick the submission sheet that had been prepared. Platoon Seven was the last to submit their work and she hoped that it wasn't a sign of who was going to take the last place in the competition.

As soon as she came out of the SAED office a few minutes later, her cell phone rang again. She glanced at the phone screen and saw that Okechukwu was calling her back. It warmed and chilled her at the same time. She was happy that he was calling her back, but scared that he was calling her to end things with her.

She picked up, cleared her throat, and said, "You called back."

Okechukwu didn't say anything.

"Hello?" she said.

He still didn't say anything. It was strange because she could hear his voice. And it wasn't only his voice. He was with someone else. A female. Oluomachukwu obviously didn't know who it was, but fought the pool of tears that tempted to swell in her eyes. She then had to stop because she didn't know why she was about to cry. Okechukwu had told her that he was going for a meeting, so it could have been a meeting with a female colleague or client.

Okechukwu had called her by mistake, and instead of hanging up, she listened intently, her curiosity getting the best of her. The voices were sort of muffled, though, as if the phone was trapped somewhere tight, like it had been placed in a pocket or in a bag, or had fallen between chair cushions. Chair cushions could only be in a house, and not in an office. Oluomachukwu shook the unwanted thoughts out of her head and concentrated on the conversation.

"Well, she was just saying that she wants to come back home." It was Okechukwu's voice and Oluomachukwu knew he was talking about her. "I don't know why she is in a hurry."

Of course he knew why, Oluomachukwu said to herself and rolled her eyes.

"I'm sure she is tired of camp," a female voice replied. The voice was very low and soft, as if the person wasn't using any effort to speak, as if relaxed on a couch or lying down.

Oluomachukwu did not know who it was, but it was clear that the person knew her.

"She shouldn't be such a baby about it, everyone goes through it. If she has made the choice to do it, then she should stick to it." It was Okechukwu.

The person he was speaking with laughed, and with so much confidence and authority that Oluomachukwu felt it was Akunna, Okechukwu's older sister. And Akunna did not really like her after the Abuja stand-up, so she wasn't expecting anything nice from her.

"So are you going to get her from camp?" The female voice was very soft and sweet again, almost inaudible.

"No, there's an Ebola threat," Okechukwu started. "So they won't let anyone come out and go back in like before. It's even good. I don't want her out."

"Ah, that's your cousin *nau*. Why would you say that?" The female laughed.

Oluomachukwu was suddenly confused. It couldn't be Akunna, she would never say such .

"Well, she's not really my cousin." Okechukwu's voice was stern.

"Wait, I thought that she was your cousin all along, and I was giving her NYSC tips before."

Oluomachukwu immediately knew that it was Idara, because Idara had given her NYSC camp tips. She also knew that Okechukwu definitely wasn't in any meeting.

"So does she like you?" Idara asked. Her voice was no longer soft and sweet, but brute, beast-like. And before he could reply, she asked, "Do you like her? Because people talk or sound unnecessarily mean about people they really like, and that's why I'm suspicious."

"We are just family friends that can pass for cousins."

Oluomachukwu's heart almost stopped at that instant. She could have just hung up, but she did not. The pool of tears that she had been trying to blot out was now welling up in her eyes. She started walking towards the female hostel entrance.

"You can pass for cousins, but it doesn't mean that you are cousins." Idara paused. "And don't tell me that you've been secretly dating her."

"Where did that come from now? Why would I have to date her, when I have you, Idara?"

"So what am I missing?"

"I'm just upset with her because she went to Abuja for just one day and slept with two of my friends."

"What?" Idara exclaimed. "She did?"

Oluomachukwu was shocked as she listened. The well toppled over and the tears streamed down her face. She almost started sobbing, but she didn't want her voice to alert Okechukwu, and Idara. She also didn't want to stop listening. She wanted to hear it all.

"Yes. Please, how desperate can a girl be?" Okechukwu

added, stabbing her deeper into the chest.

There was a brief pause.

"Whom did she sleep with?" Idara asked. Any girl that liked to gossip or enjoyed gist in general would have asked that, Oluomachukwu included.

"Kayode and Nnanna."

"Ah! Isn't Kayode married, and Nnanna practically married? She's really desperate oh."

"Maybe she didn't know they were, but in one night? Nnanna, I can understand, but she just met Kayode. And they are both my friends. I gave her Kayode's number to help her with her NYSC registration."

"Hmm." Idara sighed, then laughed. "I hope she does not sleep with every guy in the camp."

"That's her business," Okechukwu retorted. "And the business of the guy that she eventually ends up with."

Oluomachukwu had heard enough. She hung up, and went towards the entrance of the female hostel. As she was going in, she noticed three armoured trucks drive into the camp and move towards the parade ground, just in front of the hostel. She didn't know what was going on, until she heard some happy girls yelling "*Allawee, allawee,* finally." She then figured that they were bullion vans carrying a lot of money to the camp.

The bullion vans came with over forty million naira, which was a sum of 19,800 naira multiplied by the 2,031 Corps members, whether present or absent. So they really needed heavily guarded security officers to protect the cash.

The sound of the bugle filtered the air at that moment and for the first time Oluomachukwu actually saw the bugle blower as he walked to strategic points and blew it. It was time for SAED group activities. As SAED groups started setting up, the people who came with the bullion vans also started to set up to distribute the money.

Oluomachukwu had gone for her SAED activity, but she was inactive. She spent the whole time thinking about what Okechukwu had said and how Idara had laughed. She cried from within and her stomach churned. She felt like throwing up a couple of times, and that was how it was for her until the SAED activity was over and she got her SAED attendance card signed.

By the time SAED activities ended, different sections under the canopies had been fully set up for distributing the allowance, just as it had been set up for the first two allowances that had been distributed, with number codes pinned to the top of the canopy. It was also time for the lecture on NOA —National Orientation Agency — after which was another one on Collaborating Partners, but it seemed like neither was going to hold, because flyers were shared for the NOA, and the partners seemed to be the ones to share the allowance. The bugle sounded again and the OBS speaker made an announcement for everyone to go to the parade ground with their NYSC badges to collect their allowances.

Oluomachukwu was too upset to think about money at that instant, so she went back to the room to rest for a while first, then said to herself that she would go out for the money later. She was glad that the door wasn't locked when she got there. She then laid in her bed and slept off after draining all the tears in her.

***

By the time she opened her eyes, it was dark outside. She reached for her phone in her waist pouch and checked the time. It was a little after 7:30pm and the whole camp was very noisy — people were yelling and screaming, as if they were under attack in the camp. She got out of bed instantly, startling one girl that was standing by the door and talking on the phone.

The girl looked very calm, so Oluomachukwu figured that there was no crisis. She took a few seconds to reorient herself, then asked, "Hi, please, what is happening? Why is everyone yelling?"

The girl took her time to answer, then eventually said, "There's Miss NYSC and Mr. Macho competition going on."

The girl resumed talking on her phone and didn't hear when Oluomachukwu thanked her. Oluomachukwu wore her rubber trainers and ran out of the room. She was still not feeling any better than she was before she fell asleep, but she wanted to watch the contest, especially Platoon Seven's representatives. As she ran out of the hostel, she pulled out her phone and sent Nkiru a text message asking her where she was. Nkiru was at the back of the stage, helping Sister Mary prepare Eugenia and Kelenna for the contests.

By the time Oluomachukwu got there, the contest was almost over, but Nkiru told her all that had happened. The Miss NYSC contestants had come out the first time in their white shirts and shorts, tennis shoes and cap. Some jogged in, some marched in and some attempted to do cart wheels and backflips on the stage.

The second time they came on the stage, they marched, because they wore their NYSC ceremonial kit: khaki pants, NYSC crested tee shirt, khaki belt, NYSC cap and jungle boots. They also had their badges hanging over their necks and their hair packed in buns. When all of them were lined up, the MC carried out some marching tests on them, like giving three hearty cheers, slow and fast march. It was to know if they had been paying attention during the camp activities or not, or even attending them.

After that, there was a traditional attire display and the contestants came in, danced to a song of their choosing, then went to line up. When all ten of them had danced and lined up, they introduced themselves and described what tradition they were representing. Eugenia wore an *iro* and *buba*, representing the Yoruba tradition.

The final display was the evening gown. Contestants came out one after the other, smiled, posed for the camera, then went to line up. After that, the MC called them out one after the other to ask questions. There was a tray of fifteen numbers from one to fifteen, and each contestant picked one random number, then answered the question that was asked.

Oluomachukwu arrived at that instant, and from where she stood, she was able to hear the questions and answers, and see all the contestants. Some of the questions were a bit difficult, and others, quite simple. Eugenia had picked a relatively simple question, but gave her answer speaking very fast, as if she was anxious.

Oluomachukwu looked at Eugenia's dress, it wasn't all that spectacular, but it was okay, just average. It was quite long, so Oluomachukwu couldn't see what shoes she had on. But it appeared to be pretty high, because she looked like she had climbed a small stool, looking very tall. When the question and answer session was over, all the girls left and freed the stage for the macho men.

Just like the girls, the guys had come out in their white shirts, shorts and tennis shoes, all muscled up. Only about four out of the ten contestants were really muscled up. Some of them came out and tore their shirts, ripping it from the front neckline to the bottom. Some did hand stands, while others did one-hand press-ups. The crowd had screamed and cheered at the guys as they came in, one after the other.

After that, they had worn the NYSC ceremonial kit and gone through the same exercise as the female contestants. Nkiru mentioned that some of the guys had flopped, by marching with their right legs and arms in the same swing, instead of left and right. Some had forgotten how to give three hearty cheers and some kept marching even after they were asked to halt. All that didn't stop the girls from screaming and cheering.

The next display was the traditional outfit, and just like the female contestants, they introduced themselves and said what tradition they were representing. But they didn't do any traditional dance.

The final display, which Oluomachukwu witnessed, was the evening wear. Some people had fine three-piece suits, some had regular suits, and about two people didn't wear anything close to suits. They were part of the guys who didn't have muscles, but had to represent their platoons. They were asked questions as well, and most of them answered correctly, including Kelenna. In fact, Sister Mary and the others believed that there was hope for their representatives; if not first place, at least something close.

The final display was combined. All twenty contestants came out — the female contestants standing in front, and their corresponding Mr. Machos standing behind them. They stood, smiled and waited for the judges to compile their results. As they waited, Oluomachukwu heard some people saying that Platoon Nine's Mr. Macho was going to win. Not only was he the most muscled up guy in the camp, he had been asked a seemingly difficult question and answered it flawlessly, making all the girls scream. The judges were also going to use the public's interest in each contestant as a bonus point. But it was difficult to say who would win the Miss NYSC.

A few minutes later, the judges made their decision and the MC took the results and got on the stage. He was to call out the runners-up one after the other, give them a gift and make sure they left the stage until there were three contestants each remaining — three for Miss NYSC and three for Mr. Macho — then he would call the second runner-up, and eventually the winner.

There was much anticipation until the MC called out the first people who were to leave the stage, and they were both Platoon Seven's representatives. Sister Mary almost collapsed. In fact, all the people that had been helping with the make-up, change of clothes and preparations almost passed out. They hadn't expected to take the last place, and Oluomachukwu didn't want to believe that the camp officials were still angry with their platoon for the drama-day-bad-joke.

One after the other, the MC sent off contestants until only six people were left, and as expected, Platoon Nine's contestant won Mr. Macho, and the whole camp went crazy, clapping, yelling, whistling and cheering for him. Oluomachukwu didn't know who won the Miss NYSC, and she didn't bother to know. There was disappointment written on the faces of everyone in Platoon Seven. Eugenia almost started crying, but said she was happy it was over.

Oluomachukwu returned to the back and helped them pack up all the things they had brought and used, in utter silence. No one said a word and Oluomachukwu was even scared to cough and break the sad silence that burned through the air.

Without saying anything, Sister Mary packed up her things and walked away, murmuring to herself and saying that she would go to the Socials Committee Head the next day and demand an explanation.

Around the corner, some people were complaining about Platoon Nine and how they were winning every competition. Oluomachukwu hadn't really been following all the competitions, so she couldn't tell what or how many Platoon Nine had won.

Some were saying that Platoon Nine instructors had influence over the decision-making or that they had bribed the officials to always win the contests. Oluomachukwu couldn't control the half smile that cut across her cheeks when she heard all the allegations.

When they were done arranging, she went back to the hostel with Nkiru. Nkiru too was highly disappointed with the results, and wished that she had participated instead of Eugenia, because there was no way on earth she would have taken the last place. The evening killed her mood, as she went back to the hostel to sleep.

Oluomachukwu was glad that they didn't have to go to *mami* market to hang out that night, because she, too, was still in a bad mood over Okechukwu. She bought herself some fruits and a bottle of water then went back to the room to lie down and cry herself to sleep.

C. M. OKONKWO

CHAPTER TWENTY-TWO: DAY EIGHTEEN

Friday, 22nd August 2014

Oluomachukwu got up feeling worse than she was when she went to bed. Her eyes were twice its usual size and red, the evidence of lack of sleep and over-crying. She sat up in her bed and felt around her cloth-pillow, and there were still a couple of phones under it. She pushed them down as usual, then put her own phone to charge.

While the phone was charging, she checked it for the time. It was 3:50am. She had woken up earlier than usual, again, and she had hardly even slept. She also noticed that there was a text message on her phone, and had a feeling it was Okechukwu texting her with another silly and false excuse as to why he hadn't called before or sent her a text message.

Unfortunately, or maybe fortunately for her, the text message was from Juachi. He wanted to meet with her and Anita after the morning drills to have another discussion about their business plan and the division of roles, as the presentation was going to hold that afternoon by 12:00pm.

Oluomachukwu thought that he was in too much of a hurry, because the top four platoons hadn't been picked yet for the final stage, which was the presentation, but she replied with a simple 'O.K.,' then went about her morning duties.

She drank up her big bottle of water in large gulps until she had replenished all that she had lost, crying. She got her things ready for her bath, carried her bucket and bathing bowl, and tied her wrapper around her breasts, then went to the bathroom, glad that it was empty. And for the first time, she took her time to have her bath, and most of it was spent thinking. She couldn't stop thinking. All of a sudden, camp life had gotten sad and distasteful, even *mami* market was the least on her mind. She wanted to leave the camp, but the main issue was finding where to stay, because Okechukwu's house was now out of the question for her. After what she had heard, there was no way on earth she was ever going to go back to his place, unless it was to pack her things.

She didn't know where else to go. The only thing she could do was to call her mother and ask her of any of her relatives or friends she could stay with until she got a place of her own. She finished taking her bath, then went back to the room.

It was still quite early, so she put on her underwear and inner clothing, laid down, tucked herself inside her duvet cover and gazed into the springs on the bunk bed on top of hers.

Oluomachukwu didn't know that she had fallen asleep, because when Nkiru bounced on her bed, she woke up in a fright, looking around as if she was misplaced. When she saw both Nkiru and Ogo looking at her, she hissed, and they laughed.

"Were you having a nightmare?" Nkiru asked.

Oluomachukwu shook her head. What she was feeling was worse than a nightmare.

"You look so unhappy. Did something happen?" Nkiru pushed further.

"Or is it because of the Miss NYSC and Mr. Macho contest results?" Ogo laughed.

Oluomachukwu couldn't hide the smile that pressed on her lips. "Of course not. I couldn't care less about that. I heard that Platoon Nine is going to win almost, if not every contest in this camp, so it's not worth my emotions."

"So what is worth your emotions?" Nkiru asked.

Oluomachukwu didn't know what to say, and didn't want to say anything. She made faces and puffed air out of her mouth, as she was thinking about it, then got saved by the sound of the bugle. The sound rang in their ears and head, as if the bugle blower was standing just outside their room door.

"Oh, no, not that trumpet or whatever you girls call it again," Nkiru said.

"Bugle!" Oluomachukwu and Ogo yelled concurrently.

"I'm going to either steal that trumpet, or bugle, or snatch it out of that man's hand when he is playing it, then run into the female hostel. It's a noisy nuisance."

Oluomachukwu and Ogo laughed, but Oluomachukwu was glad that they had forgotten that they had asked her a question. Nkiru and Ogo got up and went to get ready for the morning activities, while Oluomachukwu went to the parade ground, as she didn't want to get into any form of trouble. It took about twenty extra minutes, coupled with several OBS announcements for everyone to come out to the parade ground. A lot of people were punished, but not Nkiru and Ogo. They used the route inside the hostel, then passed the back, just like Oluomachukwu and Ogo had done once before. Ogo then ran to her own platoon, while Nkiru ran to stand on the line close to Oluomachukwu, smiling victoriously as though she had just evaded multiple land mines on an enemy territory.

Before Oluomachukwu could ask Nkiru what was going on, and what was making her smile, Nkiru spoke. "It felt so exciting running through the back and hiding from soldiers. I saw some other Corps members doing the same thing."

"Right." Oluomachukwu rolled her eyes. "Why are you even on the parade ground today? It is unlike you."

"Well, Platoon Seven is on duty today and I want my badge." Nkiru laughed. "And besides, I have to meet with the cooking team after morning drills."

"Of course, we are on duty today." Oluomachukwu rolled her eyes again. "I have to meet with the business plan team as well."

They both smiled at each other, unable to explain why they were smiling. Maybe it was the fact that their platoon depended on them for something or that they were just busy.

Shortly after that, the morning ritual commenced with the Morning Prayer, the National and NYSC Anthems, and the Meditation from a Platoon Seven representative. One of the girls from 'Two' recited it and Oluomachukwu thought the girl was nervous. Anyone would have been nervous and probably would have spoken faster than the girl was speaking. She was incomprehensible.

After the ritual, 'Madam MC' came out to make three important announcements. Firstly, some Corps members were yet to collect their allowance from the previous day. The bank representatives and bullion vans were going to leave by 12:00pm, and anyone who didn't get their own allowance by then was going to have to forfeit it.

Oluomachukwu remembered that she hadn't collected her own, so she made a mental note, and supported it with a reminder on her cell phone, to collect the money after her meeting with Juachi and Anita.

The second announcement was for those who were sending some of their belongings to their homes via their visiting family members or friends. Apparently, guests had been visiting the Corps members with foodstuff and soft drinks, which they were asked to drop off at the gate, while some Corps members were sending home the things they had bought or had won to avoid having plenty of things to carry on the final day in the camp. 'Madam MC' said that it was not to be allowed henceforth, and that was in order to avoid theft. She believed that some Corps members would steal things from their rooms, pretend the things belonged to them, then send the things back home. That behaviour was not acceptable.

The final announcement was the result of the business plan submission. Four platoons had been picked, including Platoons Seven and Nine, and the members of the four platoons screamed, clapped and cheered. Oluomachukwu instinctively looked to her back and saw Juachi staring at her. He had been convinced that their business plan would make it, and it did. And at that, she felt a modicum of joy, one that the thought of Okechukwu could not hamper.

After all the three announcements were made, the Drill Instructor took the microphone and asked Platoon Seven Corps members to leave the parade ground and report for their duties. As Oluomachukwu and her teammates jogged away, they heard the DJ begin to play his Nigerian music mix.

***

Duties were assigned by Auntie Vera and Sister Mary, and those who still had competitions or things to do were put on Sanitation or Kitchen duties. Oluomachukwu had been on Kitchen duty before, so she opted for Sanitation this time. She was put on morning Sanitation duty and was going to clean immediately, so that she would be free for the rest of the day. Anita and Juachi, too, were put on Sanitation duties, so that they would also finish their duties before the 12:00pm timeline for the business plan event.

The Sanitation duty took less than one hour to get completed. Oluomachukwu and three other girls were put on the ground floor and asked to sweep all around, then mop the place with dirty water that had no drop of soap in it. The mop stick had only a few strands of thread left on it, so that the head of the stick scratched the floor. It was a difficult, almost impossible cleaning mission, but they were able to finish it up in time.

When Oluomachukwu had checked in with one of the cleaning coordinators that they had finished, they were allowed to go upstairs or do whatever it was they wanted to do. Oluomachukwu decided to go upstairs and get her international passport, just in case it was needed for the collection of the allowance. She already had her badge on her, but she didn't want to have to go upstairs again.

Nkiru and three girls were cleaning the fourth floor, under stern supervision from one of the local cleaners. She also hadn't collected her allowance, so she gave her badge to Oluomachukwu, then went to the room quickly, which was luckily open, to also get her international passport. Oluomachukwu then went outside, and by that time, the bugle had already sounded for Bath and Breakfast, and the bank representatives were under the canopies, waiting for Corps members to collect their money.

Oluomachukwu checked for her own State code range, found it, then went there. It went relatively fast, because there were not much people queuing up. She took her own money, which had been put in a slim brown envelope and sealed. She then asked if she could collect Nkiru's own allowance and was told that it was illegal, if not fraudulent. Nkiru was to appear by herself before 12:00pm for her money. Oluomachukwu took out her phone, called Nkiru and relayed the information to her. She then waited for Nkiru to come to the parade ground, gave her the badge and international passport, and waited for her to collect her allowance. After that, Nkiru went back to her cleaning, while Oluomachukwu went to meet with Juachi and Anita.

The meeting was very short. Juachi just said he wanted to tell them who would do what for the presentation. He was going to introduce the team and present the company, goals, values, and so on; Anita was going to talk about the marketing strategy, the positioning and competition, while Oluomachukwu was going to talk about the staff structure, the finances, and then conclude with the risk management. Oluomachukwu wondered why they couldn't have done the meeting over the phone, or why Juachi didn't just send them text messages, then she realised that he didn't like to spend his airtime. It seemed like no one in the camp liked to. When the meeting was over, she went back to the room to rest pending the time the presentation was to start.

And before she did, she kept her allowance inside the inner section of her box, wrapped between her underwear and pantyhose, which she had never used. When she had securely locked the box, she got on her bed and slid into her duvet cover to rest.

Oluomachukwu had just begun to fall asleep when the OBS speaker's announcement frightened her. The speaker was calling all business plan representatives to the parade ground. They were to dress in their ceremonial kit, without the khaki jacket, and then report immediately to the parade ground to start the presentation.

She reached for her phone in her waist pouch to check for the time, it was 8:50am, and she wondered why there was an announcement when the programme was to start by 12:00pm.

The OBS speaker also called other Corps members to come out to the parade ground to watch the competition. Oluomachukwu thought it was strange. She pulled out her cell phone and called Anita. Anita was in *mami* market, probably eating, and hadn't heard the announcement. She said she was going back to the hostel immediately to put on her ceremonial outfit and report to the parade ground as well. Oluomachukwu then called Juachi, who picked up the call immediately. He had already gone to confirm the announcement, and it was certain that the event was to hold by 9:00am, and not 12:00pm as formerly announced.

Oluomachukwu got dressed in her ceremonial outfit and held her hair up in a bun. Juachi had also told her that proper personal presentation was going to be a plus for the final results — so it was the ceremonial kit and no waist pouch. She got ready, and by the time she went outside, it was 9:11am. The canopies had already been set up for the event. All the bank representatives and bullion vans were already leaving, earlier than planned, and Platoon Seven Environmental duty Corps members were rearranging the chairs quickly. The crowd space was filling up gradually as everyone was expected to be there.

On the parade ground, there was a canopy where the judges were to sit, and there was another canopy for the twelve representatives, three for each of the four teams. The chairs were lined in columns so that each platoon was in a column. Juachi took the first seat, Anita sat in the middle and Oluomachukwu sat behind. There were also three chairs in the centre of the parade ground, flanked by the canopies. The presenting teams were to take a seat on the stage to present.

The programme started shortly after every one of the representatives was present. The event's host did some talking and made some speeches before the main show began. While the speeches were going on, Oluomachukwu felt her phone vibrate in her pocket. She took it out and saw a text message from Tracker.

"You look so beautiful sitting there."

Oluomachukwu instinctively looked towards the crowd and around, wondering where Tracker was seated, and conscious that the whole crowd of Corps members could be looking at her. Her pulse pumped and her heartbeat quickened at that instant and she hoped that the event would be over and done with as soon as possible.

She contemplated replying to Tracker, but before she did, her phone rang in her hand and it was Okechukwu calling. Her heart stopped for a bit. She felt even more nervous than she was before. She contemplated answering it, then eventually did.

"Hello?" she whispered.

"Hey, why are you whispering?" he asked.

"I'm on a mini stage, waiting to present a business plan that I worked on with some of my team members in my platoon."

"Okay, let me allow you focus on the presentation," he replied, and it was obvious that he was trying to avoid her. For all she knew, he could have called her by error or out of pity or even guilty conscience.

"No, you can talk," she said.

"I was just calling to check up on you and to tell you that I miss you."

She hadn't actually planned to verbally attack him, but her emotions took the best of her. "Oh, please, Oke. What type of missing is that? You never call or text me, you just leave me hanging, then call once and want to run off, then say you miss me."

Okechukwu didn't say anything.

"I didn't think you even had anything to tell me." She sighed. "Look, I just want to know what it is you are doing and why you are calling me. The other day you called me, you—" She stopped when she realised she was going to talk about the conversation she had heard of him and Idara. He wouldn't have known about it and it wasn't the right time for her to confront him, but thinking about it again made her upset. In fact, she was feeling destabilised all of a sudden, and didn't know how she would manage to present her part of the business plan.

"The other day I called, what happened? And what day was it?" he asked.

Oluomachukwu totally ignored his questions, then said, "I guess you are right, maybe you should let me focus on my presentation."

"Okay, fine." He sounded exasperated, and she didn't know why. He had no right to sound in any way negative.

"Fine, talk to you whenever," she replied.

"What does that even mean?"

"It means that I have to go now and whenever you call we can talk." She hung up after that, as it was almost time to start the presentations.

She received an instant text message from him, and she opened it immediately to read.

"What's up with you? You are acting hostile ."

She didn't bother replying, she locked the screen of her phone and put it in her pocket, then focused her attention to the event.

One after the other, each platoon came out to present their business and defend the plan. Oluomachukwu had drifted out during the first two presentations, thinking of nothing else but Okechukwu and Idara's conversation, and how much of a betrayer Okechukwu was. Not to forget, a pretender and a double-dater, a cheat just like his friends.

On a normal day, she could just forget about him and move on with her life, but the fact that she had heard what she heard was preventing her from moving forward. The thought of someone having such horrible ideas about her troubled her.

Her platoon defended after the second one and she reluctantly dragged her feet to the mini stage, looking lost. Fortunately for her, Juachi had done all the talking and defence, so both herself and Anita didn't have anything to say. In fact, the presentation was so nice that one of the judges asked Juachi to contact him much later after the event. Platoon Nine defended next and were so grilled with questions that people wondered how they had made the top four list. No other platoon had been asked that many questions, so people felt it was going to be the fall of the platoon finally.

When all the teams had finished presenting, a Nigerian comedian called Elenu, whom Oluomachukwu had never heard of, was invited to keep the crowd busy while the judges worked on the results. He made everyone laugh as he made jokes about Nigeria in general, and two of the businesses that had been presented. By the time he was done with his skit, the results were ready.

The organiser came out and called the results, starting from the fourth and third places. The first two platoons to have presented took third and fourth, Oluomachukwu was not really sure which was which. Only Platoons Seven and Nine were left for the final result. The organiser smiled first before he announced that Platoon Nine had won the contest.

The Platoon Nine representatives jumped and shouted, while their platoon members roared in the crowd, happy that once again, they had taken the first place. Every other platoon contested the decision, as they were all sure that Platoon Seven had won the competition with their unique business idea. Platoon Nine's business idea was in fashion designing and making cheap clothes for the masses, while Platoon Seven had picked 3D printing.

And much to everybody's surprise, the business plan competition organisers gave each of Platoon Nine's three representatives two milllion naira to support their business, because they had mentioned that all they needed in their make-belief business was five million naira. Platoon Seven, on the other hand, needed a little over six million naira.

The organisers said that if Platoon Seven's capital was six million naira or less, they would have won the contest. The ridiculous part was that no one had mentioned the six million naira prize prior to the competition, and nobody had actually thought of setting up the businesses in reality.

They had invented business ideas solely for the contest. So whether the organisers were really going to give out the prize money or the winners were really going to set up the business was unknown to anyone in the camp. It was to remain a mystery.

As Platoon Nine members were invited to receive their prize, the DJ played the same song he normally played whenever there was a contest and a winner was picked —

Stand up for the champions. Platoon Nine representatives, all smiles, went to receive their prize money amongst other prizes like small generator sets, pillows and 50,000 naira for their platoon. Platoon Seven representatives were given tabletop cookers, pillows and a cheque of 15,000 naira for their platoon. The third place team got rechargeable fans, pillows as well, and 10,000 naira for their team, and that was how the event ended.

Oluomachukwu, together with Juachi and Anita then proceeded to take pictures with other contestants, with the business plan organisers and judges, and with their platoon members.

***

The rest of the day went quietly, apart from the bad mixture of music that flooded the camp, from the DJ and also from *mami* market. There was supposed to be SAED group meetings, but the business plan competition had taken the slot. After that, there was an hour dedicated to Personal Administration and Oluomachukwu still didn't know what it was. And judging by the way the camp life was gradually coming to an end, she didn't think she would ever know its purpose.

After that, there was Jumat service for Muslim Corps members, which was to run for an hour, from 1:00pm to 2:00pm. Oluomachukwu used the opportunity to go back to the room to rest for a while. She was still upset about the Okechukwu incident and upset at the fact that it was eating into her happiness, and she didn't want to feel that way anymore.

The bugle sounded for Lunch and Siesta, and it was accompanied by the OBS speaker's monotonous voice. The camp kitchen was serving beans and yam porridge, and Oluomachukwu wasn't interested. In fact, she hadn't even had any breakfast and wasn't prepared to eat until all the uneasiness she was feeling left her.

After Lunch and Siesta time was over, finals for all the sports activities were scheduled except for football, which was to hold in a couple of days. Volleyball semi-finals and finals were played on the same day. Athletics and table tennis finals were also played. There were also martial arts and man-o-war competitions, which Platoon Seven took second place. Oluomachukwu actually wasn't interested in knowing all the winners or losers, but whenever she was told what position Platoon Seven took, she was willing to listen.

When all the contests were over about two and a half hours later, the bugle sounded for dinner. Oluomachukwu didn't go for dinner either, she stayed on her bed to brood. Nkiru and Ogo had come to talk to her a few times, asking her if she wanted to eat or hang out in *mami* market to celebrate her second prize for the business plan contest and she said "No."

They also asked her why she was feeling down and what was going on with her, as they had noticed her erratic behaviour all day, but she refused to tell them anything. She said that she needed one more night to think about everything that was on her mind, then she would be able to have fun again. They both agreed and left her to be by herself.

***

The room was very quiet when it was about 7:30pm, but Oluomachukwu could hear a lot of noise from the camp market of people having fun. She started crying, and she didn't know how to get out of her sour mood. Just then, her phone vibrated, she checked it and saw that there was a text message from Okechukwu, and her tears dried up immediately.

"Hi, I hope the presentation went well, and I still don't know why you were sounding very strange today."

She didn't want to reply at first, but got tempted and

eventually did. *"I don't know what game you are playing. You can't be acting like you want to be with me, when you are screwing someone else."*

"I don't understand what you mean by that. What is wrong with you?"

"Yes, you do understand, and nothing is wrong with me. You know deep down within that heart of yours that you have someone else, so why are you fucking pretending?"

She knew that the text message sounded harsh, but she didn't care.

"Temper, temper... I don't like your language or tone. If you have something to say, then better say it."

"You are disgusting. There. That's what I have to say."

"Don't insult me, because you wouldn't like me when I'm angry. I'm not in a gaming mood right now."

"I don't care what mood you are in right now." She hit Send. She wanted to upset him on purpose, so that he would feel some hurt as well.

He didn't reply, instead he called her. He called, once, twice, three times and the phone rang out each time. She wasn't in the mood to talk to him.

"So now you won't pick up my call and let me know what is wrong with you." His text came in almost immediately after the third call rang out.

"You are trying to double-date and it's disgusting... that is what is wrong with me. You are not better than your friends, Kayode and Nnanna." She was still not sure when to officially bring Idara into the equation.

"And yet you slept with both of them and would also sleep with me in a snap of my finger if I asked you to"

Okechukwu's reply hit Oluomachukwu so hard that she would have staggered if she were standing. There and then, her eyes started to well up again, and she started to get upset again. Her intention had been to upset him and it backfired on her.

"Fuck you and fuck off, you fucking loser."

She hit Send, then switched her phone off immediately,

because she didn't want to know what else he had to say. She was now too upset. In fact upset was too mild a word to express how she was feeling. She was capable of hurting someone, anyone, or even herself at that instant and there was nothing anybody could do to cheer her up. In fact, she didn't feel like hurting just a random person, she felt like hurting Okechukwu for hurting her.

She was sad and also very embarrassed that she had practically forced herself on someone she thought loved her. She trusted him and even shared her ugly secrets with him, and all the while he already had his mind on someone else.

She laid on her bed thinking deeply, but she didn't cry again. She tried to force herself to cry, but the tears didn't come out. Maybe she was suddenly hard hearted or maybe her subconscious didn't want her to shed any more tears for him. She stayed that way, staring up at the springs that supported the bed that Ijeoma, her ex-bunkmate used to sleep in. She also heard the twirling of the fan, and it sounded louder and faster, like there were two fans. She stretched her neck and checked, there was now a new fan.

She had told Foyin about the fan just the morning before and it was already fixed. Even in her anger, she commended the NYSC for that. She then laid back in her bed and stayed that way until she was done feeling angry and disappointed, and decided to go to *mami* market to have a few drinks on her own, and with a lot of money to spend.

A few drinks turned into a lot of drinks. She drank everything from red wine, to beer, to cocktails, to Orijin and to Kiss Mix. She had never tried Kiss Mix before, but all the different flavours tasted very nice, so she stuck to the brand for the rest of the evening. She then stood at a corner, next to a loud speaker and danced all by herself. Some guys came to ask her to dance, but she refused. Some even tried to grab her and dance with her by force, but she pushed them away and hissed.

While she was dancing, she started to roll her waist and turn around seductively. That was when she caught glances with Kayode. He was at a table with some people that she didn't know, probably camp officials. There were also a couple of girls at the table, and conversations were going on here and there at the table, but he was looking intently at her, as if observing her, as if craving her. So she looked away immediately, then danced away from where his eyes could still be on her.

Her head started to spin from all the alcohol and the lack of food, and everything was woozy around her, but she still danced around until she couldn't recognise the faces of the people she was seeing around her. Not that she didn't know the faces, she couldn't just see them at all; everything was blurry.

She started to count her steps, because it was as if she was moving in slow motion. She felt like her body was slanting and when it was as though she was about to fall, someone held her arm and walked with her. She didn't know if her mind was playing games with her, because things seemed to be moving around her. When she looked at the person that was walking with her, she didn't see a face.

She didn't know when or how she ended up in one of the dirty stalls at the back of the camp market with a guy she didn't know. Her vision was getting clearer, but her mind was too cloggy to react. She wanted to ask him who he was and how they got there, but the words did not come out. Just then, the guy held her waist and pulled her closer, then tilted her head up, and she realised that he was about to kiss her. She managed to turn her head to the side and protested.

"Please, stop," she said, but she was the only one that heard what she had said.

Her voice echoed in her own head and remained there. The strange guy tried to still force a kiss on her lips, but she pushed him away weakly and turned her head to the side again. His lips landed on her neck and she shrieked. He then held her head firmly and started kissing her. Just then, her eyes began to clear up and she mustered up some energy to fight him off. She tried to scream, but the sound didn't come out from her mouth.

"Stop it, please," she pleaded, then pushed him again.

This time, she heard her own voice when she spoke, and it was evident that the strange guy had heard her too, because he told her to shut up. He began to get a bit aggressive. He grabbed her and pulled her closer again, trying to force-open the button of her shorts and undo her zipper. It was when he attempted to put his hands in her shorts that someone forcefully pulled him away from her from behind. It was Kayode. He had arrived in the nick of time.

The strange guy fell on his backside and immediately stood up, trying to ram into Kayode and knock him down, but Kayode moved a step to the side and the guy ran into one of the poles that held the stall together and banged his shoulder into it.

"If you dare get up again, you'll be severely dealt with tonight and I'll make sure you get arrested," Kayode yelled at the strange guy.

The strange guy had intended to get up, even with his aching shoulder, to fight Kayode, probably thinking that Kayode was a stall owner or one of the sellers in the camp market, but he stopped when he realised that Kayode was a camp official, especially as he stood firm and didn't move and also spoke with authority.

"Just try and make one more move and I'll show you that I didn't become an NYSC official overnight," Kayode threatened, just in case the strange guy wanted to try his luck again.

The strange guy stepped back.

Kayode stretched forth his hand. "Give me your badge, right now."

The strange guy didn't move. He knew that if he gave his badge, it would be the end for him in the camp or even in the NYSC scheme. He looked around and made to run, but Kayode set a foot in his path and he fell face down. Kayode then bent down, removed the badge from around the guy's neck and told him to get out. When the strange guy ran off, Kayode turned to look at Oluomachukwu. She was at a corner, shaken up, shocked at what had happened and angry at how she had let things get out of hand just because of her emotions, how Okechukwu had made her feel. She felt stupid.

Kayode tried to hold her arm, tried to help her steady herself, and then walk her out of what now seemed like a dungeon into the main market, but she shrugged his hand away.

"Leave me alone," she said. "You're not different from that guy that tried to force himself on me. In fact, you're worse than him. All of you."

Kayode was offended. "Please, Oluoma, don't say that. I would never force myself on you or on anyone. Never. I noticed you were drinking too much and a lot of people were looking at you. When you went out of my sight, I had to look for you. Did something happen?"

Oluomachukwu closed her eyes and shuddered, as the incident came back to her like it was happening again. She opened her eyes, but she didn't look at Kayode. "Nothing happened," she lied. "But I'm sorry."

Kayode was confused. "What are you sorry for?"

"I should be thanking you, not accusing you."

"It's okay. I'm not just someone you know. I'm also an NYSC official and part of my job is to look out for Corps members, and it involves protecting, helping and assisting Corps members or people in need."

Kayode tried to hold Oluomachukwu's arm again and she didn't shove him away this time. He held it, then they left the stall and went back to the main camp market.

By the time they got there, a little fight had broken out

between some male Corps members, who were evidently drunk, and some man-o-war officials, who perhaps, were also drunk, over table reservation, drinks and girls — girls that had already left their table because of the fight. In fact, the girls were running to safety towards the hostel, while soldiers came to calm everything down.

The Camp Commandant sat not too far away, watching everything that was happening and how the soldiers were handling the fight. He hardly ever wore his uniform, so he always blended in with the crowd to observe things and people, and know what steps to take next. He looked on as the soldiers started sending Corps members back to their rooms, probably thinking of the best type of punishment for all parties involved in the fight.

And as if the soldiers had read his mind, they started collecting badges from the Corps members and man-o-war officials in order to identify them much later for further action.

When Kayode approached the Camp Commandant's table, he looked up, then noticed that Kayode was with someone. He looked at the person, and was startled to see Oluomachukwu. She looked distraught. He looked at their hands — Kayode was holding her. He then looked at her again, then looked back at Kayode, and wore a confused, suspicious and worried look.

"Is something going on here?" the Camp Commandant asked. He had actually gone from confused and suspicious to worried, very worried.

Kayode didn't say anything. He asked Oluomachukwu to wait for him just a few tables away while he spoke with the Camp Commandant, who was now sitting at the edge of his seat, wondering what exactly was going on.

"What is going on?" the Camp Commandant asked, as soon as Oluomachukwu walked towards a table and sat on it. She was looking at both of them.

Oluomachukwu watched Kayode as he was talking and

explaining things to the Camp Commandant, who sat still and listened attentively, one hand was on his chin and the other across his belly, supporting one elbow. Kayode then put the badge he had seized on the table, and the Camp Commandant looked at it first, before he snatched it, and then dismissed Kayode.

He got up after a couple of seconds and went to meet Oluomachukwu. He asked to walk her back to the hostel and she followed him. Her head was still throbbing and her mouth was reeking of alcohol. If he had gotten any closer to her and perceived her breath, he would have vomited.

Even in her state, she was still able to walk a straight line and her vision was getting a bit clearer. It was just the reality of what had happened that woke her out of her high state of intoxication.

"So how are you feeling?" The Camp Commandant's voice brought her mind back to him.

"I'm fine," she replied without looking at him. It was as though she was speaking to the red sand that covered the camp market ground.

"What happened to you back there?"

She did not answer, because she thought that Kayode had already told him, so she kept looking at the red sand.

"I want to know what happened."

She responded, but not immediately. She took her time, but eventually told him what had happened in summary, then ended it by blaming herself for drinking too much. The Camp Commandant did not say anything yet. He just walked her towards the volleyball court area, where there was light, bright enough to read.

"The culprit..." he said, and looked at the badge he had collected from Kayode. It must have been very difficult to read what was on the yellow badge at night, because he narrowed his eyes. But he managed to find what he was looking for, and continued, "Segun is his name. He would have to be decamped and severely dealt with. In fact, he would not be allowed to complete the service year, and I will make sure he is banned. We do not condone such acts in this camp or anywhere else for that matter."

Oluomachukwu was super shocked. She wasn't sure if it was the same Segun she had met in church; the same Segun she had refused to give her number to; the same Segun that said he loved the way she danced and that he noticed that she drank a lot. She was tempted to ask the Camp Commandant if she could see the ID, but didn't. Only time would tell if it was really the same Segun.

C. M. OKONKWO

CHAPTER TWENTY-THREE: DAY NINETEEN

Saturday, 23 rd August 2014

Oluomachukwu woke up with a hangover, and at that instant she started to regret coming back to Nigeria, coming to the NYSC Orientation camp, meeting Okechukwu and Nnanna again, and also meeting Kayode. She regretted everything and couldn't wait to go back to the UK at the first opportunity she had. She had cried herself to sleep the night before, and was dehydrated when she woke up. She felt around her bed and saw an almost empty bottle of water. It had just a few drops in it and she took it down immediately.

She sat up in her bed and was shocked to see Nkiru awake, also sitting up in her bed and watching her in a creepy way. Nkiru didn't attempt to move or go over to Oluomachukwu's bed as she normally did. Oluomachukwu got the message and stood up. Her legs were shaky, but she managed to go over to Nkiru's bed and sat at the foot of the bed. Nkiru still didn't react.

"What's going on?" Oluomachukwu asked, not sure what Nkiru was thinking or feeling, or if she was thinking about or feeling anything.

"I should be asking you that," Nkiru responded. "You were acting funny all through yesterday, so Ogo and I proposed to go to *mami* market with you to cheer you up and you said no. We left you in the room and went to *mami* market, but when we came back, you weren't here. You then came back after the Lights Out call, looking ruffled, drunk and weird. You still didn't want to tell us what was wrong, but you cried yourself to sleep. So, you tell me, what is going on?"

Oluomachukwu didn't say anything. She was actually mesmerised at how Nkiru had talked very fast, and in a whisper, and didn't even stop to breathe. She looked up at Nkiru and Nkiru was staring at her, so she looked at her fingernails. She always did that in the past, when she was very nervous or when someone was expecting her to say something. She hadn't done it in a while, and was surprised at herself for doing it while Nkiru was talking to her.

"Are you going to say something or are you going to keep looking at your fingernails?"

Oluomachukwu looked at Nkiru's face, then at her own fingernails again, then back at Nkiru's face, and sighed. "I am fine. Nothing is wrong," she lied.

"You can't tell me that, because you just thought about what was wrong right now, but you feel that I' m not worth knowing about it. Isn't it?"

Oluomachukwu was shocked at how Nkiru could have guessed that, because she had indeed been thinking about what was wrong, while looking at her fingernails. Her story was a bit on the complicated side and it was too much to share, and she wasn't sure Nkiru was the right person to share it with. After thinking briefly, she said, "That's not true, Nkiru. Please, I'm fine, and I really appreciate your friendship so far, and I would never think that you are not worth knowing things about me."

"Then why don't you just tell me that you are not ready to share, and I'll wait for you until you are? It beats lying to me and telling me that all is well when it's obviously not. "

"That's fine." Oluomachukwu managed to smile. "And I'm so sorry. My mind is just in a lot of places right now. Once I figure myself out, I'll let you know."

Nkiru shrugged. "That's fine."

Oluomachukwu looked around, biting her lower lip. "What's up with everyone? No morning drill today?"

"I don't think so. There's meant to be Endurance Trek this morning from 6:30am to 2:00pm, but I'm not too sure it would still happen." Nkiru corked her head towards the window, and Oluomachukwu followed it and saw that it was windy outside, as if it was going to rain.

At that moment, the sound of the bugle rang round the hostel, and Oluomachukwu looked at Nkiru immediately. "I thought it wasn't going to hold." Oluomachukwu rolled her eyes.

Nkiru shrugged a second time. "I guess we better get ready, then go and find out."

Oluomachukwu got up from the bed, then as she got her things ready for her bath, Nkiru went and slapped Ogo on the buttocks and told her to wake up. Ogo grumbled as usual and eventually got up. Other girls in the room also woke up reluctantly, grumbling as they did.

Oluomachukwu hurried to the bathroom, and luckily it was empty. The surprise bugle call had not woken a lot of people up. The OBS speaker kept making announcements, asking everyone to go out for an important message and an impromptu lecture, since there was not going to be an endurance trek. The endurance trek hadn't been cancelled because of the cloudy weather, but because of safety, security and health reasons.

There were no morning drills to the joy of many, but it had taken a record-breaking time of more than thirty minutes to get everyone out of their rooms. Since in their minds, there was not going to be morning drills, they had not prepared themselves to wake up. By the time the last batch of people were coming out, the bugle blower played the national anthem that still sounded nothing like the anthem. Even in their tired states, and with croaked voices, some Corps members still sang 'Hold something' when the bugle blower got to that particular part.

After that, 'Madam MC' came out and led the Morning Prayer. And after the National and NYSC Anthems, she called out the Platoon Eight representative to recite the Meditation. When that was over, she announced that there was not going to be an endurance trek in order to ensure the safety of everyone, because with the Ebola threat, it was not safe. But the main purpose of the emergency call wasn't for the information on the trek, as most people already knew that it wasn't going to hold from the day before, the emergency call was for an address from the Camp Director and a last-minute lecture that had been set up.

Platoon Eight Corps members didn't leave the parade ground to report for their duties, because they, too, had to partake in the lecture, so only the camp kitchen prepared breakfast, but the Corps members were going to serve it much later. It was going to be bread, boiled egg and tea, either way, so it didn't require much preparation.

When 'Madam MC' was done with her talk, she handed the microphone over to the Camp Director, who was frowning for the first time. It was sure that something had happened again or that she wasn't happy with the sudden air of nonchalance she and other camp officials perceived amongst the Corps members.

The Camp Director started her address by expressing her distaste in the event that happened the night before in the camp market, and everyone looked at one another, wondering what she was talking about. She then said that a male Corps member had lured a female Corps member to the back of the camp market and attempted to rape her, then condemned the male Corps member. At the mention of that, there was sudden unrest and discomfort among the crowd and people started to murmur.

Oluomachukwu felt embarrassed at that moment and a flush of ice cold air went through her body, making her shiver and giving her goose bumps. The culprit hadn't tried to rape her, but just tried to force-kiss her. She shook when the thought came back to her, then she admitted to herself that the force-kiss could have led to something worse if Kayode hadn't been there to stop it. She hoped that the Camp Director wouldn't call names. She could call the name of the culprit, but not her own name. She would practically pass out if everyone knew that she was the victim and perceived her as such. She wouldn't be able to handle all the attention, pity and even negative accusations from people who always blame victims for their attacks.

The Camp Director allowed them to finish murmuring before she continued her address. She went ahead and warned all female Corps members to be careful and be mindful of the people around them, and that they should also drink moderately or not even drink at all, so that they wouldn't fall into any type of danger. She made sure to warn them that even friends couldn't be fully trusted, both male and female, so they had to always be on alert and leave where they were if they ever felt uncomfortable.

After the address, there was an impromptu lecture on Security Awareness and Education. It seemed to be the perfect time to bring up the topic. A green and white mini handbook on the topic was also distributed to everybody, and a guest security officer and a medical specialist came to speak about violent crimes and mitigations, and specifically about preventing sexual assault and what actions to take to minimise risks. Everybody kept quiet and listened intently, some thinking very deeply, some shedding silent tears.

Oluomachukwu stood there and fought back her tears, when she turned to look at Nkiru, Nkiru had a worried look on her face, so Oluomachukwu smiled at her and she smiled back, but it was a consoling kind of smile. After the lecture, the Camp Director announced that the culprit had already been decamped that morning, removed from the NYSC scheme, banned, and handed over to the authorities for further action.

Nobody gasped, nobody murmured, nobody reacted. It was as if everyone was reflecting on their lives and how lucky they were for being neither the culprit nor the victim. Some of them were probably wondering who the culprit and the victim were. Oluomachukwu, too, wondered who the culprit was, but would not have wanted to come face-to-face with him. Within a couple of minutes, the crowd was dismissed and everyone went quietly to their various destinations. Platoon Eight Corps members went to the volleyball court to report for their duties for the day.

***

Oluomachukwu went back to the room quietly, while Nkiru went to meet with the cooking contest team at the back of the dining hall to finalise on what they were going to buy for the cooking, and how they were going to set up and decorate their table. The cooking contest was to hold that evening, so she was going to be busy all through until it was time for the show to start.

When Oluomachukwu entered the room, Ogo wasn't back yet, so she was happy that she wasn't going to have to explain her previous behaviour to her. She removed her rubber trainers, then slid inside her duvet cover and got comfortable in her bed. She brought out her cell phone, wondering why it hadn't vibrated since, when she realised that the phone had been switched off since her last nasty message to Okechukwu. She turned on the phone, and much to her surprise, there was nothing from him.

She locked the phone screen and stowed it under her new pillow — the one she had won — when the phone vibrated. She pulled it out and looked at the screen, it was Okechukwu calling. She didn't pick it up, she just looked at the phone ringing until it rang out. She did the same thing for the next five calls that came in, then stowed the phone away again. And as soon as she closed her eyes, the phone vibrated again, but not for long, so she looked at the screen again and saw a text message.

"Hi, Oluoma. I know you are still angry with me for reasons unknown, but I need to talk to you because I'm worried about you. Let me know that you are okay, and I'm sorry for what I said yesterday. I admit I was out of line and I shouldn't have judged you based on what you had told me. Please, pick up ."

Oluomachukwu thought for a second, then replied. *"I am fine, thanks. And don't worry about yesterday. I've long forgotten about it."*

"What exactly have you long forgotten about? What I said yesterday or what happened to you last night? I am feeling guilty about it. Please, pick up ."

Oluomachukwu saw the reply and her heart almost exploded in her chest. She took a few seconds to catch her breath, then called Kayode immediately.

"Hi, Oluoma, are you okay?" Kayode asked.

"Did you have to tell Okechukwu what happened to me?" she replied, sounding very agitated.

Kayode sighed. "I'm sorry. I was worried about you, so I thought I should call someone you were close to, so that they could help you."

"It was just a forced-kiss..." Oluomachukwu lowered her voice when she realised that she was speaking too loudly. She then whispered, "It was just a forced-kiss. I don't want this turning into a pity party. You didn't have to tell him."

"Clearly." Kayode snapped. "He said you two had an argument, and he thought he was at fault. He felt that you went drinking because of what he said to you."

"He didn't have to tell you that either."

"Oluoma, please, calm down. You are still upset about yesterday and that's why you're finding faults in everything. I know you don't want a pity party made out of this, but you cannot tell that it is really affecting you. Talk about it and free your mind, it will make you feel better."

Oluomachukwu rolled her eyes, even though Kayode couldn't see her. Her phone started to beep at the same time. She looked at the screen and there was an incoming call from Okechukwu. She thought about what Kayode had said to her and decided to talk to Okechukwu. "Okay, Kayode. I'm sorry for yelling at you. Thanks for the help."

"It's no problem. Just call me if you need someone to talk to," Kayode replied.

"I will. Bye." She quickly hit End Call and switched to the incoming call before it went off.

"Hi, Oluoma," Okechukwu said, even before she said anything.

"Hi, Oke." She sounded detached. She was still upset with him.

"I'm so sorry to hear that you were attacked in camp. I never expected such a thing to ever happen in there."

"I was drinking," she replied. "I had drunk a lot and on an empty stomach."

"It doesn't give anyone the right to force himself on you. And I know I'm responsible for your drinking. So technically, I'm responsible for the attack."

Oluomachukwu didn't say anything.

"Please, talk to me. We can talk about yesterday and any other day, and I promise I would never use what you tell me against you, ever again."

"It's actually my fault that everything happened. I was very upset. You called me by mistake and I heard your conversation with Idara, about me."

It was now Okechukwu's turn to keep quiet. It was as though the mysterious tongue-eating cat had jumped out of nowhere and eaten his tongue.

"I don't know why you were leading me on when you had your mind on someone else. It was painful to hear you both talk and laugh about me," Oluomachukwu continued.

"I'm sorry," Okechukwu finally said. "I guess I was just trying to be careful in case you found someone else."

"But you told me not to fall in love in camp, while you still had Idara."

"I had recently started dating Idara and I didn't want to leave her until I was sure that you were mine."

"And after I told you that I wanted to be with you, you told her what I had disclosed to you, and the two of you laughed at me." Oluomachukwu sighed, frustrated.

"Look, Oluoma, I really want—"

"I don't want to know what you want," she interrupted. "But I cannot continue with you and yes, I went drinking because of you. There, I've said it. So I've suffered the pain and moved on."

"I see. But can we go back to the way we used to be? Good friends?"

"I guess we can." She shrugged. "I have to go now. I'll talk to you later."

Okechukwu said "Okay," and she hung up. When she put her phone down, she started to cry, but this time it was tears of joy and of freedom. And as she cried, she made a decision not to stay in Okechukwu's place for the service year. She was glad to have him as a friend again, but wasn't going to live with him.

She thought about what to do, as she knew no one else in Lagos, then called her mother in London, finally. She didn't give her a lot of information, just the basic: coming back to Lagos, registering for the NYSC, her experience with roadside robbers at Oshodi and camp life. She said nothing about the sinister trio that had caused her pain or the forced-kiss incident.

She then asked her mother if there were any friends or relatives of hers that she could live with until she got her own place before the service year ran out. Her mother had obviously asked her why she no longer wanted to stay with Okechukwu, and in order not to go into any long detail, she told her mother that Okechukwu had a girlfriend living in the house with him and she didn't want to cause them any discomfort. Her mother bought the story, told her that she would make phone calls, then call her back.

When Oluomachukwu was done talking to her mother, she spoke to her father as well and her younger brother and sister, whom she missed dearly. And before she hung up, her mother said a long prayer for her, like Nigerian mothers normally did, then wished her well.

***

After Oluomachukwu was well rested, she went to the back of the camp kitchen where Nkiru and her teammates were cooking, to see how they were doing. They used the man-o-war village to cook because there was enough space there.

The NYSC Cooking Contest Committee had given all the platoons the meals to prepare and the foodstuff, so they all basically had the same menu. So the differences would be in the taste of the food, the extras in the food, the creativity in the menu, by thinking outside the box, and the layout of the table.

Oluomachukwu stood there and watched them cook, and occasionally she would give Nkiru a hand with what she was doing. Nkiru was making a special stew for the *ofada* rice she had cooked, and while the stew simmered, she sat on an almost broken chair and drank a can of Coke that Oluomachukwu had bought for her from the camp market before joining her.

"So, how are you feeling now?" Nkiru looked at her, searching her face for clues.

Oluomachukwu smiled. "I'm feeling much better now, thanks."

"That's good, because it means you can finally tell me what has been prickling you for the past two days." Nkiru laughed, the same way she always did, holding her tummy with her head tilting backwards.

Oluomachukwu laughed, but it was Nkiru's contagious laugh that made her laugh too. "I guess so."

There was a sudden silence.

"Oh that reminds me," Nkiru started. "Sister Mary was here not too long ago, and she is much better now."

"Much better?" Oluomachukwu was confused. "What was wrong with her?"

"Remember she almost went into depression because of the Miss NYSC and Mr. Macho results. She said that she had invested her time and energy to make it work and didn't know why we took the last place."

Oluomachukwu laughed. "Seriously? She would go into depression because of something as lame as that? It's just a competition. I'm sure the Eugenia girl and Kelenna have long moved on."

"Well, Sister Mary was too upset, so she went to the contest officials and they told her that we didn't take the last place."

"Really?"

Nkiru nodded. "Yes. We were actually fourth place, both Kelenna and Eugenia. They called from the fourth place to the tenth place, and that was why Platoon Seven was called first."

"Oh."

"Yeah, so Sister Mary calmed down when she heard that, and she's telling everyone that cares to listen. She also told Eugenia and Kelenna so that they wouldn't feel too bad."

"I'm sure they don't care." Oluomachukwu laughed, and Nkiru also laughed.

They stopped laughing when someone grabbed one of their shoulders each from behind, startling them. They turned backwards simultaneously and saw Ogo, smiling at them sheepishly.

"What's tickling you?" Nkiru asked.

"I'll get to that soon, but first of all..." Ogo looked at Oluomachukwu. "Are you okay? You have been acting strange of late, but judging by the way you were laughing just now, it appears that you might be feeling better."

"I am, thanks," Oluomachukwu said shyly, hoping that Ogo wouldn't ask for details. And she didn't.

"Anyway, I was with the CMD not too long ago and he gave me some more gist concerning Fadeke."

"I have even long forgotten about her. Is she still in the camp?" Oluomachukwu asked.

"I was just going to ask the same thing," Nkiru added.

"Not anymore, she isn't," Ogo replied, making both Oluomachukwu and Nkiru look at her in an odd way. She continued, "The State Coordinator asked her to go home today, so you are not likely to see her things in the room when you get there."

"That's interesting," Oluomachukwu commented.

"Yeah." Ogo nodded. "The State Coordinator took her time, but finally decided not to do anything, since Fadeke and Mr. Kayode were both consenting adults. However, she did reprimand Mr. Kayode, and inform his wife all the way in Abuja, because she knows her very well. His wife said that she was disappointed in him, shocked that he was even in the camp, when he said he was going to Kaduna State for Training."

"What?" Nkiru exclaimed, as she burst out in laughter, holding her tummy and tilting her head backwards, the same intoxicating way she always did. Oluomachukwu also laughed.

"In fact, his wife even threatened to leave him and told him not to come back home to her and their two young children," Ogo concluded with that.

"Two young children?" Oluomachukwu was surprised. "That bastard is sure full of surprises, excuse my French."

Both Nkiru and Ogo burst out in laughter this time, but Oluomachukwu didn't. For a brief second she was lost in her thoughts. She felt schadenfreude at the information concerning Kayode. It was definitely going to rattle his marriage and cause him pain, a lot of pain... The same pain he had caused to many.

If she had ever thought of paying him back, that was

enough payback for him. Karma was surely going to show its face one way or another, and in unexpected ways.

***

When they were done goofing around, Oluomachukwu decided to allow Nkiru to get back to her work. Ogo, on the other hand, wanted to go to the tailor at the back of the camp market to pick up a new set of khaki pants she had ordered.

Apparently, Corps members who didn't like what their khaki pants looked like asked tailors to buy them material and sew them new ones, and Ogo was one of those who did. She asked Oluomachukwu to accompany her there, but Oluomachukwu hesitated, since it was at the back of the camp that she had been force-kissed. It was bright, and many people were outside, so she had nothing to worry about. When Ogo attempted to beg her again, she willingly agreed, then they went together.

She stood in front of the tailor community section and looked around the back of the camp, probably for where exactly she had been on the night she was force-kissed, but she had no idea. She zoned out as Ogo tried on her new khaki pants, but then she was brought back to reality when someone stepped on her. The pain stung that she winced and looked up angrily at the person.

She wanted to verbally attack the person, but stopped when she looked at him from head to toe, and back to the head. He was tall and very fit, a Corps member, but that didn't matter because he had the most handsome face she had seen in a while. She looked at him, speechless, as she took in his features: nicely trimmed hair, caramel-coloured even-toned skin, well shaved and light brown eyes.

"I'm very sorry," the guy said, and his baritone voice sounded like melody to the ears.

"You are welcome," Oluomachukwu said, then realised that she shouldn't have said that.

At that instant, Ogo turned back. She must have heard the 'I'm sorry' and the rather awkward 'You are welcome' that followed it. She saw the guy that was looking intently at Oluomachukwu and exclaimed. "Tobenna!"

The guy turned his stare from Oluomachukwu to Ogo, with his eyebrows raised, as if he was trying to figure out who Ogo was. "Oh, hi," he said, then turned his stare back to Oluomachukwu.

"What's going on?" Ogo looked back and forth at both Oluomachukwu and Tobenna.

"He stepped on my foot, so he was just apologising," Oluomachukwu replied, looking at Ogo, then at Tobenna.

"And then you said he was welcome?" Ogo asked, and laughed, making Oluomachukwu feel a little embarrassed. She pulled Oluomachukwu's hand and said, "Anyway, I'm done. We can go back to the hostel now."

Oluomachukwu glanced at Tobenna again, and he was looking at her too. She immediately felt something inside her, but shrugged it away, as she didn't want her mind to start thinking way ahead of her. Tobenna stood there and watched her as she turned away and left without saying any other thing.

"I actually like the cutting of these pants. The line was done perfectly well and the fitting is nice, it hugs me very well..."

Ogo held up the khaki pants and started talking about them passionately, but Oluomachukwu had already lost her, looking backwards occasionally to check if Tobenna was still there. He was, and he was looking in her direction.

When Tobenna was finally out of sight she brought her attention back to Ogo who was still rambling on about the khaki pants, then interrupted her.

"How do you know him?" Oluomachukwu asked.

"What?" Ogo exclaimed, then paused for a couple of seconds, looking at Oluomachukwu, then the light bulb in her head switched on instantly. "Oh, you mean Tobenna?"

Oluomachukwu nodded.

"I don't know him. I saw him on the parade ground once, and someone was trying to get my attention, then asked me to help her get his attention. She said his name was Tobenna." Ogo shrugged, then she held up her khaki pants again and was looking at the hem.

Oluomachukwu was disappointed... disappointed at the fact that Ogo had pulled her away when she didn't know who Tobenna was, and also disappointed that she, herself, hadn't said anything to him before she walked away, even though he was staring fixedly at her.

Ogo finally kept her khaki pants in the plastic bag the tailor gave to her, then turned to look at Oluomachukwu. "Why are you asking?"

Oluomachukwu shrugged. "No reason. Just asking. He looks familiar," she lied.

"Oh, okay," Ogo replied. "I have seen him only once on the parade ground, so maybe you might be lucky to see him again. But he is so cute, so a lot of girls were looking at him that day."

"I see." That was the only thing Oluomachukwu said in reply, then they went back to their room to rest until the cooking contest was to start.

***

The day moved pretty fast, and when it was about 5:00pm, Oluomachukwu went outside to check how the preparations were going. The parade ground was looking rather beautiful and colourful, as platoons had started to set up their canopies and decorate their tables. Some platoons didn't have any canopy, because others had already rented all the good ones from *mami* market.

As Oluomachukwu approached where Platoon Seven was going to be situated, she saw Sister Mary coordinating things. Eight of Platoon Seven Corps members were carrying a dirty white canopy, two holding each pole, which they positioned over the table where the food was going to be placed. Beside the table, but a couple of inches backwards, two rows of about one hundred chairs were neatly arranged for Corps members to sit and support the cooking team.

One of the girls from 'Two' was carrying a crate of canned Fanta, while the platoon president and Auntie Vera followed behind, carrying a crate of canned Coke and an empty cooler respectively, to put the drinks in. Someone else brought bags of ice for the cooler, and another person carried two packs of bottled water.

They had rented tablecloths, napkins and a small flower vase with artificial flowers to add to the table. Someone sat at a corner, writing the name of each dish on a very small rectangular shapped cardboard paper. His handwriting was spectacular, as if he had studied calligraphy in school, and Oluomachukwu figured that it was probably the reason why he was the one assigned to do the labelling.

The platoon had also rented one set of four plates, cups, wine glasses, cutleries, soup bowls, desert bowls for four NYSC officials-cum-judges, and just enough serving bowls and serving spoons necessary.

Oluomachukwu darted her eyes to her left side, where Platoons Eight, Nine and Ten were situated side-by-side. Her eyes popped open when she saw the Platoon Nine stand. They had hired a professional *asun* meat maker to add an extra touch to their table. The *asun* meat maker brought his grill and set it a few meters from their table, then put a full goat on it to grill. In fact, all eyes were on that stand after they saw the man setting up.

Oluomachukwu looked back at her platoon members when she heard some of them talking in a very low tone. One asked if it was allowed to make something that wasn't on the menu, and another said it could have been possible. Another then asked how Platoon Nine had even managed to buy the goat and hire the *asun* meat maker, and another person responded, saying that Platoon Nine had won almost every competition in the camp, and each came with a prize money. Therefore, so far, they had accumulated enough money to even buy five goats.

Shortly after all the setting up was done, the judges started to make their tour round all the tables, with camera men and photographers following them, recording the event and taking photographs. There were four judges, but about fifteen men and women did the tour, each wanting to taste what had been cooked. The extra judges, who hadn't been accounted for, carried their own plastic plates around and took small helpings to taste.

It took the judges almost two hours to make the tour round the parade ground because each time, they had to stop and ask questions, and there was a lot of food to taste — a starter, four different main dishes and a dessert, each to be multiplied by ten platoons, plus the *asun* meat on Platoon Nine's stand.

When the judges were making their way to Platoon Seven's stand, Auntie Vera quickly told them to rehearse a personalised greeting for the judges. Once the judges approached the table, the whole crowd of supporters were to stand up immediately and say the greeting, then remain standing until the judges were done tasting.

The whole supporters group stood up suddenly and at the same time, when Auntie Vera gave the signal, and the judges were startled. It took them a few seconds to realise that the Corps members were just trying to greet them, and were not attempting to leave. They eventually smiled heartily as they waited for the supporters to finish their greeting, then they responded in kind. It seemed like that stunt had won them an extra point.

Oluomachukwu looked at Nkiru as she explained what they had cooked and how they had cooked it, in a clean British accent. Oluomachukwu smiled. Just like Nkiru, she had left her accent at the camp gate, only to be used when necessary. It was necessary for Nkiru then, as one of her aims was to captivate both the stomach and the mind. The men looked at her as she spoke, smiling as the words came out of her mouth, prompting them to even eat quickly to check if the food tasted as sweet as her voice did.

When the judges were done tasting, they thanked all Platoon Seven Corps members, then moved on to the next table. After the whole exercise, everyone waited patiently for the judges to reconvene to the stage and discuss. They deliberated for a while discussing seriously that one would have thought they were strategising on the adoption of a new National policy.

Finally, the results were ready and the Cooking Contest Committee Head came out, microphone in one hand and a big sheet of paper in the other. She cleared her throat and began to speak, thanking everyone for their participation, commitment and hard work. She also mentioned that the decision-making was not easy, as everyone had done well, but in every competition, there was always a winner.

She proceeded to call the results and from the tenth place. Oluomachukwu could hear the sound of hearts beating as she called the platoon numbers one after the other, until it was Platoons Nine, Seven and another platoon left, Oluomachukwu wasn't sure which. She had tried to hear, but people were screaming too much after each platoon number was called. In fact, it was other platoons that screamed, happy that their platoon number had not yet been called. The screaming reduced as the numbers reduced.

When the fifth place was called, the four remaining platoons still in the competition screamed. The same thing happened when the fourth place was called, the three remaining platoons screamed and Platoon Nine screamed the most. They seemed to have outnumbered all the other platoons on the parade ground. They screamed so loudly that Oluomachukwu didn't know what the third place platoon number was.

The Cooking Contest Committee President kept quiet and smiled, waiting for everyone to calm down before she announced the final result. It was now down to Platoons

Seven and Nine, again, and before Oluomachukwu could breathe in and out, she called Platoon Seven as the second place, and all Platoon Nine Corps members, instructors and soldiers included, started to jump, scream and jeer, happy that they had won, as though it was a surprise. The grill and large goat that gave taste to their stand already won them the first place before the contest even began.

Platoon Seven Corps members, on the other hand, looked gloomy, too gloomy for a team that had taken the second place. They could have also shouted and cheered, but the voices of the Platoon Nine team overshadowed theirs. Oluomachukwu went to the front of the platoon stand to Nkiru and hugged her tightly. She congratulated her and told her to smile. She also went to hug the other cooking team members, since it was a joint effort from them. They were each given gifts, and a second-place prize money was given to them.

Before everyone dispersed, the cooking team started to share what was left of their food for interested platoon members who were hungry. Some had already started to protest, asking why the team hadn't cooked for the whole platoon and both Auntie Vera and Sister Mary rebuked them, asking if they were the judges.

The grumbling Corps members compared their platoon to Platoon Nine, whose cooking team started sharing *asun* meat in small plastic plates with a little portion of food to their platoon members. They had cooked a lot, and it was clearly because they had money to buy more things. Auntie Vera got angry and asked the angry Corps members to go and join Platoon Nine if they so wished. They obviously couldn't join, and Platoon Nine obviously wasn't accepting anyone new either.

After the angry Corps members were done grumbling, they took the plates that were being passed around with plastic spoons, then tasted the food, taking one or two spoons each and passing it on to the next person. When the degustation was over, the cooking team cleaned up, while some of the guys went to return the canopy.

Oluomachukwu was glad that it didn't rain, as it would have completely ruined the event and the evening.

***

Oluomachukwu and Nkiru went back to their room; none of them were in the mood to go to *mami* market for celebration. Nkiru was knackered and Oluomachukwu was still not ready to go to *mami* market to hang out or have drinks. She still wanted to give herself some time before she went there again.

Ogo had gone to the clinic ward to hang out and party with the medical team, because some of Platoon Nine's doctors were there, celebrating.

Nkiru had slept off almost immediately after she had taken a bath, while Oluomachukwu stayed awake for a bit, thinking about everything and nothing. And in that relaxed state of body and mind, the beauteous image of Tobenna came to her mind and she smiled softly.

She did not know exactly why she was thinking about him, but she remembered him stepping on her, and sighed. It felt like a magical step to her and that was what she tagged the encounter as — 'a Magical step.'

And with that thought, she slept off, deeply. She didn't even wake up or notice that Ogo had returned, right after the Lights Out call. The only time she woke up from her nice dream was briefly when she heard banging on the window of their room. She opened her eyes and saw a Hostel Administrator was going round, and checking that everyone was okay.

The Hostel Administrator banged on the window again and said, "Open this window." She continued and banged on the second window. "Open this window too."

Foyin woke up and was looking towards the window, obviously confused. After she had registered who was talking to her and what the person was saying, she opened the windows by her side, then went to open the windows by the side of the bunk beds opposite hers.

The Hostel Administrator went on to say that someone had fainted in another room, because it was too stuffy, so she wanted all the windows to be opened.

After that, Oluomachukwu drifted back into sleep and slept happy.

CHAPTER TWENTY-FOUR: DAY TWENTY

Sunday, 24th August 2014

Oluomachukwu's delicious sleep was interrupted in the early hours of the morning when she heard screaming. She jolted up from her bed and looked around, squinting in the darkness of the room. Only the light in the corridor provided visible guidance, just enough to see the silhouettes in the room. Some of her roommates woke up as well and were sitting up on their beds, and even in the darkness, she saw Foyin get up quickly to go and check if the door was locked. It was clear that Foyin didn't know what was happening, but her instinct was to lock the door.

Most of the girls started to get paranoid and afraid that something was happening, and some even said they were not going to leave the room in the morning until NYSC officials announced via the OBS that it was safe to do so.

Oluomachukwu picked up her phone and checked the time. It was 4:35am, which was about the time the Wake-Up call was made for morning drills, only that there wasn't going to be any drills that morning, since it was a Sunday. She also wanted to know what was going on, so she dialled

Ekene's number, who was on the third floor, to ask her if she had heard anything. Surprisingly, Ekene picked up the call immediately.

"Oluoma," she said. "What's up?"

"Why are you whispering?" Oluomachukwu asked.

"Oh." Ekene didn't notice that she had whispered, but then again, she had intended to. "We are all afraid here. Someone was screaming. I think they left the door open in one room and some guys went in."

"What?" Oluomachukwu exclaimed, and everyone who had heard her in the room turned to look at her. "Do you know what room?"

"I'm not sure," Ekene replied. "But someone from my room went to check it out just right now. It came from my floor."

"She wasn't afraid?" Oluomachukwu was shocked. She would have never gone to check out what was going on.

"Yes, she was, but we saw some female soldiers coming upstairs, and that was why she was able to go and check what was going on."

"Oh, okay." Oluomachukwu sighed. "So who were the guys?"

"We don't know, because they managed to escape."

Oluomachukwu was a bit doubtful. "How? In a heavily guarded camp with soldiers?"

"They ran to the second floor, which is about the same level of the fence and jumped over it."

"Wait, are you serious?" Oluomachukwu's eyes popped open at the realisation. "Please, what did they come for? Hope the mission was not accomplished." She swallowed hard as she asked the question, refusing to think of what the response might be.

"What else would they come for? They were looking for envelopes."

"What envelopes? I don't understand."

Ekene laughed. "Oluoma, stop acting slow. They were looking for *allawee*. Guys have been spending their money and girls have refused to spend theirs. I heard that they even ran away with about five or six waist pouches so that their efforts would not be wasted."

Oluomachukwu laughed. In fact, she burst out in laughter, as her roommates looked at her. When she was done laughing, she thanked Ekene for the information, hung up, then went ahead to explain what Ekene had just told her. Some laughed, some said they were going to bury their money, while others said they would carry the money on them at all times. Others even said they would not leave the money in their waist pouches, but in their bras, while some were indifferent — they didn't laugh or comment, they simply went back to sleep.

Neither Nkiru nor Ogo had woken up the whole time, and Oluomachukwu was surprised. She understood that Nkiru had cooked the day before and Ogo had gone out celebrating, and obviously drinking, but she didn't think anyone could sleep all through that much screaming and panic. In no time, the room became dead silent again, and Oluomachukwu also drifted back to sleep.

***

By the time Oluomachukwu woke up, it was bright outside, and a ray of sunlight was piercing through the torn mosquito net on the window beside her bed. It was so intense that she thought her hand would burn if she held it out to the sunray. She didn't know exactly what time it was, but she figured it wasn't 11:00am yet because Ogo hadn't left for mass. Ogo was sitting on her bed, applying her make-up, and Oluomachukwu was surprised at how invigorated she looked.

"Hey," Oluomachukwu said, smiling.

Ogo stopped applying the eyeliner on her lower eyelid, took her eyes off her mirror and looked at Oluomachukwu with a raised eyebrow. "Why are you smiling?"

"Because someone had fun yesterday." Oluomachukwu

winked at her.

Ogo hissed. "You are not serious."

Just at that instant, Nkiru walked into the room and Oluomachukwu hadn't even noticed that she wasn't there earlier. And as usual, she went directly for the foot of Oluomachukwu's bed, bounced on it and smiled.

"Finally awake," Nkiru said to Oluomachukwu.

"I should be saying that to both of you," she replied.

Ogo stopped applying the eyeliner to her other eye briefly, then asked, "Why would you say that? We have been watching you sleep for the past two hours, and when I came back last night you were fast asleep."

"First of all, we would talk about last night later, that is, your outing. And secondly, I woke up in the early hours of the morning because I heard some serious screaming."

"Really?" Nkiru asked, while Ogo packed up her make-up things. Her eyes were heavily made up and the black eyeliner she used made her look like a trainee witch.

Oluomachukwu nodded. "Someone was screaming on the third floor, so I called Ekene to ask what happened, and she told me that some guys came into the hostel and entered a room."

"Oh, no." Nkiru shook her head several times. "I just hope they didn't..." She didn't complete her sentence, but Oluomachukwu understood, and shook her head.

"They actually came to steal money. They were looking for *allawee*."

Nkiru and Ogo burst into uncontrollable laughter, then Ogo said, "Those guys have been spending their money on girls, and now they want it back."

"Hmm." Nkiru sighed. "How did the guys get access into the female hostel when there are security officers at the gate?"

"Probably the same way they escaped, from the fence."

"Those high fences?" Nkiru was doubtful.

"It could have been an inside thing," Ogo said. "Maybe male Corps members. They can come into the female side of the hostel from the bars that are dividing both hostels."

Both Oluomachukwu and Nkiru nodded.

"That's true." Nkiru finally believed. "It could even be the soldiers or those people that sell in *mami* market. They should know the hostels so well by now. Good thing we even have the small security we have, if not, it would be a different story."

Out of nowhere, Foyin walked up to Oluomachukwu's bed and said, "Me, I don't believe that guys stormed into the hostel, because no one else saw them, only one girl, so until I see the girl and she tells me by herself, I will not believe."

"But you stood up immediately to check if the door was locked," Oluomachukwu pointed out. She also almost called Foyin a 'Doubting Thomas,' or rather, a 'Doubting Foyin,' but she restrained herself.

"Of course I did," Foyin said. "In times of uncertainty, you think of safety first. Act first, then ask questions later, like I'm doing now." With that she walked away, and went back to where she had come from.

There was a brief silence, and after a few seconds, Ogo broke the silence. "Oluoma, aren't you going to church?"

Oluomachukwu held her breath, because she instantly remembered Segun, then what had happened at the back of *mami* market. She knew that Segun had been decamped, but she didn't think she could risk going to the church and seeing him there.

"Oluoma, are you okay?" Nkiru asked, waking her out of her sudden thoughts. "You look like you have just seen a ghost."

Oluomachukwu opened her mouth, and then started to babble. She then took a couple of seconds to pull herself together, then said to Nkiru, "I'm fine," and to Ogo, "No, I'm not going to church today. I'm not in the mood."

"You aren't in the mood to go to church? Really?" Ogo asked.

Oluomachukwu didn't say anything immediately. Her

words hadn't come out the right way, but she didn't want to explain what she really meant. Instead, she said, "I'm simply not in a good mood this morning, but I'm always in the mood to praise and worship God."

"Okay," Ogo said, then buckled her waist pouch and made for the door. "See you girls later."

***

Oluomachukwu and Nkiru went to get breakfast. Nkiru went to get what was served in the camp kitchen — *akara* and *akamu*, while Oluomachukwu went to buy Gala, a plastic bottle of Fanta and two bottles of drinking water. They had agreed to meet at the hostel entrance, then go back to the room to eat.

When they were back in the room, Nkiru sat at the foot of Oluomachukwu's bed, her legs folded together, as if she was meditating, then started to eat, quietly.

Oluomachukwu would throw fleeting glances at Nkiru, wondering what was going through her mind, and Nkiru would do the same. In fact, they were both wondering what was going through each other's minds. The fleeting glances turned to intent stares that when Oluomachukwu's phone rang, they were both startled.

Oluomachukwu replaced the cap of her bottle of Fanta, wrapped up her remaining Gala and looked at the phone. It was her mother calling, so she jumped out of her bed. "I'll be right back."

Nkiru nodded, and Oluomachukwu rushed out of the room. The call was supposed to be a brief one, because her mother just wanted to give her feedback. But the call was also an unfortunate one, because she didn't get good news. According to Oluomachukwu's mother, all her relatives lived outside Lagos, and the only ones that lived in Lagos were away for the summer holiday and were not to return until after summer, so Oluomachukwu would have to stay somewhere, maybe in a hotel, until then. The only other option for her was to deploy to another State in Nigeria and start working there.

Oluomachukwu thought about it briefly and all the options were unacceptable. She didn't want to redeploy, she didn't want to stay in any hotel and wait, and she definitely didn't want to stay with Okechukwu. As she was thinking about it, her mother interrupted her thoughts again and asked her to manage in Okechukwu's place until her relatives returned or until she got her own place. Oluomachukwu agreed, even though she wasn't going to stay with him, then thanked her mother, sent greetings to her family and hung up.

When she went back to the room, Nkiru had already finished eating and had put her plate and bowl aside. She had also gone back to her own bed and was sitting on her pillow.

"That was a rather long call," Nkiru said. "Is everything okay? You look disappointed."

Oluomachukwu raised an eyebrow, wondering if her emotions were that easy to detect. She seemed incapable of hiding anything, as both Nkiru and Ogo kept reading her reactions.

Nkiru tapped the bed, and said, "Come and sit down let's talk."

Oluomachukwu was afraid. And like a child going to her mother for a scolding, she went to Nkiru's bed and sat down. She had suddenly lost her appetite, so she put her remaining Gala and Fanta aside. She sighed deeply, not sure if she should open up to Nkiru or not. But she was highly overwhelmed. The camp was coming to an end and it felt like her life was also coming to an end. She looked around the room and every other person seemed distracted doing one thing or the other.

"Oluoma?" Nkiru prompted her, waking her up from her reverie. "What's wrong? You can tell me anything."

Oluomachukwu sighed again. "I was the *mami* market back stall victim that the Camp Director talked about on the parade ground yesterday, and I strongly believe that the guy from the church, Segun, was the culprit."

Nkiru's mouth hung wide open, as she blinked rapidly, shocked at the unexpected blow that had hit her awfully hard. She cringed suddenly and Oluomachukwu knew that she was uncomfortable. And before Nkiru could regain herself and say something, Oluomachukwu continued with what she was saying.

Oluomachukwu started by telling Nkiru about Abuja, about Kayode and Nnanna, and about Dunsin as well. Nkiru's mouth still hung open, as she analysed the whole situation and began to comprehend Dunsin's unspoken connection to Oluomachukwu. Oluomachukwu also talked about Okechukwu, and how she had decided to date him, before she heard his conversation with Idara. She even went further to explain their exchange of text messages, showing them to her as evidence. She then added the part where she had cried herself to sorrow until she could cry no more, and that was then she decided to go drinking and ended up with a stranger in a dirty stall. Oluomachukwu didn't know where she got the courage from but she gave Nkiru details of how everything happened, up until when the Camp Commandant mentioned the culprit's name.

Oluomachukwu didn't stop there.

She went on to explain how the camp was coming to an end and how she feared she would then be homeless, because she didn't want to stay with Okechukwu anymore. She told Nkiru about the phone calls to and from her mother for help with accommodation, and how it had been disappointing — she didn't want to redeploy, and she didn't want to live in a hotel and open herself to danger. The only thing she could do was to wrap up the NYSC programme, go back to the UK, then return to Nigeria when she was better prepared.

And with that, Oluomachukwu finished the story and waited for Nkiru to say something or at least close her mouth before an insect flew into it.

"Wow," Nkiru finally said. "Just wow."

Oluomachukwu kept quiet and watched Nkiru for a short while. Nkiru then asked if she could hug her, and Oluomachukwu let her. They sat down there on Nkiru's bed in a tight embrace, then Oluomachukwu started to cry, but quickly blinked the tears away when the hug came to an end. She wiped her face quickly with the back of her hand.

"I don't know what to say. This is just too much , and to think you were going through all of this on your own in such little time." Nkiru shook her head and sighed, while Oluomachukwu nodded.

"I'm so sorry about the *mami* market incident. I should have been there for you. I knew you were not happy, so I should have insisted you come with Ogo and I, instead of leaving you here on your own."

"You couldn't have known what would happen, but it's fine now." Oluomachukwu smiled. She was truly feeling better now.

"You don't have to go back to the UK, redeploy or do any of that nonsense."

Oluomachukwu was amused, and she almost laughed. "What do you mean?"

"You can stay with me. I live in Ikoyi with my parents and my older brother, and they are all laid back and very accommodating. I'm not saying this because they are my family, but they are really cool people. Plus you would be safe and comfortable."

Oluomachukwu smiled happily. "Thanks, I'll be happy to stay. That takes care of all my problems, then."

Nkiru also smiled. "I'll let my parents know, so that they can prepare for you, and my brother will come and pick us from here on the last day."

Oluomachukwu hugged Nkiru again and thanked her, and at that moment, she saw a sister and a friend in Nkiru.

***

Oluomachukwu and Nkiru remained in the room and spent a while chatting and laughing about everything and everyone, especially in the camp. They revisited their most embarrassing, funny, ridiculous and happy moments, and that was when Oluomachukwu remembered her 'magical stepper,' Tobenna and told Nkiru about him.

She also thought that Nkiru would be able to help her locate Tobenna since she hopped from platoon to platoon, but Nkiru was not able to. She said she was yet to see any guy with that description. She would have had to bag him otherwise, since she was single.

They both laughed at that.

While they were chatting, Oluomachukwu's cell phone rang. She looked at the screen and saw a number she did not recognise. She did not want to pick it up, but Nkiru urged her to, and she eventually did.

"Hello?" Oluomachukwu said, uncertainty in her tone.

"Hi, Oluoma, it's me, Chinedu."

Oluomachukwu did not know any Chinedu. "Okay?" She still sounded uncertain, clueless.

"I'm in your platoon... Platoon Seven. Or don't you remember me?"

Oluomachukwu coughed, because she did not want to say either yes or no.

"Please, I need to see you urgently," Chinedu said.

"What? Why?" Oluomachukwu was very confused. She looked at Nkiru, and Nkiru just stared at her, mouthing things that she didn't understand.

"Can you just meet me in front of the hostel right now, please? I'll explain to you when I see you. It's very urgent."

"Well, I guess. Okay." Oluomachukwu hung up before it got any weirder. She then turned and looked at Nkiru. "I don't know who the hell that was."

Nkiru burst out in laughter, tilting her head backwards and holding her tummy. "I think you need to stop giving out your number."

"No, I think both of our platoon presidents or any of those sports or socials representatives need to stop giving out my number." Oluomachukwu laughed.

"So what did the caller want?" Nkiru sounded eager for some gist.

"The person said that he wants to see me and that it is very urgent." Oluomachukwu emphasised on the 'urgent' by raising the first two fingers on each of her hands and bending them three times to each syllable as she said 'ur‑gen‑t.'

"Interesting." Nkiru laughed. "You better go and find out what he wants. Maybe there's a new contest he wants you to participate in."

"Ah. I hope not." Oluomachukwu got up and put her phone in her waist pouch. "I think I'm done with contests. Besides, it's only the football final and the March past left, and I'm not keen on either. See you soon."

Oluomachukwu took her time and went downstairs, wondering who Chinedu could be. She didn't know who she was looking for, so for all she knew, the person could be there, watching her while she looked around aimlessly.

As soon as she got to the front of the hostel, Cleaner approached her.

"Hi, Oluoma, thank you for coming to see me."

"What?" Oluomachukwu never expected Chinedu to be Cleaner, but then again, she didn't know his real name. Nkiru had mentioned it once, but she didn't register it in her head. Plus if she had told Nkiru that it was Chinedu that had called, Nkiru would definitely have known.

"I said, 'thank you for coming to see me,'" Cleaner said again.

"Oh, okay. It's no problem." Oluomachukwu suddenly felt uncomfortable, but didn't know why. Maybe it was the way Cleaner was looking intently at her or the fact that he had noticed stains between Nkiru's legs when no one else did.

"Weren't you expecting to see me? Or you didn't know it was me?"

"Of course I know who you are." Oluomachukwu chose to respond diplomatically. "So how can I help you?"

"We have two days left in this camp. I think I'm in love and I don't want this opportunity to fly past me." Cleaner went straight to the point.

Oluomachukwu opened her eyes wide, totally shocked. "What do mean?" she stuttered.

"I want your friend Nkiru. I think I'm in love with her. In fact, I know that I am. I have tried to tell her a couple of times, but whenever she sees me, she runs away or pretends to be on the phone, or even hides, and I always notice. What am I doing wrong or does she have someone else?"

Oluomachukwu had no option than to laugh. Cleaner had no idea why Nkiru never wanted to see him, and from the chat they had had earlier on, Nkiru wasn't currently in a relationship. "Oh, Cleaner. Not everyone fancies the idea of dating while in the camp."

"What did you just call me?"

Oluomachukwu almost did backflips. She didn't realise she had slipped and didn't know that Cleaner would catch it, but he did. "I didn't call you anything."

"You did. Was it 'Cleaner?'" Cleaner raised an eyebrow.

"Oh. That's just an expression."

"Okay." Cleaner said. He wasn't in the mood to push the topic further. "So what about dating in camp? What is wrong with it?"

"You know people don't really fancy the whole 'corper love' thing."

"Why are you sounding like being a corper is a disease? Aren't we all corpers and are we going to remain corpers for the rest of our lives?" Cleaner was sounding upset, as if Oluomachukwu had stabbed his ego.

"No need to get upset. I'm just telling you as it is."

"I'm sorry." Cleaner sighed. "Please, can you give me

her number or give her mine to call me? Nobody seems to have her number in this bloody camp and I really need to talk to her."

Oluomachukwu took a few seconds to think about it, then pulled out her phone and opened her contact list. She held the phone to Cleaner and he copied out the number. When he was done, he thanked Oluomachukwu and went towards *mami* market, while Oluomachukwu went back to the room.

"I just saw Chinedu," Oluomachukwu announced as she walked into the room.

Nkiru jolted up from her bed. "You mean Cleaner?"

"Yes, I mean Cleaner." Oluomachukwu rolled her eyes. "And if you had told me his real name, I would have known I was going to meet him."

"What? Noooo." Nkiru sat up. "He was your urgent meeting?"

Oluomachukwu raised an eyebrow and gave Nkiru a sarcastic look.

"But I told you his name was Chinedu *nau*."

"That was eons ago. How on earth was I supposed to remember?" Oluomachukwu rolled her eyes again.

"Okay sorry. So what did he want?"

"You."

There was absolute silence.

"What do you mean by 'you?'" Nkiru asked when she finally got herself back.

"He is in love with you and doesn't want to blow the opportunity before you leave camp. And just in case you want to shake your head and say you are not interested, and that he is a corper and that corpers are useless players, I already gave him your number."

"What?" Nkiru exclaimed. "How would you..."

Nkiru completed her sentence, but Oluomachukwu did not hear it, because at that instant, the OBS speaker was making an announcement, a rather strange announcement.

Oluomachukwu and Nkiru listened attentively, surprised.

"*...Please, come to the volleyball court now. He is waiting. I repeat. If you are the girl who a guy stepped on yesterday in mami market, in front of where the tailors are, please, come to the volleyball court now. He is waiting. Thank you.*"

Oluomachukwu and Nkiru exchanged glances, then Nkiru got up from her bed and jumped happily, unable to hide her happiness. Some of their roommates looked at her, wondering why she was so excited, then turning back to do what they were doing. When Nkiru was done with her jumping, she went and sat back on the bed.

"Are you done?" Oluomachukwu asked.

"Yes, I'm done, and what are you still doing here?" Nkiru asked. "Let's go and meet the magical stepper. This is the best news ever."

"What best news?" Oluomachukwu laughed. "You had better go and meet Cleaner, and talk to him."

"Leave Cleaner for now, when he calls I'll talk to him, but now, you need to go downstairs to the volleyball court before your magical stepper leaves."

Oluomachukwu sighed, not sure she wanted to go, but Nkiru was able to persuade her. She got up, wore some make-up, and then arranged her hair properly. She even changed her shorts and made sure they were tighter and shorter. Her tee shirt was already rumpled, so she put on another one, and at that instant, she felt like Cleaner. She smiled at herself for the inside joke. By the time she was ready, about five minutes had gone by and she hoped that Tobenna was still waiting for her.

She and Nkiru hurried outside and went through the back of the hostel to the volleyball court, so that people wouldn't see her. When they got there, they were shocked. Not only did they not see Tobenna, they saw half the girls in the camp on the volleyball court. In fact, the only reason why the other half of the girls weren't there, was because marching rehearsals were going on for the contest that was to hold the next day.

TWENTY-ONE DAYS

Oluomachukwu stood on her toes and stretched her neck to check if she would see Tobenna in the crowd, but it was impossible. The girls had probably enveloped him or driven him away with their presence. They were so many of them that some soldiers, both male and female, had to come and control the traffic, so that they wouldn't cause a mini stampede or any accident. Oluomachukwu shook her head. She hadn't expected the crowd and would have been very embarrassed if everyone knew that Tobenna had been waiting for her. At the same time, she wondered why those girls would go there, hoping to meet Tobenna, when it was clear that Tobenna knew exactly who he was waiting for. She tugged on Nkiru's shoulder and both of them left the volleyball court inconspicuously.

Oluomachukwu sort of felt unhappy as they went back to the hostel. She also wanted to go and make her own announcement at the OBS, but feared that the same thing would happen — that half the guys in the camp would go there. She also thought of putting up her number on the notice board, anything that would connect her to Tobenna again.

Alternatively, she could go to the OBS and announce her phone number. She headed towards the OBS office with Nkiru, then changed her mind and went towards the female hostel instead. If Tobenna was truly hers, then she would meet him again before the end of the camp, she thought to herself.

As they got to their room and sat on Oluomachukwu's bed, they heard someone running from afar and very fast, then the person ran towards their room, pushed the door open and barged in. It was Ogo, she was panting, as if she had just run a marathon.

"Is everything alright?" Nkiru asked.

"No, I mean, yes," Ogo answered Nkiru, then looked at Oluomachukwu. "I just heard an announcement from the OBS. Tobenna is in love with you. You are the one he stepped on." She smiled.

That statement caught the attention of the girls in the room, but none of them said anything.

"And if you are coming from the volleyball court area, you would notice that half the girls in the camp are there."

Ogo went to sit on the bed with them. "Really? I came straight from the clinic ward, so I didn't see it."

"That's true, speaking of the clinic ward, I said that we would talk about your last night outing later on and this seems like the perfect time," Oluomachukwu said. "What's up with your Americana boyfriend?"

Ogo inched backwards on the bed, then asked, "What do you mean?"

"Hmm." Nkiru sighed. "I also noticed it too. You are not on the phone like you normally are, and you have been spending too much time with the CMD of late. Should we be worried or is there something we don't know?"

"Well, Martins is very sweet, that's all I can say," Ogo replied.

Oluomachukwu and Nkiru let out a prolonged hiss simultaneously, and Nkiru asked, "What is this one talking about?"

"I wonder," Oluomachukwu replied.

Ogo sighed. "James isn't serious. If I don't call him, he won't call me, and he has been claiming to be busy for a while now and I don't have that kin d of time. Maybe he is really having fun and I'm here acting like a 'devoted wife.' I decided to stop calling him and said to myself, when he is missing me, he would call me, and he hasn't. So, in the meantime, I shall have fun too."

"Oh, okay," Oluomachukwu said, suddenly feeling a bit guilty that she had asked about her boyfriend.

"Well, I guess if he's not serious, then there's no point wasting your time," Nkiru added.

Ogo stood up. "Let me go back to the clinic ward. I heard the announcement and couldn't wait to come and tell you, even though I came late." She laughed. When she was by the door, she stopped, turned back and looked at

Oluomachukwu. "By the way, I saw Segun in church and he said hello. He is also wondering why you have stopped coming to church."

Oluomachukwu felt bubbles in her belly at that instant as Ogo walked away and Nkiru even noticed it. She was sort of relieved or glad that it wasn't the same Segun that had force-kissed her, and she also didn't know how, but realising that gave her a bit of satisfaction, a bit of closure. Nkiru reached out to her and squeezed her hands, and they both smiled.

***

The rest of the day went lazily for Oluomachukwu and Nkiru, as they sat in bed, talking, laughing and snacking. There weren't that many activities going on in the camp, so they remained in the room until it was dinnertime and time for socials activities. They went to *mami* market to have dinner and went with Ogo and Ekene, like old times. And also like old times, Tracker came to their table with a few of his friends and bought them alcoholic drinks.

Nkiru, Ogo and Ekene wanted to eat Indomie noodl es, but Oluomachukwu didn't. Right after she had tasted the noodles prepared by Golden Penny about a week earlier, she added it to the list of food she was never going to eat outside of a home. In fact, she was going to be the only person to prepare it for herself, because she didn't enjoy cold or soggy noodles. She ended up buying chicken and chips, and when they were done eating, Tracker garnished their table with small chops and more bottles of alcoholic drinks. They then started to munch away, drink and talk.

While they were all talking, Nkiru's phone rang and she raised an eyebrow at the strange number. She picked it up and looked surprised as she spoke. She turned towards where Oluomachukwu sat and mouthed 'Cleaner' to her. Oluomachukwu smiled at her a nd gave her a thumbs-up, hoping that Nkiru would give him a chance.

After what Tobenna had done in the camp by making an announcement at the OBS, everybody could be given a chance to prove themself.

Nkiru spent some time talking on the phone, or rather yelling, because the music was way too loud to hear and be heard. A few minutes after she was done talking, Cleaner showed up, pulled a chair and sat beside her. And as the music played, Oluomachukwu looked round her table at all her friends as they talked, laughed, ate and drank, looking happy. She, too, was happy at the fact that they were all happy, and she smiled. So they had fun until the Lights Out call, and they all went to bed with a happy mind.

At least Oluomachukwu did.

CHAPTER TWENTY-FIVE: DAY TWENTY-ONE

Monday, 25th August 2014

Oluomachukwu woke up with mixed feelings. She was happy and sad at the same time, and she felt it could be the same for other Corps members as well, since it was the last day they were going to spend in the camp. Things seemed different, as she had gotten used to the life already. She didn't mind staying there for another three months, but clearly not with the current state of the bathrooms and toilets. If the NYSC officials could change that, then they would have problems chasing her out.

For the first time in camp, Oluomachukwu had woken up after the bugle Wake-Up call. They had had two days of no morning calls, so everyone had gotten too comfortable. She sat up on her bed and looked round, and everyone was still sleeping. She did not want to go to the parade ground without taking her bath first, so she decided to hurry up and do it, hoping that the bathrooms wouldn't be flooded with girls who had also woken up late.

Without wasting any time, she got out of her nightwear, tied her wrapper around her breasts, and carried her bath things. Before she left, she woke Ogo and Nkiru up, and when she was sure that they were fully awake, she hurried out. There was a queue when she got to the bathroom, but it wasn't anything she hadn't seen before. She had even expected to see more than a hundred people there, but it was far from it.

She stood by the door and waited for her turn as she brushed her teeth. At that instant, she remembered her first few times in the bathroom and the image of 'Fucking Space' crossed her mind. She wondered where the girl was, and concluded that she had certainly found herself another bathroom and space to monopolise. Oluomachukwu also hardly ever saw her on the parade ground anymore, and was happy because she didn't know how she would react towards her.

By the time Oluomachukwu was done brushing her teeth and rinsing her mouth into a toilet bowl, Nkiru walked into the still crowded bathroom with her bath things in hand and toothbrush in her mouth, brushing vigorously, as if she was trying to cleanse her mouth of something sour. Ogo came in afterwards, looking sleepy. Oluomachukwu took her focus back to Nkiru and smiled, as she imagined that Nkiru had kissed Cleaner in her very happy moment and regretted it by almost blistering her mouth.

A few minutes later, a space by the sink was freed, and Oluomachukwu went there to have a quick bath. Although Nkiru and Ogo had come later than a lot of people, they, too, tried to squeeze their way into the bathroom, close to Oluomachukwu, claiming that they wanted to use the sink. When they were done brushing, they used the opportunity to also have a quick bath beside the sink, then got out of the bathroom.

The bugle sounded again and again, followed by OBS announcements for everyone to come out to the parade ground. As Oluomachukwu got ready, she wondered what time the OBS speaker had woken up and gotten ready, because the person was always there in time to accompany the bugle blower, especially very early in the morning.

Oluomachukwu, Nkiru and Ogo got ready and quickly ran out of their room to the parade ground. When they got there, the parade ground was almost empty, just like it had been once before when Corps members had drunk too much the previous night. The bugle blower kept making the call and soldiers had mobilised to the hostels to bring everyone out. The exercise took longer than expected, and when the parade ground was filled up again, one hour had gone by.

'Madam MC,' who was dressed in her workout gear, came out and whined again about everybody's behaviour and reluctance to come out to the parade ground when called upon, because it was the last day in the camp. She also said she was capable of prolonging their stay in the camp for another month, and everyone grumbled. She told them all to shut up and continued complaining about way too many other things, but Oluomachukwu had already totally zoned out. She had gone to the end of the Platoon Seven line with Nkiru to gist about her discussion with Cleaner from the previous night.

Nkiru and Cleaner had spoken extensively about their prospective relationship, and she was actually thinking of considering him. But before she made her final decision, Cleaner promised her that he would show her something later in the day that would help with her decision, so she was waiting for it. After their mini chat, Oluomachukwu and Nkiru kept quiet and listened to what was going on.

The morning activities went as usual: Corps members recited the Morning Prayer, then the National Anthem and the NYSC Anthem were sung. After that, a Platoon Ten representative came out to recite the Meditation.

When that was over, 'Madam MC' read the programme for the day like she always did each morning. But it was the first time Oluomachukwu actually paid attention to it. There was not going to be any lecture for the day, there were just going to be activities and finals for all contests. The football final and other sports activities were going to hold. Registration for some SAED and CDS groups was open and was going to take place in the SAED office, which was just by the entrance of the male hostel. The State Coordinator was also going to be around by 4:00pm to debrief all the Corps members, then there was going to be the marching competition after that. 'Madam MC' also indicated that dinner would hold as usual from 6:30pm to 8:20pm, then socials activities from 8:30pm to 10:30pm when the Lights Out call would be made.

Some Corps members started to grumble and 'Madam MC' told them to keep quiet, but they were not yielding. In fact, they started to grumble even louder, as if they were trying to remind her of something that she had missed in the programme. It took both Oluomachukwu and Nkiru a few seconds to realise that they were asking about the Bonfire night. Oluomachukwu and Nkiru looked at each other, as they had no idea what it was about.

"Bonfire night would not hold, thank you," 'Madam MC' stated in a yell that rattled the whole camp, making everyone protest seriously. And without saying any other thing, she gave the microphone to the Drill Instructor for him to start the drills and walked away to stand at a corner, waiting to commence workout.

Some Corps members and soldiers standing close to Oluomachukwu were talking about the Bonfire night, so she decided to eavesdrop, so that she could know what it was about and why it wasn't going to hold. Apparently, on the third or second to last night in the camp, depending on what camp it was, there was normally a large gathering in the evening. The gathering was done in the field area of *mami* market, where a huge bonfire would be set up in the middle of the field and all Corps members would be seated according to their platoon number round the bonfire.

An MC would be there to compère the event, and each platoon would be called upon one after the other, to dance round the fire, chanting some songs. If Oluomachukwu didn't know better, she would have compared the image to ritualism or even an initiation gathering.

The songs ranged from what was usually played and sung during drills and workout to all sorts of other songs, and during the song-chanting period, drinks, finger food and biscuits would be shared amongst platoons, and each platoon was responsible for providing the refreshments.

If a Corps member went to another platoon, the Corps member would not be served. Oluomachukwu imagined if any platoon would turn Nkiru down, since she had hopped round platoons throughout her stay in the camp. Everyone was also expected to put on their white shirts and shorts, for the Bonfire night, but for the first time, they would be allowed to wear any footwear they liked.

One of the Corps members, who was discussing about the Bonfire night, concluded by saying that the specificity about the event was that there was no Lights Out call, so everyone could go to bed whenever they wanted or not go to bed at all. Another Corps member added that it was a rumour. Her older brother had served a year ago, and he, too, had heard talks about no Lights Out, only for them to be chased into the hostel before 10:00pm by soldiers.

As for the reason why the Bonfire night was not going to hold during Batch B, people heard that the last Bonfire night for Batch A Corps members had been a big scandal — the whole camp went completely crazy. There was no Lights Out, so Corps members didn't take the initiative to go to bed. They stayed up all night, even after the fire was put out, partying, drinking and having sex, until soldiers took charge and sent everyone to the hostel.

The next morning, used condoms were littered around *mami* market, empty bottles scattered around everywhere, and all sorts of unidentified objects lay across the camp. Some people had even forgotten their white shorts and shirts, and underwear on the parade ground, and a lot of things went missing, or rather a lot of things were stolen, such as cell phones, wristwatches, wallets, untagged crested NYSC caps.

A lot of people had spent their allowance and finished it on Bonfire night, and some people stole other people's own to spend on girls, food and drinks. After that, some people proposed to the NYSC to give out the allowance on the last day, just after the Closing Ceremony and at the same time of the collection of Posting letters. That way, nonchalance, delinquent behaviours and stealing would be curbed. Instead, the NYSC decided to completely cancel the event until further notice.

Oluomachukwu already imagined herself in a Bonfire night just by hearing the description alone and it sounded interesting. She only regretted why the NYSC hadn't left it on the schedule and at least tried to manage it better. By the time she turned her focus back to the parade ground and the Drill Instructor, Platoon Ten Corps members had already filed out of the parade ground to the volleyball court to meet with their platoon instructors for their duties. The Drill Instructor had taken the microphone and had started singing the usual workout songs, revisiting the ones that he used before, and that Oluomachukwu liked.

Oluomachukwu turned to her left side and noticed that Nkiru had joined in on the jogging, along side Cleaner, so she also joined in and participated fully, singing along with every other Corps member.

***

Oluomachukwu and Nkiru went to collect breakfast in the camp kitchen. They were serving bread, boiled egg and tea. Nkiru didn't have a '10 ON DUTY' badge pinned on her shirt, as she didn't file out with Platoon Ten Corps members when they did, so she wasn't able to take more than one egg, but Oluomachukwu gave hers to her. Nkiru also took the diluted tea that tasted nothing like tea, while Oluomachukwu bought coffee from a coffee vendor and diluted it, because it was too sweet, as usual. When they had gotten their breakfast, they went back to the room.

Ogo was already in the room eating her breakfast when Oluomachukwu and Nkiru entered. She smiled at them, then raised an eyebrow at Oluomachukwu when she saw the small loaf of camp bread in her hand. "You are eating breakfast from the camp kitchen today?"

Oluomachukwu shrugged. "I can't remember the last time I used my meal ticket, plus I am tired of eating Gala."

"And I'm sure you gave your share of boiled egg to this egg-junkie," Ogo said, throwing a funny face at Nkiru. She then threw a tube-like thing on Oluomachukwu's bed. "I bought two tubes of margarine in *mami* market, because the bread is too dry."

"Oh, thanks." Oluomachukwu smiled, as she took the margarine, opened it and squeezed its content into the middle of the bread that she had cut open haphazardly.

Ogo took a boiled egg she had hidden under her pillow and gave it to Nkiru. "I got this for you. I got one extra because I'm on duty today, and I didn't see you join our platoon today."

Nkiru went to take the egg and smiled. "I just felt like jogging today, and thanks for thinking about my love for eggs."

They all laughed, then kept quiet and started eating. And as they were quietly munching away, only the sound of their chewing filled the air, until Ogo spoke.

"Hmm, can you imagine, just when I entered the room one girl was crying. She said her 15,000 naira was missing." Ogo pointed to the left end angle of the room. "It's the girl that stays on that bunk, on the top bed."

Nkiru almost choked and Oluomachukwu laughed.

"How?" Oluomachukwu asked. Neither she nor Nkiru knew the girl personally, but they did know that she had at least three friends she always hung out with.

"I think she said it was stolen. When she mentioned it, everyone started panicking, then went to their boxes to check if their money was still intact."

"But wait, girls," Nkiru said, when she swallowed the combination of bread and egg she had in her mouth. "Isn't it the same girl that buys a lot of things in the room? She's always buying small chops, ice cream, meat pies and other junk food."

Both Oluomachukwu and Ogo laughed.

"And she also has a lot of friends that hang out around her, so she should start by asking all of them."

Ogo nodded in agreement. Oluomachukwu shrugged her shoulders. Idara had told her that people stole, and her allowance, together with the remaining money that she had brought to the camp were still stowed away in her box, as she had kept them.

"You know, I also panicked when the girl said that her money was missing, and instinctively, I went to open my box," Ogo started. "But I stopped half way when I realised that it could have been a tactic for people to check their money, so that the real thief would know where it had been hidden. For all I know, the girl might not have lost any money."

Nkiru and Oluomachukwu laughed this time, then Oluomachukwu asked, "So what did you now do?"

"I just acted like I was looking for a pair of socks in my bag and pulled it out." Ogo laughed as well. "And when no one was looking, I hid the envelope properly behind some scrap paper in the hidden zip area of my box and zipped it up."

"That's very serious," Nkiru commented. "Because of 19,800 naira?"

"Of course." Ogo rolled her eyes. "But if it's nothing to you, then you can pass yours to me."

Before Nkiru could comment on what Ogo had said, her phone started ringing. She looked at the screen and immediately smiled, and Oluomachukwu had a feeling she knew who it was.

"That must be Cleaner, right?" Oluomachukwu asked,

and Nkiru nodded.

Nkiru then picked up the 'what would be a very curt phone call,' and it sounded official. "Hi... Yes, I'm fine... And you...? Okay... When...? When is it...? Oh, really...? Okay, I'll come out now... See you." She hung up.

"Spill," both Oluomachukwu and Ogo said.

"Spill what?" Nkiru feigned ignorance.

"If I slap you, *ehn*." Ogo raised her hand, as if she was going to slap Nkiru, and they all laughed.

"He just said that he wanted to show me something, and that we would go and watch the football final together afterwards. Platoons Seven and Nine are playing, and I already forgot, even after the announcement was made this morning."

"What an interesting choice of date," Oluomachukwu mocked.

"You're not serious." Nkiru got up and started to clear up the bread wrapper and egg shells to throw in the bin. She then put the cup she had used to drink the diluted tasting tea by Oluomachukwu's bedside. "Please, wash my cup for me when you are washing yours."

Oluomachukwu hissed. "And what exactly happened to your hands?"

"I have a date, my friend," Nkiru joked. "Please, help me."

Oluomachukwu laughed. "Okay, no problem, se e you. I'll probably see you much later at the field for the football match."

"Alright, see you then." She waved to Oluomachukwu and Ogo, and they waved back.

Shortly after Nkiru left the room, Ogo also left to go and spend some time in the clinic ward with the CMD. Oluomachukwu still had about thirty minutes to wait before the football final game started, so she decided to rest in the room for a while. She got into her duvet cover, but after about twenty-five minutes, a thought came to her. She got out of bed, and went to open her box, searching for where she had kept her allowance and her other cash. Sadly, she admitted to herself that Ogo's chat about theft had gotten to her, and inasmuch as she had tried to blank the thoughts out of her mind, she couldn't. She had to check if her own was still intact.

She was just about to panic, when she realised that she had dumped the envelope in the area directly under the front of the box cover, where she put her underwear. She checked, and the envelope was still the re, untouched. She wanted to open it and remove the money, then replace it with rolls of toilet paper, but she stopped. She thought about it again and concluded that 19,800 naira wasn't really worth the hassle. She zipped up her b ox and went back to her bed to lie down a bit when she heard the sound of the bugle, accompanied by the OBS speaker's anno uncement for the football final.

***

The turn-up was unbelievable that one would have thought it was the World Cup going on. The field was full of both Corps members and camp officials, and the judges had set up a table on the left-hand side, just by the centre line of the field, right where Nwanyi Imo's food stall was normally situated. White lines had been drawn around the angles of the field and over the red sand, to get a replica of a real football field.

Oluomachukwu stood at a corner, looking for where to sit or stand. She couldn't see Nkiru anywhere, and Ogo hadn't planned on showing up. She also didn't know if Ekene was going to be there or if she was eve n interested in football for that matter.

A set of about one hundred chairs had been arranged in two parts behind the goal post that backed the parade ground and was sandwiched on the other side by the canopies where the photographers had their workstations. The chairs weren't fully occupied, but it could have been quite difficult for anyone to squeeze their way through if they didn't already have a reserved seat there. The other goal post backed the back part of *mami* market, so there was no space for chairs.

Oluomachukwu moved towards a shop where phones were being charged, stood on her toes and started to look around. It was almost time for kick off, so a camp official, who was kitted up to be the referee, came to the middle of the field and called out the two teams. They came jogging out and went into formation, while one player from each team went to the centre of the field to meet the referee. There were about eight or less players per team, it wasn't really sure. They just looked too few. Maybe it was because the field was too big.

Shortly after the whistle was blown for kick off and the players started to run around, Oluomachukwu heard her name. She turned around and saw Cleaner smiling at her. He was holding three plastic bottles of Fanta.

"Hi," Oluomachukwu said.

"Hi." Cleaner made to hug her and she allowed herself to be hugged. "Nkiru is sitting over there." He pointed to the chairs that were neatly arranged behind the goal post. "They are for the supporters. One part is for Platoon Nine and the other part is for Platoon Seven."

"Oh, okay," Oluomachukwu said, looking over at the seats, checking if she would see Nkiru.

"Come let's go, she said you would be coming, and it's a good thing I found you."

Cleaner gave Oluomachukwu one of the plastic bottles, then held the other two in one hand. And just like an older brother leading his younger sister to cross the road, he let out his free hand to her and led her to the area where Nkiru was sitting. Nkiru jumped and smiled heartily when she saw Oluomachukwu arrive. Cleaner then gave one of the drinks to Nkiru and the other one to Ekene who was also there and sitting by Nkiru's left side.

Oluomachukwu sat between Ekene and Nkiru, and

Cleaner sat by Nkiru's right side, then they all enjoyed the game. It looked more like street football because of the red sand and the dust that almost blinded everyone. The whole field was animated with Platoon Nine supporters singing, drumming and oppressing Platoon Seven, as usual. Almost two hundred of them showed up, while Platoon Seven's supporters were not even up to fifty — they hung loosely between thirty and forty.

Platoon Nine supporters sang and cheered all through the game as Platoon Nine scored the first goal and was leading. But shortly afterwards, Platoon Seven equalised. Platoon Nine scored again, almost immediately, denying Platoon Seven the time to rejoice, but then, Platoon Seven equalised again and had enough time to rejoice. The scores remained the same until the end of the game, and it was time for penalty shootouts.

The penalty shootouts were so intense that they kept everyone on the edge of their seats, but then, they ended in Platoon Seven winning the cup. It was very satisfying for Platoon Seven to finally win a competition and at least once before the end of the camp. Football, like every other sports activity, was one of the only contests that the camp officials didn't have to decide on a winner and deprive Platoon Seven the opportunity of winning because of their failed joke during the drama contest.

After Platoon Seven players were given the cup, the few supporters they had ran directly into the field to celebrate with them, and together they ran around the field, holding the cup high and stopping at intervals to take snapshots from the hawk of photographers that flooded the field. A team of drummers, led by a Platoon Seven Corps member, had been rehearsing not too far from the field, so they diverted and entered into the field, playing as the supporters danced.

Platoon Seven was given a prize money, which the players had planned to spend on anyone in the platoon who came into *mami* market later that evening to celebrate with them. They kept on dancing and walking round the field until the team of drummers left and the bugle call was made for lunchtime.

***

Lunch was *jollof* rice and fish. Oluomachukwu didn't like to eat fish, so she shared her tiny piece of fish between Nkiru and Ogo, then ate only the rice. After eating, they decided to rest for a while before it was time for the State Coordinator's debrief. Ogo lay on her bed, while Nkiru shared Oluomachukwu's bed with her.

"So?" Oluomachukwu started, when they were both comfortable on the bed.

"So, what?" Nkiru asked. "Who are you talking to?"

Oluomachukwu sat up. "Who else?"

"Don't mind her oh." Ogo also sat up. "What was the something that Cleaner wanted to show you?"

"Oh." Nkiru laughed. "You girls didn't forget?"

Oluomachukwu and Ogo wore straight faces, and it made Nkiru laugh even more.

"Okay, okay, fine, so I agreed to give him a try." Nkiru covered her face with her hands.

"What?" Oluomachukwu and Ogo both exclaimed.

"He told me how serious he was, then showed me a message from his mother. I even spoke with her on the phone."

"Really?" Oluomachukwu raised an eyebrow, and at that instant, she wished she had met Tobenna on the day he made the OBS announcement, and that he would also show her messages from his mother and connect them via phone.

"Yes, and that's not all. He showed me his mother's pictures on Google."

"Why is he showing you that?" Ogo asked. "And why is his mother even on Google?"

"Well, because she is an Ambassador and she is having

an award show in Ghana... and they've invited me." Nkiru smiled sheepishly and covered her face again.

"Oh wow," Ogo said, then nodded, impressed. " That's really something."

"Well, happy married life," Oluomachukwu said, and they all laughed.

Not too long afterwards, the bugle sounded for the State Coordinator's debrief. All three of them got out of bed, grumbling, put on their tennis shoes or trainers, and went to the parade ground.

Unlike during the morning bugle call, Corps members came out to the parade ground on time and it was filled up quickly, even before the OBS speaker could start making any announcements. They all sat on the ground — some using handkerchief, face towels or handbooks, and others on the bare floor. In fact, some smart ones took off their tennis shoes or trainers and sat on them for more comfort.

The State Coordinator started the debrief by greeting the Corps members, "Good morning gentlemen, Corps members," to which Corps members laughed and made jest of her, saying that it was almost, if not already evening.

The State Coordinator laughed, then told them that in the military, it was always morning, and not afternoon or evening. She then greeted them again, and when they said "Good morning" to her, she asked how things had been going in the camp. When the Corps members responded in chorus that everything had been going all fine, the State Coordinator made the mistake of congratulating Platoon Nine for wining almost all the competitions.

Just then, someone yelled, "PDP," referring to one of Nigeria's ruling political parties — Peoples Democratic Party. And the whole crowd, except for Platoon Nine members, of course, replied, "Power."

"PDP," the person yelled again.

"Power," resounded in the whole camp, followed by uncontrollable laughter.

Nobody expected that — not the Corps members, not the State Coordinator herself, not the camp officials, not the soldiers, not the camp sellers that went around the camp, waiting to sell their goods. They all joined the Corps members in the laughter. The State Coordinator continued laughing, and she shook her head as she laughed.

When everyone had calmed down, she asked them a few more questions, then gave information about activities concerning the following day, which involved the Closing Ceremony, collection of Posting letters to take to their employers, opening of NYSC official bank accounts and monthly clearance activities. She told the Corps members not to try to pay any money or bribe anyone to get posted to offices of their own choice, because such acts were prohibited and punishable by law. She also told them that the information had been pasted on the notice board, so they were free to go and consult them.

Before she wrapped up her debrief, she told the crowd that the NYSC Batch B-Stream 2 Corps members would not be coming to the Orientation camp the next week as scheduled, because of the high level threat of the Ebola virus. She then urged all Corps members to be watchful, and report any suspected case to doctors or policemen, she wasn't really sure which. At that instant, Oluomachukwu remembered the woman in *mami* market who didn't want to sell rubber trainers to her a while back, because she was so sure that there was going to be a 'Stream 2' the next month. She then felt like going to the market, just to laugh at the woman and poke her tongue at her.

Right after the address, the marching competition was to take place. Corps members were asked to move under the canopies where Platoon Ten Corps members on Environmental duty had prepared before the debrief. And after everyone had moved, the contest started and it was a lovely display of more than ten minutes for each platoon. The Corps members cheered and clapped as each platoon displayed, they but didn't fail to laugh when each platoon made a mistake. When Platoon Nine came out to display, Corps members booed them whether they were doing the right thing or not, and it was rather surprising that they did not miss their steps or get distracted even once with all the booing.

At the end of the competition, Platoon Seven entered the top four semi-finalists. Platoon Nine was also there, as usual. Platoon Five members, who had trained extensively for the competition and were quite outstanding, were also picked, and then there was one other platoon in the top four.

Oluomachukwu, as well as every other Corps member in that camp knew that Platoon Five deserved to win, so if any other platoon took the first place, specifically Platoon Nine, then it would be a case of favouritism. The results were given out shortly afterwards, and Platoon Five won the contest. The whole crowd roared and laughed, aiming it at Platoon Nine. In fact, they made so much noise that no one heard what platoons took second, third and fourth places.

Before the event ended, the Marching Committee Head reminded the four semi-finalists that they were all going to display again at the Closing Ceremony the next day, even though they already had a winner. Prizes were awarded to the first three platoons, and with that, the crowd dispersed for dinner.

***

Oluomachukwu and her friends didn't go and collect dinner in the camp kitchen, even though they didn't know what was being served. Platoon Seven football team had already reminded them to go straight to *mami* market, so that they could start eating and drinking early, and have enough time to hang out before it was time for Lights Out.

Platoon Seven's football team's self-appointed captain

took everyone's order and went to arrange for the food and drinks, even for Ogo who wasn't in their platoon. Ogo was in Platoon Ten, but she spent way too much time with Oluomachukwu and Nkiru that she could even pass for a Platoon Seven Corps member. She had come to the camp market with the CMD, who was visiting the place for the first time, looking around like the novice that he was. Ekene was also there talking with Player, even though she knew that he was a player, and Nkiru was with Cleaner... sitting on his lap.

Oluomachukwu looked around, and even in the midst of people, loneliness enveloped her. She wanted to go to the OBS again at that instant to ask Tobenna to meet her, but she didn't do it. She actually couldn't do it. Instead, she sat there, brooding to herself. At that moment, she knew that she needed a friend, even Tracker would suffice. She looked up in front of her and saw Tracker approaching. She smiled at him and almost stood up, but she saw that he had come with another girl. She sat down immediately and acted like she was adjusting herself on the seat. He came and greeted her, then went to get a seat at another angle of the table and sat with the new girl. He had come with a goal of getting someone before the end of camp, and if Oluomachukwu wasn't interested, he was going to get another person.

After Oluomachukwu was done feeling very lonely, she started dancing on her own, and having all the fun she could. The night went on like that, with drinks and music, not forgetting the four regular songs they played in camp, and they partied until the killjoy bugle sounded across the camp and sent everyone back to their rooms.

C. M. OKONKWO

CHAPTER TWENTY-SIX: NEXT STEP

Tuesday, 26th August 2014
Oluomachukwu woke up feeling happy that camp life was finally going to be over. There was going to be a Closing Ceremony, just like the Opening Ceremony that they had had on the third day in the camp. The Corps members were expected to wear their ceremonial kit, pack up all their things, clean out their rooms a nd go out to the parade ground.

After the Closing Ceremony, they would then collect their Posting letters from their platoon instructors, then leave the camp for their service year.

Before Oluomachukwu had her bath that morning, she packed up all her things, leaving only her ceremonial outfit. Someone passed a broom from the far end of the room and each person swept their corner and passed it down until the whole room was swept. They then arranged their things, had their baths and went out to the parade ground.

The bugle had sounded later than usual that morning, because there wasn't going to be any early morning drill. However, there was the Morning Prayer, and the National and NYSC Anthems. After that, the Camp Director came out to make announcements on what was next and then wished everyone the best. The State Coordinator was also around to address the Corps members on the next step of action and wished them well as well. When that was over, everyone went to sit under the canopies, at the designated sections for their respective platoons.

The last four finalists for the march past remained on the parade ground to display all that they had learnt, and even though the winning platoon had already been picked, which was Platoon Five, they still made sure they wowed everyone with their display. It seemed as if the platoon members had trained for a whole year for the competition.

Everyone watched and clapped for them, and when Platoon Nine started to march, everyone booed them and laughed. Oluomachukwu didn't march, but at that instant, she wished that she had. She looked intently at the Corps members, searching for Tobenna, but she didn't see him anywhere. She was getting worried, because after that day, there was no way she was going to find him again. She wished she had gone to the volleyball court to meet him two days ago or gone to make her own announcement. She wished she could turn back the hands of time, she wished he would come out one last time to make another announcement at the OBS; but none of those happened.

When the march past was over, every platoon gathered at their regular position under the canopies and waited to receive their Posting letters. It seemed like a very big deal, because people were eager to know where they had been posted to, or rather, they wanted to check if they had been sent to the Ministries or Local Government offices, but not to schools to teach.

Oluomachukwu was indifferent. If she were sent to a school to teach, she would take it with open arms; if she were sent to a farmland for agricultural development, she would also accept it, if she was needed at road safety to control the horrible Lagos traffic, she was willing to oblige. She had decided to serve her country to the fullest, and after the wonderful experience she had gotten while in the camp, there was no regretting signing up for the NYSC programme anymore.

As she scouted the area for Tobenna, she felt her cell phone vibrate in her khaki pocket. She immediately pulled it out, probably hoping it was him, although they had not exchanged numbers. It was Okechukwu calling.

"Oke," she said.

"Hmm." Okechukwu sighed. "You sound very happy. Excited to finally leave?"

Oluomachukwu laughed. "Actually, no. I'm truly happy about the wonderful experience I had, even though there were ups and downs. It was still amazing in the end."

"Oh, yeah?" he asked.

"Well, I never expected it to be this way, and I'm glad I came and stayed until the end."

The image of Tobenna crossed her mind and it warmed her internally, making her smile, making her lost for a few seconds, before Okechukwu spoke and brought her back to Earth.

"Okay, good," he said. "Anyway, I'm already outside. Since you didn't give me any time to come and get you, I figured I could come in the morning."

"Oh," Oluomachukwu replied.

"What? You don't seem too excited," he pointed out. "Don't you want to go home anymore or you don't want to go home with me?"

Oluomachukwu didn't want to go home anymore. She actually wished the camp time could be prolonged, and that she could spend another three weeks or more there. She also wanted to find Tobenna and collect his number. She then contemplated going to the OBS again to make an announcement, but she didn't.

"Hello?" Okechukwu said. "Are you still there? Which one is it?"

Oluomachukwu came back to reality and remembered his questions. Without thinking twice about it and without feeling sorry about it either, she said, "Actually, you came quite early. I was just about to collect my Posting letter. I thought we would be done by 11:00am, but I didn't put a lot of things into consideration, like the rain and the queue to collect the letters." After a brief pause, she added, "And I don't want to go back with you."

Okechukwu was taken aback by how she had ended her reply with no warning. "What do you mean?"

"I'm not staying with you anymore."

"I don't understand," he said. "I thought we had settled things. I am not chasing you out of my place. My home is your home, no matter what happens."

"Thanks, I'll be fine. We'll still be friends, but I'll rather not live with you. I'll come and pick up my things over the weekend."

"Where are you going to stay?"

"With my friend in Ikoyi."

"Your friend?" Okechukwu was actually more worried about if the 'friend' was male or female.

"Yes, my new friend... and I trust her."

"Wait, just after twenty-one days in camp?" he asked and sighed. At least the friend was female.

"Actually, it's just after nineteen days. I met her on the third day, after the Opening Ceremony, and she has been an amazing friend since then. Apparently, the length of friendship doesn't determine anything."

Okechukwu understood the message she was trying to pass along to him. "Okay, that's fine. Take care of yourself then and call me when you want to come and pick up your things."

"I will," Oluomachukwu replied. "Goodbye, Oke."

"Please, no goodbyes, and certainly no calling of names in a dramatic way," he said immediately. "See you later. I prefer, 'see you later.'"

Oluomachukwu laughed. "Okay, see you later, then." She hung up and tucked the phone in to her khaki pocket.

As Oluomachukwu walked towards the canopy where Platoon Seven Corps members were gathered, she heard

TWENTY-ONE DAYS

an OBS speaker make an announcement. Platoon One was on duty again, but none of them wanted to go out and do Security or Environmental duties. There were no Kitchen or Sanitation duties on that day.

A camp official also went to make an announcement, urging Platoon One instructors to make sure that their platoon members came out for their duties.

Oluomachukwu was sure that Platoon One members felt cheated. Every other platoon had two days of being on duty, and not three, but at the same time, the second day in camp wasn't that busy and Platoon One didn't really do much. They had been on duty only halfway through the day, so it was only normal that they did another half day on the last day.

***

Oluomachukwu stood among her platoon members and listened to the instructions Auntie Vera was giving. The instructions had already been printed out and pasted on the notice board, and Oluomachukwu had taken a few snapshots of them, but she still had to wait and listen to Auntie Vera, because she was going to give out the Posting letters after she was done with what she was saying.

Auntie Vera had finished giving the instructions, and instead of sharing the Posting letter, she kept talking. "So, like I just said, in case some people didn't read the notice board or listen to me, this is what I said..."

Some impatient platoon members started grumbling loudly, distracting Auntie Vera from what she was saying.

"Keep quiet," Auntie Vera yelled. "Don't think because this is the last day that you can act however you want. I have the right to seize these Posting letters and send all of you home until next month, and you would not get your allowance for the month."

"Ah, no oh!" at least one hundred Platoon Seven Corps members exclaimed in unison, so loud that other platoon

Corps members turned to look at them.

"Just try it and see." Auntie Vera sounded harsh. "Just interrupt me one more time and you'll see if you'll get your Posting letters."

Everyone immediately kept quiet that one would have thought they had just entered a library.

Auntie Vera continued with what she was saying. " So after you receive your Posting letter, proceed to your Place of Primary Assignment, which is your PPA, as indicated on the letter, and that's where you will be working for your service year. You'll then collect an Acceptance letter from your employer. When you are done with that you'll have to go and open a Savings Account with the bank, and at the branch that the NYSC has designated to you."

"Excuse me, ma," one guy said from the crowd. "How do we know what bank and what branch the NYSC has designated to us?"

"You see what I was saying?" Auntie Vera asked. "The information has been on the notice board since last week."

The boy said nothing.

"Anyway, there's a list of NYSC approved banks, and for each bank, different ranges of State codes have been provided. So depending on your State code, you will know the bank you should go to."

Oluomachukwu put her hand up and said that she had taken a snapshot of the list, and she was willing to share it with everyone much later. She just wanted the woman to carry on with what she was saying, so that she could share the Posting letters and release them.

As if Auntie Vera had read Oluomachukwu's mind, she continued, "So after going to your PPA and opening your bank accounts, please, report to your Local Government Inspectors, who are also known as LGIs. Their names and phone numbers will be provided on your Posting letter s. Also, make sure you provide your phone numbers in use, in case you need to be contacted. When you meet your LGI, you'll register and submit your Acceptance letter and original bank form; they will serve as your clearance for next month and payment of your allowance. And failure to follow all the bank instructions might result in the non-payment of the stipend, or the allowance as you know it to be."

Some platoon members exclaimed, frightened at the possibility of not receiving the 19,800 naira, and making Corps members from other platoons turn to look at them a second time.

"Keep quiet," Auntie Vera yelled. "Do the right thing and you won't have any problems. Anyway, so subsequent payment of your allowances will depend on the submission of your monthly and CDS clearances between the first and tenth of every month."

Someone shouted from the crowd, and asked, "What if we are rejected at our PPA?"

"You will collect a Rejection letter from your employer and take it to your LGI. You will also be expected to write an application letter to the NYSC secretariat through your LGI, and if you have any place in mind where you would want to work and you are sure that you will be accepted there, add a request letter from the place."

"Even a private company?" someone else yelled from the crowd.

"No," Auntie Vera replied. "Only government offices and agencies in these four core sectors — Rural Health, Primary and Secondary Education, Rural Infrastructural Development and Agricultural Development.

After she had finished explaining, some one else from the crowd, a guy, yelled, "Can we get a request letter from a private company if paraventure we get rejected in the new government office or agency?"

"Can somebody please knock that boy on the head," Auntie Vera asked, then hissed. "Were you sleeping when I just explained that you cannot bring a request letter from a private organisation?" She emphasised on the 'cannot,' then hissed again, while looking at the boy from head to toe several times, as if she was disgusted.

If Oluomachukwu was standing close to the boy, she would have helped Auntie Vera knock his head twice, not only for asking the question a second time, but for using the obsolete word 'Paraventure,' and sounding like an archaic man from another generation.

***

Before Auntie Vera handed out the letters, she gave her platoon Corps members tips for collecting their monthly allowance throughout the service year. The first week of every month, between the first and the eight of the month — even though it was first and tenth written on the notice board — they were to collect a Clearance letter from their employer, then take it to their LGI, sign a load of papers and books, and put the letter in a file. Some people already knew that the files were sold at 120 naira in some NYSC Local Government offices, and Clearance letters were also sold at 100 naira. When they asked Auntie Vera about it, she told them to shut up.

She then told them that they would have a CDS card to always give to their CDS instructors after each weekly meeting. If the Corps member was going to join a SAED group in place of CDS, they were going to get a SAED card that already had months and dates printed in it, with slots for the instructor to sign. If the Corps member was going to join a CDS group in the Local Government office instead, they were going to receive a CDS card, which had the same interior as the SAED card, but a slightly different exterior. The same Corps members that had questioned Auntie Vera before said that the CDS cards were sold for 200 naira in some NYSC Local Government offices, and just like before, Auntie Vera told them to shut up.

The complaining Corps members were still very sure of themselves, because they knew other Corps members who were in Batch A, registered in February of that year, and had had to pay for almost everything, from CDS cards, to Clearance letters, to files. Auntie Vera wasn't interested, so she ignored them. When she was done passing along all the important information, she wished the Corps members well, then dismissed them.

Oluomachukwu and Nkiru went back to the room and everyone was there. They didn't know everyone, but they assumed that they were all there. Well, Ogo was there, and she was the one they really knew. Oghene was also there, and still eyeing the three of them angrily. Dunsin was there as well, trying to avoid eye contact with Oluomachukwu. Apparently, she had come back to the camp to collect her Posting letter. She had also come to the room because she wanted to say goodbye to some of their roommates before leaving.

One of the girls proposed to say a prayer and started to pray even before getting a response from anyone. She said a lengthy prayer, binding and casting any evil that wanted to take anything away from any of them. She then prayed for all the good things that life had to offer to them and everyone kept yelling a resounding 'Amen.'

After the prayer session, they had a goodbye session and some of them exchanged phone numbers, BBM pins and emails, just in case. Some also had to exchange names, since they didn't all know each other.

When Oluomachukwu was done preparing her things to be carried downstairs, she waited for Nkiru and Ogo, so that they could all go downstairs together. While she was waiting, Dunsin came to her bedside and asked to speak with her privately.

Nkiru glanced at Oluomachukwu, then at Ogo and at Dunsin. Ogo did the same thing, glancing at Nkiru, then at Oluomachukwu and at Dunsin.

Oluomachukwu stood up and went outside.

"This may seem a bit awkward, but when I went home to Nnanna, I learnt a lot."

Oluomachukwu didn't say a single thing. For Dunsin to

have mentioned 'Nnanna,' it meant that she had definitely learnt a lot, especially about Abuja.

"I knew Nnanna had cheated on me in Abuja and he kept denying it. He didn't want to tell me who it was. And frankly, I didn't care. I just wanted to pay him back. And the only way that I could do so was with Kayode, because I knew it would hurt him. I asked Kayode to post me to Lagos, instead of Abuja, and I also asked him to come to Lagos camp for three weeks. His time here was more like a volunteer work, because he has a high rank in the NYSC normally, and that was why he had his own personal room. I didn't suspect anything about you until Kayode said that he had slept with you. I thought it was just a random thing until he said that it happened in Abuja and that you were Okechukwu's cousin."

Oluomachukwu wanted to comment, but instead she kept quiet and listened, because she really had nothing to say.

"When I went back to Abuja two weeks ago, Nnanna and I argued about everything and spoke our hearts out, and that was when he said that he had cheated on me with you."

Oluomachukwu froze. "I'm sorry, I didn't know he was engaged then."

"I know. He said that too. It wasn't your fault. It is our issue to deal with, anyway."

There was a brief pause.

"We are no longer together. I called off the wedding, as I don't think I want to be with a husband who cheats on me and makes me cheat on him as well. Better a separation than a divorce."

Oluomachukwu looked at Dunsin's finger and noticed that she had no engagement ring on; the ring she had once seen on the first week in the camp. It was now gone.

After a brief silence, Dunsin said her goodbye, wished Oluomachukwu well and was ready to go. Oluomachukwu did the same, then went back into the room. She looked at

TWENTY-ONE DAYS

Nkiru and Ogo, and Nkiru immediately understood what had happened, but Ogo didn't, and she also didn't ask any question.

When Nkiru and Ogo had finished packing, they all carried their things outside. Oluomachukwu and Nkiru had to wait for Nkiru's brother to arrive, while Ogo left. She was going to take public transportation and had to leave early. She hugged both Oluomachukwu and Nkiru tightly, and promised to keep in touch with them.

***

Oluomachukwu didn't look at her Posting letter when she got it. She had folded it in two and taken it up to her room where she put it in her handbag. She had removed her waist pouch and transferred its contents to the bag. She and Nkiru waited outside for about ten minutes when Nkiru's phone rang and her brother said he was around. She asked him to drive into the camp, so that it would be easier to load all their things into the trunk. As he entered, he was shocked to see that her things had doubled in the camp, as she had left home with just a hand luggage. She later told him that she had bought some things while in the camp, like the green dress and shoes for the Miss NYSC contest, and she had also won second prize in the cooking competition.

When they were done loading their things, they sat in the car, and as Nkiru's brother fired up the engine, he asked, "So, where were you girls posted to?"

Nkiru said "To the Eti-Osa Local Government office," while Oluomachukwu shrugged.

Nkiru's brother obviously hadn't seen her, because he didn't turn to look at her. So he asked another question.

"Weren't either of you sent to a primary or a secondary school to teach?" He laughed.

Oluomachukwu didn't feel it was funny, but she didn't sound rude when she asked, "What's wrong with going to a primary or a secondary school to teach?"

"Nothing," he responded, looking at her from the rear view mirror. "So where then?"

"I haven't checked it yet." Oluomachukwu reached for her Posting letter and started going through it as Nkiru's brother drove out. "Wait, please, wait," she called out after a couple of seconds, startling him.

He hit the brake so hard that they would have bashed their heads into the windscreen if they had not fastened their seatbelts.

"What is it?" he asked, turning back completely to look at her.

"There's an error on my Posting letter," she retorted. "They got the spelling of my names and my qualifications wrong."

Both Nkiru and her brother sighed.

"Is that why you wanted to get us into an accident?" Nkiru asked, and laughed.

Oluomachukwu laughed, then hopped out of the car, while Nkiru's brother reversed the car and found a place to park.

Oluomachukwu was directed to the dining hall, which doubled as the registration hall, and saw a queue of people waiting to complain about something. Some complained about how they had been posted to areas that were very far from their residences, and how impossible it was going to be to get there. Some others wanted to relocate, and some, like Oluomachukwu, had spelling errors on their letters.

After waiting for another thirty minutes, she finally got her letter rectified, then ran off. She went to say goodbye to the Camp Commandant and every other person she wasn't likely to see again within the service year, including Auntie Vera and Sister Mary, and surprisingly Kayode. She also saw Mummy Dorcas — who she had met on the first day in camp — in the registration hall and said goodbye to her. She then ran towards the gate, where Nkiru's brother was parked, and jumped into the car.

She buckled her seatbelt, then said, "Thanks, they have modified it now. I was also posted to the Eti-Osa Local Government office."

Nkiru's brother nodded, while Nkiru turned to look at Oluomachukwu and smiled at her, but didn't immediately turn to face the road.

"So are we good to go?" he asked.

"Good to go, good to go, good to go, sir!" she and Nkiru replied, and laughed out loud.

"You both aren't serious." Nkiru's brother hissed, also laughing.

And as they drove out, Oluomachukwu started to feel sad about leaving the camp and about not seeing Tobenna again. Nkiru noticed something when she had turned back the first time, then she turned back again to verify it. She raised an eyebrow, making Oluomachukwu concerned. She then leaned back so that she was close to Oluomachukwu.

"There's one guy staring at you from that car parked in the corner. I noticed he has been staring at you since, and even when you entered the car, he kept looking at the car. Is that your magical stepper?" she asked, whispering.

Oluomachukwu turned around and was shocked to see Okechukwu's face. She thought he had left ever since, but he had actually waited there for her to leave, watching her sadly, as he felt he was going to lose her friendship forever, maybe. He knew that the next time he would see her again would be when she came to his place to pick up her things.

Oluomachukwu turned back and looked at Nkiru, then shook her head. "That is not my magical stepper." Nkiru did not look back again as they left, and Oluomachukwu watched as Okechukwu also drove off and went his own way.

***

When Oluomachukwu woke up the next morning, she forgot that she was a Corps member. In fact, Nkiru had woken her up to get ready for her journey to her PPA and to the bank, where she was to go and open her account, but she didn't want go. She wanted to continue sleeping. She didn't know the last time she had up to six hours of sleep without interruption.

And as she lay there, she wondered what PPA was, and why she had to open an account. When Nkiru tried to pull her out of the bed, she woke up and reality dawned on her that the NYSC life was just about to begin.

The Orientation camp had only been the tip of the iceberg.

She got ready and left about the same time as Nkiru. She took a taxi, because the bank that had been designated to her was in Ikeja, and Nkiru wasn't going her way. Since her PPA was in Ikoyi, she thought to do the farther one first, then concentrate on the PPA next. It could have been a good plan, but first of all, she spent hours getting to the bank, and when she eventually got there, it took the bank hours to open the account for her. Their systems had been slow, and they had to wait and get authorisation for every step of the process.

And to make matters worse, even after keeping her for over two hours, she wasn't immediately given an account number. She couldn't understand how the system worked, but what she didn't know was that it normally took at least two weeks to receive a bank account number via email or text message after an account was opened. She was also advised to request for a free ATM card made specifically for Corps members. It usually had 'NYSC' written on it.

She left the bank, frustrated. She got another taxi and headed back to Ikoyi to sort out her PPA, hoping that it won't give her as much headache. Before she got there, she decided to call some of the people she had met in the camp to check if everything had gone well with them.

Some of them had already opened their bank accounts and had gone to their PPAs as soon as they left the camp the previous day, making her feel somewhat unserious. In fact, some of them had already made at least six trips, to and fro, in two days.

Some of them had been rejected by their employers for no reason, while some were told that they were too late... even on the first day, because the employers had already gotten the maximum number of Corps members needed. Others were told that the employers did not normally hire Corps members.

Oluomachukwu wondered why the NYSC would send Corps members to places where they were not wanted or needed. But then again, she figured that the NYSC could not know every institution that needed Corps members, so they sent Corps members around to propose their services, by selling their skills and years of experience, and if they were needed, they were engaged, and if not, they were sent away. The only problem was that it was difficult to have many years of experience, especially as a recent graduate.

However, Oluomachukwu knew that there was a way around the dilemma, so she made a mental note to ask the NYSC secretariat to form a research group and put a team in place — even if it was going to be made up of Corps members — to research on all the PPAs that the NYSC normally posted Corps members to. The group would then draw up a list of the PPAs, liaise with their employers, and ask if they needed Corps members for the service year and the exact number of positions that would be available. That way, the NYSC would work with numbers and not worry about Corps members being rejected or having to spend months and months, looking for a PPA.

When Oluomachukwu got to her Local Government office, she walked in and wasn't surprised to see a queue — there were queues everywhere, and a couple of Corps members had come, hoping that they would be among the 'wanted' people before the office filled all their vacant spots. Oluomachukwu absent-mindedly joined the queue, attention glued to her phone and chatting with Nkiru. She was so engrossed in her chat, that she didn't hear when an officer asked everyone to move backwards, because the office was getting crowded.

Oluomachukwu stood there as others moved back, and the guy in front of her stepped on her. She was pissed off and was prepared to verbally attack him as he prepared to turn back and apologise, and when he turned around, she saw Tobenna, as handsome as she had remembered when she first saw him in the camp. She smiled from within and she could also feel him smile from within. Evidence was in the fact that they maintained eye contact for almost five seconds before he apologised to her and she accepted it immediately. There was nothing more exciting and great than knowing that they were going to spend a whole year together in the same PPA, and hopefully at the same CDS group — thanks to the magical step that brought them together in the first place, and this step that was going to keep them together.

*** Eleven months later ***

Neither Oluomachukwu nor Tobenna knew how it happened, but eleven months down the road of the NYSC journey, they were heading to the altar to tie the knot. Meeting at the camp had been the beginning, and meeting again at their PPA had sealed the deal. And during the eleven months preceding their wedding, they had worked together, dodged CDS group meetings together, played together, done everything together and even moved in together after dating for about six months.

At the seventh month of dating, Tobenna proposed to Oluomachukwu on her birthday in the presence of some of their colleagues, family, friends and platoon members.

The engagement party had been an interesting one, as Oluomachukwu had the feeling that she was back at the Orientation camp once again, in *mami* market. They started planning the wedding during the two months that followed the engagement and almost everyone mobilised in order to make it a success. And to top it all up, the NYSC gave her and Tobenna a wedding gift in form of a financial package for their wedding ceremony. It was a practice of the NYSC to do so whenever a Corps member was getting married to another Corps member within their service year.

Some Corps members had heard about the wedding gift offer before, but never believed. Oluomachukwu and Tobenna's wedding was an evidence of that. Some other Corps members even joked about getting married before the end of their service year, just to get a wedding package as well.

On the day of their wedding, Oluomachukwu couldn't contain her joy, and the same was said for Tobenna. They knew they had made the right decision, and they thanked their stars each day for it. Oluomachukwu never thought anything like that would ever happen to her, and before she said "I do," she thanked her lucky stars one more time for helping her make the decision to serve her country.

She had all that she wanted that day — her husband, of course; her family. Her parents and her siblings had flown to Nigeria for the wedding; her new best friend, Nkiru. She had come with Cleaner; Ogo was also there with Martins, the CMD; and so was Okechukwu with Idara. Kayode was also present at the wedding, alone, and so was Nnanna. She had reconciled with everyone and had peace of mind on her day. The Camp Commandant didn't miss it as well.

After they finished the church service, they moved to the reception hall for the follow-up, and before the end of the party, a whole lot of the Corps members present said that they had a special number they wanted to sing to the couple. Oluomachukwu was suspicious, but agreed to it.

When they all gathered at the centre of the hall, some holding microphones in their hands, they started to sing.

They go born mumu, they go born mumu,
If corper marry corper, they go born mumu.

The whole crowd burst into laughter and only Corps members — old and new, could understand the meaning of the song. Only those who had gone to any Orientation camp got the joke. It took them all a while to calm down from the outburst of laughter.

Oluomachukwu and Tobenna also laughed, but before they could protest, the Corps members changed the lyrics of the song and started singing.

They go born better, they go born better,
If Oluoma marry Tobe, they go born better...

Just then, someone yelled, "*Oya*, hold something... hold something... hold something... hold something..." and the crowd went crazy after that.

***

At the end of the service year, Oluomachukwu created her own tag for the NYSC: "Now Your Suffering Ceases."

*****

GLOSSARY

Abeg — Oh please; Please
Amebo — Gossip
Ahn-ahn — Expression of surprise, shock, bewilderment
Ajuwayah — Stop; Halt
Akamu — Pap; Ogi; Fermented cereal porridge
Akara — Bean cakes
Allawee — NYSC monthly allowance/stipend
Amala — Yoruba cuisine made out of yam flour and/or cassava flour.
Area boys — Street boys; Touts; Riffraffs
Ashawo — Prostitute
Asun — Native goat meat, roasted and cut into tiny bits, boiled and stir fried in pepper sauce.
Biko — Please
Buba — Blouse in Yoruba native attire
Buns — A snack similar to puff-puff, but made with more flour.
CBN — Central Bank of Nigeria
CDS — Community Development Service
CMD — Chief Medical Director
Dey — The verb 'to be' (am, are, is)
Do someone — Sleep with or have sex with someone

Eba — Ground cassava made into a thick mould with hot water
EFCC — Economic and Financial Crimes Commission
Ehen — Aha
Ehn? — What? Can also be used as emphasis
Ewedu — Soup made with Corchorus leaves and eaten with amala.
Forming — Pretending
Gisting — Chatting; Gossiping
Iro — Skirt in Yoruba native attire
Johnny-just-come — Newbie; Fresher; Novice
Keh? — How?
Lesbo — Lesbian
LGI — Local Government Inspector
Mallam — Word used to address Hausa men, although an honorific title for Islamic scholars.
MDG — Millennium Development Goals
Moimoi — A Nigerian steamed bean pudding
Na — It is
Nau — Used to emphasise or stress a point
NOA — National Orientation Agency
NIM — Nigerian Institute of Management
NYSC — National Youth Service Corps
OBS — Orientation Broadcasting Service
Ofada rice — Rice produced locally
Ogas — Bosses
Okpolo — Frog
Otondo — Idiot; Learner
Oya — Okay; Alright
PDP — Peoples Democratic Party
Poopoo — Poop
Puff-puff — A snack similar to doughnut; Sweet dough deep-fried in oil until golden brown
PPA — Place of Primary Assignment
SAED — Skills Acquisition and Entrepreneurial Development
Selling someone — Confusing someone

Sha — At least
Sleep-sleep — Someone who sleeps a lot
Strong thing — A lesson, as in teach someone a lesson
Tufiakwa — God forbid
Una — All of you; You people; You all
Wetin? — What?
Wor-wor — Very ugly
Yawa go gas — There would be trouble

C. M. OKONKWO

OTHER BOOKS BY THE AUTHOR

<u>Novels:</u>
The XIth Hour, Thriller/Suspense, 2013
Thirteen Suspects, Erotic/Suspense, 2014
Dim Noo Abroad, Desperate Women Series #1, Drama/Suspense, 2014

<u>Novellas:</u>
-The Angela Hunter Series, Young Adult/Mystery
#1, Closed Door, 2013
#2, Jammed Door, 2014
#3, Locked Door, 2015

<u>Short stories:</u>
Ziora's Surprise, Mystery/Suspense, 2013
Finding Love, Romance/Suspense, 2015

AUTHOR'S NOTE

If you wish to keep in touch with me or give me some feedback on my book, please use any of the links below. I'll be happy to hear from you.

For more information about my books and my ongoing projects, visit my website: www.cmo29.com

Follow me on Twitter: @CMO2904

Send me an email: cmo2904@gmail.com

Thank you for reading, and I hope you enjoyed it!

Printed and bound by Printing & Packaging Aids (NIG.) Ltd.
Lagos, Nigeria.
www.printpackaids.com
ppaaidsltd@yahoo.com